The Street Orphans

Mary Wood was born in Maidstone, Kent, and brought up in Claybrooke, Leicestershire. Born one of fifteen children to a middle-class mother and an East End barrow boy, Mary's family were poor but rich in love. This encouraged her to develop a natural empathy with the less fortunate and a fascination with social history. In 1989 Mary was inspired to pen her first novel and she is now a full-time novelist.

Mary welcomes interaction with readers and invites you to subscribe to her website where you can contact her, receive regular newsletters and follow links to meet her on Facebook and Twitter: www.authormarywood.com

BY MARY WOOD

The Breckton series

To Catch a Dream
An Unbreakable Bond
Tomorrow Brings Sorrow
Time Passes Time

Proud of You

Brighter Days Ahead

The Street Orphans

The Generation's Wars

All I Have to Give
In Their Mother's Footsteps

The Street Orphans

Mary Wood

PAN BOOKS

First published 2018 by Pan Books
an imprint of Pan Macmillan
20 New Wharf Road, London N1 9RR
Associated companies throughout the world
www.panmacmillan.com

ISBN 978-1-4472-6751-5

1 3 5 7 9 8 6 4 2

A CIP catalogue record for this book is available from the British Library.

Typeset in ITC Galliard Std by Palimpsest Book Production Ltd, Falkirk, Stirlingshire
Printed and bound by CPI Group (UK) Ltd, Croydon, CR0 4YY

To my friend and avid reader of my books Jane Taylor. A special person who will be so missed, not only because she was loved dearly, but because she brought so much into the lives of expats living in and around Camposol, Spain. All of our lives were enriched for having Jane a part of them. Rest in peace, dear lady.

PART ONE
Lives Ripped Apart
1850

1

Ruth Dovecote

A Shattered Family

'Eeh, Ruth, will you hurry yourself? It's nigh on nightfall and we've to find shelter.'

'Ma, I can't. You go on. I'll rest awhile and catch up later. Leave a message at the inn when you find somewhere to bed down, so that I know where to find you.' Shouting her answer to her ma sapped more of her strength than Ruth could spare, as she battled against the strong, bitter January wind that whistled around the mountainous hills of Bowland.

Ruth's one good leg wobbled. Thinking she was going to topple over, she leaned heavily on her crutch. Her underarm burned as the crutch rasped against her armpit. Despair threatened to engulf her. The weight of her club foot seemed to become heavier with every mile they walked – and they had trundled many miles these last days.

Turned out of their tied cottage on a remote farm within days of their da taking his last breath, Ruth, her ma and her four siblings had now reached the narrow high-peak road of Lythe Fell on their way to Blackburn.

It had been an accident that had taken their da. A strong man, he'd been to market in the nearby small town of

Pradley, which lay topside of Slaidburn, north of the Forest of Bowland. He'd stopped at an old well on the edge of the town to haul up a bucket of water for the old horse pulling his cart. The sides of the well had collapsed, taking him thirty feet into the ground. He'd been in freezing-cold water up to his neck for two days before the rescue workers brought him to the surface. With many bones broken and pneumonia setting in, he'd stood little chance.

Their da's boss, a rich landowner, hadn't considered the grief that her ma and Ruth and her siblings were suffering, or the plight the family would now be in. Within an hour of Da dying, the agent for the estate had served notice on them to quit their cottage and had ordered them to leave within twenty-four hours of the funeral. They had no money and had been left with just the clothes they stood up in, plus an old pram. The undertaker had taken everything they owned, in payment for their da's burial.

Ma had a cousin in Blackburn who she thought might help them. When she'd last heard from him, two years since, he'd told her how the town was flourishing with the rise of the cotton-mill industry. This held the hope that Ma and the lads and Amy could get taken on at one of the mills. Ruth's task would be to care for them all and look after Elsie. It all sounded good, if very different from the life they had led so far, and Ruth wasn't without her worries as to how it would all work out. But she knew they would never be able to find the kind of work on the land that they were used to. Farm work paid little to the menfolk, and nothing for the labour of women and young 'uns, who were expected to work as part of the deal to gain a cottage with the job.

They had taken few rests as they walked during the day-light hours in the unforgiving weather conditions, and had

had to keep to the highway, because of Ruth's difficulties. The road was little more than a track, and it stretched their journey by many more miles than going over the top would have done. At night they had huddled together and bedded down amongst the bracken.

By nightfall this day they hoped to reach Clitheroe, as Ma thought it was within ten miles now. There, they planned to beg some shelter and food, as the last of the bread and preserves that Ma had packed for their trip had run out the night before. Hunger and cold slowed their progress – Ruth's more than that of the others, as her affliction, already a hindrance to her, worsened with the effort of walking such a long distance.

Looking up, she saw that her ma was three hundred yards ahead of her. Behind her ma trailed her sister, Amy, her curly hair frizzed even more than usual by the way the wind had played with it. Amy hated it and thought Ruth lucky to have long, dark hair. Amy's wouldn't grow long; it became too tangled and Ma had to cut it. It reminded Ruth of a bowl of soapsuds all bubbled up, and though Amy wouldn't have it, it set off her pretty face and huge dark eyes. At fifteen years of age, Amy was younger than Ruth by three years. No one would take her and Amy for sisters, if they didn't know them to be. There was nothing about them that resembled the other.

Amy held the hand of four-year-old Elsie, a delicate child, who was slow to learn new skills. Seth, fourteen and a bit, and ten months younger than Amy, and George, just nine months younger than Seth, were up in front. Seth pushed the pram that had carried them all as bairns, and which was still needed for Elsie as she tired easily.

Two handsome lads, Seth and George looked very much

alike and had the same appearance as Ruth, with their dark complexions, black hair and shining blue eyes. They were different in character, though. Seth had a gentle nature and preferred to reason problems out rather than argue his point. He tended to be shy and rarely put himself forward. George, though quick to lose his temper with people, had a wonderful way with animals; in contrast to his short fuse, he also had a good sense of humour and at times was so funny with his antics that he'd have you wetting yourself.

The five of them were the only survivors of the ten children Ma had birthed; one of these children, and two miscarriages, accounted for the gap in age between Ruth and her first three siblings. Twin boys and another two girls had died between George's birth and Elsie's. Ruth had helped at the delivery of all of them, from Amy down, and still felt the pain of their loss.

'By, lass, I can't go on without you. I—' The howl of the wind took away Ma's words as she stepped off the grass verge to walk back towards Ruth.

Ruth opened her mouth to urge her ma to go on once more, but fear changed what she was about to say. 'Ma! Look out, Ma!'

The coach had come from nowhere. The horses reared. Ma cowered. Her body fell to the ground. The hooves of the startled animals pounded down on her. The screams of terrified children and the whinnying of the stallions filled the space around Ruth. Her own scream strangled in her throat. Horror held her as if she'd been turned to stone, but then desperation moved her body and urged her forward. 'Ma . . . Naw, Ma!'

All around her went into slow motion, and it seemed she had to claw her way through invisible barriers as she tried to hasten. When at last she neared them, the horses swayed. Their hooves lost their grip on the muddied road and the carriage went onto its left wheel, before banging down onto its right. The violent motion catapulted the driver from his seat and over the cliff. His holler held the knowledge of his own imminent death. The carriage didn't right itself, and the crashing and splintering of its wooden structure drowned out the sound of the desperate driver.

A face appeared at the window of what was left of the carriage: a lad, his hair curled tightly to his head, his eyes holding a look of terror. Mud splattered Ruth as one of the horses tried to keep its grip, but the animal lost the battle and slid over the edge, pulling the coach almost upside down. The face disappeared. The three horses remaining on sturdy ground reared against the weight of the one dangling below. Steam rushed from their nostrils. The whites of their eyes glared their own terror and compounded Ruth's horror. Finding her voice, she shouted orders. 'Amy, come and help me. Seth, George, get Ma away.'

Leaning her weight onto her crutch, Ruth stretched her body to enable her to reach the handle of the door. It resisted her pulling it open. 'Amy, climb up. See if anyone is alive.'

'But, our ma? Eeh, Ruth, Ma's—'

'Leave Ma to the lads. They'll take care of her. We must help those in the carriage afore it goes over the edge. Hurry, lass.' Ruth's heart didn't encourage her to take these actions – it wanted her to go to her ma – but something in her knew it was already too late and, if she didn't help the occupants of the carriage, it would be so for them, too.

'Get up, Amy, lass, go on. That's reet. Can you see if anyone's alive?'

'Aye, there is, Ruth. A young man, but I'm not sure about the lady. She looks dead. She – she's bleeding from a cut on her head.'

'Tell the lad to climb out. Tell him!' Turning, Ruth saw Seth and George standing over the tangled, unmoving body of their ma. Her heart clamoured with despair at what she knew to be the truth, but she had to save the lad in the carriage. She couldn't let him die. 'Seth, George – here, quick! Amy, come down and let me lean on you. Seth, take me crutch, and you and George climb up with it to the window. Get the young man to take hold of the crutch, then pull him out. Go on, me lads, let sommat good come out of today.'

It didn't take long to get the young man out, but he'd not let them think they couldn't save his mother.

'Please try. Mama is breathing. She is alive!'

'We can't. I'm sorry – there's nowt we can do, as she ain't able to help us. She's unconscious. We wouldn't manage. It's impossible.'

'Do it, or I'll have you all up for murder, you scum! What were you doing on the highway anyway? You caused this. You should keep yourselves to the bridle paths.'

Ruth felt her anger rising, but common sense stopped her from giving full rein to her temper. What she'd thought of as a lad, because of how small he was, she could now see was a man of around twenty-five years of age. He was in shock and was reacting as all toffs would. Though she needed to take heed of what he said, as he could have them all sent down if he wished – hanged even.

But how could she get the woman out of the swaying cab, with the horses still pulling in all directions, and the whole lot likely to go over the edge of the cliff at any moment?

8

'I'll unleash the horses, Ruth. I knows how to do it. I learned that time when our da's boss made me work with his stablehand for a while.'

'But they'll kick you to death, Seth.'

'I'll help.' George chipping in with this comment offered Ruth some relief from her fear for Seth. George would be able to calm the animals. His confidence helped, as he instructed, 'Come on, Seth, get between the back of the horses and the carriage. I'll try to soothe them.'

Before the lads could act, the toff spoke. 'Unleash the one hanging over the side first. It cannot be saved, and its weight is a danger.'

'Aye, Sir, that is me plan.' Seth touched the brim of his cap in a mock-salute.

'"My Lord" – not "*Sir*"! You are addressing the Earl of Harrogate.'

Ruth clenched her fist. The ungrateful devil! And them with their ma lying dead, not ten feet away. He showed no compassion. Her glance over to her ma's body showed her the pitiful scene of Amy sobbing and Elsie looking bewildered and afraid, her wide eyes staring at the raging horses. Their plight undid Ruth. Hatred for this man, and all he stood for, trembled through her and spat from her before she could stop it: 'You're nowt to us. Us "scum" don't recognize the likes of you toffs. We should have left you to rot in hell!'

His hand sliced her face. His foot kicked her crutch away from her. The mud, though wet and squelchy, didn't cushion her fall, but slapped hard against her, knocking the breath from her.

'You'll pay for that, cripple. You'll pay dearly.' Rage puffed his face, making him appear ugly and evil. As he turned from her, his hand went inside his jacket. Ruth's fear intensified at the sight of the pistol that he now brandished towards her brothers, as they made as if to charge at him. The click of the gun as he cocked it, ready to fire, resounded around Ruth. The Earl's voice shook with anger and fear. 'Get back! Get those horses under control – now.'

Ruth knew the threat from the Earl was real. Though she hadn't seen him load his pistol, he could have done so before starting his journey, as these toffs were always afraid of coming across robbers. Terrified of what the impetuous George might do, and of the consequences for him, she drew in a painful breath. 'Naw! George, leave it. Go with Seth, see to the horses.'

George did as she bade him, and within moments his uncanny knack with animals showed in the way they became calm.

Seth freed the dangling horse, but despite the shouted commands of the young man, he didn't unleash the others; instead he listened to George, who was telling him to leave them, as he wanted to try and drive them forward, to pull the remains of the carriage gradually from the edge and out of danger. Ruth closed her eyes, praying that he would succeed.

The scraping noise told her something was happening. When she dared to look, she saw with relief that George had accomplished what he'd set out to do. But her relief was short-lived, as the searing tragedy of her ma's plight came to her. Dragging herself along the ground, Ruth reached the grass verge where her ma lay and looked into the unseeing, once-beautiful eyes. 'Oh, Ma . . . Ma!'

Elsie's wails penetrated Ruth's grief. Reaching for her and

Amy, she held them close, but the Earl's voice brought her attention back to what was happening behind her.

'You there, get over here and help my mother!'

Picking up her crutch, the Earl threw it towards her. Ruth crouched over her sisters, afraid the hurtling crutch would hit them, but it sailed right over them. Gathering her wits, she spoke as calmly as she could. 'Amy, lass, pass me crutch to me and help me up. Don't be afraid. We've to do as he bids. We'll see to Ma later.'

'Is – is she . . . ?'

'Aye, lass. Ma's gone.' She said this as though she were talking about something else, as neither her ma's death, nor the crying of her sisters, touched her in the way it should have done. It was as if she'd been taken out of her own body and put inside one that shielded her from all that could hurt her. But then it had to be so. Somehow she had to be strong for them all.

With Amy's help, Ruth managed to get up and hobble over to where the Earl's mother lay on a rug on the ground. It surprised Ruth to see that the lady wasn't as old as she'd first assumed, and she realized that she must have been very young when she birthed the Earl.

'Do something!'

Ruth stared down the barrel of the gun, saw the Earl's finger on the trigger. Sweat dripped off his face.

'Ruth!'

'Stay back, George, lad, it's all right.'

On George's movement towards her, the Earl turned swiftly and aimed his gun. 'Do as she says, urchin.'

Ruth held her breath. George froze. The Earl turned, his gun once more pointing at Ruth. 'I've heard it said that cripples like you have powers. Well, use them now. The likes

11

of you were hanged for being witches in the past, and still should be, in my opinion.'

'I'm naw witch, M'Lord.'

'Oh? And you'll be telling me next that your brother there is not a sorcerer, when only such a one could have calmed those horses. I would be within my rights to shoot you all, and have a mind to do so.' The weak sun, which gave no warmth, reflected on the barrel of the Earl's gun as he trained it on George. 'And us within spitting distance of Pendle Hill, where they hanged a whole bunch of your kind a couple of centuries ago.'

His words filled Ruth with the fear of the time when people in Pradley had whispered about her having evil powers, and that she should be sent away. It had been after one lad had been teasing her. Losing her temper, she'd turned on him, telling him no good would come to him. The lad had fallen ill just afterwards and, in his delirium, had screamed her name in terror. The atmosphere had darkened from that day, as many gave her a wide berth. Some even spat in her path. What this man had just said about Pendle Hill deepened her fear. *Please, God, save us; save me brothers and our Amy and me little Elsie. Don't let this devil of a man kill them.*

'Get on with it or they will all die.'

Ruth's fear turned to terror, as she saw the gun was now pointed at Elsie. The child had no concept of the danger she was in, as she ran over to Seth. The movement spooked the Earl. A crack resounded through the valley, echoing off the hills.

Amy screamed. Ruth's heart banged against her ribs. But then relief flooded through her as she saw that no one was hurt.

12

The Earl smiled as he reloaded his gun. 'Just to show you that I mean what I say.'

Bending over as best she could, Ruth touched the lady's forehead. She stirred.

'See! It is as I said – you are a witch! You only had to touch her and—'

Pushing back her hair, which had come loose from the ribbon Ma had tied in it, Ruth looked up at him and saw him properly for the first time. 'Puny' was how she'd label him. His bones jutted from hollow cheeks, his lips were feminine in their fullness, and she could see that his hair hung in false curls held with pins, some of which had escaped and now looked hideous. The depths of his black eyes held terror for her and, in that moment, she knew she was damned if his mother lived, and yet damned if she didn't.

The thought came to her that this would be the fate of her sisters and brothers as well. With this, her anger – fuelled by fear for herself and her siblings – caused her to grab her crutch and swing it with all her might. Catching the back of the Earl's knees, her blow floored him. Lunging towards him on all fours, Ruth scrambled across him, holding his body down with her weight. Her eyes glimpsed his pistol, now loosened from his grip. Grabbing it, she mustered all her strength and smashed it across his head.

The gaping, bloodied gash on his forehead shocked her back to reality. Gasping for breath, she stared in horror as the Earl's head rolled to one side, as if independent of his neck. His breath gasped from him in a rasping, gurgling sound. He didn't draw it back in. *Oh God! No. No . . . I've killed him!*

'Ruth! God, Ruth, lass, what have you done?'

'I didn't mean to kill him, Seth. I didn't. I just wanted to knock him out, so we could get away.'

A moan caught their attention. The lady moved her head, but didn't open her eyes.

'What're we going to do?' Seth's whisper held tears. His fear spurred Ruth into action. Pulling her crutch towards her and grabbing the piece of ribbon she'd lost from her hair – a precious memento now, as her ma had won it when the fair had visited – she put her hand out to Seth, who helped her up.

A flash of memory came to her, as she held onto the ribbon – her ma's words: 'I'm choosing you over Amy or Elsie for the ribbon, lass, as it will help to keep you cool, to have your hair tied back. Never cut your hair, our lass. It is your crowning glory. Look at it: it reaches your waist. It suits your beautiful oval face and complements your blue eyes. You need it to distract people from your affliction, and to let folk see as you're a bonny lass, despite that foot of yours.'

Shaking the tear-jerking recollection from her, Ruth brought her attention back to their current situation. 'Seth, you and George get the Earl's body back into the coach. Hurry, afore his ma comes round proper. Put him in a position that he would likely be in if he'd been killed in the accident. Go on, me lads.'

Hobbling over to the lady, Ruth placed herself between her and the carriage, because although the lady had sunk back into deep unconsciousness once more, Ruth felt afraid that she might still open her eyes and see what they were doing.

'Amy, lass, bring Elsie to me, and then get sommat to

disturb the mud to hide the trail of the lads dragging the body. A stick or something will do.'

'But, our Ruth, anyone'll know as he were out of the carriage afore he died. He'll be covered in mud, and there's mud on his boots.'

Fear of the truth of what Amy said stopped Ruth in her tracks for a moment. When a solution came to her, she knew George wouldn't be in favour of it, but their situation was desperate – hers above all, as now the noose would be her certain fate.

'We have to attach the horses again and drive them over the cliff to take the—'

'Naw!'

George's horrified gasp showed Ruth the enormity of what she'd proposed, and she knew she wouldn't be able to achieve it.

'We have to do sommat to cover up what really happened, George. We have to.'

'I think I knaw what we could do, our Ruth.'

Ruth didn't dismiss Amy. The lass had a clever brain. She could even read and write, and she'd only had the miller's lad to teach her what he'd learned in school.

'We could just push the seating area of the carriage over the edge, with the Earl inside. Then, when he's found, the state of him will give no clue to him having left the carriage before he died. And it won't be too heavy for us to shift, now that it is detached from where the trunks are stored. We could say as we'd managed to get the lady out, but then had to unleash the horses as they were in danger of shoving the rest over the cliff. But just as we did so, the lightest part of the carriage went over, with the unconscious man still in it.'

'Yes, that could have happened. You're reet, lass. By, Ma

15

allus said as you were the brains of the family, our Amy. Reet, me lads, that's what we'll do – just as Amy says – and I can help, if I get me back against it.'

'Naw, you shield the lady's view, Ruth, just in case. And mind our Elsie an' all. Me and the lads'll manage. We're strong.'

Ruth did as Amy suggested. She knew her own strength was limited and would more than likely be a hindrance. It wasn't just her foot that was crippled, as the bottom of her spine also had a curve in it. Though it wasn't much of one and it didn't bend her over, unless she was tired, like now, the curvature did cause her pain almost beyond endurance at times. She held Elsie to her, and the crashing sound of the carriage against the rocks undid her. Her body trembled. The dry sockets of her eyes filled with tears as the full impact of their plight hit her. She looked in fear at the lady, but she hadn't moved. The thought came to her: *God, what now? What now?*

There was no doubt in Ruth's mind that they had to take the lady down to Clitheroe and get help for her, but what trouble would that bring down upon them? The fear this caused increased the shaking in her body.

2

Katrina Arkwright

Released from a Dreaded Event

'I won't marry him, Mama!'

'My dear Katrina, Father will be so disappointed if you don't marry Lord Bertram Rollinson . . . He is the Earl of Harrogate, for heaven's sake!'

'No! And I don't care about his title or *who* he is, or what he represents. He is puny and disgusts me. His manner is effeminate and his breath smells. Ugh! The very thought of him repulses me. Why, Mama, why must I?'

'Darling, he is such a good catch. Your father is so pleased about the Earl choosing you as his bride. Lord Bertram is sought-after by every female of standing who is of marriageable age.'

Katrina doubted that her father had anything to do with it. A self-made man, he was accepted in society only because of her mama, who was born a lady; and although Katrina knew it pained him that Mama was no longer fully accepted, being so meant far more to her mama than it did to Daddy.

'This is such a good opportunity for you, Katrina. Most girls of twenty-one have been spoken-for at least for a couple of years. And you will be such a help to your sister. Marcia will get to meet someone of worth, as you will be in the social circle that you should have been in by birthright – and that will involve us all.'

'Mama, you – of all people – should understand how I feel. You were born a titled lady, and Grandpapa sold you to Father: a lower-class person made good. And that is what is happening to me. Lord Rollinson is trading a title for me, and Daddy's acceptance into society circles, just to get his hands on our money. How could you wish this to happen to me?'

'Because I know that such arrangements can work. Mine has. Yes, I had to marry your father, because Daddy was in so much debt, and by marrying me off to one of the richest men in England, he and my family would be saved. And, as it happened, your father wanted greater things for himself, so he was a ready target. What the poor darling didn't realize was that you don't get into the aristocracy by buying into it, but only by birth; and so he never managed to raise himself, only to lower me. You are different. You are from the aristocracy on my side, and marrying back into it will raise you up. You will become a titled lady.'

'How contradictory is that: you want, for me and Marcia, what you didn't want for yourself! It is all for Daddy, so you say. Well, I don't believe you, Mama. And this is too high a price to pay for what *you* want. Besides, it didn't work for Grandpapa – his debts crippled him in the end, and took him and Grandmama to an early grave, so what is to say that our money will work for bloody Lord Bertram?'

'Don't swear, darling. It doesn't become you. Anyway, my father was a gambler; Lord Bertram isn't. His father was and so is his brother, the Viscount Frederick, but that isn't the cause of the decline of their wealth. Not altogether. The coming of the Industrial Revolution may have helped men like your father to advance themselves, but those who depend upon the land and their estates are not in a good position – except those who had funds to invest in manufacturing in the beginning. All the big money is centred on the towns. Just look how Blackburn has grown. When I was a young girl, it was nothing more than a large village. It is a—'

A tap on the door interrupted her mother and increased Katrina's frustration. If she could only bring her mama round to her side, she might stand a chance! There must be some way out of her situation. There had to be. God, she couldn't marry that sickly nanny-boy. She couldn't.

Wistlow entered, at her mama's bidding. Trying not to show their butler there was anything amiss, Katrina turned her back and walked over to the window. Her feet sank into the hand-made Indian rug as she went – a rug so huge it could almost be called a carpet. Its rich blues, golds and reds gave a splash of colour to the otherwise subtle creams and soft blues of Mama's sitting room, without interfering with the elegance that Mama surrounded herself with. An elegance reflected in the carved deep-mahogany furniture and the beautiful chandelier, which held as many as forty candles.

The view from the window brought some peace to Katrina. The mountains of the Pennines, with their snow-capped peaks, formed a backdrop to frost-tipped trees and acres of land covered in bracken, which was wearing its browns and rusts of the winter season. Wistlow's words shattered that moment's peace and brought her attention back to the present.

'Ma'am, there is a policeman here. He has some bad news. Should I send him to the factory to talk to Mr Arkwright, or summon Mr Arkwright here?'

'What does he want, Wistlow? Has the policeman told you?'

'Only that there has been an accident, Ma'am, but he did say it wasn't a family member and that he is here as part of his investigations.'

Though this was alarming, Katrina couldn't think how this accident could concern them, if her father wasn't involved, or indeed Marcia, who was at this moment travelling home from finishing school.

'Did he indicate whether the accident happened at the factory?' her mother asked, but then answered her own question, 'No, of course it couldn't have. He'd have gone there, not here.'

This set Katrina wondering: *So who then? Good God, surely not the Earl and his mother, who are on their way to see us? Though that might solve my problem, if it was serious enough.* This thought soon changed to: *Let it be. Please let it be the ghastly Earl.*

Mama's anxiety caused Katrina a feeling of guilt, as it was obvious that the same thought had occurred to her and distressed her. Her face had paled and her voice shook. 'Oh dear, it can only be . . . No, it can't be, not my dear Eleonore.'

Lady Eleonore, the Earl's mother, had been a friend of Katrina's mother since they were girls at the same school in Belgium. A French nobleman's daughter, Lady Eleonore had met and married the elder Earl of Harrogate, now deceased. Her sons, the new and despicable Earl, Lord Bertram, and his brother, the Viscount Frederick, couldn't be more different, if they were born to entirely separate families. Katrina rather liked the handsome Frederick and wouldn't have baulked at marrying him.

It wasn't just his looks – tall compared to Bertram's short height; dark hair to Bertram's fair; and, well, Frederick was altogether French-looking. Whereas Bertram . . . Oh, she didn't want to think about him, other than to wish he'd be conveniently disposed of in some way.

It didn't take long for Mama to recover herself and instruct Wistlow to take the police officer to the kitchen and offer him some refreshment. 'And then send an urgent message to Mr Arkwright. Tell him to come home at once, Wistlow.'

After Wistlow had left, they sat in silence for a moment. Katrina had sunk down onto the light-blue, French-influenced couch and looked up at a picture of her mother adorning the chimneybreast above the huge open fireplace. This room, although cool in summer with its many windows and French doors that opened onto the garden, needed the roaring log fire to be kept alight to maintain the heat at this time of year.

The spitting and crackling of the logs blazing in the hearth drew her attention. Trying to dispel the horrid thought she'd had, she looked into the depth of the flames and watched the dance of the sparks on the soot-covered fire-bricks behind them. She remembered herself and Marcia playing a game of claiming a spark each, and willing it to last longer than the other ones. She and Marcia had been so close in those days – how did it all change?

They had spent quite a time apart because when she returned from finishing school, Marcia – two years younger than herself – left to attend the same school. The change in Marcia when she returned for a school break had dismayed Katrina. Now, although she loved her sister dearly, she was wary of her scheming ways.

21

A small sigh from her mother broke into Katrina's thoughts. 'Would you like a drink, Mama? Because I could do with one.'

Mama leaned forward and rang the bell on the table in front of her. 'Yes, dear, I certainly would. I feel so worried. I am certain it is Eleonore, but what could have befallen them?'

'Robbers maybe, or a lame horse rearing. Who knows?'

'You don't sound very concerned, Katrina, and that isn't like you. You may not care for what happens to Lord Bertram, but Lady Eleonore—'

'I know. I'm sorry, Mama.'

Her mother nodded. The ringlets caught up in a bunch on the back of her head did a little jig as she did so. Still beautiful and very elegant, her mama showed little sign of her age. Her hair shone in a youthful way, with very few grey strands peppering its jet-black colour. Her oval-shaped face had a delicate, vulnerable look, and sweeping lashes framed her hazel eyes. Everything about her – from her creamy skin to her slanting shoulders and tiny, but in-proportion figure – was a picture of loveliness. Not that she was all sweetness and light, as she appeared to be; she was a woman who knew what she wanted, and she could twist her husband around her finger to get it.

In some of that, Katrina knew she was describing herself. In looks and figure, that is, she was the epitome of her mother as a young woman, though she knew her nature was more like her father's: determined, strong-minded and stubborn; in her youth this had been interpreted as being wilful.

Wistlow had only just finished serving their drinks – gin with lemonade for Mama, and a sherry for herself – when a commotion started up in the hallway. Father's loud voice could be heard shouting, 'Where is everybody? I'm bloody summoned home and there's no bugger here to greet me!'

Mama raised her eyebrows, but remained seated. Wistlow moved in a sort of scurrying action towards the door. Too late: Daddy had already entered and almost threw his cloak at the poor man, followed by his tall hat, which Wistlow caught with style, making Katrina want to clap her hands and shout, 'Bravo!' – though she knew better than to do so at this moment.

'Come and sit here, dear.' Mama patted the seat next to her.

Daddy calmed immediately, smiled and sat down. 'Sorry, dear. I'm just very worried. What's happening? Why the summons?'

Mama told him about the policeman and why he was here. 'We don't know who is involved or why it is of interest to us. Only that it isn't a family member, and that we are part of his investigations. I thought you would want to handle it yourself.'

'My love, you're shaking. What are you afraid of?'

'That it might be Lady Eleonore. Oh, Robert, I couldn't bear it if she—'

'Now, now.'

Mama leaned heavily on Daddy's shoulder as he tried to comfort her. 'We'll not meet trouble afore it meets us. Where is this policeman fellow?'

Her father, though a huge man in stature, with his clothes, demeanour and manners telling of his extreme wealth, still had a Lancashire tone to his voice, which somehow was at odds with the rest of him, and could be so pronounced that you would think him a worker in his mill, instead of the owner. For all that, she liked the accent, and it didn't matter to her that her father still showed his roots. She suspected it mattered to Mama, as she was always correcting him. This time, though, Mama stayed quiet.

'By now he should be on his way to your study, dear. I instructed Wistlow to see to the man's refreshment and keep him in the kitchen until you arrived, and then to take him to your study.'

'Right. Yes, that's the best place, I'd say. Well done. Are you wanting to come t'office with me? Hear at first hand what this is all about, eh?'

'Can I come too, Papa? After all, it could concern me.'

'Erm . . .' Her father looked towards Mama. His way was to defer to her in all such matters. To Katrina's delight, her mother agreed. *Thank goodness. At least I won't be left wondering.*

Walking in the garden some thirty minutes later, snuggled in her fur coat over a long brown day-frock, Katrina felt great sadness for the plight of Lady Eleonore, lying unconscious in a cottage hospital in Clitheroe. That lovely lady's life hung in the balance, and yet she had no idea that her son was dead. Despite this, Katrina had to admit that her sadness for Lady Eleonore vied with the joy she felt for herself in being released from a fate she had thought of as worse than death.

Her father had ordered that a doctor should be in constant attendance and that, as soon as Lady Eleonore could travel, she should be brought to their house. It appeared that it was an entry in her diary that had brought the police to their door. Father had immediately sent a wire to Viscount Frederick, to tell him the news. Poor Frederick. Once again Katrina admonished herself for feeling glad to hear of Bertram's demise, when Frederick and his mother had so much to contend with.

Anger entered her as she thought of the peasants who had caused the accident. To her mind, they had no thought for others. There was no excuse for walking on a road that was for the use of horseriders and horse-driven vehicles and had very few passing places. But for all that, she shuddered to think what their fate might be; after all, it sounded as if they were all very young.

3

Ruth

A Fruitless Search

Ruth stared into the terrifying, impenetrable darkness of the room in which she'd been locked. Her mind jumped from one thing to the next. But it was mostly occupied by where her sisters and brothers were.

The journey to get the injured lady somewhere she would receive help had been hazardous and heart-wrenching. The lads had managed to make a kind of stretcher out of the remains of the back end of the coach and between them they'd lifted her onto it, before tying it – and the lady – securely on top of the pram and fixing that to the horses. They'd found everything they needed amongst the debris scattered around: belts from dressing gowns, and some leather belts rolled and tied, plus a blanket to cover her with. And although the contraption was unsteady, George had managed to soothe the horses along the way, so that the journey didn't cause the lady any further injury.

It was the burden of the third horse, which was not needed to pull the pram, that had broken their hearts. Somehow they'd managed to lift their ma's body and secure it over the horse's back. Five orphans, lost in grief, doing what they thought best.

On the way Ruth and Seth had made up a story, which they all had to learn by heart and not stray from. Elsie was instructed over and over again to stay dumb. No matter what was said to her, she was to shake her head and keep her lips clamped together.

Their story was simple and most of it was the truth; they were to lie, though, when it came to what had happened to the Earl. They were to say they hadn't been able to save the young man before the carriage went over the cliff. And they had to remember that they wouldn't know who he was, so they mustn't mention his title, no matter what they did.

A shudder went through Ruth's cold body. It had all seemed so simple. But on arriving at a small hamlet, they'd knocked on the door of the first house – a large house, where they thought someone of note might live. Someone who would help them. Instead, the man who answered the door asked them their business in a cold, suspicious manner.

Ruth had told him their story, thinking that once he knew, he would be more kindly towards them, but instead he'd told them to wait. The huge door had shut on them with a snap that had sent worry through Ruth. She'd been right to fear. Within moments the man returned with another man, and together they lifted the lady off the pram and took her inside, telling the siblings not to budge.

Seth had urged Ruth to let them make a run for it, but although she was apprehensive, Ruth had refused, as she couldn't think why asking for help should bring trouble down on them. They'd done the right thing, hadn't they?

When the door of the house had opened again, she'd

wished with all her heart that she had taken Seth's advice. The man growled at them that they were all to come inside. He showed them into a small room, with one wall containing shelves from floor to ceiling stacked with provisions, the sight of which had been torture to their starving bellies. Tins of meat and jars of preserves lay side-by-side with bags of flour and stacks of tins containing sugar and tea. The other three walls were whitewashed. Against one of these was a cold slab holding tubs of lard and dripping, and a leg of lamb. On the brick floor stood flagons of ale, and bottles of wine lay in a rack. Above these hung a cooked ham, which had had slices cut from it. For a moment Ruth had been tempted to seize hold of it and let each of her siblings take a bite. But she'd resisted and had huddled them close to her.

No matter what their fate, or what they were thought to have done, to put starving children in such a place seemed a cruel act.

They'd stood awhile not speaking, each taking in the feast before their eyes, as Ruth reminded them to stick to their story. The door had opened during her telling and a voice had boomed out, 'And what story is that then, scum?'

Ruth had looked into the beady eyes of a very fat man. His clothes spoke of him being a gentleman, but there was nothing gentle about him. His face was purple with rage. Turning, he'd bellowed, 'Is that idiot returned yet, Dorking?'

The man who'd first opened the door to them had appeared. 'He is, Sir.'

'Good. Has he brought the doctor?'

'Yes, Sir, the doctor is with the lady now.'

'Tell him that when he has administered to her, he is to come to my office. Now, take these wretches to the barn

28

outside. Whatever possessed you to put this dirty, thieving rabble in my pantry? You're more of an imbecile than I thought, Dorking!'

'Sorry, Sir. I thought to lock them in, and this was the only place I could do that.'

'Hmm, yes, I believe they would try to escape. Have that brute of a man stay with them. The one who carries out the repairs – what's his name?'

'Gadling, Sir.'

'Yes, that's him. Tell him he has my permission to clout any of them if they try to escape.'

When a bear-like man took them to the barn, they'd been relieved to find the horses there and had snuggled up to them for warmth.

Ruth had felt her fear deepen with every moment, and her fear was justified, as not an hour later a policeman arrived and asked them how they came to bring an injured lady to the home of the Honourable Judge Yarrow.

That name was a feared one even as far as Pradley, and it struck terror in Ruth. The judge was known for his harsh dealings. A lad from Pradley, not ten years old, came into her mind. Caught stealing fruit from a market stall, he'd been sent away from his family to a land called Australia, which was said to be on the other side of the world.

Ruth had tried to explain, had tried to tell her story, but her fear had tongue-tied her. Little Elsie had blurted out, 'It were the horses. They jumped up and made our mam dead, and a man made us—'

Seth had tried to save the day. He'd interrupted and calmly told the man what they had rehearsed, but their fate had been sealed. Hours later, and well into the night, Ruth had been transported here, to this hellhole; and the others, she knew not where.

Since being shoved roughly into this room, which she likened to a cell, Ruth hadn't moved. Now she felt forced to, by the urge to pee. Shuffling along to the end of the stone slab she was sitting on, she found the wall. With the help of her crutch she hobbled along it.

As she made her way along the cold, damp, rough surface, the cocoon of shock that had protected her cracked, and her senses awoke to the stench of stale urine mingled with sweat. Bile rose to her throat. Swallowing left a sting that caused her to cough. A tremble of cold and horror shuddered through her. Walking in the direction of the strength of the smell, she counted her steps. Ten paces before her foot kicked something tinny, which made a sound like a gong. Liquid splashed over her foot. The stench increased. Ruth retched but, with an empty stomach, only stinging bile came up from her. Tears streamed from her eyes as she choked on the vile-tasting liquid. Somehow she controlled the spasm and forced herself to use the bucket. It was already full, and adding more urine made the contents spill over the side and run around her feet.

Her tears turned to tears of despair. Unable to sustain the standing position she'd had to take, she slumped on her crutch. But the angle she'd held the crutch at, while relieving herself, made it slip. She landed heavily on the floor. Her hair soaked into the foul sewage that she lay in.

For a moment she lay still, begging God to let her die. But then a picture of her sisters and brothers came to her and she knew she had to live, for them. She had to try and save them all. With this thought, some courage came back to her. Writhing in pain, she somehow managed to retrieve her crutch and stand up. Counting the steps back to the stone bench, she sat down and tried to clear her mind. Everything depended on her getting out of here, but how?

A noise woke Ruth, who had not been conscious of falling asleep. A clanging, banging sound. Opening her eyes, she saw that a trickle of daylight was forcing its way through a high, barred, filthy window, allowing her to see her surroundings.

The din increased. The sound was like screaming cats, with the background of a thousand tin cans banging on metal. In front of her was a door with a hatch. That too was barred, but light shone through it. Hobbling towards it, Ruth tried to see out. Horror gripped her as she peered through it. A woman with black-as-night beady eyes sunken into bloodshot sockets stared back at her, from behind the bars of the door opposite. Gnarled, pockmarked and with warts on her cheeks and her nose, she made a sound that was more like a growl than a human voice. After several grunts, she became agitated and her hand, with nails like claws, came through the bars. Curses of evil poured from her, directed at Ruth, which had Ruth shrinking back from the hatch. *Where am I? Oh God, please don't say I'm in an asylum!* Tales of folk being locked up in such places and never heard of again taunted her. She begged God for help.

A different sound brought her out of her despair: that of a cart being wheeled along cobbled ground. Without looking across at the woman, Ruth peered out of the hatch once more. To her left she saw a man pushing a trolley full of bowls, the contents of which must be hot, as Ruth could see steam rising from each one.

31

At each cell the man unlocked the door, viciously pushed the inmate back with a long pole that had a crosspiece on the end, then shoved a bowl into the cell, quickly locking the door again. He waited at each one until there was a knocking from inside, when he opened the door once more, shoved the inmate back, then leaned in and took the slop bucket, putting it to the side of the cell door while he locked the door once more.

It seemed to take an age for the man to reach Ruth's cell, during which time a plan had formed in her mind. She only hoped she had the strength to accomplish it and she knew she'd have to move quickly, attacking him before he could push her back with his rod.

Her heart clanged as she heard him lock the cell next to hers. How was she going to stand long enough to use her crutch as a weapon?

His shadow splashed across the hatch. The key grated in the lock. Ruth's heart pounded even faster and, though she was cold to her bones, sweat trickled down her body. What if she failed?

The door creaked. She knew she had to act now. As the door opened, she lunged her whole body forward, shoving the man's rod to one side and digging her crutch deep into his belly. His body crumbled beneath hers. His breath reeked as it left his body in a gasp that Ruth thought he'd never draw in again. His face registered shock and fear.

Lifting the top half of herself – something she was always able to do, having gained strength in her upper torso to compensate for the weakness of her lower body – Ruth grabbed her crutch and, as if ramming a pole into the ground, brought the end smashing down into the man's face.

His head rolled, in much the same way as the Earl's had

done earlier, drawing Ruth out of her rage and filling her once more with the horror of her actions. Looking down into his shattered, bloodied features, she thanked God that the man was still breathing.

The silence that had fallen erupted into a cackling of pleas and screams. Ruth looked around her. At every hatch, wild faces appeared. Screams of 'Save me' mixed with shrieking laughter and name-calling.

As if given super-strength, Ruth knew what she must do. Unhooking the keys from the man's belt, she managed to get up and make her way along the corridor of hell. Dodging the globs of phlegm that were spat at her, and ignoring the stench of the slop buckets, she made it to the gated door at the end. It took a moment to locate the correct key, but she concentrated on the task as the racket behind her increased in volume. At last the door creaked open. Ruth froze. What if there were more staff outside? Could she fight them all off in her near-exhausted state? But once she pulled the heavy door closed behind her, there were no more people, just another corridor with a room off to the left. The room held a table and a stool. On the table was a pile of papers, and that was all.

When she reached another door, she fumbled with the keys once more and eventually made her way along the corridor, with a series of doors leading off it. One door at the end of the last corner that Ruth turned stood open, and beyond that was another gate-like door that led to the outside.

The smell of food cooking, and the sound of cooking pots clanging, came to Ruth as she neared the open door. A woman's voice called out, 'Is that you, Trevor? You done all the slop buckets already? Well, I have a pot on the hearth. I'll make you a drop of tea.'

Ruth cringed against the wall. She could now see that the gate-door beyond the kitchen stood ajar, but could she make it through without being seen? Looking behind her and then in front of her again, she was seized by panic. Would the woman come out of the kitchen, when she received no reply? The thought of being taken back to that cell, and worse – now having on her head the crime of assaulting the guard – propelled Ruth forward.

'Trevor? Trevor, what's wrong . . . Hey, what are you up to—'

Using her crutch, Ruth shoved the woman with all her might, in the same way she'd seen the guard do. The woman lost her balance and fell backwards. Ruth swayed. The floor came up to meet her, but before she hit it, she grabbed the handle of the door and steadied herself. The woman's eyes held terror as she stared up at Ruth. Ruth snarled in the way she'd seen the other inmates do. The woman cowered away, curling herself in a ball and screaming, 'Don't hurt me, I'll not stop you leaving. Please don't hurt me.'

Somehow Ruth managed to close the kitchen door, then couldn't believe her eyes as she saw there was a key still in its lock. Relief flooded through her at the sound of the lock clicking into place. Removing the key, she carried on towards the gate-door, sheer willpower overcoming the horrendous pain that was racking her body.

As her hand grasped the handle of the door, she caught sight of a woman's coat hanging on a nail. Taking the coat down, she threw it outside, knowing that she wouldn't be able to hold it while she found the key to lock the gate-door behind her.

Agony permeated every part of her, with the relief of knowing she was free. Through uncontrollable tears, Ruth saw she was in a courtyard. In the centre of the stone-flagged yard stood a well. The blackened, rust-covered pump looked enormous, but she was used to such a contraption. One of her tasks back home had been to see to the supply of buckets of water for her family from the well in their garden. Pumping it up from the ground had contributed to her body's upper strength.

She knew she mustn't think of the pain she was in. The only way of living with it was to block it from her mind, and she did that now. Leaning against the wall, she steeled herself to make it to the well, draw water and wash her face, hands and feet.

Shivering against the cold of the icy water, she used what strength she could muster to empty a bucket of it over her head. With chattering teeth, she donned the coat. Several sizes too big and reaching the floor, it wrapped comfortingly around her, and its belt tied around her twice, but held the coat in place. Searching in the pockets of her clothes, she found her ribbon and fixed her wet hair into a ponytail. Her last task was to swill down her sandals. This done, her feet squelched into them, but the cold made her oblivious to the dampness.

Some warmth entered her as she made her way towards the gate that led to the outside world. Getting through the gate itself posed no problems, and no one was about. A little way along the road, Ruth threw the bunch of keys and the kitchen key into the bushes, before taking in her surroundings.

The building she'd just left was a huge, rambling old house with bars at every window. As she walked round to the front she saw a sign saying 'Merchant Street, Union's Workhouse Hospital' – the place where they put those considered not normal. A shudder trembled through her, as she realized her thoughts about the place were confirmed. Now, though, she had to get as far away from here as she could.

It was afternoon by the time Ruth allowed herself to rest. Her journey had taken her along busy high streets, where she'd begged a crust from a kindly-looking lady sweeping the path outside a bakery shop. The lady had seemed afraid of her, but had given her a piece from a warm loaf. Ruth had smiled her thanks, and this had the effect of warming the lady towards her; but then an awkward moment had followed as she'd asked where Ruth came from and where she was going. Ruth had been sorry to rush away, but was afraid to answer the woman's questions and was wary of the deeper prying that might have ensued.

Coming to a narrow, cobbled street, she went to walk down it, thinking that it looked as though it housed folk of her own standing and she might get some help. But the stench of the place – the same stinking smell of sewage as where she'd come from – had her changing her mind. Instead, exhausted, she sank down on a bench and allowed herself to lean back and rest, thinking for the first time that she had no need to fear.

The shabbiness of her surroundings meant that she was unlikely to come across anyone who would be curious about her. This thought hadn't died before a young girl approached her. 'What you doing there, dressed like that? Eeh, you look reet funny, lass.' The girl's eyes rested on Ruth's crutch. 'You a cripple, then? By, you'll find no one to beg from around these parts, though I could take you somewhere you'd make a good bit of money and have food an' all.'

Ruth found the girl to be a strange creature. Her face wasn't natural, in that it was painted with rouge, as were her lips. Both in a bright red. Her blonde hair looked like straw. Combed high on her head, it hung in straggly bits around her face. Her clothes showed a lot more of her than they should and seemed to be far too tight for her. But for all that, she had a friendly nature and hadn't been repulsed by Ruth's club foot.

'You're a pretty thing. Ma Perkins will rub her hands together at the sight of you. Eeh, the gents pay well for someone a bit different. You ever been with a man, eh?'

'Naw. And I'm not sure what you're offering, but I could do with a drink and some food, if that's what you mean.'

'Aye, I do. Come along with me. The house is only just down the road. Ma Perkins will put you reet. She's kindly, if you keep on the right side of her. Just do as she asks of you and your life will change.' The girl gave a funny little laugh, but, although wary of her and what she was getting into, Ruth liked her.

'I'll give owt a try, ta. Me name's Ruth – what's yours?'

'Lottie. Does you need a helping hand?'

'Aye, I could do with a lift. If you put your arm underneath mine on me good side, that'd be grand. By, I'm glad as I met you, Lottie.'

'You never said what you're doing here.'

'I'm just wandering. I got separated from me sisters and brothers and I keep hoping to see them, or at least where they may have been taken.'

'Who took them?'

Pulling herself up, Ruth cautioned herself. Could she

really trust this girl? 'Oh, I – I mean, if anyone found them. Anyroad, I'll carry on looking after I've had a bite to eat.'

The girl let out the funny little laugh again. It seemed to convey a message, but Ruth had no idea what it meant.

Inside the house, enlightenment began to dawn on her. She'd never seen anything of a whorehouse, but she'd heard of them, and had once heard her da telling her ma of one in Blackburn. He'd been into the market with some livestock, and a girl had approached him. He and Ma had laughed till they cried at the tales her da had come out with, but Ruth hadn't understood all they'd said. Now, as she stood in the hall of this three-storey house, she knew she was in such a place. Everywhere was decorated in a ruby red. Velvet curtains hung over the many doors leading off the hall, and each was tied with gold braid. Half-clad girls sat on the stairs, giggling down at her, as she stared at the buxom woman who greeted her.

'I'm Ma Perkins. Lottie here tells me you're a virgin, girl. That right?' The woman had bright-red hair. Her face was even more made-up than Lottie's was, and her frock was cut so that her two huge wobbly breasts looked set to escape.

'I – I . . . That's none of your business. Lottie said she was bringing me here for a drink and sommat to eat.'

'You'll get that, all right. But first you need a bath and to get into some proper clothes. You're going to bring me in a mint – that is, if you're a virgin. Now answer me question!'

Feeling intimidated, Ruth nodded.

'No man's ever laid a finger on you, is that true?'

Ruth nodded again.

'Good. Lottie, take her to the bathroom and give her a good scrubbing. Dress her in that white gown. We're going to make a packet from her, especially as she's a cripple an' all. I know a few who like it a bit different. Go with Lottie, there's a good girl. There's some nice stew for you, when you're ready. That is, if a punter hasn't arrived by then. Janet, run to the gentlemen's club and put the word out, love.'

As the woman spoke to all and sundry in one sentence, Ruth found her own voice. 'But I don't want to go with a man. I won't. I'll be off, and you can stuff your stew!'

'Now, now. Here, Lottie, take her bloody crutch from her. She'll have to do as we say, then.'

'If you do that, I'll fall on the floor. I can't stand up without it. Please, let me go. Please.'

A slap sent Ruth reeling. 'Do as you're bloody told, girl. Pick her up, Lottie, and get the bitch ready.'

Ruth's face stung; her body, already weak, folded. Two girls helped her up. They spoke kindly to her, bringing her to tears. With no strength to resist, she went along with them, all the while praying to God to help her, as He had done earlier. But this time He didn't answer her prayers, and there seemed no way out of what she thought might lie in store for her.

4

Frederick, the New Earl of Harrogate

In His Brother's Footsteps

'Mama must be brought back to Beckstone Abbey. Bertram should never have moved her out, on his succession. It wasn't as if he had a family to put in residence there, for God's sake! This house needs repairs that are beyond our purse. I, as the new Earl, will see to closing it at once.'

Frederick and his uncle, Jacobite, the family lawyer, were in the dower-house. The house was a short drive along a leafy lane from Beckstone Abbey, which was situated just outside Northallerton. A sprawling mansion, Beckstone Abbey – the Rollinson family's country seat – had a long history. After being sacked and taken from the monks who had built it, it had been given to an ancestor of Frederick by Elizabeth I. Why, it was not known, but rumour had it that this ancestor was numbered amongst Elizabeth's favourites, with a special place in her heart. Frederick loved the tales of the first Earl of Harrogate and, from his picture, which hung in the great hall of the Abbey, knew that he resembled him in appearance, even though he had inherited the look of his French ancestors, too.

Not having been home since his father's funeral just over

a year ago, Frederick was shocked to see the conditions that his mother had endured. In dire need of replastering and decorating, the dower-house walls showed signs of damp, and mildew blackened a patch behind his mother's sofa. The furniture was shabby and the carpet ragged. Frederick was appalled, and not a little angry with his late brother. 'What the hell was Bertram thinking, Uncle? I wish I had come home sooner. I would have at least tried to dissuade him from making Mother live here. But I just couldn't face seeing the place without Father here, and with Bertram lording it over me. Now I wish that he could do so.'

The pain of his brother's loss brought a lump to Frederick's throat. Though Bertram had been such a different character from him – staid in his ways, which often caused arguments between them – he wasn't a bad brother. They just had a different outlook and their values were different, too. Bertram thought everyone could better themselves if they tried, and loathed those who didn't. He took no heed of their circumstances and was repulsed by the poor. Frederick always thought that was born of fear. They themselves had been so close to poverty and had faced losing everything. But to Frederick, Bertram's point of view was hypocritical; he saw no reason to hate those who were already poor, just because you were afraid of joining their ranks. However, Bertram was a bitter man. He found it hard to hold his head up in society when his purse couldn't run to what his peers had. He'd been determined to find a bride who could provide him with the money the family so dearly needed. Frederick hadn't thought he stood a chance, as there was nothing attractive about Bertram.

Not a strong person, Bertram had suffered many illnesses as a child, and for some reason had never developed physically

41

in the same way that Frederick himself had. This lack of height also contributed to his manner, as he tried too hard to assert himself, which made him come across as much harsher than he really was. But for all his faults, Frederick had loved Bertram; and, yes, looked up to him, if he was truthful.

A cough from his uncle brought Frederick out of his thoughts. Composing himself, he apologized and asked his uncle to continue.

'Bertram had plans to completely overhaul the dowerhouse, once his finances would permit. His priority, and your mother's, was to keep your fees paid. They both recognized that you needed a trade. His motive, and your mother's in residing here, was so that Bertram would have no obstacles in the way of bringing a new bride home. He wanted to be able to offer a home free of any encumbrances, and for his wife to have freedom in how she ran things and the way she wanted to do the renovations that were needed.'

Guilt entered Frederick. He knew that his education was a strain on the family purse, but that didn't excuse Bertram's decision. 'But to even consider letting Mama live here! She will be fetched immediately from hospital and restored to the comfort of her own quarters at the Abbey.'

'I agree, Frederick – it was a bad idea of Bertram's; he could at least have waited until he had the funds to do up the place first. But as for bringing Lady Eleonore home immediately, well, that will be the decision of the doctor who is taking care of her. He may not allow her to travel for a while. I am sure the Arkwrights will make her comfortable until then.'

'But with this place closed, I can afford to have a nurse

to care for Mama twenty-four hours a day. Her doctor *has* to agree.'

'Your finances are not that simple, my dear boy. Closing this place and ridding yourself of the extra staff is just one of the changes you need to make. The Rollinson fortune has diminished to the value of what little land is left, and the leased properties standing on it. Not only have death-duties taken their toll – and there will be more of them to pay – but also your father made some very bad investments. I tried to encourage him to put what money he could spare into the cotton industry, but he thought it traitorous to those of his farmers who lived and worked on your land and had lost a big part of their livelihoods.'

'I know, and he was right in a way. My father was very young when automation began to take over and, as he always did, he took a romantic view of it all and saw himself as the champion of his own father's tenants. He remained steadfast to the idea that the factory system should never have been allowed, and that it was the cause of the death of the cottage industries with which many of our tenants' wives supplemented the family income. But Father had not enough foresight to realize that if he failed, or rather the family business did, then they would, too. If he had invested and prospered, then compromises could have been found. Look at the growth of Blackburn. More food is needed to sustain the many people flocking in to work in the factories. Father could have helped his tenants by using his profit from investing in the mill industry to increase their arable and animal farming of the land, and everyone would have bene-fited.'

'You are right, of course. But no, they took the most stupid action they could. And I, being the younger son,

43

couldn't bring any influence to bear, though I tried, God knows, I tried.'

Frederick knew that his uncle was referring to the misguided decisions and actions taken by his father and grandfather. They had funded the tenants to riot, which resulted in the smashing of the power looms at Carr's mill – all to no avail, as there was no chance that the factory system would not go ahead. Their actions led to them having to sell the land that those same farmers had leased from them. Land that had been in the family for centuries.

'Anyway, we cannot change history, but it angers me that your father made things worse and brought the estate almost to its knees, as his soft-hearted ways led him to allowing rents to get into arrears, which – coupled with his gambling habit – ate into what was left and practically bankrupted the estate. You need to watch those traits, Frederick, as you have inherited them both, my boy.'

Frederick knew what his uncle referred to, and felt deeply for him. Being the second son, Jacobite had to take up a career or be faced with becoming a vicar; and he could only advise his family in their financial affairs. He'd rarely been listened to. Frederick had been looking at a similar future himself, as he too was the second son. He had taken steps to avoid being forced to become a man of the cloth. *The very idea makes me laugh. Good God! Nothing could be further from my nature.*

Well, he was no longer the second son, although he couldn't contemplate the enormity of the task facing him, as the concerns that his uncle had outlined weighed heavily upon him.

He'd not had an unpleasant life to date. His allowance hadn't come up to that of some of his peers, but he had done well at the poker games, winning more often than losing – to the point where some at his club had barred him from their tables. His genius in maths helped. His interest in the subject had been piqued by his mother's talk of knowing the eminent mathematician Siméon Denis Poisson in her youth in France. Frederick had wanted to emulate the man, and had studied his theories. One of the eminent gentleman's papers, in particular, had been very useful: 'Poisson's contribution to Fourier analysis, definite integrals, path integrals, statistics, partial differential equations and calculus of variations' – very handy in applying the mind to a game of poker. Not only that, but Frederick's chosen path lay within it, as he wanted to become a professor of maths. He was in his third year at Oxford, but this awful tragedy would change all that. Now he had responsibility for a near-bankrupt estate! And it didn't sound as though his uncle had a lot of faith in him, which wasn't altogether fair.

'I am not like my father, Uncle. We differ in that I am a winner at the tables. That has stood me in good stead whilst trying to manage my finances on a pittance. But that aside, where *do* I stand? What about Mama's money?'

'Practically gone. There was little left of her family's fortune after the French Revolution. Your maternal grandfather was astute enough to get out what he could, but the bad management of this estate has dwindled it away. The saving of everything – even the earldom, come to that – was due to the prospective marriage of Bertram to Katrina Arkwright. Her father was to put things right: shares in his many businesses, a very large dowry, and a legacy after his and Lady Ver— I mean, Mrs Arkwright's death. The residue of his estate, after his second daughter had been taken care of, was to come to Bertram and Katrina. A considerable amount

– and huge collateral to offer the bank. All our problems would have been solved.'

'Well, I don't think Bertram and Katrina were in love, so maybe I could step in?'

'Yes, I'm glad that has occurred to you, as nothing had been announced and the coming union was, as yet, known only to close family. And as I happen to be Arkwright's family and business solicitor, too, there was no other legal party involved, either. All of which means that you could take Katrina's hand without any scandal, and I can arrange that.'

'Thank you, Uncle. Poor Bertram, I know from his letters that he was very excited to be marrying Katrina. I will miss him. He was a good brother – I know he had his ways, but he loved me and I loved him. And poor Mother adored him, which shows in her agreeing to move out of the Abbey. She would want to give his marriage every chance, although she is also very fond of Katrina, and I believe they would rub along well together. Bertram's death is going to break her heart. I could personally string up the bloody family who were responsible!'

'Oh, I think their fate is sealed. Whichever way you look at it, it was their fault and therefore the charge will be murder on two counts. I would say that, unless there are some under-fourteen-year-olds amongst them, none of them will escape the gallows.'

Later that evening, sitting alone in the largest drawing room of Beckstone Abbey, Frederick found it hard to take in all that had happened.

In his times of trouble, relaxing in this room always settled him and gave him comfort. It had a shabby elegance about it. Its grand gold-and-silver brocade suite had faded and worn long ago, and the wine-coloured, elaborately patterned carpet had become threadbare in patches, for this room had always been the hub of the family and many feet had trodden it. It was a room where the men had smoked their cigars after the ladies had retired to a smaller sitting room, in the days of the rich gathering for dinner. Then there had been the recitals. He'd sat through many, played on the piano in the corner by one or other talented – or sometimes not – young lady showing off her skills. Now, it seemed a lonely place and its familiarity didn't soothe his aching inner self.

This morning had been the start of a normal day. With his brother absent when he'd arrived from Oxford, he'd planned to make the most of his solitary state and do a bit of fishing, as he hadn't been to the lake in an age; and after that he'd thought he'd perhaps track down the gamekeeper and indulge in a little shooting. Maybe even bag something that Cook could prepare for him, with the fish he'd have caught earlier as an appetiser, as there wouldn't be anything big enough in the water at this time of year to make a meal. The prospect had been very pleasing to him. Now he wallowed in misery and felt very alone.

How his mother would feel when she came to, he couldn't imagine. In fact he should go to her. Yes, why it hadn't occurred to him to do so immediately he didn't know, but then he had been in deep shock. And with his uncle wanting to collect some things for his mother, it had seemed a good chance to chat with Jacobite and at least be with one of his family.

He would set off first thing tomorrow. But before that, he must acknowledge the Arkwrights' telegram, which had delivered the bad news to him, and at the same time give them warning of his impending visit.

Crossing the room to his mother's desk, he sat down to compose the note. With it done, he allowed his thoughts to mull over things once more.

Maybe while he was in Blackburn he could see how the land lay with regard to the arrangement for Katrina's marriage to Bertram passing to him. He couldn't see any objection to it. He had none himself. He rather fancied Katrina, as it happened. She was very beautiful and, from what he'd seen of her, had a good sense of humour and a pleasant enough demeanour. Yes, they could fare very well together – better than he imagined she would have done with Bertram. The thought occurred to him that Katrina might even be relieved at the turn of events.

Funny how the world goes round. Katrina's mother had been forced to marry a commoner to secure her family's seat, and now he was having to do the same. Not that Katrina was altogether a commoner – no, she would be acceptable, by way of being the daughter of a lady, even though her mother had given up her title to marry for money.

His thoughts turned to the accident. He had very little knowledge of the family who had caused it. His uncle had told him what details he knew, but Frederick's anger had clouded his thoughts. Why were the family on the highway? They must have known how dangerous it was, and what could happen if they came across a carriage! But then the Bowland Hills were hardly a major route for traffic. Maybe the family thought to make their journey easier than crossing the hilltops would have been.

A small trickle of pity towards them entered him. He wondered how old the children were and how they felt, having seen their mother killed, and what it was like for them in a cold jail. He would ask after them. Maybe even go and see them. He needed to hear exactly how it had all happened. With this settled in his mind, he felt much more relaxed.

Taking what used to be his father's chair near the log fire, he rested his feet on the fender and raised his arm to tug on the cord of the attendance bell. The summons was answered within minutes.

'You rang, M'Lord?'

The address surprised him; he hadn't yet got used to being the new Earl. 'Yes, Crowther, I'd like to partake of a brandy, if you would see to that for me.'

'Very well, M'Lord. And may I say how sorry I am at what has happened, and convey the condolences of all the staff, M'Lord?'

'Thank you, Crowther. And thank the staff for me. I will have a few instructions shortly, as I am going to see my mother tomorrow. In the meantime there is a telegram I need sending.'

With the door closed on Crowther and the dusk just beginning to throw shadows across the room, Frederick's earlier sense of being alone crowded in on him. A spark spat out and landed on the part of his ankle that was exposed. The pain of the burn triggered a tear that had threatened since he'd been told the dreadful news. Trying to blink it away didn't help. Before he could stop it, a whole deluge of tears was released, causing his body to fold and leaving him feeling weak with despair.

A tap on the door got him sitting up straight and blowing his nose with vigour, before giving the command to enter.

'I've taken the liberty of having a hot bath prepared in front of the fire in your room, M'Lord.'

This had the effect of soothing Frederick. 'Thank you. That will be most welcome, Crowther. Oh, before you go, I wish to pen another telegram. This time to Lord Bellinger.'

Simon Bellinger was the same age as himself, though a damn sight richer! They had mixed in the same circles since childhood, as the estate that used to be in Simon's family was situated not far from Frederick's family home. Simon's father had been more astute than most of the aristocracy of the time, and hadn't been precious about the family pile, but had sold it on the death of his father and had invested most of the money in a cotton mill. Now Simon's family owned several of them, and a new country estate just outside Blackburn.

Frederick intended to ask Simon if he could stay with him whilst he was in Blackburn. It would be less embarrassing than staying with the Arkwrights. The question of the marriage arrangement shifting to him would need to be discussed, but it wouldn't hang over him every minute of the day if he stayed elsewhere. Yes, he'd be better as a visitor than as a lodger, even if his mother was in residence in the house. And it would leave him free to make arrangements to have Bertram's body, which still needed identifying, brought back. Besides, he could enjoy some lighter moments with Simon. He'd not have to stand on ceremony all the time or make small talk.

Maybe there would be a chance of joining Bellinger's poker table. The players in his circle had serious money to lose. And why the thought came to him, Frederick didn't know, but if the game did happen, afterwards he would go to the whorehouse that Bellinger frequented. Bellinger had

50

often invited him, but as yet Frederick had remained a virgin and relieved himself, when it was necessary to do so. Perhaps it was the right time to become a proper man. Yes, a new life awaited him. He might as well start it by finding out what it was all about, and what would be expected of him in that department, if he married Katrina. According to Bellinger, the ladies of the whorehouse were the best of teachers.

5

Katrina & Frederick

A Deal is Struck

Katrina couldn't believe the turn of events. Part of her was sorry, of course, for what had brought it about, but a large part of her was filled with excitement. Frederick, the new Earl, would be arriving at any moment, and Papa had received a communication from the Rollinson solicitor, Frederick's uncle, to ask if he would consider a new betrothal – whether his daughter was disposed to consider a match between Frederick and herself. Katrina smiled. *Yes, I find myself very much disposed towards the idea.*

'Oh, Mama, I am so happy, and yet I feel guilty for being so. I know I have only met Frederick on a couple of occasions, but I did find myself attracted to him.'

'Well, my dear, it is an ill wind, as they say. But for our part, your father and I are very happy, too. We wouldn't have forced you to marry Bertram, God rest his soul, but Papa would have been very disappointed – and I for him. At last you will be in the position you should have been from birth, and it all bodes well for you being very happy, too. I am so pleased, and now it should be an easy task to get Marcia settled. Suitors will be knocking at her door in their droves, due to the connections that she will have through you, and with the elevation of our position.'

This little speech confirmed what Katrina had always known about her mama: that it was she who missed her former life so much and hated living on the fringe of society, not Papa wanting to elevate himself. And it was this desire, from the wife he loved deeply, that had driven her papa to try and drive her into marriage to the repulsive Bertram.

Her mother's voice cut into these thoughts. 'You look very pretty, dear. That blue suits you. Now, I must go up and talk to Lady Eleonore. She was feeling much better when I looked in on her this morning. She has no broken bones, thank goodness, and the cut on her head looks as though it will heal nicely, but the poor darling has black eyes and is bruised all over.'

'Does she know?'

'No. In his communication Lord Frederick said he wanted to be the one to tell her, but I think she suspects. She hasn't asked after Bertram, only muttered about her poor baby.'

'Baby!'

'We mothers always think of our children in that way, as you will find out, my dear.'

'Mama . . . well, about that I – I don't know anything about having babies or—'

'Really, Katrina! That isn't a subject for discussion. Having said that, don't worry about it. Everything will come naturally, and Frederick will know what to do. It isn't proper for a young lady even to think about it. I'm very surprised at you.'

With her face flushed, Mama left the room, leaving Katrina blushing with embarrassment. She'd known it wasn't proper to ask, but she had been worrying about that side of things ever since it was first proposed that she should wed. What did happen between a man and a woman in bed? And how did it result in pregnancy? Oh, it was all very frightening.

Having been shown into a grand drawing room and partaken of a glass of ale with Arkwright, Frederick found that he rather liked the man. Straight-talking and with no airs and graces. And even though it was clear he wanted his family to rise in their social standing, he came across as an honest and fair man – easy to deal with and a good fellow altogether. Frederick was surprised, though, that Mrs Arkwright hadn't managed to get her husband to speak the Queen's English, or at least to moderate his northern country accent a little. Surely she would know that it, alone, would bar him from certain circles. Even he would find it an embarrassment to introduce Arkwright to his friends, and he was known for his liberal attitude towards such things. Besides, the way Arkwright spoke masked the intelligence the man obviously possessed, and gave credence to those who would say that new-moneyed folk were vulgar in the extreme.

Into these thoughts came the realization that Arkwright had paused in his conversation and was refilling their glasses himself! Though Frederick often wanted to relieve his servants of their duties and felt capable of carrying out these simple tasks, he would never do so. His butler would feel affronted, and as if he hadn't any worth. Arkwright had a lot to learn.

When the man spoke again, he changed the subject from business to the matter they both knew was at hand: 'Now, lad. As sorry as I am about everything, there are things we need to discuss. You know that your uncle has contacted me?'

A tinge of embarrassment flooded through Frederick at this. Suddenly it seemed in very bad taste for them to have even thought about the new arrangement within hours of learning of Bertram's demise.

As if sensing his thoughts, Arkwright said, 'Naw, lad, there's nowt to be ashamed of. I long since learned how them in your class go about these things. I have a good teacher in me wife. Marriage in your society is no more than a business contract that can at best sometimes turn out well for both parties, and at worst solve a lot of problems. I were lucky, and I hope you will be an' all.'

'Are you saying that you agree to it, Sir?'

'Aye, I am, and I think as you'll fare very well together. You're a handsome chap and, from what me wife tells me, a very agreeable one. Katrina can be a handful – takes after me in her ways – but you look man enough to sort her out; not like that brother of yours, God rest him. She'd have taken him in, chewed him to a cud and spat him out.'

Frederick didn't know whether to laugh at this or not. He certainly felt like doing so, as he didn't detect any malice in what Arkwright had said and could acknowledge the truth of it.

'Very well. I'll meet Katrina and court her a while, make sure she is of a mind to have me as her husband.'

'Oh, she'll have you all right. Her mother tells me she's right taken with you.'

'Thank you, Sir.'

'Same terms apply, but I'll say to you what I were going to say to your brother. In return, I want me other lass introducing to the right circles. I want me and me wife to be included in the right circles, and I want you, lad, to learn some of me trade. I want to leave me business to someone as cannot only handle it and know what it's all about, but can improve it as well and start to take over from me, so as I can spend more time enjoying what me hard graft has got me.'

'As far as taking a hand in the business and learning the ropes, you will find me very well disposed. I am a mathematician in my third year at Oxford, with a view to becoming a professor, but the idea of that was born from my circumstances, and the repulsion in me at becoming a man of the cloth, as was my fate if I had no trade. I am fascinated by industry and will be a willing learner and very happy to take over from you – that is, if I come up to the mark. Now, Sir, I find you a straight talker and, as such, imagine that you can take as well as give out, so I have a condition of my own to put to you, if I am to introduce you to the "right circles", as you phrase it.'

'Oh? And what's that then?'

The harshness of this response had Frederick cringing. Had he misjudged the fellow?

But then a grin lit Arkwright's face and he beamed at him as he said, 'Quite right. Start as you mean to go on. Let's have it then, lad. What condition have I to meet?'

'It's about the way you speak, Sir. You will never be accepted in the upper circles – and don't forget, mine will sometimes include Queen Victoria herself – whilst you talk with such a broad accent. It marks you as uneducated and uncouth, which I know you are not, but others won't even bother to get to know you, to find out. And they will shun your wife and daughters, just in case courting them will lead to having to court you.'

'Good God! Well, I—'

'I am sorry if I have offended you, Sir.'

'No, lad.'

'And on that subject, whilst we are alone you may address me as you like, but the proper address is "My Lord". Even family will address me in that way when others are around. If you are talking of me, you—'

'All right, la— M'Lord, I get the bloody picture. You lot have always been so far up your own arses, and yet few of you have a penny to call your own.'

At this, Frederick couldn't help himself: his laughter bubbled over and came out as a roar.

Poor Arkwright looked nonplussed for a moment, then joined him, taking his hand and shaking it with a strength that no one had ever used before. 'Eeh, you had me going then, lad!'

With this, their friendship was sealed. When he could speak, Frederick said, 'I thought you would explode, Sir!'

Calming down, the man he now thought of as his soon-to-be father-in-law became serious once more. 'You're reet, I will have to do sommat about how I speak. Young lass as is our Queen will think I'm from a foreign country, as she's never been up this end of her country, and isn't likely to. But you knaw, lad, I didn't come by what I have easily, and that's nowt to do with speaking one way or t'other. I was a putters-out – I dropped raw cotton off to the spinners in the cottage industries, but I saved all I earned, and when the first automated spinners were invented, I bought into one. Me fortunes grew from that, and from me own bloody hard work. And I'll tell thee sommat, lad, I'm not a nobody, as me dad was a distant relation to Richard Arkwright, who was a brilliant inventor and who funded the invention of the water-powered spinning wheel, and died an extremely rich man. But having said that, I take what you say on board, and I'll speak with Mrs Arkwright, see what she can do for me. She's never criticized me, never – well, not criticism as such. She has tried to correct me at times, but I took no bloody notice. She should have insisted and put me right before now. Can't understand it; she usually gets her way with everything. Anyway, let's go and find the ladies, and then I expect you would like to see your mother.'

All of this surprised Frederick. 'I admire you, Sir, and I am honoured that you are to take me into your family. I will work hard, too, and make you proud of me. And yes, I'm not looking forward to telling my mother what has happened, and if you will give me your leave to, I think I should do so as soon as possible. Maybe the ladies would excuse me if I went up first, and then mct with them?'

'Just as you like, lad . . . um, M'Lord. Eeh, thou knaws, when we're on our own, it'll allus be me calling you "lad". I won't be able to help meself – you've to allow me that respite to be meself.'

'I agree. Besides, I rather like being that, to you. It will make for a special relationship between us.'

'You're alreet, you knaw that? In fact you're all I could wish for in a son-in-law. I have faith as you'll make my Katrina very happy. You have a way of accepting compromises and, with my lass, you're going to need to. Like I told you, she can be headstrong.'

They both laughed – a laugh that said they were companions in the face of the women in their lives. Frederick had a feeling his new life was going to turn out really well. But first he had to deal with what was happening in the present, and that weighed heavily upon him.

6

Frederick & Ruth

A Chance Meeting

As he sat at the poker table later that night, Frederick thought about the day's events. The whole thing had gone rather well. Mother had of course been devastated, and the doctor had been called in and had given her something to put her to sleep for a while. When she'd woken she'd come to a calmer place, and Mrs Arkwright had been a great help to her.

Katrina had been most agreeable – fun, even – and every bit the lady. Yes, they would jog along very well, he thought. He certainly found her highly attractive. She'd flirted with him, which he'd enjoyed. He knew he'd have no problem being a good husband to her, and she had explained that she was very happy with the arrangement, though she felt great sadness at the loss of his brother, which he'd found rather sweet.

Because of this, when they left the club later and he tucked his winnings into his wallet, Frederick thought twice about his earlier plan. 'Count me out of the extra activities you have planned, Bellinger. I'd rather just go back to yours and get my head down.'

Bellinger was having none of it. 'Come on, Freddie, old boy. Don't get cold feet. It's time you introduced your cock to a fanny. You can't be a virgin when you get married, dear fellow. Make a right mess of things, you will.' His ridiculous laughter echoed around the narrow street, making it impossible for Frederick to maintain the indignant stance he'd taken.

Instead he took the same line. 'You are very crude, M'Lord. It is unbecoming. At least my cock won't be riddled with poxy diseases, as yours has been on more than one occasion.'

'Oh, don't. Don't remind me, M'Lord. Ha, that sounds funny. I have had the right to that title for ages, but you . . . well, I think "Viscount" suits you much better. Anyway, all you have to do is inspect the goods first, and then get the whore to wash in your presence. Not only can you be sure she is clean by doing this, but it is pleasurable as well. Besides, once you have an idea of what's what, you can go for the virgins. They are not diseased, they give enormous pleasure and they don't expect much, so you can just enjoy yourself. Expensive, though, and not without a certain amount of guilt, especially if they cry.'

'Cry? Why should they cry?'

'Good Lord, you really are a novice. You do know that it hurts a woman the first time?'

Not wanting to appear to have no knowledge of this fact, even though he hadn't heard it before, Frederick laughed it off. 'Of course, but I didn't expect they might cry! I don't think I could bear that.'

'Oh well, you'll have to go gently then. But that's not for me. I like to push my way through and get on with it. Bugger the tears – they're being paid well.'

This whole thing was sounding more distasteful by the minute. These women might be selling what they had, but they didn't deserve to be hurt to that extent. And what about Katrina? My God, he'd have to find out more, without making a fool of himself, before he took her for his bride. He couldn't stand the thought of reducing her to tears.

Before he could protest further, Bellinger called a cab over. A two-man hackney – not a comfortable ride, after consuming copious amounts of brandy. Relief at the journey coming to an end outweighed Frederick's trepidation as they reached an area of town that he'd never ventured into before.

Nothing about the place endeared itself to him: an even narrower street than the one he'd left, and the whole area had an overbearing stench clogging the air. So bad was it that he had to take out his kerchief and cover his nose.

'Good God! Where are we? It smells like a sewer.'

'And that's just what it is. Welcome to Bott Lane. Ha, never was there a more appropriate name than that, my dear fellow, because here the women will lay on their botts for you, and empty what comes out of there into the gutter outside their house.'

'Really, Simon! I haven't heard you talk like this since we were schoolboys. It doesn't become you. You must be drunk. You're disgusting!'

'Telling it how it is, Freddie, M'Lord. Come to think of it, that title does suit you. You have all the stuffiness it implies. You need to undo a button or two and give yourself some space to breathe. Lower your nose a little and have some fun, for goodness' sake. Come on, this is the place.'

As they went to step onto the lowest stair of five leading

to the front door of the house, the door opened. What he first thought of as 'a creature', hunched over a crutch and crying, had him stepping back and almost knocking Simon over.

'Watch out. Hey, get out of the way, cripple! Go and do your crying elsewhere. You—'

'Don't, Bellinger. Here, Miss, let me help you.' The moonlight caught in the most beautiful blue eyes he'd ever seen, as the girl looked up at him. Soft strands of long, dark hair brushed his hand as she flung it back, giving him a glimpse of a face that glistened with tears. A perfect face, from the gentle arch of her eyebrows to the slant of her nose, and lips that had the shape of a sweet, soft bow.

For a moment Frederick held her eyes with his, and as he did so, he became aware of every part of himself, in a way he never had before.

'Let me go. Please, Sir, I ain't one of them. I were tricked into coming here. I – I have to find me brothers and sisters.' The girl tried to pull away, apparently desperate not to be taken back inside the house.

'Leave her go, Freddie. She's scum. Come on, we've a task ahead of us – and a very pleasurable one.'

'No, you go ahead. I'll make sure she's all right, then I'll join you.'

'What? Are you mad? Oh well, on your head be it. I have a pressing need that I have to see to. But take care, there are some weird characters around these parts, and she looks like one of them.'

'I'm not—'

The gentleman who had said he wanted to help her shushed Ruth and helped her down the steps. His kindness didn't give her the feeling that he was planning on doing what those inside the house were up to.

'Has someone hurt you, Miss?'

'Me name's Ruth and, naw, I didn't give them a chance to. I hit out with me crutch, but they had a mind to do things to me. To sell me, to the likes of you and your friend.'

'What are you doing here then? Are you not willing to work here?'

'I—' Her legs gave way beneath her as she began to answer him. The last step took her weight with a jolt that reverberated through her whole body.

Strong arms caught hold of her. 'Oh dear, you're exhausted. Have you eaten?'

'They fed me last night, but the woman who runs this house said she wanted me more compliant, and then she'd take care of me needs.'

'Stay here, sit on the step for a moment. I saw a pie-man on the corner as we turned into the street. I'll go and get you one of his pies. You'll feel better once you've had something to eat.'

'Don't leave me here, Sir. Please. If they see me, they might drag me back in. They were saying as I'd fetch a good price from anyone who had a leaning towards wanting to do stuff with a cripple. They wouldn't take naw for an answer. This lass brought me here yesterday. She found me sitting on a bench and said as them as run this place would feed me. I just need a little rest, then I have to find me brothers and sisters.'

'Come along then. If I help you, do you think you could get to the end of the street? It's only a couple of hundred yards.'

'Aye, I could, if you've a mind to have me hanging onto your arm on me good side.'

He didn't make any objections, and yet it must be something he'd never done before: walking with – let alone touching – a pauper. And a crippled one at that.

At the end of the street he set her down on the bench she'd sat on earlier and called the pie-man over, giving the man short shrift when he tried to joke as he handed over a pie and pocketed the money given to him: 'Eeh, having to feed 'em first now, eh? That's sommat as I've not seen afore. I hope she's worth it.'

'Be off with you, you insolent—'

'I'm going. Keep your hair on and, if I were you, I'd keep your trousers on an' all. There's sommat not right with that one.' With this, he darted away.

'I'm sorry about that, my dear. Now eat up, and then tell me all about your sisters and brothers and why you are looking for them.'

During Ruth's telling of her story of the happenings on the Bowland Hills, and how she'd escaped from the asylum they'd thrown her into, he didn't stop her, but more than once uttered, 'Oh, my God.'

Now, at the end of her story, tiredness weakened every bone in her. Pain creased her back and her gammy foot. The tears that had stopped, with the hope that had crept into her as someone with a bit of clout showed her some kindness, now stung her eyes and wet her cheeks.

The gentleman didn't speak for an age and, when he did, he asked her if she'd allow him to find her some lodgings for the night and trust him to make enquiries in the morning as to the whereabouts of her family.

Though she wanted with all her heart to begin searching

that moment, Ruth knew it would be fruitless and that she might even be arrested again and thrown back into that place. 'What if they find me? They must be looking.'

'They won't look now. I'll go to the police station, once I have you settled, to make sure. Stay here a moment while I hail one of those cabs over there.'

Though it frightened Ruth to think of him going to the police, she could do nothing about it. She hadn't the strength. She hadn't even enough energy to get up on her own two feet and, when he realized this, he lifted her into his arms.

Despite her tiredness, as he carried her across to the cab she felt as though she was on a cloud. As if everything that had gone before was of no consequence, and that her life was beginning at this moment. As the cab driver lifted his oil lamp, the light lit up the gentleman's face. Ruth caught her breath as his eyes locked onto hers. At that moment she felt as if the whole world had melted away, leaving just the two of them.

7

Ruth

Taking Flight

Sinking into the clean linen sheets that enveloped her in comfort, Ruth felt for a moment that she couldn't stay in this hostel and would have to get up and out again and look for the young 'uns. But that moment left her, only to hit her in the face when she woke after what seemed not ten minutes, but was in reality hours later, as now it was morning.

Panic gripped her as she went to sit up and the pain searing her back wouldn't allow her to. The thought of her siblings, and where they might be, filled her with anxiety.

The low winter sun shone through the windows. Someone had opened the curtains and Ruth could see, through the haze of thick muslin nets that still shielded the windows, that the room she was in was on the ground floor.

Looking around her, she took in her surroundings. To her it was a palatial room, with its beautiful polished furniture. There was a chest of drawers in one corner, a huge wardrobe and a washstand on the far wall. The walls were panelled in wood and matched the floorboards that edged the square carpet, which was patterned in shades of grey and blue with some green and cream. And the bed! Three people could have slept in it, in comfort, it was that big.

A young girl stood by the bed with a jug of hot water and what seemed like a pile of fluffy towels.

'Here, Miss. I've nearly filled your bath.' She handed Ruth what she could now see wasn't a pile, but just one towel. The softness of it was alien to her, as always before in her life she had only dried herself on hessian cloth.

'What time is it?'

'Nigh on ten, Miss. The gentleman who brought you here said we weren't to disturb you until you woke, then we were to lay on a bath for you and give you a hearty breakfast. You must have served him well, lass.'

'I didn't . . . I—' Oh, what was the use? Folk would think bad of her, no matter what. She had the young 'uns to think about. 'Look, Miss, I can't stay to have breakfast. I have to get on me way.'

'Well, you can't leave. The gentleman gave strict instructions that you were to be kept here till he came for you, otherwise he'd not pay us our due. He said to tell you not to worry – he'll have everything sorted when he comes back for you later this morning.'

Ruth didn't argue. Something about the gentleman she'd met last night, and who had done all this for her, told her that she could trust his word.

The thought of a bath appealed. She'd never had a bath – not one where she could lower herself into the hot water. That Lottie had washed her last night, but she hadn't sat her in the bath, merely sluiced her down, like her ma used to.

'I'll need a hand, if you'd be kind enough to hold me while I sit, please.'

The girl hadn't objected and now, as Ruth lay back in the

bath, she thought herself in heaven. Her ma came to mind again and an ache overwhelmed her. *Oh, Ma. Ma!*

Swallowing back the tears that threatened, Ruth tried to be strong. Ma would want that of her.

When she'd told the gentleman about her ma and how they'd brought her body down on the back of the third horse, he'd said he'd make enquiries at the hospital about her and find out what had happened. But Ruth knew she'd no need to wonder. Most likely they'd sent her ma's body to a pauper's grave. They didn't mess about, not when folk like them passed on. They soon had them under the ground, afraid of disease. It wasn't like that for the toffs. It seemed the toffs weren't considered diseased. No doubt they'd bring that Earl of Harrogate's body back and give him a funeral with all the honours.

Never in her life had Ruth been violent, until that moment when she'd struck him. Trying to protect her siblings had tapped into instincts that she hadn't known she possessed. She'd killed one man and near killed another, as she felt certain she'd really hurt the guard who'd been on duty in the asylum.

Her heart weighed heavy with the guilt of what she'd done. *Oh God, I didn't mean to kill that man, I was only trying to look after the young 'uns. Forgive me – forgive me.*

'Let's get you out. There's some porridge and slices of bread, and some tatties fried off, for you downstairs.'

The girl's voice cut into Ruth's despair. She might think of Ruth as a whore, but she wasn't treating her like one.

'Ta, lass, I'm grateful for your help.'

'Eeh, God gave you sommat to contend with, with that foot, lass. But then he gave you a face and a figure to set men's hearts racing, so no doubt you'll do all right for yourself. And you haven't made a bad start. An earl, no less. He introduced himself to us as the new Earl of Harrogate! Eeh, I wish I could get meself one of them. Here, lass, here's your crutch.'

Her words struck terror into Ruth and her breath caught in her lungs. *My God, the new Earl of Harrogate! He must be the younger brother of . . . No, he can't be! Such coincidences don't happen, do they?* But logic told her that's exactly who the gentleman who had helped her was, and now the thought came to her that his kindness was a cover – a way of making sure she stayed where he'd put her. *Oh no! He's going to bring the police! I have to get out of here.* If she didn't, she knew she would be sent back to that cell she'd escaped from, and would face further charges of assaulting the guard. She had to escape before the Earl returned. She had to find Seth and George and Amy, and poor little Elsie.

Forcing herself to speak in a matter-of-fact way, Ruth told the girl, 'Look, lass, I'm reet now. I'll get meself dressed and come through in a mo.'

'Right-o. Just come along the corridor, pass the bottom of the stairs and go through the first door on the left. That's the saloon where we serve breakfast.'

As soon as the girl had gone, Ruth hobbled over to the bed where her clothes were laid out. Her back hindered her, as it was stiff with pain. It took an age to get on the silk pantaloons that she had been given by that woman at the whorehouse. And she was all thumbs when it came to her corset. She'd insisted that they let her keep her corset – a garment her ma had bought her from a passing peddler. It had taken everything her ma had in the pot for a rainy day, but Ma had an idea that it would help to support Ruth's back, keep it from bending over too much and ease the pain she experienced. Ma had been right. Life had changed quite a lot, once she began to wear the stiff-boned garment. Ma had said it was worth the struggle – and the going without – to get it for her. Ruth couldn't think of not wearing it.

Becoming anxious, as dressing seemed to be taking forever, Ruth caught her boot in the hem of the long grey skirt of the dress, which showed more than a bit of her bosom. A jagged tear ripped through the material. Fighting back the urge to cry took all the effort Ruth could muster, but this silly incident undid her. By the time she'd wrapped herself in her own shawl and reached the window, the brimming tears had misted her view.

The quiet of the place unnerved her as she looked at the sash window. She knew she wouldn't be able to open it without making a lot of noise. Holding onto the window-frame, she used her crutch to knock the catch until it was free.

The sound of the window sliding up had her holding her breath. Thank goodness the sill was low. She'd throw her crutch out first, then sit on the sill and twist her body until her feet were dangling outside. The drop was only a few feet, but it might as well be twenty feet to her. She'd try to land on her good foot. Slither, rather than jump.

For a moment when she landed, Ruth sat on the grass. Her fists and teeth clenched against the agony the drop had caused her. Wiping her tears on the back of her hand did no good, as more followed them. They ran down her face, compounding her despair. Where would she go? How should she set about finding the others without going to the police? It was hopeless.

Cold seeped into her, freezing her to her very soul. She'd have to move.

Crying out against the pain, she managed to get to her feet. Her armpit, which was still sore, felt bruised as she leaned on her crutch. It took everything Ruth had within her to reach the road. But which way to go? The sign pointed to Clitheroe one way and Darwen the other. In that moment it came to her that her quest to find the others was too dangerous and hopeless a task. The guard had taunted her with the prospect of her going to the gallows. Well, now it would be a certainty, after what she'd done to him. What use would she be to the young 'uns then? What use could she ever be, if it came to that? Even if she found out they weren't in prison, but in some orphanage, there was nothing she could do. Nothing!

Whatever she tried would only expose her to recapture. Better that she found help somewhere away from here.

Her thoughts turned to Whalley Bradstone, the local butcher back in Pradley. He'd shown an interest in her. He'd even asked Da if he could take her, but Da hadn't wanted her to go. He'd worried that she'd become a lackey, as Whalley was known to be looking for someone to take the place of his ma. She had a few-score years under her belt, and some said she were in her nineties, but still Whalley kept her working and complained that she was too slow, despite her chopping meat and cooking and cleaning from dawn to dusk.

Ruth had been grateful to her da, but now – as she saw it – Whalley was her best bet, as she had no idea where her ma's cousin lived. She hadn't thought to look for her ma's purse when they'd lifted her onto that horse; it was likely the address would have been in it. And none of their possessions had been offered back to them, when that policeman took them from the house where they had sought help. So now she knew no one else in the world who might take her in, other than Whalley. Most folk she'd ever known shunned her or cringed from her, and besides, she could keep making discreet enquiries about the young 'uns if she went to Whalley. She'd make it a condition that he help her. She knew Whalley often took a cart to Blackburn with his wares and brought back livestock. She would make it clear to him that no one in authority must be made aware that it was Ruth who wanted to know. He'd have to say that he worried after their welfare, after hearing about an accident they'd been involved in. And he'd have to agree to take the young 'uns in, an' all, if she could get them back. This thought didn't worry her, as she knew Whalley would be willing. He'd see them as free labour.

A small element of hope entered Ruth. Even though the thought of being with Whalley – a fat man three times her age – repulsed her, and the idea of going to his bed made her feel sick, at least she'd have shelter and warmth and food, and the possibility of getting the young 'uns back. And she knew that Whalley wouldn't let those who would do any harm to her get anywhere near her. He'd shown that in the past. There was once a time when a gang of lads were following her. Their name-calling had hurt her, just as much as their stone-throwing. Whalley had chased them off with a meat cleaver, and they hadn't bothered Ruth for a while. He'd see she was left alone to live in peace.

A flurry of snow landed on her face as she turned towards Clitheroe. Getting back to Pradley meant she had to get back over the Bowland Hills. The thought of the journey brought her to the point of wretchedness, with her whole body screaming against ever going near those bleak highways again, but then determination came over her.

Come on, lass, you've to do this. Oh, aye, there's a chance of me starving or freezing to death, but there's also a chance I can make it. And then, at the end of the day, what other choice have I?

8

Amy Dovecote

Young Shoulders Bear the Unbearable

Amy sat on the dank floor of the prison cell, her skirt soaked through with Elsie's urine.

Quiet now, Elsie had screamed till her lungs must have been sore, then sobbed till she was weary, with very little sleeping time since the cell door had banged closed behind them two days ago, leaving them in the dark. And now, as she slept, Elsie's body heaved a sob every few minutes, but worse than that was her coughing. Even in her sleep a croup nearly took her breath away. And, to compound Amy's worry, Elsie's little body felt hot and yet shook with shivers. Elsie had clung onto Amy, sitting on her knee for most of the time, and had reverted to wetting herself as if she were a babby again. Her cries for their mammy were pitiful, and ground into the open sore of grief that was clogging Amy's every thought. To her it felt as if everything had been ripped from her – even her tears, as she hadn't cried many. But then she had to be strong for Elsie and the lads.

Neither Seth nor George had spoken much, though she'd heard the odd sniffle. She'd not let on that she knew they cried – that would've embarrassed them.

Shifting her position to ease the aching of her body, Amy's mind turned to Ruth. *How will she ever get out of that place they took her to?* And then in her despair, even though she knew it impossible, she begged, *Oh, Ruth, please come and get us. Please!*

A picture of Ruth as she'd last seen her came to her, compounding her despair. Ruth had been exhausted by the time the policeman questioned her, and she had begun to make little sense as she attempted to make their story sound convincing. With that and her affliction, they must have thought her mad. When they'd dropped Ruth off at that frightening, huge dark building, Amy had been glad that the lads and Elsie had fallen asleep and hadn't seen what she had. She hadn't dared to ask questions, but had looked on in terror as the officer had manhandled Ruth and shoved her through the door of the building when it opened. As the horses pulled the cart back through the gates, she'd seen the sign that had told her what the place was. Her heart had pounded with the fear this aroused in her. Didn't they put loonies into workhouse hospitals? Ruth had often been called one of them, because of her affliction, but she wasn't a looney, she wasn't!

It had been a good while before the horses were halted, and she and Elsie and Seth and George had been pulled off the cart. Amy had looked up at the building they were being ushered into, and had seen an old house, large and rambling, with a sign that said 'Police Station', lit by a burning flame inside a blue glass lamp.

No one had talked to them to explain anything. Their names had been given by the officer who'd brought them in, and were written down by a clerk sitting behind a desk that was so tall, Amy could hardly see over it.

In the cellar where they'd been led, she'd seen several heavy doors leading off a dimly lit corridor. One stood ajar, and it was into this room that they had all been shoved.

It was then that all hell broke loose, as one of the officers had tried to take Elsie from them, saying something about her going to an orphanage. Elsie had clung onto Amy's legs and screamed and screamed. And a din like none Amy had ever heard started up, as other prisoners cat-called, swore or banged on the bars of their cells, yelling at the officer to leave the kid alone. The officer had given up and growled at her that the magistrate would decide, when they came up before him.

'Is our Elsie alreet, Amy?'

'Naw, she ain't, Seth. Her cough's bad.'

'Aye, I don't like the sound of it.'

'Happen they'll get help for her, when they come next.' These words had hardly died on Amy's lips when she heard keys jangling. 'Eeh, someone's coming. D'yer reckon as it's for us?'

The murmur of noise, as other prisoners awoke, gained momentum as they reacted to the presence of the jailer and yelled and banged on the bars of their cells once more. Part of Amy wanted it to be their door that was opened, but most of her didn't, as she feared what would happen next.

Warmth enveloped her as Seth and George crept towards her and clung onto her, edging themselves as near as they could, giving her strength, as now she wanted to protect them all. 'Don't worry, we'll be reet.'

Brave words, but not heartfelt, as Amy's heart dropped with the turning of the handle to their cell and a man's voice shouting, 'Get up out of there, you. Come on. There's someone here to see you.'

Ruth! Eeh, our Ruth's come to get us! I knew as she'd find a way. Amy's heart sang with hope, but it was dashed at his next words, aimed at Seth and George, 'Not you two, just the girls. You're to face the magistrate this afternoon, and will be up in front of the high judge on the morrow, I shouldn't wonder.'

'Naw! I'm not going without Seth and George. Naw, get off me. Seth! George! Naw-w-w-w. Naw!'

'By, you're a feisty one. Come here when I tell you!'

Amy's head stung as the jailer grabbed her hair and dragged her to the door. Her screams rasped her throat and burned her chest. The slab-stone floor smacked the breath from her body as he flung her as if she were nothing. *Oh God, Elsie! Elsie . . .* In the moment he'd grabbed her, she'd let go of Elsie. *Where is she? Where's Elsie?* 'ELS-S-IE!'

A hand grabbed Amy's arm and yanked her up. The sound of Elsie's crying brought her some relief, as the cry was pitiful, but not one that she would give if she'd been hurt. Looking around her, Amy caught sight of Elsie leaning against the now-closed cell door. She reached out to Elsie, taking her hand in her own. Drained of strength, Amy knew she wouldn't be able to lift Elsie, even though she now held her little arms up towards her.

'You stink, the pair of you. Not fit to be in the presence of the gentleman who has come to see you. Though why he has, I've no idea. The likes of you scum, having visits from an earl!' His spit landed on Amy's shoulder, and sprays of it hit her face. Her stomach retched, but the reaction halted as the guard grabbed her hair again and yanked her head back-wards, ricking her neck. Dragging her into a cold room, he lifted his lamp high and sat it on the sill of a small window near the low ceiling. The glow from it showed her that they were in an annexe, covered from floor to ceiling with dark-green brick-shaped tiles. From a slab in one corner protruded an iron pump. Under this stood an enamel bowl, dented and with large lumps of its white coating chipped.

'Pump some water into that bowl and wash the kid and yourself. Here, you can use that to dry on.' Amy caught the rough piece of hessian that he'd thrown towards her.

How she managed to pump some water through, she didn't know, but as she began to peel Elsie's clothes from her to prepare her for a wash, her earlier fear gripped her. Elsie's body was hot and clammy, and yet still she shivered. Her face had blotches of red standing out against the other-wise stark white of her skin.

Cleaning Elsie as best she could, Amy took a larger sheet of hessian from the pile on a shelf next to her and wrapped it around her sister's body, before sitting her on the slab. 'Sit still, our Elsie, there's a good lass. I'll just wash meself, then I'll dress you.'

'Take your clothes off. Go on! You need more than a wipe-down.'

'Naw, I'll not. Not while you stand there gawping. I can manage with them on.'

'I said: get your clothes off. Do it, and be quick about it. We can't keep that gentleman waiting, can we? He's brother to that one as you murdered. No doubt come to spit on you and revel in whatever your fate is; but whatever he wants, he commands respect and you're not going up stinking like that.' Turning and opening a cupboard, he pulled something out. 'Here, put this prison gown on when you've washed, and wrap this one around the nipper. You can tie it around her with the belt.'

'Turn around then, Mister. We can't get past you or owt, so you've no need to watch.'

'I decide what happens down here.' The vicious swipe he aimed at Amy knocked her into the wall, banging her head and rocking her vision. But still she held her defiant stance. 'Naw, I'll not. Not whilst you're looking, I'll not!'

Reaching out towards her, the jailer grabbed her arms. Struggling and kicking didn't help Amy. His hands tore the thin rag of her frock from her, leaving her standing in her petticoat. But that didn't stay in place for long, as it went the same way as her frock had.

Holding her arms across her chest, she could feel the fleshiness of her soft breasts, which had begun to emerge a year ago at the same time as her monthly bleeding had shown. She did all she could to hide them, but her thin arms would only cover her nipples. The jailer was still close to her, his breath panting a foul smell in her face.

'Nice. Now, get washed down, and I might take a bit of you afore I take you up.'

She knew what he meant. Growing up on a farm didn't leave any gaps in knowing how the world went around. The animals were always at it and, if they weren't, then they were helped to, at breeding time. And she knew the look he had in his eyes – she'd seen it in her da's, when he courted her ma before bedtime. And always on those nights she'd heard the squeaking of the bed and the moans of pleasure coming from her da as he took her ma. Her ma would be shushing him, but giggling as she did so, and making her own noises that showed she were enjoying it. Amy had tried to block out what was happening, but being in the same room as them, it hadn't been easy and she'd got used to it. Though of late she'd felt a funny feeling down below, whenever it happened, and this had her touching herself and then feeling a deep shame. Now she could see that same lust in the jailer's eyes, and it terrified and disgusted her. She went to turn towards the basin, but he stopped her. His hands grabbed her arms and forced them down. His eyes insulted her body. She lashed out at him, but he caught her and twisted her arm behind her. Pressed up against the slab, Amy couldn't move. The muscles in her arm burned. She bit back the moan that tried to escape from her, as his body jarred her into the slab.

'Leave go of me, you pig! I'll tell the gentleman, if you touch me.'

'Ha! He'll not believe you over me.' This in a harsh voice gave way to a softer, hoarser tone. 'Nice. Eeh, lass, you feel nice.' His hips gyrated against her, his hardness rubbing up and down her buttocks. Dampness seeped through her knickers.

With all she had in her, Amy twisted around and, ignoring the agony this caused to her arm, lifted her knee. His holler increased her fear. His body doubled over and the cheeks of his face reddened as he looked up at her, and tears filled his eyes. As he sank to his knees, she grabbed another large piece of hessian, wrapped it round herself, seized Elsie and pushed past the jailer. Where her strength came from she didn't know, but to the background of the catcalls of the other prisoners, she ran across the stone floor and climbed the stairs as if she were an athlete. The door at the top stood ajar. She pushed against it. Its weight resisted her and bruised her shoulder, but on her second push, it opened. Before her lay another flight of steps. Her fear compelled her forward and stopped her from noticing Elsie's weight. At the top, she found another door. Despair nearly undid her as she discovered it was locked. Banging on it with her fist, she screamed till her throat was scorched. When it opened, she fell through it and landed on the floor.

'Good God! What the devil?'

'It's all right, M'Lord. I've got her. Here, lass, what are you doing? How did you get up here? Where's Constable Brown?'

Conscious that the towel had slipped from around her, Amy tried to pull it up to cover her bare breasts, but it was trapped beneath her. 'He were trying to . . . he were going t – to rape me!'

'Eeh, I doubt that. He's a married man, our Constable Brown, and an honourable one. By, lass, what game were you playing, eh? Did you egg him on or sommat? What have you done to him, you dirty little scum?'

Elsie cried out at that moment – a throaty sound that set off a fit of coughing, causing the sergeant to step back from them. 'Eeh, lass has got the croup. Keep away from her, M'Lord. Give you all sorts, these scum do. Excuse me whilst I go and wash me hands.'

'Send for a doctor at once, Sergeant! What goes on here? Look at them. These are children, for God's sake!'

The gloved hand of the gentleman took hers. With his help, Amy rose. He kept his head turned away from her. 'Wrap yourself up, girl.'

Amy wrapped the hessian back around her body, grateful that the gentleman showed her some respect.

'That's better. I'm the Earl of Harrogate. I believe you were involved in the killing of my brother?'

'Naw. We didn't kill anyone, M'Lord. It were an accident.' Pictures of Ruth bashing the young man with his pistol turned Amy's stomach with repulsion and fear. Needing a distraction, she looked around for Elsie, who was huddled on the floor, her breathing laboured, her face burning a bright red. Amy went to her and picked her up, fear for her sister gripping her heart.

'She looks very poorly. How long has she been like this?'

'It started soon after they put us in that cell. She's been through a lot, for a bairn. We all have. Afore me da died a few weeks back, we were a settled, hard-working family; now we're orphans and—'

'I know. I met your sister.'

'Ruth? Where is she? What did you do to her? She didn't mean to—'

'What? What didn't she mean to do?'

'Nowt. She never means to do owt. It's others as goad her, cos of her affliction.'

'I see. Look, I want to help. I'm not here to persecute you. From what I have heard from Ruth, you all tried to help my mother as best you could. Yes, you were partly to blame, as you should never have been on the highway, but I understand why you were. Ruth told me that, too.'

'We had no choice, M'Lord. And . . . and me ma—'

'I know. I'm sorry.'

'Is – is our Ruth still in that asylum?'

'Asylum? Is that where they took her? Good God!'

Amy could only nod. The enormity of their plight hit her, as if the shock shown by the Earl had brought it all home to her for the first time. It was too much to bear. 'You said you wanted to help. Please get her out of there, please.'

'She *is* out.'

Listening to the Earl tell her what had happened to Ruth, Amy felt her despair deepen. *Ruth has near killed another man! Kind, gentle Ruth. None of it seems real.* But where was

Ruth now? And why was this gentleman so concerned? Something about him seemed nice, and she wanted to trust him.

'I took your sister to a guesthouse for the night, but when I called there, before coming here this morning, they told me she'd gone. Climbed through a window and disappeared. Where do you think she would head for? And why would she leave like that? I only wanted to help her.'

The gentleman sounding so desperate as to where Ruth might have gone made Amy wary. Why should he care? He could only want to hand her in. What other motive could he have?

'I don't knaw where she'd make for. She knaws no one hereabouts, and she can't walk far.' This last thought compounded her fear. If Ruth tried to get back to Pradley, she'd never make it. Not on her own, she wouldn't, but where else would she go? None of them knew where their ma's cousin lived. Amy's mind went from one conclusion to another, as she thought of how Pradley held nothing but fear for Ruth. The folk there looked on her as evil. But what about Whalley Bradstone? No, Ruth wouldn't go to him. She'd said she found him repulsive. *Oh, Ruth, where are you?*

'Look, you're all in. Come and sit on this bench. I'm going to get you and your sister out of here.'

'But what about me brothers? They did more than any of us to try and save your ma. Our George stopped them horses from pulling the carriage over, whilst Seth unhooked them. It were very dangerous. They could have been killed, but they didn't care, they just wanted to save your ma.'

'But Ruth said the carriage did go over, and that you all managed to get my mother out, but it went over with my brother still inside when you unleashed the horses. Is that right?'

Shocked at how easily she'd forgotten to stick to the story, Amy could only nod her head.

'I have to know the truth, girl. I can't protect you and get you out of here if it isn't true that you tried to save my brother. Now, what exactly happened? Was my mother out of the carriage before you unleashed the horses?'

'She were, M'Lord.' This time, in her telling, Amy told it how they'd planned to tell it – well, how she'd planned it. It had been their only way. *Ruth didn't mean to kill the Earl, she didn't!*

'Right, if that's the truth, then I will help you. And we *must* find Ruth. I can't bear to think of her out there . . . I – I mean, well, in her condition she is in danger. She may fall prey to the likes of those in that house I saw her in, last evening.'

Still unsure whether she could trust this toff, Amy said nothing.

'Please think. There must be somewhere!'

'I'm sorry, M'Lord, but I don't knaw. I'm worried sick over her. And over me brothers. Please help them.'

'Well, look, I'll try. I'll get a lawyer, but the sergeant was only willing to turn you and your sister over to me. He said they must be seen to make someone account for the accident, so that people will feel they do aim to keep the highways safe. The public still haven't much faith in the idea of the county having a police force. It is early days, and so far the police seem to be costing the country a lot of money and not getting many results. They are anxious to show that they are protecting us, especially those in the upper classes,

84

as it is us who pay our taxes, and it is us who are making the most fuss about their worth.'

'But Seth and George didn't do owt wrong. They didn't. They did their best. Please save them – please.'

'I have said I will do what I can. You have my word on that and—'

The door opening, and the sergeant and the doctor entering the room, cut the Earl off mid-sentence.

As she sat next to the hospital bed that Elsie lay in, Amy tried to keep awake to watch over her sister, but her eyes kept closing, despite her mind racing and screaming possibilities at her as to what might happen. Would Elsie pull through? Would Ruth and her brothers die? Ruth of cold, hunger and exhaustion. And the lads . . . No, she couldn't turn her thoughts to that. That lawyer would find a way of getting them off or, if not, would at least make sure they only got a prison sentence. They wouldn't hang them, they couldn't.

At times she'd thought, *What if Ruth is dead?* She knew in her heart there was every likelihood of this, if Ruth had set out on that journey over the Bowland Hills – especially as she'd be afraid to keep to the highway and would take the bridle path over the top. *Oh God, I don't want that to happen. Oh God, help me – help us all . . .*

The flickering light from the candle that the nurse had left by Elsie's bed glistened on the beads of sweat on her glowing red cheeks. Dancing shadows made Elsie's eyes look sunken and her little face gaunt, deepening Amy's worry. Closing her eyes, meaning to say the rosary over and over, but only getting as far as the first decade of Hail Marys, she found sleep overwhelming her.

At some point in the night a noise roused Amy – a rasping sound that would haunt her forever – but sleep clawed her back into its depths before she could react to it. When she did open her eyes again, the moon had taken over from the candle in throwing light over Elsie.

For a moment it seemed that her little sister was at last in a restful sleep, but she was too still. Too silent. Her face resembled the texture of the wax that had melted into a smooth puddle and set, where the candle had been. A lacy pattern made by the moon shining through the frost-covered window spread over the tiny form, making an almost magical picture of loveliness. Amy could only stare at the serene, angelic look on Elsie's beautiful little face.

The scene held her captivated and in a wondrous place, until somewhere behind her a nurse called out to another, and reality took root inside her. Her moan came from deep within her. She could do nothing to stop it turning into a piercing scream as it reached her throat.

Someone helped her out of the chair as her joints seemed to have locked and her body didn't want to work. *Elsie . . . Dear, sweet little Elsie, gone.* The reality of what had happened hit her. She couldn't bear it and let the blackness that sucked her in take her, as she sank into a deep faint, welcoming the oblivion it offered her.

9

Ruth

Meeting the Hill Farmer

Ruth huddled against the wall of the cave. Cold numbed her, deadening the excruciating pain that had racked her body as she'd stumbled along. Willpower had kept her going, and the reason behind this strong urge to make it was the force that had given her the strength to get this far. For herself, she felt wretched and would have gladly given up and let death take her, but she had to find a way of saving the others. She had to! And for that, she'd suffer anything.

These thoughts were at odds with what she knew to be the reality of their situation. There was little hope that she could do anything to help her siblings. Acknowledging this finally caused her to curl her body up into a ball, as trembling sobs of despair coursed through her. But weeping hadn't helped. It had only compounded her desolation, so she'd fought against giving in to the heartbreak that engulfed her and instead tried to find some hope, some strength to carry on.

Hunger gnawed at her, as did thirst, but both vied with the cold. Closing her eyes, Ruth rested her screaming mind for a moment, though she dared not go to sleep for fear of never waking again. Despite these thoughts, she must have drifted off, because when the sounds of another being nearby came to her, they startled her awake. Hardly daring to breathe, she listened. Had someone followed her? Or was the sound that of a wild animal?

Keeping stock-still, she listened, feeling great relief mix with her apprehension as the kindly tones of a man talking to his horse drifted into the cave.

'Come on, me lass. We'll not get any further in this darkness. I'll tether you to your favourite tree. It'll give you shelter, and there's still some grass under it for you. There you go. I'll unhitch the cart, so you can have your freedom. By, it's cold the neet, me lass.'

The rasping of a match on stone brought a small flicker of light towards Ruth. This was quickly followed by a brighter one, as the sounds of an oil lamp being pumped and brought up to full power came to her. Her body wouldn't move, though she didn't feel any fear. Something told her this man wouldn't hurt her. She'd ask him for help. But though she tried to call out, she could only manage a croaky sound.

'What were that? Who's there?'

Thank God he'd heard her. Trying again, this time a moan was all her throat would release, but it brought him nearer, and the light from his lamp now bathed the space around her in a soft glow. She could see his outline. He looked huge, fat even, but had the stance of a younger man than she'd first thought, from his talk with his horse.

Still, she didn't feel threatened when he asked, 'What're you doing here, eh?' His lamp blinded her as he leaned further over her. Her body cringed away from it. 'Christ! It's a woman! Eeh, lass, don't be afraid. I'll not hurt you. Me and

Aggie, me horse, we come this way regular. I bring a cart-load of me vegetables and me milk cans over, to sell in the early-morning market.'

The man's logic in thinking that if she was afraid, this explanation would make her less so, marked him out as harmless. Though Ruth's dry throat still wouldn't let her talk to him.

'Here, I'll get you a drink o' water, lass. You sound reet parched.'

The cool water choked her at first, but as Ruth swallowed some of it down, it soothed her and brought some life back into her. As it did so, her body shivered against the cold.

'Eeh, lass, I'll fetch you a blanket and then I'll make a fire. We need to get you warm.' It didn't seem five minutes later that flames licked the wall of the cave near the entrance. 'There, that's better. I allus set me fire against the wall – gives more warmth that way, as the rocks heat up an' all. Look, you can see where it has blackened them from me previous visits. Mind, smoke's a problem, but you can sit out of its way.'

The flames warmed every part of her, helping Ruth to unfold her body, limb by limb.

'That's better, lass. Now, can you tell me why you're here? Naw, on second thoughts, don't do that yet. I shouldn't have asked you. Wait a while whilst I get some hot water on. I have tea, though I don't suppose you have ever tasted it afore. You'll like it. It picks you up some. And I have some of me ma's stew an' all. She allus makes me some for me journey, along with chunks of her best baking of bread. I'll soon have it all on the go. I'll just take some water to Aggie and put a blanket over her. She'll need it the neet.'

As her bones relaxed, Ruth felt this was a nice man. He

made her feel safe and cared for. She'd tell him the truth of it – but not about her killing the Earl. She'd not tell him that, for fear he was a God-fearing man and would think it his duty to give her up to the police. But the rest, and her worries for her brothers and sisters . . . she'd tell him all of that.

The steam from the hot tea he handed her dampened her cheeks as she lifted the enamel mug to her lips.

'There you go. Now then, me name's Josh, short for Joshua. And like I said, I'm a farmer. I have a farm some ten miles afore you reach Pradley. Me land is on the edge of the Bowland Hills, but on the other side from here.'

His voice further soothed her as he told her how he made this trek to Blackburn once a month to the markets, but also sold his wares at Pradley market. He went on to describe where he lived. 'Some of me land is flat – well, flat-ish – where I grow me vegetables, but most of it is high ground where me sheep graze. Me and ma's house is up high an' all. It has lovely views, though, and it's peaceful. Not many visit, as it is a bit of a steep climb. But I've done it all me life now, and I'm used to it. I have to walk Aggie up and down it, as it's safer to lead her than to ride on the cart, though she's a strong carthorse and has managed some good loads. Now, that's who I am. What about you, lass? What plight does you find yourself in, that you must take shelter in a cave, eh?'

'Me name's Ruth, and I have tasted tea afore. Nowt like this, though. Ma—' Just to mention her ma brought a great sadness to her, but she swallowed hard against the constriction of her throat and continued, 'Me ma used to say as what we had were the sweepings from the deck of the ship that brought the tea over the water, but it were thirst-quenching and hot. I come from Pradley, though we never went to market. Me da did, with sheep and stuff, but we ate the produce of the farm me da worked on. It were a hard life, but, well, we were happy in a way.' To Ruth's shame, she found that despite her best efforts not to, she was sobbing by the time she'd told all.

'Eeh, lass, you've sommat to cry over there. Let it all out. It'll do you more harm keeping it in. So now you've nowhere to go – well, except to this butcher fellow. Aye, I know of him and I crossed paths with your da an' all. Nice man, your da. But that Whalley Bradstone . . . Eeh, I wouldn't like to think of you hitched to him. He ain't looking for someone to love and care for. He's after a slave. He'd kill you off, as you don't look strong to me.'

'I – I can do a lot of stuff, but I have this curve in me back and this foot—'

'Aye, I can see, lass. And that's where the mystery is with Whalley wanting you, as you wouldn't be a lot of use to him. I'm thinking it were more lust, as you're a beauty. You may not look your best just now, but I can see as you're an attractive lass and have a nice figure.'

This was said in a matter-of-fact way that didn't alarm Ruth. He might have been talking about the merits of Aggie as much as about her own merits.

'I don't usually dress like this. Them as I told you of, they put these on me. I ain't got any others.'

'I realize that. Look, lass, you can come home with me, if you have a mind to. Ma would like that. You'd be company for her, and could help her with her mending and other little jobs as you could manage, like feeding hens and collecting eggs, and maybe a bit of churning, though we'd have to see about that. She's a good 'un, me ma – hard-working and of a sunny disposition, but she's getting on a bit; she'll be sixty next, and she gets lonely when I'm off on me treks. And in return for your help, you'll be fed well and will have warmth and a room to yourself. And when I make me visits to Blackburn, I'll make enquiries as to your family. How does that sound, eh?'

'Aw, ta, Josh, ta ever so much.' Ruth had to fight against the tears coming again, but she managed it. 'And I'll make it up that hill of yours. I can, if I put me mind to it. I came across the Bowland Hills, walked all the way from Pradley to near Clitheroe, though I couldn't manage the steep bridle paths.'

'Naw, and you won't manage the hill to mine, neither, but Aggie'll give you a lift up it and bring you down, when you needs to. That's settled, then. And with you nice and warm and fed, and having some prospect for the future, you should sleep well the neet. I have some bales of straw on me cart; I'll get one in and make a mattress of it for you.'

Lying on the soft, sweet-smelling straw, once she'd managed to tame any prickly bits that dug into her, Ruth couldn't believe her luck. She was saved. And the life in front of her sounded like heaven. She'd not have to give herself to Whalley Bradstone, or fear those in Pradley town, who would throw stones or call her names. Nor would she be in fear of one of the lads in the town kicking her crutch from under her arm as they sped by her, leaving her rolling on the ground, unable to get up until someone who dared touch her stopped and helped her, or one of her brothers came looking for her – but then she'd also be away from all of those she loved most in the world. And though she'd never see her ma and da again, she prayed to God that one day she'd be reunited with her sisters and brothers.

*

It wasn't much after dawn when Josh woke her. 'We've to get on the road, lass. I've made some more tea. It's just brewing. Here, have this slice. It'll put a lining on your stomach. Stays fresh for days, does Ma's bread. I've put a bit of dripping on it. You need some fat in you on these cold mornings.'

The tea warmed her and the bread tasted delicious. Pork fat, she'd have said, though Josh hadn't mentioned keeping pigs. She hoped he did, as she liked pigs. The saying 'mucky as a pig' weren't true. They were clean animals in their habits; they just liked wallowing in mud.

'Does you need a hand up, lass?'

'Aye, I do, ta.'

'Right, there you go. Now, I'll get meself busy with Aggie, while you does what you needs to.'

Her cheeks flushed at this, as she knew what he meant. She didn't say anything, but she went into the bushes as she had a strong need on her to relieve herself.

It took the rest of the day to reach Josh's house, even though Aggie got up to a good trot on the smoother and straighter parts of the road. The last bit of the journey Ruth did with her heart in her mouth, convinced that she'd fall off the cart and over the edge of the cliff at any moment. 'Eeh, Josh, why did your forebears build up here?'

'You'll see when you get there. It's the only bit of our land we own that's suitable. We need the lower fells for the crops, as they get plenty of moisture down there and a fair bit of sun in summer. But up here we have a kind of "table" of land, and the field for the cattle. That slopes, but only as much as they can cope with. Sheep are different: they can roam steep terrain, though we do lose a few to the elements, and the odd one slips and falls to its death. But up top we have enough space for our barns and the dairy, and a pen for our pigs.'

'Eeh, I like pigs!'

'Ha, so do I. They're canny, are pigs. And they give us plenty of meat for ourselves, and for the market, as do all our animals.' He spoke with pride and love. Aye, she could tell Josh loved his work and his home; it shone through every word he spoke. 'We have a run for the hens, though you might fall out with the cockerel we have. He's a noisy blighter. Mind, he's nearly had his time, and he'll be in one of Ma's stews soon. He's not doing his job so well; he just crows loudly about it, but doesn't get on with it, so we'll be bringing in a younger one afore long.'

She laughed at this. She felt at home with Josh. The daylight had shown that what she'd thought of as his large girth turned out to be muscle, not fat. His thick, unruly blond hair and bushy eyebrows looked almost white against his tanned, weathered face. His eyes matched what she thought of his nature – kindly. Pale blue, they twinkled when he laughed. Altogether, she thought Josh a handsome man who she'd put at around thirty, though he could be younger, as his hard-working life hadn't done him any favours. It had calloused his hands and aged his skin, making it rough and thick-looking. Not that it mattered what he looked like, because Ruth liked him – liked him a lot. All of Josh, even down to the smell of him, which had wafted towards her when he'd lifted her up onto the cart. A fresh, outdoor smell – that of a clean man, but one who was always around animals and the land; and a familiar one that brought back memories of her da. But despite this sad memory, happiness was settling inside her, as was hope, and that was all down to Josh.

Though they had only just met, she could feel something between them: an ease in each other's company and an awareness of each other. Not that Josh had the same effect on her as the new Earl of Harrogate had done. The memory of the moment when the Earl had stared into her eyes sent a tremble through Ruth, evoking a feeling that she couldn't define. It had given her waves of anticipated pleasure that had rippled through her body.

Oh, she was being silly! Nothing could come of it. But she knew that if it turned out that Josh wanted her and asked her to wed him, she'd do so gladly. *Eeh, what am I thinking? I've only just met him.* She giggled at this thought. Josh looked back at her, his eyebrows raised, but didn't quiz Ruth as to what had amused her. If he had, she'd have told him it was down to excitement and the feeling of being safe. And some of that feeling was due to him not showing any revulsion at her affliction, and that boded well for her, as that was all she ever wanted from folk.

The first sight of the house pebbled her arms with goosebumps and had the hairs standing on end, as its bleakness filled her with foreboding. A large house, it stood as if in defiance against the elements. Its grey stone walls hadn't weathered well: they had dulled with the constant hammering of the extreme weather conditions that prevailed in the area. Snow lay on the rooftop, and icicles hung from the windows like teardrops. The wind howled around the building and those surrounding it, and as it gushed through the narrow gaps between the buildings, it moaned in a long, drawn-out sound of despair. Doors creaked, and one of them banged and opened, then banged again. The fragile hope that Ruth held within her died, and trepidation took its place.

'Aw, lass, don't look so scared. You're seeing it at its worst. Come spring, you won't know the place. Daffodils dance all around the garden and the sun brightens everywhere. Anyroad, you'll find it warm and inviting inside, no matter what the weather. Lean towards me. I'll catch you and help you down, lass.'

She didn't speak. The feeling the place evoked hadn't left her, and Josh's next words compounded it.

'Eeh, it's not this place that should have you scared. It's over yonder, Pendle Hill. Can you see it in the distance, over there, that large hill in the direction of Clitheroe? That's where—'

'Aye, I knaw.'

'Well, the poor devils taken there still haunt it, they reckon.'

His laugh didn't lighten what he'd said, as Ruth could feel the presence of the women burned as witches and hear their wails and screams. And with the feeling came the curses of those back in Pradley, and a dread seeped into her . . . of what, she didn't know.

Turning away, she looked over Josh's shoulder as he lifted her down, keeping her eyes on the house as he lowered her. The curtain twitched, just for a second – no doubt his ma, peeking at what he'd brought home with him. Before Ruth had her good foot on firm ground, the door opened and framed a large woman, almost as big as Josh. She had to bend to get through the door. A crisp white pinny, which looked as though she'd just donned it, covered the front of her long grey frock. Grey curls escaped from under her mobcap. A question creased her square-looking face.

'Eeh, lad, what have you done? Who's this as you've brought home, then?'

'I'm Ruth, Missus. Josh said as I can be of help to you and—'

'Help? What help can a cripple be to me? Josh, have you lost your mind?'

'Now, Ma.'

'I may be a cripple, Missus, but I can do a lot of things, and I'll be no trouble to you. I can cook and mend and sew, and Josh said as I could feed the hens and collect the eggs, so them things'll be useful to you, won't they?' Ruth could hear the plea in her own voice, and could almost touch the hostility in Josh's ma's.

'More like you'll be another burden, lass. With that gammy foot and, by the looks of you, unable to stand straight, you'll need looking out for, more than you'll contribute.'

Disappointment filled Ruth. Josh had said as his ma had a sunny disposition. Well, she might have with him, but she wasn't about to extend it to her, by the looks of it.

'Ma! What kind of a welcome is that, eh? Ruth's out on her feet, and aye, she will need help for a few days, but after that she'll be a help to you.'

'Huh!'

This parting huff of disdain compounded the dread that had settled inside Ruth. Part of her was wishing Josh hadn't brought her here, but if he hadn't, she doubted she'd have been going anywhere other than to hell. Because she'd surely have died and, no matter how she looked at it, she was a sinner. A killer on the run.

'Don't pay any heed to me ma. She can take a bit of persuading to any changes I want to make. I've been on about

97

getting her help for a good bit now, but she's resisted. She'll not like it, cos she'll think I went ahead without her wanting me to. But when she hears circumstances of how I came to bring you here, she'll come round.'

'Aye, well, we'll see. I'll do me best to please her.'

'Reet, that's good. But you're not a prisoner here, lass. If you don't settle and you don't feel happy, I'll take you down to Pradley and you can take your chance with Whalley Bradstone as you planned.'

As she hobbled towards the house, Ruth knew she wouldn't be doing that. However difficult it was to live with Josh's ma, she'd put up with it, cos she liked Josh, and she knew he'd help her find the young 'uns. Besides, she'd be safe up here. But then why did she have this feeling of trepidation in the pit of her stomach – especially when she looked over at Pendle Hill? Her body trembled at the very name of the place and the thought of what had gone on up there. Aye, it might have been two hundred years since, but to her it was as if she were part of it. She couldn't get the fate of the Pendle Witches out of her head. She could almost hear their cries of despair as they faced their death, on what had become a sinister and frightening hill to her. The sound rolled around her in the howls of the wind, striking terror into her heart. *What if folk begin to think of me as a witch?*

Pulling herself out of such a nonsensical thought, Ruth gathered all the courage she had left and entered the house. What met her showed her the truth of what Josh had said. The house did hold a warm welcome. It wasn't just the physical warmth from the huge cast-iron cooking stove, set into a recess in the wall opposite the door, but the brightness from the three windows dressed with fresh-looking, light-green curtains and, added to that, the smell of baking, which comforted and gave a homely feel. Above the stove were three rows of shelves. The top shelf held all manner of preserves, the next one down dry ingredients, and the lowest one had a row of gleaming copper cooking pans. Under this hung every cooking implement you could name, from ladles to spatulas and a rolling pin. Against the back wall stood a scrubbed table, the biggest she'd ever seen. One end had two places set, the other held a pile of papers and magazines, which made her think that one of them – or both – must be able to read. She hoped it was Josh, as maybe he would read to her like Amy did. *Eeh, Amy, lass . . .*

Before the deep pain that stabbed Ruth's heart at this thought could take hold and undo her, Josh's ma said, 'Well, come in, lass, and shut out the cold. Me name's Nora, Nora Bottomless.'

This tickled Ruth and lifted her spirits, but she tried to suppress the giggle that rose in her. She hadn't thought to ask Josh his surname, and now she knew why he hadn't offered it.

'Aye, I can see as that's amused you. Not an apt name for someone like me, who has a backside to rival any as you've ever seen, but there it is. Sit down, lass. I'm sorry about me not being welcoming just now. It were a shock that Josh went against me wishes, and to see as he'd picked you – a lass who don't look like you can be of much use. But I shouldn't have acted like I did. I've a brew on. I expect you could do with a mug of tea?'

'Aye, I could; ta, Missus.'

'"Nora," I said, and "Nora" it is. You may be here to work, but you're not me servant and I'm nobody to be addressed by owt other than me name. Now, here's your tea.

You can tell me a bit about yourself whilst you sup it. Where do you come from, and have you family?'

Sitting back on the wooden rocking chair and comforted by the soft cushion under her and at her back – cushions that matched the curtains, in that they too were of a light green, though these were of a soft velvet fabric – it took Ruth a moment and a large gulp of the hot, sweet tea before she could answer. 'If you had asked me that two weeks ago, I'd have told you I had a da and a ma and two sisters and two brothers, and we all lived on a farm in Pradley, as me da were a labourer there. But, well, me da died . . .'

More than once during her telling she had to stop, drink some tea and compose herself, but Nora never once interrupted. At the end of her tale there was a silence, which lasted a good half a minute before Nora said, 'Eeh, lass, that's a sad tale.' From the pocket of her pinny she drew out a huge white hanky. 'Here, lass, dry your tears. You've landed on your feet. There's a home here for you, for as long as you wants it. And a safe one an' all, as anyone looking ain't going to find you here. As for them young 'uns – your sisters and brothers – well, Josh'll keep his word and make some enquiries. He knows folk, does Josh, and among his acquaintances are a few of them policemen. He'll find out sommat for you.'

Ruth nodded. She hadn't realized she was crying, but now it was all brought into focus, she felt a sob take her that jolted the very heart of her.

Josh didn't remark on this as he entered the kitchen at that moment. He just went past her and stacked the logs he'd brought in with him, in a neat pile next to the brass coal scuttle that stood to one side of the Aga. His words were aimed at his ma. 'We'll need to keep stoked up the neet, Ma. By, it's enough to freeze hell over out there.'

'Ha, that's a new one. Well, lad, you have done well to bring lass here. We're what she needs, and I have to say it, lad, you were right about the help she'll be, when she finds her feet. She were brought up on a farm, so she knows what goes on. Now, get another place set and you can tell me all the news of what's happening in Blackburn whilst you eat.'

The wink that Josh gave Ruth spoke volumes. She managed a smile and felt her unsettled heart ease a little at the lovely grin he gave her back. This sealed the thought that she'd be all right here; these were good people. *If only* . . . But then, if she were to keep her sanity and be of any use to Nora and Josh, she mustn't think of 'if only' – because if she did, it would grind her into the ground.

10

Amy

The Assizes

Amy glanced around. In the public gallery, she saw the Earl of Harrogate. He looked smart in his three-quarter black coat, chequered waistcoat and grey trousers. His white cravat tied high around his neck accentuated his dark good looks. He sat with the other toff, his friend, Lord Bellinger, whose house she'd been staying in. The Earl had arranged everything and, before she knew what was happening, she'd found herself in the staff quarters of Lord Bellinger's house, learning how to do the chores that his household staff carried out. The Earl had told Amy to learn as much as she could and then he would find her a job in service. Working as a scullery maid wasn't what she wanted to do, but somehow she didn't care. Her own fate was of little importance.

Her action of pulling her shawl further around her shoulders wasn't to block out the cold, but to help hold herself together. Little Elsie's face came to her – angelic in death as in life, and holding a promise that she would always look out for Amy. She knew Elsie would have the means to, for God would want to have such a cherub by His side and would listen to her requests. *Eeh, Elsie, lass, ask Him to make things reet and get me and the boys back with Ruth. But if that's not to be, then beg of Him to please save Seth and George from the death-penalty. Please . . .*

The jangling sound of keys and iron chains stiffened her body. Her eyes fixed on the top of the stairs leading up from the cells. Two heads appeared. Amy's throat tightened. She'd not clapped eyes on her brothers since three weeks ago, when the magistrate had committed them to stand trial. Seth spotted her first. His once-chubby cheeks were gaunt and sunken, and his eyes, looking bigger than she remembered, stared as if unseeing. A nerve twitched under one of them. Then George's head turned in her direction. Amy caught her breath in her lungs. *Oh, dear God!* Strong-willed George had cuts and bruises on his face.

Swallowing hard, she tried a little smile and a nod, to send them hope. The sharp tapping of a wooden hammer on the clerk's desk made her jump. A silence had fallen, but it was broken by the sound of everyone in the court rising together as the clerk bellowed, 'Please be upstanding for his worship, Judge Cradgley.'

A man with an unreadable expression came through the doors behind the bench. His red-blotched face, with its large bulbous nose, looked hideous in the long, tightly curled wig that sat squarely on his head. The clerk and the lawyers bowed towards the judge. Amy did the same, but was glad to see that he then indicated they should sit, as she didn't think her wobbly legs would hold her much longer.

'The defendants will remain standing.' This, from the clerk, was followed by another bow towards the judge, who then spoke for the first time.

'Seth Dovecote and George Dovecote, you are charged

along with another, Ruth Dovecote, who is not in court today, but has been put under warrant for her arrest.'

A sound of protest came from the gallery, having the effect of stopping Amy from voicing the one that rose in her. *Does the Earl not know that Ruth is to be charged an' all? It doesn't seem like it. And, if he does, surely he would have told me?*

The judge had paused and looked up towards the gallery, before continuing, 'And has two counts against her, which shall be heard by this court upon her arrest. Seth Dovecote, together with George Dovecote and Ruth Dovecote, you are jointly charged that, on 12th January 1850, you did knowingly act in a manner that could cause harm to others, by walking on the highway. Your behaviour resulted in the death of the Earl of Harrogate, Lord Bertram Rollinson, his unfortunate driver, a Mr Vernon Orton, and in injuries to Lady Rollinson. How do you plead?'

The answer of 'Guilty', though said together, came out in different tones: Seth's pitifully, George's with defiance. Though it shocked Amy to hear them pleading guilty, at this moment she was more concerned about George's attitude. She willed him to look contrite.

'Very well. As you have admitted this charge, it falls to me to pass a sentence on you. But before doing so, I want it recorded that any such sentence does not automatically apply to Ruth Dovecote, who is to be further charged with causing grievous bodily harm to one Trevor Sugden, whilst executing his duty of keeper in charge of the welfare of the mentally insane in Merchant Street, Union's Workhouse Hospital. And that the warrant for Ruth Dovecote's arrest carries this additional charge.'

Seth and George looked over at Amy as this was read out,

shock showing on both of their faces. But then in Seth's expression she read a question, and she knew he must be wondering how it came about that she had got off scot-free. The judge's next words told them. 'It is known that there were three other members of the Dovecote family on the highway at the time of the accident. Let it be recorded that Amy Dovecote, sister of the accused, has been shown the leniency of the victim's brother, in thanks for what she and they did to save the victim's mother. The other two members of the Dovecote family, and present at the scene, were Mrs Rose Dovecote, killed in the accident, and an infant, who had not reached the age of knowing right from wrong and shall not be named, nor shall her presence be recorded.'

Though pain stabbed Amy on hearing her ma's name, it vied with relief that the judge had not mentioned Elsie's death. That would have shocked Seth and George to the core, and most likely would have tipped George over the edge, rendering him incapable of keeping his temper. As it was, there was still a chance for them. The Earl had promised he'd do what he could to get them a lenient sentence, but an outburst from George could ruin that.

Her breath stayed painfully in her lungs, held there in suspense, as the moment was now upon them when her brothers' fate would be sealed.

'Seth Dovecote and George Dovecote, the charges against you carry the sentence of hanging—'

The intake of breath around her sounded like a death-knell. *Please, please, God, I beg of you, help them. Elsie, lass, if you can hear me – pray, lass, pray.* Amy's eyes fixed on the judge. She knew that if he were to pass the sentence of hanging, he would reach for his black hat. He remained still, his voice not wavering.

'However . . .' At this one word, Amy's breath came out of her in an audible sigh. The judge glanced up at her, but didn't comment, though his eyebrows were raised in disdain. The few seconds' delay this caused held her locked in a state of extreme anxiety. At last he continued. 'The new Earl of Harrogate, Lord Frederick Rollinson, has requested that some leniency be shown to you, given the actions taken by you both, in that you calmed the horses long enough to get his mother out of the stricken carriage and, further, your attention to getting her somewhere she could receive help. And so, Seth Dovecote and George Dovecote, I therefore sentence you both to deportation.'

A moan from Seth took up the split-second silence that followed this. George put out his hand towards Seth, but the prison officer standing with them knocked it away. No matter, Seth had seen the gesture and straightened his stature in response.

As the judge's voice droned on about the British Penal Colony in Australia, where they would be sent for a period of no fewer than five years, Amy gave in to her body and let it fold. Relief mixed with deep sadness at the prospect of never seeing them again; it was too much of a burden for her, for she'd heard that folk never came back from such a place. But as the sentencing came to an end, she was determined to help her brothers by standing straight and giving them a smile of encouragement.

Once the boys had been taken down, she hurried over to the Earl, but was warded off by Lord Bellinger. 'Get away with you, girl – are you not satisfied? Leave my Lord Rollinson in peace now. He has his grieving to do. He has done his duty by you; now be off!'

Not to be put off, Amy begged, 'Please, M'Lord, I just

need to ask if I can see me brothers – please. I'll not see them again after today . . . Please.'

'You are lucky that you will know they are alive. If I had my way, they would hang – and you and your sister with them. Now, realize when you are in receipt of all the favours to be granted, and take your leave.'

'No, let her alone, my Lord Bellinger. Amy, sit down, I will see what I can do.'

Moving away from the furious Lord Bellinger, whose voice she could hear giving the Earl an earful of a lecture, Amy sat back in her seat and prayed with everything that was in her.

Silence settled around her as everyone left the court, leaving her alone in this huge room with a ceiling that seemed as if it must touch the sky. Every move she made echoed back from it, engulfing her in fear of what this courtroom stood for. She prayed. *Please, God, let me never sit here again and hear our Ruth being sentenced. Because there's naw chance she'd get off with owt lighter than the gallows.* With this thought, her imagination showed her the hopelessness of Ruth ever having made it across the fells of the Bowland Hills, as surely she must have tried to do.

The Earl had ridden out the day after she'd met him, to look for Ruth. He'd gone as far as he thought Ruth would have got. Why he should do this, she had no idea, because he had no malice in him when he set out, nor had he sounded angry when he hadn't found Ruth, only desperately concerned. This was strange, for a man of his standing. She could understand him wanting to find Ruth to hand her in, but she'd known this wasn't his intention. It wasn't like one of the toffs, to care about her kind. Mind, she had to admit the Earl was different from any she'd ever heard of.

Giving up on trying to understand his reasons for everything, Amy let her mind drift through all the sorrow that got her weeping when she was alone at night. And now she had more sadness on top of it all. How would she cope with the lads being in a place she couldn't imagine, and with never seeing them again? But then, that were better than having them dead. Her ma used to say that in life there was always a glimmer of hope. *Oh, Ma, what hope have I now?*

With this question, she realized how she'd changed. Not many weeks ago she'd been so young – a normal fifteen-year-old helping her ma at home and working on the farm alongside her da. Life hadn't been easy, and she'd been facing the prospect of having to leave soon to find paid work, because her da had said that, although he'd kept her at home longer than most, they needed the extra money she could bring in. He'd said in his kindly way, so as not to make his words hurt, that the family had missed out on any extra coming in, with Ruth being unable to work. *Poor Da, if he knew what was happening, he'd be so sad. He tried to keep his family fed and warm, and worked from dawn till dusk for us.*

Funny, but the trek across the Bowland Hills to the big town of Blackburn had taken over from the heartache of losing him and had helped her to cope with the grief of his loss. It had felt like an adventure to her. She hadn't been able to wait to see what Blackburn was like.

Well, she knew now, and it were no big deal. She preferred the country, with its fresh smell – not that you got much of that when you went near the cowsheds! But still, it had been home, and for the most part she'd been happy and carefree. Now she knew what it felt like to be alone, and facing a lifetime of being so. Fighting the despair of her situation and the plight of her brothers, Amy told herself:

I have to face it, I have no choice. Aye, and I'll have to take up the Earl's offer and go into service. Me life's mapped out for me by circumstance. The thought didn't sit well with her, for she'd hoped to work in an office, or to take up teaching young 'uns. She could do that, with the learning she had, and she knew she could take in as much knowledge as she needed to, so that she could qualify. But now she had to think of how being in service would provide a roof over her head and keep her belly full. Aye, and keep her that busy that she'd have less time to think. Less time to grieve. She had to be grateful to the Earl, for looking out for her welfare and for all he'd done for Seth and George.

Amy knew what life in service would be like, as she'd had a taste of it in Lord Bellinger's home. His housekeeper had set her to work at helping with all and sundry. She'd hated most of the chores that the girls of her age did: dunking laundry in the yard, cleaning and setting the fires and, worst of all, emptying all the piddle-pots.

Looking up at the ceiling, Amy felt a thought shuddering through her: *Eeh, naw – don't let that be me fate!*

'Come on, out of there!'

Shock at hearing this said in a sharp, commanding tone rendered Amy speechless for a moment. She looked down to see a court official standing at the bottom of the steps leading to the gallery. 'I have to stay, Sir. The Lord Rollinson, the Earl of Harrogate, is coming back for me.'

The court official gave her a disbelieving look. 'That's as may be, but the court sessions are over for the day, and I'm charged with locking up. You can wait outside.'

'But if the Earl comes back, you will tell him where I am?'

'Aye, if I see him. But you're best to wait by the desk out

there in the corridor. If this Lord Rollinson *is* coming, that's most likely where he'll ask for you.'

Amy wriggled. The bench she was sitting on in the corridor had made her bottom hard. A good hour must have passed, and the building was emptying of people, and still the Earl didn't come. *What if they've taken the lads elsewhere, ready for their journey? Oh God, please bring the Earl to me.*

'We're locking up now, Miss.' The voice of the court official came to her again. 'And I've checked outside and there's no carriages in the courtyard. Your Lord has long since gone. So, let's have you on your way now.'

'But he said he would come back. I have to wait.'

'He's not in the building, and the prisoners have been taken away. There's only me here, and I'm ready for the off.'

Shocked to have her worst fears confirmed, Amy stood. The stiffness in her limbs pained her, but she held herself steady. 'Where would they take the prisoners, Mister?'

'Back to their prison cells at the police house, until their punishment can be carried out. Them for the gallows will be hanged at midnight; them for prison sentences will be sent on the morrow to different prisons; and them for deportation will be on their way to the docks at Liverpool.'

'What, already? Naw, they can't. I have to see me brothers.'

'Them two as were up last? They're gone. I saw them taken out to the prison wagon with the rest, about thirty minutes since. You've no chance, lass.' He guided her towards the doors and gently pushed her through. 'Get off home and be quick about it. There's some reet rogues come out at neet around these parts.'

Outside, the cold didn't just sting Amy's skin, but whipped into the very heart of her, cutting right through her thin coat. It brought to the fore her hunger and thirst. Remembering that she still had the halfpenny the housekeeper had given her, to get a mug of tea, she looked longingly at the glow of a brazier further along the road. *A tattie-man*. As she came up to the blazing fire, the heat of it seeped into her. One of the shadowy figures huddled around it called out, 'Eeh, lass, what're you doing out in this? Come and have some hot tea. Only a farthing a mug, and it's good stuff an' all.'

'Aye, I will, and I'll take one of them tatties, if you'll take another farthing for one.'

'Glad to. There ain't many folk about, so I'm cutting me prices to get rid. Here you go. Sit on that box there.'

The hot mug warmed Amy's hands and the steam rising from it blurred her vision. Putting it down, she took the hot tattie handed to her and had to juggle it, as it threatened to burn her hands. When it had cooled a little, biting into it gave her the taste of creamy potato and smoke-burned crispy skin. Delicious! For a moment she forgot her troubles, as she filled her belly and allowed the low chatter of the group to lull her into a comfortable place.

The sound of the distant rumble of a carriage along the cobbled road brought her back to the real world and the pain it held. She hoped, with all that was in her, that it meant the Earl had come back to bring her some good news.

Looking back in the direction of the courthouse, Amy saw that a glow of light still surrounded the building. The silhouette of a horse and carriage drew her towards it. Lifting her mug and taking a last gulp of the tea, she rose and, still clasping her tattie, ran towards the carriage. 'I'm here, I'm here . . .'

A gentleman alighted and looked towards her. She could

see, from his height, that it wasn't the Earl. Her pace slowed with the disappointment this brought her. Then some hope rose in her again as she saw it was Lord Bellinger. Maybe he had a message?

'Ah, so you didn't give up, I see? Well, come along. Lord Rollinson had an engagement and, by the time he'd sorted out an arrangement for you, he couldn't wait around to tell you what had happened. He charged me with delivering the news to you, as I was coming back into town.'

Coming up to him, she saw that he had a smile on his face. And he'd used a pleasant voice to her, which hadn't been her experience of him when she'd heard him barking orders out to his staff. But then most folk did have a good side, and maybe he was showing his now. 'Has the Earl said as I can see me brothers, M'Lord?'

'He has, but everything has to be paid for. Girls like you know that. So first I am going to take you to a house that I know. They will teach you how to pay for whatever you want. And I will be your first tutor.'

'I don't want to go to naw house. I'll go back to the kitchens till—'

'You're no longer welcome there. I am not prepared to house one of your kind. Your brothers are paying the price for you getting off scot-free, and I don't want to stand the cost of keeping you. You owe me already. Now, get into the carriage, and hurry up about it.'

'Naw. Please, M'Lord, tell me about me brothers and I'll be on me way. I'll not go back to naw house. I'll take care of meself. I'll get a job in mill.'

'Not if I have any say in it, you won't. I own three of them, and I can influence those who own the others. Now, do as you're told. It is freezing out here and it's not much warmer inside the carriage, so we need to get going as quickly as we can. Come along. This is the best solution. You'll enjoy what goes on there and will be well looked after. There's a few who are partial to young ones – myself included. I'm looking forward to the treat of taking you. And after I'm done, I will tell you what you need to know about your brothers and will pay you well.'

Panic gripped Amy. Looking back along the street, she saw that the light from the brazier had lessened and those who had been standing around it had gone; most had shifted as the carriage approached, no doubt fearing it was the police. As she looked in the other direction, she saw nothing but a blanketing darkness. She'd take her chance with the brazier; at least there'd be some warmth for a while. Turning, she ran towards it.

'Your choice, but a stupid one. I'll tell the Earl I didn't see you.'

Tears stung like ice on Amy's cheeks as she sank down on the pavement next to the dying flames of the brazier. *Oh, Ma . . . I want me ma. Ma, help me, help me.*

11
Ruth & Amy

Contrasting Destinations

'Eeh, lass, give over. There'll be nowt left of table top – you're scrubbing the layers off it.'

Some of the tension in Ruth released as she laughed at this, from Nora. She'd been here four weeks now and had settled well. She and Nora had a good relationship, one that pleased Josh and comforted Ruth.

'That's better. Now wipe them suds away while I make us a brew. Then you can sit a mo and rest your bones. And stop glancing at that clock. Josh will be here when he gets here and you can't make a difference to that, no matter how much you will it.'

'Aye, I know.' Admitting Nora was right didn't stop her wishing that Josh would walk in the door this very minute; but beyond that, she hoped he'd have good news. And just maybe, if her prayers were answered, he'd have Amy and Elsie with him. Josh had left the day before, after setting his rams with the sheep that had reached their oestrus cycle. She smiled at his reaction, when she'd known that he meant they were coming on heat, though he was always pleased when she showed her knowledge of farming matters.

He'd told her that he had learned the term by reading *Farming Weekly* and had liked the sound of it. She'd learned it from the vet who'd had to come out to a sheep that was struggling to give birth. The vet had thought the sheep was lambing far too early, and had asked when the ewe had had her oestrus cycle and had been serviced.

Josh had laughed again when Ruth told him how she'd been really dumb, thinking the vet was referring to a pedal cycle, until he explained. She'd joined in the laughter and it had been another moment to seal their friendship.

In such a short time Josh was becoming like a second skin to her. He was that easy-going and hadn't spoilt anything by making a pass at her or anything like that, and she was glad of it, as she wasn't ready for that. A voice inside her tried to say it would be different if it were the Earl, but she quietened it. It was daft to think like that.

Finishing her tea, Ruth realized she needed to be somewhere on the road so that she could see Josh approaching. It would be like she was doing something to help him get here more quickly. Her chores were all done – twice over, if the truth be known – but keeping herself occupied helped.

The boulder she sat on had warmed a little, with her staying in the one position, but the wind howled just as strongly as it had done since she'd arrived up here, and chilled the very bones of her. Nora had made her bring a blanket with her, when she'd not been able to persuade Ruth from trying to meet Josh on the road. 'It's a daft idea, lass,' she'd said. 'You'll be cut in two, out there on the brow. And though you'll get it quicker, news'll be same, whether you hears it ten minutes earlier or not.'

Giving in to Ruth, after seeing how determined she was,

Nora had filled a billy-can with some hot broth and had insisted on the blanket. Both were welcome. Sipping the last of the broth, which was no longer hot but still comforted, Ruth pulled the blanket tighter around her and scanned the horizon. Prayers swam around in her mind – some pleading, some bargaining and, in amongst them, a few threatening ones. None of them eased her worry.

At last she saw Josh in the distance. Her heart thudded, but as he came nearer, her anticipation left her. He was alone.

'By, lass, what're you doing up here? Though I shouldn't ask, as I know the answer.'

It wasn't just the cold that stopped her answering. Part of her didn't want to know – the part that dreaded the worst.

'It ain't all bad, lass.' At Josh's telling of the lads' fate, Ruth's life seemed to end. 'Naw. Naw!'

'Don't take on, lass. It were the better option, and part of the pardon bargain that the Earl of Harrogate made.'

'But I'll never see them again!'

'He didn't have many choices open to him as to their fate, thou knows, lass. A pardon from the gallows is probably all he could get for your brothers. He managed a full pardon for your sisters. And I reckon it were only your fear made you think he were going for the police, to hand you in that day.'

'Aye, happen. I hadn't looked at it like that. But what of Amy and Elsie?' The news of the lads had ripped Ruth apart. Now all she had to cling on to was her hope that he had news of what had happened to her sisters.

'I didn't get any news on Amy. She were seen in the court, but not again afterwards. And they hadn't heard of her at the two convents I visited, but there *is* sommat I found out.' Her heart sank at his next words, and its thumping slowed as fear trembled through her. 'I have some bad news, lass. I'm sorry. Look, let's get up to the house.'

'Naw, tell me. I – I have to knaw.'

'Awe, me little lass . . .'

The endearment compounded her fear. Josh had never expressed his feelings. Now, in the moment when he had a burden he didn't want to give her, it seemed that he needed to. Turning, he tethered the horse to the rock next to her and then, opening his coat, put out his arms to her. Her body moved into his, willing that she would find all that he'd said – and still had to say – was not the truth.

Holding her close, with his coat wrapping her into him, Josh became her crutch. 'Me lass. I don't know how you're going to cope with this, but Elsie – well, she—'

The howl that started up in her was akin to an animal's cry. It started in her wretched soul and twisted each part of her into a painful knot of tortured agony, as Josh told her of Elsie's death. When the sound released itself from her, it took with it all that she was, and left Ruth feeling that she'd nothing more to live for.

Still Josh held her, his silence allowing her to vent her pain. His strength, her prop. She clung to him, digging her nails into his flesh. Her spittle mingled with her tears, soaking his shirt. Tears stung her cheeks as the wind lashed them, turning them ice-cold. They weren't wrung from her; they flowed like a river, a torrent of despair. She'd lost everything: her ma and da, and her brothers and Amy, and she herself would be arrested if they found her. But never to see precious little Elsie again was the catalyst for her to bleed her grief for them all.

'Come on, lass.' Lifting her, Josh knew that his heart was

full of her. Every part of her was him. He had to show her that he was someone she could depend on, and this set up a fight inside him with the part of him that would take her here and now. But the taking wouldn't be how he wanted it. She was looking for comfort, for something to hang on to, and that's all he must be at this moment.

It wasn't the time to give in to the burning desire that her closeness provoked in him. Or even to take the chance to kiss the soft skin or lick her salty tears, as every part of him wanted to do. Instead, he carried Ruth over to the horse and lifted her into the cart. There he laid her on some sacks, before fetching the blanket to cover her. When they reached the gate to the yard, he heard her call out to him. Pulling the cart to a halt, he turned to reassure her. She'd lifted herself onto her hands. He looked into her dark, swollen eyes and read a different distress in them – one she couldn't find the words to express. Although she tried, all that came out was a whimper.

Pulling on the rein, he told his horse, 'Hold still, my girl.' Aggie snorted. She didn't like this weather and could smell her stable and all it promised, he knew that, but she quietened when he gave her a lump of sugar from his pocket. 'Good girl, I'll not be a moment. You can give me that, can't you?' On the horse nodding her head, he rubbed her nose and walked back to Ruth. 'What is it, me little lass?'

Close to her now, he could make out her words. Her sweet breath brushed his cheeks in little puffs, as she sobbed out that she couldn't face his ma. 'N – not yet. I – I need a little time.'

'I'll take you into me work-shed and light the stove in there, lass. It'll soon kindle, as I allus keep it ready for when I need to work on mending sommat, or need to get away

118

from me ma.' Ruth didn't join his attempt at a laugh, at this. His heart swelled towards her with wanting to lift her sorrow – wanting to put her lovely smile back in place and, aye, wanting to hold her and give his all to her. He loved her. As sure as spring followed winter, he loved her.

The shed gave some shelter from the wind, but little else, until he lit the kindling and the flames jumped into life. They flickered soft shadows around the small area that wasn't taken up with benches and tools and part-projects that Josh was working on. He laid Ruth on the bales of straw that he kept at one end, to sit on and enjoy a brew in peace – not that his ma was a nag, or had too much talk, but at times he needed his own thoughts and this was his haven for them.

'Reet, lass, I've to see to Aggie and will go and put Ma's mind at rest, as she'll have seen us enter the yard and I don't want her agitating and coming across here in this wind. She'll catch her death.' This thought increased his worry for Ruth, as it was likely she'd take a knock to her fragile health and, God forbid, there was a chance of pneumonia, from the exposure to the elements and the shock she'd had. 'I'll not be a mo. Try to close your eyes.' She didn't speak, but he read acceptance of his plans and thanks in her eyes, just before she closed them. Tucking the blanket around her, he allowed his hand to stay a moment longer on her body, gently rubbing her back. She didn't protest. Her breathing slowed and deepened, and he knew she was near to drifting off. He hoped it would be a healing sleep, and that she would wake able to cope with her lot. *Eeh, lass, you have been sent more of a burden than most, but I'm here for you and if I can lighten your load, I will.* He wanted desperately to say the words aloud, but now wasn't the time.

Tired, Amy huddled in a doorway not far from the brazier. She'd wandered aimlessly and confused around the town of Blackburn for the last few days. She was uncertain which direction they had come in from Clitheroe, which she knew would lead her to the Bowland Hills. Crossing those would get her home to Pradley, where she had a chance of finding shelter, and maybe even Ruth.

No one hereabouts would help her. Most folk gave her a wide berth; some spat at her and others gave her a piece of their mind, calling her scum and telling her to get off their streets – if only she could, she would.

Dirt and grime clung to her and her clothes. Life these last few days – she'd lost track of how many – had been spent huddled in one doorway after another, begging for pennies and trying to glean some warmth and shelter.

Each day she managed to get a farthing or a halfpenny – enough to buy a tattie at the brazier at night. And the man who sold them had given her a drop of tea with it, even though she hadn't enough to pay, though he'd shooed her off as soon as she had her food, telling her she weren't to sit near, for fear of putting potential customers off approaching him.

He'd been gone some time now and so, as she'd done other nights, Amy crept back over to the brazier to sit near to the heat it gave off before its last embers died away. The frozen grass had melted and blackened within a foot of the brazier, and it was a patch of this that she curled up on and drifted into sleep.

A sharp pain woke her. Twisting round, she saw the

outline of a man about to kick her, as she was sure he had just done.

'Leave me alone. I'm not doing any harm.'

'Gerrup. I need to take a look at you.'

'What for?'

'Gerrup, or you'll feel me boot again.'

Cringing away from his raised foot, Amy rolled over and stood up.

'Nowt a good wash won't fix. I'll take you in, if you're prepared to work.'

Hope seeped into her. 'Take me in where, Mister? Are you in need of a hired help?'

'Aye, that and more. Come on.'

Though trepidation lurked within her, Amy obeyed. What the 'more' could be, she didn't like to think, but the thought of shelter and a job was too big a lure to stop her following him. She could turn it down, if she didn't like it.

Brushing the sleep out of her eyes, she tried to get the measure of him. If she could see him properly, it might help her to decide whether to go with him. A short way away in front of them she could see something shining, in the direction they were heading. She would follow him until they reached it, and then she would be able to take a look at the man. The light turned out to be a gas lamp swinging in the breeze, below a sign saying 'Apothecary'. It illuminated his silhouette. 'Hold on a minute, Mister. I have a stone in me shoe.'

'Hurry up, then. I'll not hang around.'

Though one minute the light shadowed him as it moved away from him in the wind, when it came over him she could see him clearly. A man in his middle years with a paunch on him, he'd lost most of his hair, and his face had

121

the rough texture that pockmarks give. His clothes looked tailored: he wore a three-quarter coat with slim-legged breeches that didn't improve his shape, and high boots. She had him down as a man of means, but not of breeding or manners. To her, it seemed strange that he should be roaming the streets at this time of night looking for workers. And not asking if she had any training or references didn't fit, either.

'Right. Are you coming, or do I have to drag you?'

'Why should you drag me? I ain't tied to you. I can walk away, if I like.'

'Not if I have owt to do with it. I've a mind to have you, and have you I shall, willing or not. I've seen you about these last few days. It strikes me you've nowhere to go, so what I have to offer will be a blessing to you. Aye, and once you get used to it, you'll like it an' all.'

'What is it?'

'Stop asking and let's get going. Me need's a pressing one, and I'll satisfy it here and now if you keep dawdling.'

There was only one pressing need Amy knew men to have, and what little she knew of it all, they'd do anything to get it. Well, she weren't about to let this man do it to her, no matter what he offered.

She turned and was about to run, but he moved quickly for a big man. His hand grasped her arm. The wrench he gave her was so fierce that she lost her balance and landed on the ground. 'Leave me, Mister. I ain't wanting to go with you, and you can't make me.'

'Can't I?'

Her back scraped along the ground as he grabbed her feet and dragged her along. Before she could scream, he had her in the ginnel.

'Naw, leave me!' Kicking out, she caught him on the knee. For a moment he let go. Amy scrambled onto all fours and then stood up. A fist hit her in the face. The sting of it brought tears to her eyes and sent her reeling backwards. A wall stayed her fall. In desperation she raise her foot again. This time she aimed between his legs as she had done at the jailer, but the man caught her foot and upended her.

Flat on her back with the air forced out of her lungs, Amy could do nothing but take his weight as he came down on her. 'Yer forcing this on yourself. I didn't want to have yer till I'd cleaned you up. Are you clean down there?'

She couldn't answer. Panic gripped her. If she didn't get air, she'd die!

He raised his upper body. Amy gasped. Relief mixed with pain as her bruised ribs screamed against the expansion of her lungs.

'I asked you if you were clean?'

'Naw . . . I – I haven't had a wash in days.'

'I don't mean that kind of clean. Have you the pox?'

'Naw. Look, Mister, please let me go. I ain't never done it. I don't know how – you're hurting me!'

'A virgin! Well, ain't I the lucky one? I had it in me head that you were plying your trade. Right, well, this might hurt, but like I said, you'll be glad you had it. And if you're good, I'll take you on, and for returned favours I'll see as you're looked after well, with just a few chores to do in me house.' His hands groped her small breasts. 'A pretty little well-formed girl like you will give a lot of pleasure.' Leaning back once more he undid his breeches.

'Naw, please don't.' Desperate to escape, Amy reached out around her, feeling for something – anything – to hit him with, but there was nothing.

His cold hand touched her thigh and then pulled at her bloomers. Her struggle exhausted her. His breaths panted on her face, droplets of his spittle landing on her. 'Naw, don't . . .' Clawing at his face and eyes as though demented, she uttered a scream that echoed in the still night. Before she could release it all, a blow from the back of his hand sent her head jolting backwards.

The weight of him lessened. His moan told of his agony. Lifting himself to a kneeling position, he held a hand to his eyes. 'You vixen! My God, you've torn my eye sockets. I'll kill you!'

Amy could do nothing to stave off the blow. It sent her body backwards with a force that crashed her head into the wall.

The blackness that swallowed her into its depth brought a blessed relief, until the horror of all that had happened came to her in flashes that terrified her.

Images of George and Seth hanging from ropes, their eyes swollen and bursting from their sockets. Then flames licking around Ruth's feet, her flesh melting away from her face, leaving only her skull. Now Ma, Da and Elsie sailing on a sea of cloud in a turbulent boat, calling to her, but when she went to rise to go to them, she couldn't. They disappeared over the horizon.

As she was catapulted from the blackness, a terrible noise assaulted her ears. Her throat rasped and burned, bringing her the knowledge that it was she herself making the noise. A hand clamped over her mouth.

'Naw, me little one – naw.'

Opening her eyes, Amy looked into a wizened face. *The angel of death?*

A smell came to her, one she remembered from sitting

124

with Elsie in the hospital. The hand clamping her mouth hurt. She wanted to bite it, but instead she remained still and quiet.

'That's better. Now, if I take my hand away, you mustn't start again. If you do, they'll take you to the madhouse and you'll never get out.'

Amy tried to nod her head to the woman so that she would release her, but the nod turned into a shiver – a violent tremble of a shiver that seized her whole body and seemed to rattle the teeth in her head. She couldn't stop it or control it. Confusion clogged her brain. *Where am I? How did I get here?* But most of all, the terrifying thought: *who am I?*

She must have said this all out loud, because the woman answered her. 'You're in workhouse hospital, lass. Police brought you in and, as for who you are, you're Iva and I'll take care of you. You're me little Iva, and you've come back to me.'

With this, the woman covered her with something and then moved away in a shuffling manner, rather than walking, and as she did so she called back, 'Whatever you do, don't start shouting again, Iva, me lass.'

Iva? Why can't I remember being Iva, or recall the woman who seems to be saying she's me ma? Flashes of her nightmare came back to her: a young woman burning, a man and a woman, and a little girl on a cloud, drifting. *Who are they? Why does it matter so much to me that they are not here?*

When the woman returned a few minutes later, she had a blanket with her, but now Amy didn't want it, as every part of her had become hot and clammy. She needed air! Her lungs gasped for it. Panic overcame her, as her lungs wouldn't expand.

125

'Oh, me lass, no. Not this. Not the croup.'

'H – help me . . . Please, h – h – help me.'

The woman seemed frozen and oblivious to Amy needing her to fetch help. Her voice droned on, saying the same thing over and over: 'Oh, dear God, not me little Iva. Don't be taking me Iva from me again.'

12

Katrina

A Shattered Happiness

'Katrina, you look very beautiful. I find myself falling in love with you and may take you from under Lord Frederick's nose.'

'Really, Lord Bellinger, don't be so ridiculous! You, *marry*? I don't think so. At least not for a long time. Though eventually you will need to, to produce an heir.'

His amusement at this put a smile on Bellinger's face, enhancing his rakish good looks. Two ringlet-type curls had fallen onto his forehead, escaping the neat rolls of his naturally curly hair. His violet eyes held an expression akin to a cat that had got the cream. His lips remained full as they revealed his even, white teeth. He wasn't as tall as Frederick, but still gave her at least four inches, so that she had to look up at him. His voice had a husky note as he said, 'But I am smitten. And besides, you are only marrying Frederick for his title – and he you, for your money. Me, I could give you a title, and our union would be the merger of two very important families in the cotton-mill industry. Besides, we would fare well in other areas of our union, and you wouldn't have to shore me up financially, darling.'

'My Lord, this is very disloyal of you. Your poor friend is at home and unable to attend such a function, due to the propriety of his mourning and it being only two months since his brother died, and you try to steal his betrothed!'

'Betrothed? I understood from Lord Frederick that you hadn't finalized things.'

'Oh? But we are engaged . . . I mean, well, there has been no formal announcement or celebration, but there couldn't be yet, with Frederick in mourning.'

'I'm only having fun. Come into the Regency Room. I have some new artworks to show you. Lord Frederick tells me that you are a talented artist?'

'Oh no, My Lord, I wouldn't go so far as that! But I do love to paint and have a liking for Renaissance art.'

'Mmm, a bit too religious and fantasy-based for me. I like more grit in my paintings.' He lowered his voice. 'Something a bit risqué. Goya offers both, and it is one of his that I have just acquired. A nude.'

Katrina glanced around her to cover her blush. There were about fifty guests, some seated, others milling around socializing in this beautiful room. From the silk curtains to the damask covering the sofas and chairs that were arranged around the walls, everything was in a luscious silver-grey, giving a feeling of complete elegance. The floor in the centre of the room was of highly polished oak, ideal for dancing. This was edged to the walls by a pale-blue carpet. From the ceiling hung the most magnificent chandelier Katrina had ever seen. She couldn't count the number of candles it held, but each one lit up the glass that contained it and added lighting to the room that created an air of romance.

A delicious meal had been enjoyed by all, in the equally sumptuous dining hall. Three long tables had been set, with a top table for Lord Bellinger and his honoured guests – all lords and ladies, except for one elderly duke.

It was an annual occasion, Lord Bellinger's Ball, held in late March, and many more would attend later, when the entertainment and dancing would begin. Only a chosen few sat down at his table. Katrina had never been invited before. However, her new status, already known to many, had made her worthy of being added to the guest list. Frederick had urged her to accept. 'You will represent me . . . us, my dear. I would like to present you to my friends myself, of course, but everyone will understand and there will be a formal introduction of you, once a decent time has elapsed.'

This had persuaded her. And with propriety being satisfied by partnering her with Lady Henrietta Parvoil, Katrina had allowed herself to enjoy the excitement of mingling in such circles. Had she been a little too overawed and had maybe let herself down? She couldn't think how, but Lord Bellinger seemed to have a poor opinion of her.

'Katrina? Have I offended your sensibility? I am so sorry, my dear. I did not realize you were so . . . How can I put this? Prudish isn't the right word. No, innocent maybe?'

'Oh? What *did* you think me? My Lord, I am sure you do not wish to insult me, but your insinuations about my relationship with Lord Rollinson – and in thinking me someone you can talk with, in the manner in which you have engaged me – have offended me. I may be the daughter of a self-made man, but I am also the daughter of a lady. I have had an upbringing that rivals many of those here, and have attended the same schools as some of them. I am not who you seem to think I am. Now I would be grateful if you would arrange for my carriage to be brought to the front entrance to take me home. Please make the excuse that I am feeling unwell.'

With this, Katrina turned and walked out of the room, trying to maintain as much dignity as she could. Tears stung her eyes, humiliation burned her cheeks and anger boiled in her blood. It was an altogether uncomfortable feeling, and not one that was conducive to salvaging her pride.

Somehow she managed to make it to the ladies' closet – a room delicately decorated and perfumed, with another room leading off, which housed a water toilet. All very convenient, but a maid was needed to be in attendance to help with holding the contraption that the ladies had to wear under their frocks.

Her heart sank at the sight of herself: beautiful, yes, and dressed in the finest of clothes that could be bought. Ruby in colour, her gown belled from her tiny waist and was held with the aid of a cage-like stiff petticoat. She didn't need the benefit of a corset and wouldn't have worn one, but for the necessity to hold her bosom in place. The neckline of her gown showed just a tiny part of her cleavage – and that only because, being large in that department, she couldn't keep it all under the pretty white lace that edged the square neckline of the tight-fitting bodice. The sleeves of her frock were close-fitting to her upper arm and then draped to a point just below her elbow, and were also edged with lace. Around her neck she wore a diamond necklace – an heirloom from her mother's family. A matching tiara adorned her hair. All perfect and fitting for the occasion, but could this finery make her what she wasn't: 'high-born' to both parents? No, of course not, and nor could it make her acceptable to the likes of Lord Bellinger. Not to his inner circle at least, though she had always been on the fringe of it. His behaviour tonight was a reminder of who she really was. *Oh God, why did I accept his invitation? I'm a damn fool.*

A maid entered the room. 'Excuse me, Miss Arkwright, but Lord Bellinger begs to be allowed to speak with you. He has asked me to take you to his sitting room.'

'I cannot go there unaccompanied. Will you please find Lady Henrietta Parvoil and bring her to me? Thank you. Oh, and tell his lordship that I will be with him shortly.'

Henrietta's face was full of concern as she entered. 'Katrina, my dear, are you unwell?'

The daughter of Lord and Lady Parvoil, Henrietta had been Katrina's best friend at school and had always been her defender in matters of her birthright, when many of the other ladies would question her standing and had shunned her in social matters. Not that Katrina gave a jot about it all. If only her mother hadn't constantly sought to get her into those circles that she herself – or so she maintained – felt glad not to be a part of any more!

'I've had a horrid experience, Henrietta. Please help me.' Telling Henrietta how Lord Bellinger had insulted her caused Katrina mixed feelings of embarrassment and anger. At the end of her telling, a thought occurred to her. 'Oh dear, should I refuse Lord Rollinson's offer, do you think? I don't want to cause him embarrassment, and I really don't want to go through this discomfiture every time we socialize with his friends. I mean, it was different when I was just one of the crowd of acceptable guests, to make up the numbers. I could mingle with the others who had some reason for being on the fringe of society. But tonight was my first experience of being part of the honoured guest list.'

'My poor Katrina. Simon Bellinger is a cad of the worst order! How dare he treat you in a manner that, if you hadn't

131

had the sense to do as you did, would have compromised you! I will speak to Father. He won't stand for such behaviour, and if he has a mind to, he will have Bellinger cast out from many circles that he wouldn't want to be ostracized from. There are many people who have had enough of his arrogant ways. I don't know a single lady who wants Bellinger to offer for them, but he struts around as if we would all fall at his feet!'

Henrietta was far more furious than Katrina thought the matter warranted. To her, Bellinger just needed to be shown that she was worthy of better treatment, but Henrietta was moved to wanting to destroy his standing altogether! 'No, please don't do that. He is one of Lord Frederick's best friends. It might set us off on the wrong foot. Lord Frederick has already mentioned that he is to ask Lord Bellinger to be his best man.'

'But Lord Frederick should know. He would surely be mortified that his future wife was treated in such a way.'

'Let us see what Lord Bellinger has to say for himself, first. You will come with me?'

'Yes, and that is another thing. He has no right to ask you to his private sitting room without asking you to bring someone with you. I am very suspicious of that. I should be on your guard at all times when dealing with him, my dear. It is as if he has a hidden agenda, where you are concerned.'

'But why should he have?'

'Katrina, you are very beautiful, and your father is very powerful in the same industry that Bellinger is in. To get his hands on your estate would make him *the* richest man in England! Bellinger has always liked power. He knows that you are vulnerable to gossip, and any blame would lie on your shoulders if there were to be a scandal. He could use that to force you into marrying him.'

'B-but he's Frederick's best friend.'

'Lord Bellinger is not anyone's best friend. And you will do well to remember that. Now come along, let's face this ogre together. It will be quite a shock to him to see me come in with you. You did the right thing to call for me. I'm looking forward to this.'

Katrina had a feeling that there was more depth than was warranted to Henrietta's anger – and did she detect something more? Hurt? Yes, Henrietta was hurt, and Katrina didn't think it was solely because Henrietta was affronted by the way Lord Bellinger had treated her. Henrietta had once expressed her feelings for Lord Bellinger. *Oh God. Is she still in love with him?*

Lord Bellinger stood as they entered. His face revealed his astonishment at Katrina having arrived with Henrietta in tow, but he quickly hid his surprise. 'My Lady Henrietta? It is good of you to chaperone Miss Katrina. Though I must confess I am embarrassed that you have knowledge of my misdemeanour. I am ashamed of my behaviour, Miss Katrina, and beg your forgiveness. I did not mean to respond in the way I did, and it was an unforgivable slip of etiquette on my behalf. My saving grace is that I do have a deep regard for my Lord Rollinson, and I only sought to quash the thought that you had no feelings for him and that, in your attempt to climb the social ladder, you would, at the first show of admiration from another, more eligible man, have no compunction about leaving Lord Rollinson for a better catch. I was wrong to say what I did, though it has proven you to be more than worthy of my Lord Rollinson's trust and affection. Indeed, had you not been betrothed to

133

a friend, your show of spirit and dignity and your beauty would have seen me offering for your hand, as I would be entitled to. I am a worthy suitor, and your engagement has not yet been announced.'

Beside her, Katrina felt Henrietta stiffen and thought she would speak, but she remained silent.

With the shock of his veiled proposal causing her senses to reel, Katrina made a supreme effort to answer Lord Bellinger, though she had to admit that her reply would be at odds with the way he'd made her feel. His address had been given in the humblest of manners and in a seductive voice, a measure of which smouldered in his eyes.

Katrina chose her words with care. 'My Lord Bellinger, I accept your apology and hope that, in your dealings with me in the future, you will give me the respect of my standing. Your wish to put me through a test of some kind has an arrogance that speaks of your disdain for me. I would not accept your proposal in any circumstances, should it be made, and find it in the poorest of taste that you would even think of offering for my hand. I am betrothed to your best friend, who I know will be mortified by your conduct towards me tonight.'

The ugliness of what lay inside Bellinger, which Henrietta had warned her of, came to the fore at this, and his face reddened. 'If you knew the truth, I doubt you would think of that . . . that do-gooder above me. Lord Rollinson wears his heart on his sleeve! He has even fallen in love with a low-life murdering cripple! And if it wasn't for me, he would now have her urchin of a sister to contend with as well. He proposed that I should take care of her until he could install her in his house. A child, just verging on becoming a woman – it's vile, and it is ridiculous that you should consider

134

marrying him. You are not in love with him. You hardly know him. He is a sleight-of-hand gambler – a man on his uppers who is grasping at you to save his estate and his title. And, my dear Katrina . . .'

His voice lowered as if he would deliver even more revolting accusations about Lord Rollinson, but he had no need to, for what he'd just said had kicked Katrina in the stomach. It was true; she didn't know Lord Rollinson well, and now it seemed she knew him even less than she thought, though he had spoken to her of a crippled girl and her sisters and brothers. She knew they were the ones who had had a hand in Lord Bertram's death, and about the trial and the older girl having gone missing. But she hadn't detected that Frederick was in love with the girl, even though she had been surprised at his excessive concern for the family. If what Lord Bellinger had said was true, and if the way he spoke of Frederick was how he was perceived by those whom he would count as his friends, then she had been deceived!

Before Lord Bellinger could go on or Katrina could respond, Henrietta waded in. 'Do not *dear Katrina* her! You are behaving like a first-class cad, of the order of a senior boy in school who cannot have his own way. You are despicable, My Lord. Lord Frederick is an honourable man, and I cannot think why you should wish to smear his name in this way. I will be speaking to my father about your behaviour. That is if I can even find words to express your vileness. Come along, Katrina. I will go home with you. I have some things to collect from my chamber, as I was to have been an overnight guest here, but I would stay with you instead, if – if you would do me the honour of having me?'

The catch in her voice prompted Katrina to realize what was troubling Henrietta throughout all this. There had been

135

a time when Henrietta had gushed over the virtues of Lord Bellinger. Katrina felt convinced now that Henrietta still had feelings for him. Oh dear, she hoped not, as his behaviour tonight would have hurt her badly.

Furious with them and with himself, Lord Bellinger sat on the high-backed chair next to the blazing fire and pulled hard on the bell cord above him. The second footman appeared.

'Get me a brandy. A large one. And if Riley isn't seeing to my guests and keeping them happy, there will be hell to pay.' Why he said this he didn't know; it was a bit like kicking the cat. Riley, his butler, would, if anything, be over-attentive, knowing that he himself was indisposed for a time. He would be ordering the staff around, making sure everyone's glass was replenished the moment their drink reached a quarter of an inch from the bottom, and would have told the pianist to begin playing, to cover any silences. Riley could be trusted in any circumstances.

Relaxing a little with the reassurance these thoughts gave him, he spoke in a more civil tone to the footman who had furnished him with a large brandy, and instructed him that Miss Arkwright and Lady Henrietta were leaving, and to see to whatever needed doing to assist them.

With this settled, Bellinger sat back and gave in to the feeling of despair that rested in him. *God, how did it all go so badly! I'd set my heart on getting Katrina for myself. How can she prefer Lord Rollinson to me – the namby-pamby bloody virgin! Lover of the down-and-out!*

Always there had been this resentment within him where Rollinson was concerned, something that had made him pleased that the man was down on his luck in life, and he'd known he'd want to keep Rollinson there, if he could. He much preferred to have him beholden to him than see him rise to an equal or, God forbid, elevated! Even when Rollinson had been a Viscount and was titled by etiquette as 'Lord', very few in their circle had used that address, and the term 'Viscount' had been used in a derogatory way. Being the second son, and with nothing of worth to his name, had diminished Rollinson's ranking in the eyes of his peers. Bellinger had liked it that way. But now everything *had* changed, and Rollinson was an earl! And not only that, but a soon-to-be-very-rich earl. That standing would give him power over them all – something he hated the thought of. Bloody hell, it was all a bloody mess, and he'd just made it worse.

As he sat back and took another sip of his brandy, he knew his absence from his own ball would have been noted, and that he was committing a social faux pas by continuing it, but he just couldn't face going back into the hub of the party yet.

And what of Lord Parvoil? A much-respected and powerful man on the social scene. Would he listen to his daughter? It was known that if he and his wife shunned anyone, most others would follow suit. *Oh Lord, it's all turned out to be a bloody disaster!*

The prospect of facing the rest of the weekend hung heavily on him, as now he'd to spend most of it in the company of what would surely be a furious Lord Parvoil. But he'd no choice in the matter, as Lord and Lady Parvoil had nowhere else to go and wouldn't dream of leaving tonight for London, a seemingly endless journey from Blackburn. Nor, although they would allow their daughter to, would they consider staying at the Arkwrights' home, as that would elevate Arkwright's standing. Lord Parvoil had been heard on many occasions to call Arkwright 'that jumped-up ape of a man', before going on to say that Arkwright had dared to take one of their class and lower her status, till she was no longer accepted amongst them. To explain his reasoning for letting his daughter befriend Katrina, he had said, 'It is my affection for Lady Veronica that dictates my acceptance of her daughter, though of course the daughter has merits of her own and would be a good catch for anyone – even one of high standing.'

It had been this statement that had made Bellinger think of the possibility of offering for Katrina's hand himself, though why he had sought earlier to put her in the place he had always held her – that of a commoner's daughter – he didn't know.

With the endorsement that Lord Parvoil had given Katrina, Bellinger knew that he could have asked for Katrina's hand weeks ago. *I've behaved like a damn fool!*

Disappointment gnawed at him. He really *had* wanted Katrina's hand. She'd found a place within him that no one else had touched. He'd been devastated when Lord Bertram had confided in him that he had approached Katrina's father and been accepted; but then to hear of Bertram's death and have the ridiculous, well-meaning, moralistic Frederick have the cheek to speak up for her hand within hours of his brother's demise – well, it had taken the wind out of his sails, if the truth be known.

A knock at the door stopped his train of thought. 'M'Lord, Lord Parvoil would like an audience with you.'

Bloody hell! 'Please tell My Lord that I have to re-join my guests, and ask if what he wishes to discuss can wait until the morrow. Of course if it is urgent, then I will see him now.'

Urgent? The man probably wants to rip me apart! All he

could hope for was that propriety would see Lord Parvoil wait – if what he wanted to say would be disagreeable. After all, an argument at such an important event in the calendar as this ball would cause embarrassment to all.

A few minutes later Bellinger found that such considerations didn't matter to the pompous Parvoil and, much to his chagrin, he was forced to meet Parvoil in the library.

'Bellinger, this will not wait. I am extremely angry. What did you think you were playing at? To embarrass one of your guests and, even more, to insult them is bad form, but to do so in front of *my* daughter is unforgivable. Henrietta is very fond of Katrina. And, for some reason, of you! I had it in mind to approach you on Henrietta's behalf, but now she wouldn't have anything to do with you, and neither will we!'

This shocked him. He hadn't imagined such a scenario. Henrietta, good God! He'd never thought of her in that way. She was just jolly old Henrietta – always proper, of course, but also ever ready for a laugh. and a jolly good sort to boot. *What the hell have I done?* The Parvoil connection would mean far more to him than the Arkwright one – far, far more. Somehow he had to turn this around. All he could think of doing was discrediting Katrina.

'My Lord, I am gravely sorry. None of it happened in the way Miss Katrina must have put it across. That young lady had a mind to flirt with me. She sought me out and engaged me in talk about my artwork. No doubt Lord Rollinson had told her how fond I am of it. When she asked if she might accompany me to the Regency Room, where the works are displayed, I told her I would be glad to take her if she would bring Lady Henrietta along. My reasoning for that was twofold: on the one hand, I could see by her manner that she was trying to seduce me. Her recent involvement in the Earl of Harrogate's family, methinks, has made her realize she is worthy of anyone's hand – and not just someone who is desperate to be saved by her money. I also had the ulterior motive of wanting to be in Lady Henrietta's company. What you have said has gladdened my heart, as I have felt unworthy of Henrietta's hand and knew many were vying for it. I hadn't joined them, because I didn't want to be rebuffed.'

'Hmm, well, that puts a different light on things, but why then did you send for Katrina, to beg her forgiveness?'

'Miss Katrina took umbrage at me for asking her to have a chaperone present; she made it clear what her intentions were. She said, "If I do that, then we won't be alone, My Lord, and for what I have in mind, we need to be."'

Lord Parvoil looked suitably shocked, which pleased Bellinger. *I am winning the game!*

'Unfortunately, Lord Parvoil, as you must know, low breeding will out, and Miss Katrina is very low-bred on her father's side. Anyway, I told her how disgusted I was with her and that she had insulted my very best friend, the Earl of Harrogate, by her proposal, and at this she stormed off. I naturally sent for her to apologize for my outburst, which was maybe more than the way I would have dealt with this situation, had it not involved Lord Rollinson, who is very dear to me.'

'Well, the little minx! But there is something not quite right here. Henrietta was very upset, but she distinctly said that you confirmed in your apology what Katrina had said.'

'Once I saw she had Lady Henrietta with her, I could not do other than take the blame for my part, and leave what she had done unsaid. It would have been ungentlemanly of me to discredit Katrina in front of Lady Henrietta. It was enough that I knew that Miss Katrina understood how I felt about her antics, even though, to save her embarrassment, I veiled them a little, so that the meaning wouldn't be plain to Lady Henrietta, as of course I had her feelings in mind at all times.'

'Did you make a marriage proposal to Katrina?'

'I did not! She twisted my words. She made it look as if that was my meaning, and prompted me to get very angry. And, as anyone would in that situation – with the added trigger of having the woman I truly love present – I confess to losing my temper. I even vented my disgust at my friend the Earl of Harrogate's nature! I am mortally sorry at having done so. He is a friend, and now, if he continues with his plans to marry the girl, he may well hear how I feel about the way he conducts himself in his gambling habits, and about offering for his brother's betrothed before Bertram's body was even cold.'

'You mean, Katrina was to marry Bertram?'

'Yes. Purely for money, you understand. The Rollinsons are almost out on their arse, if you will forgive the expression. And the Arkwrights would sell their own daughter to get a foot back in society. It all leaves a bad taste in the mouth. However, I am a loyal person, and I will be sorry if Katrina's antics and lies lead Lord Rollinson to break our friendship. I truly value him as a friend, and have tried to guide him in the way he should behave.'

'Oh, my dear boy. This is all very bad form. We all have things we don't like about those we are close to, but we hope never to voice them. I see you have been put in a position where you had no choice. I think you will have to speak to the Earl and tell him what happened . . . May I?'

Lord Parvoil had picked up the decanter of brandy and waved it at him. Then he put up his hand to stay Lord Bellinger from ringing the bell.

'I can manage, and there is a glass on the tray. We don't need any interruptions.'

Into the silence that followed this came the satisfying glug of brandy, as Parvoil filled the spare glass standing next to the half-empty one that Lord Bellinger had discarded earlier. Taking a swallow and screwing up his eyes as the excellent, smooth liquid hit his throat, giving what Bellinger knew was a satisfying burn before it hit the stomach with a warmth that soothed, Lord Parvoil let out a long sigh and raised the glass. 'Mmm, very good. Now, as you say, breeding will out. I can't believe that Lady Veronica hasn't had more influence over her daughter than that. She seemed to be doing so. She sent both of her daughters to good schools and is seeking good husbands for them. Well, this puts a very different light on things. I will send for Henrietta to come back immediately.'

'Do you think that necessary, My Lord?'

'Yes, I do. Any other action would continue to place you in a bad light. Others saw that Henrietta was upset, and witnessed my fury as I sought you out. Besides, you indicated that you would look favourably on any proposal from me, regarding Henrietta?'

'I did, My Lord, and I would – very much so. I adore her.'

'Right, so be it. We will sort out the niceties of it all later. In the meantime, I will let folk know how you and she have been duped. After all, Miss Katrina must have known how Henrietta felt. Her aim in using her as a chaperone must have been to finally spoil her chances with you, and to discredit you. Once my daughter has been told the truth and has had time to put herself together again, her mother will obtain her consent to us making an announcement. I know that will make her very happy and will finally lay to rest any ideas that Katrina may have, of ruining things for you both. Well done, my boy. I'm proud of the way you conducted yourself, even when you must have known you were being shown in a bad light. As you say, anyone would lose their temper under such provocation. It is a wonder you didn't go even further and reveal the truth of what she'd been up to, in front of Henrietta. It must have taken a lot of self-control not to do so.'

'It did, but my consideration for Lady Henrietta's feelings was paramount.'

'That is good to know, but . . . well, speaking of self-control, your way of conducting yourself in your private life is well known. Oh, don't protest. I have been getting reports for some time. I didn't want to, but my daughter's welfare is my only concern. I haven't told her, mind, but it will have to stop. I will not have my daughter hurt, nor will I have her subjected to any humiliation – not to mention what you might pass on to her, from one of your dubious escapades.'

Lord Bellinger knew there was no answer to this. He more than deserved it; his reputation wasn't good. He was lucky even to be considered as a husband, let alone to be in line to land the much sought-after connections Lord Parvoil's daughter would bring. Not saying anything, he nodded, with just enough depth to the bow of his head to give a respectful affirmation, which was all that would be expected of him. All in all, he felt himself lucky to have got off this lightly, and that Lord Parvoil was willing to overlook his past. Not that he had any intention of changing, but he would be much more discreet. Trips to London would have to be frequent, as he could no longer play on home ground. But that would be no sacrifice. His experiences of the London whorehouses had always been far superior to those in Blackburn. *Yes, things could work out very nicely. And who knows, maybe my Lady Henrietta will turn out to be a sex goddess. I'd certainly enjoy teaching her. But if not, I won't have to bed her often – only as long as it takes to make her pregnant.*

'I'm glad that's out of the way. Now, will you join me in another of those excellent brandies, before we go back to the party?'

Lord Bellinger stepped forward. 'Certainly, My Lord. Let me do the honours.'

This time the tinkle of the liquid hitting the crystal glass was music to Bellinger's ears, as it seemed to signify the sealing of a deal. Life was good. Very good indeed.

'Henrietta, forgive me for touching on such a delicate subject, but do you still have feelings for Lord Bellinger?'

They were back at Katrina's home, and had been for half an hour or so. During that time Henrietta had been very quiet. The way in which she lowered her head gave Katrina the answer she sought.

'I – I'm so sorry that I – I put myself in the position I did. None of this would have happened if I hadn't—'

'It is of no matter, and it isn't your fault. Lord Bellinger has shown himself to be what I have always known he is. It is a good thing that I know. But yes, I am attracted to him. Well, more than that. Daddy was going to proposition him tonight on my behalf.'

'Oh, Henrietta, how can you forgive me? I should never have—'

'Please forget it. It doesn't matter really. I am almost as fond of Lord Weckstone, and he has offered for me. I will take his offer and know that, in doing so, I will be very happy. He is handsome, well-connected, rich and nice, too – everything a girl could want. A bit like your Earl, who despite his lack of wealth is a very good catch, darling, more so than his brother! That did worry me. Frederick will make you happy, I am sure.'

'Oh, Henrietta, tell no one that I was meant to marry Bertram. It will all look so bad, if that comes out. But do you really think Frederick and I will be happy? You weren't swayed to a different view by what Lord Bellinger said? I mean, well, what did you think about what Lord Bellinger said about Frederick being in love with . . . with a cripple?'

'Utter nonsense! When would the Earl of Harrogate ever come into contact with such a person. He just wouldn't.'

'But he did. He told me about it. He told me that Lord Bellinger took him . . .' As she progressed through the story Katrina wished she'd never started it, as Henrietta looked even more hurt and not a little shocked. *But she must know how Lord Bellinger conducts himself, surely?* The tear she saw Henrietta hastily wipe away told her that she didn't. But did it matter now? Henrietta had already made her mind up that she wasn't interested in the vile Lord Bellinger any longer. But then her next words showed that she was.

'I'm very hurt by what happened tonight, Katrina, and by what you have just told me. I would like to go to bed now. I have a thumping headache.'

'Oh, my dear. I'll call your maid. My maid will help her. I will get her to fill a tub for you and bring you some warm milk. Once you're settled, I'll come in and say goodnight, then tomorrow—' Katrina's mother entering the room cut her off from outlining her plans. 'What is it, Mummy? You look very upset.'

'Lord Parvoil has sent a carriage for Henrietta, and a most distressing letter saying that you lied, to put Lord Bellinger in a bad light, Katrina. He says he has now heard the truth from Lord Bellinger and it doesn't sit at all with what you have told Henrietta.'

Katrina listened in astonishment to what Lord Bellinger had said to Lord Parvoil about the whole incident. Her mother's voice shook as she read the letter out, and there were tears in her voice when she finished with: 'Oh dear, Lord Parvoil has said that when and *if* the wedding takes place between yourself and the Earl of Harrogate, would we kindly refrain from inviting him and Lady Parvoil! Good Lord, what is all this about, Katrina?'

'I – I don't know. I didn't lie, Mama, I didn't. He insulted me; he tried to lure me into a room where he had his paintings, and he made insinuations . . . He – he did! And then he did it again when he sent for me to apologize, only I asked Henrietta to come with me. Henrietta heard what he said about the Earl and—'

Henrietta stood, looking from one to the other of them. Her face held an expression of incredulity. When she spoke, dread wove its way into Katrina's heart, as she couldn't deny the truth of Henrietta's words, and it was only now that she realized how clever Lord Bellinger had been, in the way he had chosen his own words.

'Katrina, what have you done? I heard Lord Bellinger say that he had been wrong and hadn't meant to respond in the way he did, to the impression that you conveyed to him. No, don't deny it. You even tried to apologize just now, almost admitting it all. And actually, now I come to think of it, you did twist his words about what he said on offering for your hand. I can't believe this of you. You knew I had a leaning towards Simon – Lord Bellinger. How could you!'

'Henrietta? Mama?'

'Please get my things, Mrs Arkwright. I will leave immediately.' With this, Henrietta walked out of the room and Katrina's mother followed her.

Katrina sat down. Her heart thumped in her breast. *Will no one believe me? I meant to say that I shouldn't have gone, not . . . Oh dear, will Lord Frederick believe me? Oh, why did I go to the blessed ball?* But then she knew why. It had flattered her to be considered worthy to take her place amongst the high-born, and by Lord Bellinger, with whom she had to admit she felt a certain fascination. *The damned, pompous . . . Ooh, I could slap his face!* She sank back into the chair as the realization hit her: *I'm no longer worthy.*

Not only that, but she knew she would be the talk of society, thanks to Lord Bellinger's lies and her own stupidity in not making herself clear to Henrietta. And what that would mean for her future, or the future of her family, she dared not imagine.

She would write to Lord Frederick immediately and tell him exactly what had happened. It would be a test of his affection for her. If he believed her and did something about it, well and good – she would marry him. If he didn't, then she would give him a chance to get out of their arrangement. And though it might not be correct to do so, she'd try to help her case by telling him how Lord Bellinger had said that Frederick was in love with the girl who was wanted for the unlawful killing of his brother. And she would tell him how Lord Bellinger had sent the girl's young sister packing. This part frightened her more than any of it. What if he admitted some feeling for this cripple?

Oh, why has life suddenly become so complicated?

13

The Earl of Harrogate

A Feeling Not to Be Denied

Three letters sat on the silver salver awaiting his attention. One the Earl knew the contents of, as it was a formality that he had been expecting, but he still felt a tinge of delight as he looked at the royal crest sealing the envelope. With him now formally in place as the Earl of Harrogate, it was customary for Queen Victoria to ask him to attend an audience with her. It was a way of introducing him to the court.

Thrilled, he began to plan in his head how the event would go. He would have Katrina by his side, and Mother, of course – now so much better and almost back to her old self. The Queen would glide over to them, and he would be introduced as the new Earl of Harrogate, and Katrina as his intended; and Mother would be greeted and might even be singled out for a chat with the Queen, as she had always been a favourite in those circles. It would be a magnificent occasion.

Leaving the royal letter till last, when he could savour the moment, he picked up one of the two stamped as having come from Blackburn. The one he opened first was from

Katrina. The contents had him reeling between anger at Lord Bellinger and sympathy for Katrina. His anger wasn't all directed at the way Simon had treated Katrina, as some of it concerned Amy. Katrina told him about Bellinger kicking Amy out. *What must her life be like now? How could Simon go against his word and not keep Amy in his care, as he promised to do until I returned, when I would have taken her in and given her a job? Did Bellinger even take her to her brothers before they left? Or at least tell her that I had been successful in arranging for them to go to Parkhurst on the Isle of Wight, in the first instance?*

It had been very satisfactory for him to know that the boys would, once they eventually sailed to Australia, be assigned an apprenticeship, rather than going to a penal colony – a special arrangement in place for boys from Parkhurst Prison. Further to that, he intended to contact the Governor in Australia and make sure that the boys were given his address, for them to write to their sisters. That's if they were able to, but he assumed the boys would be schooled in the art of reading and writing as part of learning a trade.

Something told him that Bellinger wouldn't have taken Amy to her brothers. Simon had been very disapproving of Frederick's involvement with the family, as it was, and particularly of him thinking of taking care of them and looking for Ruth. *Oh, Ruth, what made you run away? And why do you haunt my thoughts? Oh God, it's an impossible situation – the more so because I know I can answer that question, and the one posed by Katrina. The answer doesn't sit well with me, but I am in love with Ruth. She is in my very blood, and I can't rid myself of her . . . Never! I must find her.* Mentally he scolded himself; *Stop being so bloody ridiculous.*

The reality was that he was going to marry Katrina, and should try to put Ruth out of his mind. But now, to his horror, that bloody Simon Bellinger had undone things for him by telling Katrina of his infatuation, for that must surely be what it was. What was Bellinger playing at? Did he want Katrina for himself? If he did, then he'd shown no signs of any feeling for her, and he didn't need her money. *So why then – why?*

Lord Bellinger's letter threw Frederick into confusion, giving a very different side to the tale and an altogether more believable one, for some reason. But he must remain loyal to Katrina. She was his intended and he should not doubt her. It would be disastrous to do so. Besides, he'd been friends with Bellinger for long enough to know his ways. And many times he had wanted to break ties with him, but that wasn't an easy thing to do in society. One had to tolerate certain traits amongst one's acquaintances or risk becoming ostracized by many, or finding oneself among those small groups of people who were laughed at, as they disapproved of all that wasn't Christian or godly. That wouldn't have suited at all.

Frederick recognized that he needed the Bellingers of this world to keep himself afloat, even though he knew Bellinger's cunning and how he would play every dirty trick in the book. But that wasn't so any longer, now that Frederick was a lord and was going to be rich in his own right.

It beggared belief, but Bellinger had almost admitted to his own cunning and conniving when he said that he had *landed a good prize* out of the unfortunate happenings – more like he'd been offered a fatter fish, and needed to put a different light on things to assuage his future father-in-law. Good God, the man was despicable – Bellinger himself said

151

that he now felt Katrina wouldn't be accepted in some quarters, and was only tolerated because of who she was to marry. The words appalled Frederick as he read them through again:

If, dear Frederick, you go ahead with the marriage after this, you will need your head examining. She will drag you down with her. You won't be accepted in certain circles. After all, Lord Parvoil has already said he won't attend the wedding, and that could mean the event is a social disaster.

The man was downright wicked – that was, if he was to believe Katrina's story, which had become the one he felt sure he could set more store by. It looked to him as though not only had Bellinger tried to compromise her, but when he couldn't get his own way he'd ruined her slim chances of being fully accepted and had turned them into a near-impossibility.

Seething, he went through to his office. He'd deal with the matter immediately. He would send a letter to the Lord Parvoil. He must stop this getting out of hand.

'Frederick? Is everything all right?'

'Oh, good morning, Mama. How are you, dear?'

'I am fine. I slept very well and am refreshed. Thank you for inviting me back here. I rest well in my own bed, but it is something we must discuss.'

'No. I am not having it any other way. This is your home, Mama. I won't hear of you living in the dower-house. I argued with Bertram over him putting you there.'

'I know. But when you bring Katrina here—'

'*If.*'

'Oh?'

In the telling of it all to his mother, any wisps of doubt that he still harboured were dispelled, along with a firming of his resolve to clear Katrina's name. And as he listened to her, confidence built in him that he could achieve this.

'I am sure Parvoil will retract his decision, Frederick. You have a good reason to expect a favour from him. I don't think he thought this through or considered you or me – or the standing our family has at court – when he said he would not attend your wedding. Look at how soon the Queen has invited you. Oh, I dare say when you open her letter you will find that she has allowed the proper amount of time for mourning. And when you answer, you will have to inform her of your forthcoming marriage. But it does show that she is eager to welcome you. Parvoil has never had such standing, even though he is popular with her – and would dearly love to have it. You could extend an invitation to him to the informal after-party. After all, Queen Victoria may drop in on that. And another possibility that you could mention in passing is that she might ask for an invitation to your wedding. If she does, and Parvoil has caused the most influential people to refuse to come, it will look very bad for him and Lord Bellinger, because I will personally inform her that they are responsible for smearing Katrina's reputation. Katrina is a darling girl and is incapable of the behaviour Lord Bellinger has accused her of. I will speak to his uncle. I am very cross with the boy. He is the vilest of creatures!'

Sitting back after penning his letter, Frederick felt better. Lord Parvoil had conceded a massive loss at the card table to Frederick a few years back and had written a promissory note to cover his debt. It had included shares in his business portfolio, but, not taking it up immediately, Frederick had eventually let the man off, even though he'd needed the money – an action he'd often regretted, as the shares had gone on to restore Lord Parvoil's wealth and re-establish his standing. Now it was time to remind Parvoil of that good deed and inform him of all Mother had said might happen, regarding the Queen.

This task achieved satisfactorily – and, he hoped, with a successful outcome to follow – Frederick penned a further three letters, one accepting the Queen's gracious invitation, and the other two to Katrina and Lord Bellinger; in Bellinger's he threatened to expose him fully to Lord Parvoil, whom he knew would accept his account – or, rather, Katrina's account – if it came to it.

> *So, please do not force my hand. I have approached Lord Parvoil and given him a way of retracting his earlier statement about not attending my wedding. I want you to put it around that it was all a misunderstanding. And, as much as it is abhorrent to me now, I want you to continue to consent to be my best man!*

This last stuck in his throat, as what had seemed a natural progression of their friendship was now distasteful to him, but it would seal the whole thing as being an episode to forget and would give Katrina a chance. That was something he had to make sure of: she *must* be accepted! She had to be. She would be his wife, for God's sake.

He had worried as to whether the Queen would accept Katrina, but his mother had put his mind at rest. 'Of course she will. Katrina is the daughter of a very well-connected and high-born family.'

'But what of Arkwright?'

'Darling, the Queen has a great deal of respect for those who are contributing in such a huge way to the wealth of her country, and she understands the need for some of us aristocrats to marry into that wealth. Besides, not knowing that Bertram was to offer for Katrina's hand, the Queen will assume that you have a mutual affection for each other and have made a very good arrangement. And don't forget, I will help in that quarter, my dear, so please don't worry about it. You have a formidable weapon in me, my darling son. French by birth I may be, but I have English society in the palm of my hands. Always have had.'

Frederick laughed at this, but knew that she was right and that neither the Lords Parvoil nor Bellinger were a match for Mama, when it came to who would be accepted in society – and the sooner they realized this, the better.

Turning his attention to his letter to Katrina, Frederick sat for a moment unsure how to begin. But then it occurred to him to make sure she knew from the outset that he believed her:

My Dear Katrina,

I beg your forgiveness for the way my friend Bellinger has treated you. I assure you that I have written to him in the strongest terms.

From that beginning, the rest flowed, assuring Katrina that she would be treated with the utmost respect in future. He also qualified his involvement with Ruth and her siblings as stemming from his gratitude to them for saving his dear mother:

I have no feelings for them other than pity. And I ask you,
when deciding whether to believe me or not, to consider
Lord Bellinger's behaviour towards you, his cunning and
the way he manipulates a situation.

This, he was sure, would put to bed Bellinger's vile attempt at discrediting him in Katrina's eyes.

Sitting back, his mind took up the thread it hadn't wanted to leave earlier. He desperately wanted to know if Ruth and her sister were safe.

It would take days to get a letter back from Katrina, and he had nothing pressing to do. The estate, such as it was, was ticking over, and some of the farmers were beginning to pay their rents again. They'd never catch up, and he wouldn't press them to.

So he could see no reason why he shouldn't make a visit to Pradley and make some enquiries about Ruth. In the meantime, he hoped Katrina would write and that she would be receptive to him visiting her. He needed to get his affairs in order, and that meant the wedding must be sooner rather than later. He couldn't arrange such an event by letter. Once all was organized, he would invite her here to stay with his mother for a few days, giving Katrina the freedom to explore her new home and a free hand in how she would make it her own. He didn't doubt that such a determined lady as Katrina was proving to be would want to take the reins and make the place reflect her own taste. He was looking forward to it. It would be good to see new life breathed into this beautiful place.

Pradley buzzed with activity in the market lining its one main street. The noise of traders calling out the price of their wares, of folk chatting with neighbours and of children racing around, gave an atmosphere of joviality that lifted Frederick's spirits. His journey had taken him a couple of hours – some of it over some fairly rough terrain.

Stretching his stiff legs, he wandered over to a stall selling hot drinks and sugared doughnuts. One sip of the tea he purchased had him asking for a doughnut – he needed it to take away the smoky, over-brewed taste of the tea, which had been made from water simmering on an open brazier. Fascinated, he watched the stallholder drop a lump of dough into a vat of hot melted lard, then take an iron rod and poke it through the middle of the dough. The resulting puffed-up ring took on a coat of sugar and ended up wrapped in a square of brown paper, before being handed to him. Burning his tongue, but not caring, he savoured the delicious taste and had to wipe crusts of the sugar from around his mouth more than once.

'Hey, boy, what say you have a doughnut at my expense, eh?' Frederick had spotted a lad crouched on the pavement with an empty begging bowl in front of him – his body bony, his clothes ragged and inadequate against the harsh bite of cold in the air. Blackened teeth, and not many of them, showed as the lad grinned and nodded his head. Shouting his order for another two doughnuts – he'd a mind to have a second one himself – Frederick lowered himself to sit next to the lad. 'So, what do you know? Oh, by the way, I'm Frederick, Earl of Harrogate. What's your name, boy?'

He'd never seen eyes open as wide as this boy's did, his astonishment seeming to render him speechless.

'Oh, don't worry, lad. I'm no different from you, as I beg, too. I had to ask a girl to marry me just because she's rich, and so that I can have her money. That's begging, is it not?'

Again the grin. The lips that framed it looked as red as those of the miners did against their blackened faces, as this lad was as dirty as they were after they came up from a shift.

'Me name's Finwil. Martin Finwil, but everyone just calls me Fin.'

'Right-o. Oh, here's our doughnuts. Careful, now. I gave my tongue a blister by biting into it before it had cooled a little.'

Savouring the sugary taste once more, Frederick watched in awe as the lad scoffed his without much of a to-do, and without taking any heed of the doughnut's heat. 'Tell me, lad, why are you not at your lessons?'

'I ain't never been ter no school, Mister. But that don't mean as I don't know a thing or two.'

This caused Frederick a pang of guilt. Worried as he was about his monetary affairs, he was never likely to suffer the fate of this poor lad. Maybe there would be something he could do to lighten the load of such poor people in the future. In the meantime, this lad might well be able to give him some information. 'I expect you do. You look as if you have survived thus far on your wits and, to do so, you must know most of what occurs in these parts. I wonder if you could help me? Have you any knowledge of a girl with a twisted foot? I believe she came from here.'

'You mean that cripple of a witch, Ruth Dovecote, don't yer? Well, her family are gone from these parts, and good riddance. Not that the rest of them were bad, but that Ruth had powers. She made a lad sick till he nearly died.'

'Good God, what did she do?'

'She cursed him and he took with a fever. Folk say she should be strung up, or burned, up on Pendle Hill!'

Shock held Frederick quiet for a moment. The hate the lad felt for Ruth was tangible, but worse than that, doubt stirred in his own mind. It seemed that wherever Ruth went, someone suffered. His own brother . . . No, he was being ridiculous! It was all just coincidence. Besides, uneducated people were always setting store by myths and were led by what they perceived, rather than by what was logical.

All the same, a chill went through him. It wasn't connected to Ruth's supposed powers, but to his fears for her. This lad spoke with the kind of venom that, if it became widespread, could cause a feral hunt for her, if she was known to be nearby. He *must* find her first. 'So I take it she hasn't been around this town since her family left?'

'Naw, and she'd do well not to. Folk are scared of her, and I reckon as she wouldn't last long if she came round here again.'

'Have you any idea where she might be?'

'I told yer, she took off with her ma.'

'Yes, you did. But . . .'

The lad listened to his tale, then made him regret telling it.

'Eeh, naw. We thought as the town were rid of her. The McNaughts won't like to hear she could come back. It were their lad as she cursed.'

'That's all nonsense. She was born deformed; it wasn't her fault. When something like that happens to a person, they must make the best of it. That can't have been easy, with the attitude of the people around here, by what you're saying. It sounds as though they hounded her, and I suspect you did yourself. Well, anyone's patience is going to give out under

159

that constant barrage. It was coincidence that she turned on the lad and then he became ill, and nothing else.'

'Aye, well, we know what we know.'

'Very well, I'll be on my way. But mark my words, if she does come back and any of you hurt her, I'll make it my business to have you all strung up. Do you understand?'

'What's it to you, anyroad, toff?' With this, the lad was up and scarpered before Frederick could do anything. Despite the supposed insult, he had to laugh. 'Toff' indeed!

The laugh didn't dispel his worry. He wished he could find Ruth and take her to safety. Maybe, when his finances were in a better shape, he could hire someone to look for her. But then what? Have her as his mistress? No, he couldn't do that . . . he told himself, but this didn't help, because every part of him longed for her. And all that after only a chance meeting, which put him in her company for not much more than an hour or so!

'Fresh sprouts and salted beef at the right price, Sir, and I can deliver up to ten miles by morning.'

'Your wares look good. Tell me, where is your farm?'

'I'm up on the edge of the Bowland Hills, Sir. I market here and in Blackburn – doesn't matter to me. Me position is such that I can service both. Me main business is in meat and vegetables, but I have some dairy and am hoping to increase it. If you're looking for a regular supply to your kitchens, I'm your man, Sir.'

'Lord – Lord Rollinson, Earl of Harrogate. And you are?'

'I – I, I'm sorry, M'Lord . . . I didn't realize. Me name's Josh. Josh Bottomless.'

'There's no need to be nervous, my good man. I'm the same person you hailed to your stall a few minutes ago. Just because you now know my title doesn't mean you have to

160

treat me differently. Tell me, have you ever come across a young woman afflicted with a club foot, on your travels? She'd be about seventeen, long dark hair.'

'I – I, naw, M'Lord. I've not seen anyone like that.'

Something didn't ring true about this. The man had a sweat on him, beads of it trickling down his face. 'I don't mean any harm to the girl. I just want to help her. Our paths crossed, under tragic circumstances. She ran off in fear, but she had no need to. She could have trusted me.' With the feeling Frederick had about this man knowing more than he'd let on, he felt he had to maintain a link. 'Do you read and write, Josh?'

'Aye, I do, M'Lord.'

'Well then, be so kind as to take my calling card. Contact me by letter or telegram if you do hear anything, or see her anywhere; or, indeed, her sister, who is younger and has fairer, curly hair. Very slight and thin.'

'I – I have no knowledge of them, I've only just started to come as far as this side of the hills.'

'Very well, but I'd be grateful if you kept an eye out for them. I will drop by here again sometime. I'll not need deliveries, though. Sorry, but I have some excellent tenant farmers who keep us well supplied. However, I wish you well. An enterprising man like yourself deserves to flourish.'

Walking away, Frederick felt certain that the man knew of Ruth. His whole manner gave off an air of someone hiding something. But what could he do? *I can't force him to tell. And what if I'm wrong?* But he had made his mind up: he would hire somebody to look for Ruth, and he'd tell him to begin with Mr Josh Bottomless.

*

161

'Hey, Mister, did that toff ask you about that Ruth Dove-cote? What's he want with her? He asked me an' all.'

'Mind your own business.' Josh, still reeling from the shock of having the Earl asking after Ruth and finding out that he didn't know where Ruth's sister was, regretted the way he snapped at the lad, the moment he did so. Young Martin Finwil meant no harm. He were just one of many living off their wits. He'd make it up to him. 'Here, lad, if you wants to earn a couple of pennies, give me a hand to pack me cart.'

Market wasn't finished by a long shot, but the encounter had knocked the wind out of Josh and he wanted away, before the Earl thought to return to question him some more. He felt sure he hadn't believed him, and wouldn't blame the Earl if he hadn't. The man had caught him off his guard.

Working at a surprising rate for a bony, half-starved individual, Fin amazed Josh with his strength and agility.

'I'm a good worker, Mister, as you can see. Have you any work I could do up at your place? I know where you live and it's harsh up there. I could be a help to you.'

Josh had no doubt that he would, and if it hadn't been for Ruth's presence, he'd take him on. He needed help, that was for sure. Maybe if he kept Fin to the lower fields? He could have him see to the clearing of the ground for the spring sowing, and then help with the planting and the hoeing. There was plenty that he could keep Fin going at and it wasn't possible to see the house, or any of the activity around it, from down there. But then where would the boy sleep, because he couldn't travel there, not daily he couldn't. Although there was the barn.

'Look, lad, I do need help, but can only offer a couple of days at a time, now and again, and it's a good trek to mine.'

'I can walk that, easy. I'd do it in an hour, and I'd set off early. Please, Mister, me mam and me sister are starving. Me dad drinks all he earns. I'd do a good job and be no trouble.'

'Reet, lad. Here's what I can do. I can take you back with me and you can work a couple of days picking the last of the Brussels sprouts and packing them into boxes for me trip to Blackburn next week. You can stop in the barn overnight. I'll bring your snap down to you, and there's a brazier in there which stays lit for hours; and there's dry straw to bed on and I'll bring you a blanket. Now, here's the deal. You come nowhere near to me house. You stays down at the lower-field level. Me ma gets spooked with visitors, she ain't used to them . . . and she ain't well.' The lad didn't seem to bother about this or show any curiosity. 'If that suits you, I'll pay you a day rate and make sure as your family has supplies. We'll go that way when I'm done here, and I'll drop off one of these sides of salted beef and some tatties and sprouts.'

'Eeh, Mister, ta. I won't let you down. I'll not do owt you don't want me to. And I'll work hard at what you tell me to do.'

'Right-o, let's get on with packing up.'

The fact that the lad showed no interest in why Josh wanted to leave early, which was an unusual event, boded well. The lad seemed to know where his nosy-parkering wasn't wanted, and Josh felt sure he wouldn't come snooping around the house. Yes, it would work out well. God knows he needed the help, and Ruth would remain safe – of that he felt sure.

14

Amy & Ruth

A Flicker of Hope, but a Fear Embedded

A memory of the time a ragged muslin curtain blew in the wind and wrapped around her face came to Amy as she tried to drag herself out of the sleep that held her, but her fogged brain would not show her where that was, or whose curtain it was. It only set up a battle in her to claw the feeling away.

A commotion around her seeped through the haze, and someone wiped her forehead. A whispered voice came through: 'She can't last much longer. Her breathing is much laboured.' Another answered, ''Tis rare for them to recover.' At this, her body shivered as it rejected the wet, cold cloth they swabbed her body with.

The light above her struck her eyes in a painful way, but closing them didn't help. She wanted to talk to the people around her, ask them to save her, but she couldn't, so she prayed to Jesus's mother to bring her through whatever ailed her. She'd often talked to the Virgin Mary since seeing a statue of her in a Catholic church she'd once visited. Always it was as if things got better afterwards, so maybe Mary did hear her prayers. *Please let her hear me today*.

With this thought, peace came into her and she imagined

she saw the statue gliding towards her. 'Eeh, little lady, you're lovely.' A light shone around the statue that didn't hurt her eyes to look upon. A warmth filled Amy. She held her hands out towards the figure, but it went away from her and a voice came to her with the sweetest tinkle to it.

'Not yet, little one. You have much to do.'

'What? What have I got to do? I don't understand.'

'Make a difference.'

'I can't make a difference to owt.'

But the lady had gone and a voice of this world came to her, 'We can all make a difference, lass. I don't know who that was you were talking to, but whoever it was, by, they've worked some magic on you. How do you feel now, Iva?'

'Me name's not Iva.'

'Naw, we know that, but that name has stuck to you since you came in here some four weeks back. Loopy Lil, as we call her, gave it to you. She thinks you're her daughter. Poor Iva died in this very hospital about five years ago. Now then, who are you, love? Have you any family?'

'I'm Amy. Amy Dovecote from over Pradley.' As she told her tale, more of it came back to her, as did all the folk in her dream. With this last came fear – fear for Ruth and the lads – but also knowledge that her ma and da and little Elsie were all together and safe.

'Eeh, lass, that's a tale and half, and I've heard some. But yours is the worst ever. Well, sommat or someone is helping you, that's for sure, as not ten minutes ago I wouldn't have you down as being here now. I thought your last breath was on you.'

'I – I sort of went – well, nearly, but the lady wouldn't have me.'

'Well, that's funny talk. I'll take it as you're still a bit delirious, but don't be talking like that when the doctor comes back, nor in front of Matron, as they'll have you in the madhouse as soon as look at you. You've got pneumonia, but you've come through the crisis point, so should recover. Is there owt you want, me wee one?'

'Only a drink, please. Who's Lil? Does she work here?'

'Huh, thinks she does, poor woman. But naw, she's just another inmate of the workhouse, but she likes to hang around these wards. She tries to make herself useful, but now and again everything gets on top of her and she's taken into the madhouse, as we call it. But she's a handful in there, so they like to keep her this side and let her take care of some of the lasses brought in during the night. She sleeps most of the day. That's where she'll be now, though she took some persuading to leave your side.

The girl telling her all of this looked the same age as Ruth. Amy liked her. She had a way about her that said she'd always be truthful with you. She wanted to ask her what would happen to her when she was well.

'Amy, love, your face holds the troubles of the world, but it stands need to, with your circumstances. Look, you'll be a good few days getting fit, then if you've no place to go, the board'll apply to the court to put you under the Poor Law – and that'll be it. You'll be in here till your circumstances change, which is a rare occurrence.'

'Are you under the Poor Law, Miss?'

'Aye, and me name's Lettie. I were orphaned at the age of thirteen. I were the only surviving one of me family. The typhus took them all from me. A friend of me ma's looked after me at first, but her husband took a shine to me when I reached fifteen and took his needs out of me. When I copped for a babby, I wasn't welcome any longer. She called

166

me a whore and wouldn't listen when I tried to tell her as I fought him, but couldn't stop him. I lost me babby and ended up in here. But I'm keeping meself useful and following all the rules, in the hope of being released to work in one of the mills one day and moving into one of them hostels.'

'I hope you do. But I'm sorry to hear about what happened to you, Lettie. I know what it's like . . . a man—'

'Aye, I know. You were in a mess down below. Look, lass. If it results in a babby, I ain't sure what will happen. I reckon as they'll keep you in here till you have it, then take your babby for adoption.'

'But he didn't manage it, I kicked him.'

'Lass, I reckon he must have done. You're torn and bruised and . . . well, a lot of the bruising and blood was on your inner thighs. I'm sorry to tell you that, Amy, but you'll get through it somehow. Just think on: you're alive and that's sommat, as you were left for dead.'

'But I don't want a babby. I don't. I can't. I – I don't reckon as I'm up to taking much more.'

'Don't talk like that, lass. God only sends to us what he knows we can cope with. Though why he thinks us lasses can cope with all he sends us, I don't know. Look, I like you. You're a plucky lass. If I promise to be your friend and to look out for you, will you promise to try and put up with your lot and work towards a better future, like I am?'

Amy could think of nothing better than having Lettie as a friend. It'd be like having Ruth back. This thought didn't sit well with her, as thinking of Ruth brought the tears flowing down her cheeks. *Oh, Ruth, I want you back for real. I don't want a substitute.*

'By, lass, you'll have to grow a thicker skin. What's

happened has happened, and you can't undo it.' The cloth Lettie used to wipe her face had a coarse feel, but the gentleness of her touch was akin to love, and that brought some comfort to Amy, as did Lettie's words: 'It's easy to give in. I cried meself to sleep for weeks, but then I gave meself a good talking-to and made me mind up to better meself. After that, me attitude towards everybody improved and they took me off spinning and weaving, and brought me in here to look after the sick. I get better rations and that's built me strength.' As she patted Amy's face dry, Lettie stood back a moment and said, 'Look, I need more help, so I'll ask if you can work with me. They'll listen to me, but only if you ain't having a babby. If you are, they'll put you to work in the kitchens or some such until you have it.'

'How do they find out if you're having a babby? Does it allus happen if a man does sommat to you?'

'Naw, not allus. Were it an old man?'

'Aye, he looked old. He were horrible and fat, and . . . Eeh, it makes me sick to think on it.'

'Well then, don't. Put it out of your head. Chances are he had no substance in him for making babbies, lass, so don't worry. It'll be to do with your bleeding that they find out. Have you started that yet?'

'I have had a couple, but I were late starting. Our Ruth started when she were ten.'

'Well, it makes no odds when you started. Fact is that . . .'

As she listened to Lettie explaining about how her bleeding meant she could now have babbies, Amy's despair deepened. She just wanted to die, and she wished the little lady had let her. But then some of what Lettie had said made her think of Ruth. Ruth was strong, she coped with everything. And besides, Lettie had said she would help her.

This thought brought comfort with it, and Amy knew she had to make the best of everything as it was and do as Lettie said, and work at making things better for herself.

A movement behind the bushes frightened Ruth. Leaning heavily on her crutch, she peered in the direction it had come from, hoping to see that a rabbit or a stray sheep had been the culprit. Her fear was such that her heart seemed to want to push itself out of her breast, in a painful way that got her holding her breath. *What if that lad Josh has hired has gone against his wishes and come up to the farm?*

When Josh had told her what he'd done, she hadn't liked it. She knew the lad that everyone called Fin, and knew him to be one as was always out to make mischief. He'd many a time knocked her crutch from under her, and had never let her pass without calling her names: cripple, halfwit or witch. Shuddering against this last, she looked up towards Pendle Hill and the dread in her increased. The place had always been held as somewhere to fear, but she'd never seen it until she, her ma and the others had started out on their journey, and she had never thought in a million years that she'd end up living under its shadow.

Another rustle and the snapping sound of a twig froze her thoughts and all life around her, leaving her isolated. She tried to call out, but her dry throat wouldn't respond and nothing other than a croak came from her. But although it wasn't loud, it set the intruder running, for now she heard the tread of someone or something scampering away. It relaxed her to know that whoever or whatever it was had gone, and made her able to move once more. Hobbling back across to the chicken run, she scattered the hens' food more quickly than she'd ever done before. The chorus of birds clucking their appreciation and squawking, as they flew out of her way, brought normal life back into focus. She'd been silly. It'd be an animal – nothing else.

Hurrying across the yard in a swaying movement that she knew made her look ridiculous, but helped to get her where she wanted to be faster than her normal gait did, Ruth reached Josh's work-shed. She hesitated a moment, unsure whether to voice her fears, but the door creaked open and Josh appeared. The look in his eyes as he gazed at her stilled her thoughts. For a moment she couldn't glance away or speak. In the intensity of his gaze she read a message that triggered something inside her – a feeling, a need. But then Josh spoke and his words broke the spell, though somehow she knew that what he said wasn't what he truly wanted to say.

'What is it, lass? I saw you crossing the yard as if the devil himself were after you. By, if I'd have known you could move that fast, I'd have doubled your workload! In fact I might have to consider it, now you have given yourself away.'

Embarrassment overcame Ruth and banished the last threads of the emotion that had gripped her. The thought of Josh seeing her move in a way that made her look like one of them gorillas in a flicker-book mortified her.

'By, lass, you look pretty when you blush.' Josh's voice gravelled to a deep tone that she hadn't heard before. The memory and embarrassment of Josh seeing her gait faded, and Ruth's body flooded with the sensation that had taken her when his eyes had held hers. But that feeling was short-lived, as Josh turned from her and went back inside, banging the door shut behind him.

Ruth stood for a moment. Confusion gripped her. Part of

her wanted to go to him, but fear of rejection held her back. Then a voice in her head said, 'Do it, lass. You know you want to.'

The door opened without its usual creak. Not entering the room fully, Ruth peered into the shed. The sight of Josh's dejected figure highlighted against the window stopped her progress. He was bowed forward, with his entwined hands clasping the back of his head.

'Josh?'

For a moment she thought he'd stumble, with the speed at which his body swivelled round. 'Eeh, lass.'

Something compelled them both forward and Ruth found herself in a place she'd been before, enclosed in Josh's arms. But that last time had been for comfort; this time a feeling seized her that burned through her body, as Josh guided her towards the same row of straw bales that he'd sat her on the first time he brought her here.

'Lass, I – I need to ask you something.' That same gravelly sound that had lowered the tone of his voice was present as he spoke. His eyes held hers while he set her crutch against the wall and knelt in front of her. 'Will you have me, Ruth? Will you become me wife?' His eyes held deep love. Aye, and a promise that gripped her with feelings she could hardly cope with. But these emotions weren't all that Ruth gleaned from Josh's intent look, for harboured in their depth was a respect she'd never thought anyone would feel for her.

Warmth kindled inside her, in response to the love shown to her. All she found she could do was nod her head. As she did so, Josh's face faded and the Earl's deep, smouldering eyes stared back at her. Ruth closed her eyes against the image. *No! Don't. That can never be.*

171

'Ruth?'

Opening her eyes, she gazed once more into the kind, loving face of Josh and expelled the Earl from her imagination.

'Did you nod, lass? Are you saying as you would have me?'

The moment was suspended. Then all doubts left her. 'Aye, I would. I have a feeling for you, Josh.'

'I have more than a feeling for you, Ruth. I love you, lass, and I will until me death.'

'And I you, Josh.' As she said the words, she knew them to be the truth. What she felt for Josh was a deep love – a love that she knew didn't match what the Earl had kindled in her, but it didn't have to. This love for Josh had its own strength and was born of all she knew him to be, not of a fantasy she could never hold.

'Oh, me little lass.'

This time, when Josh held her, she felt a different emotion come from him – an animal-like hunger. His lips touched hers. His strong arms supported her as if they would do so forever and ever. The sensation that shivered through her shocked her, as did the intensity of her response, as desire burned deep within her. And yet the moment had a gentleness about it. A moment that was fleeting, as Josh's hold on her tightened and he crushed her body to his. Her name on his lips sounded as if it were an instrument of pleasure. Her heart sang out a joyous acceptance. At last she felt beautiful, wanted and desired, and every fibre of her needed to give that same feeling to him.

Their second kiss was not his to her, or hers to him, but a seeking of each other as their tongues probed, tingling undeniable sensations through Ruth. She yielded to Josh, sinking into all that he offered.

Pulling away from her, he looked intently at her. His eyes asked a question. Not knowing how she knew what he meant, she nodded. His moan went into her neck, and his mouth sucked in her skin, as he gently swayed her backwards until she lay beneath him.

There was a moment of pain, but then her soul knew her very reason for being, as she allowed all that he had to give – his caresses, his kisses, his love – and, with the taking, an explosion of feelings conveyed her to a place she never wanted to leave.

Sobbing her joy, she clung to Josh, accepting him as he moaned his final pleasure and pressed into her as if he'd never leave her. 'Oh, Josh. Josh . . .'

After a moment he released himself from her and rolled off her. Neither of them spoke, their lips joining in a kiss that left no need for words. Their sweat mingled. Clinging to him, Ruth felt a peace inside her, one she never wanted to lose. *But I will – I will!* She didn't know where this thought came from, but it shattered the fragile tranquillity she'd felt, and the truth of it shivered through her.

As if he knew and wanted to deny it, Josh pulled her close. 'Nothing will hurt you again, lass, not while I have breath in me body. You're me wife now, in the only way you can be. Thou knows that. We can't do owt about making our union legal, as that would expose you, but we're bound together just as tightly as we would be if the church had blessed us and we had the certificate that stated we were husband and wife.'

'I know.'

'How does you feel about it, lass?'

173

'I know there's no other way for us. But your ma, Josh. What will your ma say?'

'Ma don't come into it, lass. But she knows me intentions. She's not altogether for it, but she said she'd accept it, if you did.'

'I accept it, Josh. I am your wife.'

'Tonight you will be with me in me bed, and that's where you'll always spend your nights. And as we did just now, we'll come together as one as often as we can. Eeh, lass, I'm a happy man. You're made for loving. I've never had owt like it.'

'Have you done it with others, Josh?'

His answer shocked her. She didn't want him to have done so, but the way he put it softened how she felt. 'A man has his needs, lass, and there's those who'll satisfy him for a payment. But never before did it mean anything other than a release. Never have I done it like we did – driven by a love that filled me soul and a need that consumed me. And never again will I take another. Doing so was just me looking for the basics in life. What we had fulfilled me as a man.'

Moving herself onto her elbow, she looked down at him. 'They say as I'm a witch. Well, I'm telling you, Josh Bottomless, if you so much as look at another woman, I'll cook up a spell that will turn you to stone.'

His laughter echoed around the shed and, with it, he raised himself. 'Come on, lass. You'll be in trouble with Ma as it is.'

'Oh, Josh, what shall I tell her?'

'You'll tell her nowt – not on your own, you won't. I'll come with you and announce our marriage. I'll tell her that we're sorry we couldn't invite her to the ceremony, but it were a private affair.' Again they laughed. It was a laughter that dispelled Ruth's earlier fears and bound them to each other as much as their coming together had.

'I'll tell you what, though, lass: we will have a celebration. One that Ma can join in. She can get her glad rags on and find sommat for you – she has trunks of stuff from her younger days, and we'll have a sing-song around the piano the neet. Eeh, we might even have a drop of me ma's home-made beer. By, lass, it'll be grand.'

'I didn't know you played the piano?'

'Aye, I does. Piano belonged to me grandma. She brought it with her when she came to me grandad. She were a canny player and taught me to play. I'll teach you, if you like.'

'Eeh, I would like. I'd really like that.' And she knew she would – to be able to make music – something she'd only ever heard when the fair had come to Pradley and a man fed a card with many holes in it into a kind of barrel and turned the handle. She'd loved it and had stood next to him for more than an hour. To her, the sound tinkling in the air had a magic to it, and it had transported her to another world. It had made her feel whole, and she'd swayed her body to its rhythm. The man hadn't laughed at her. He'd just said, 'Lass, you may have an affliction, but that's not the be-all of everything. You have music in your veins, and that will see you reet.'

How it could do that, Ruth didn't know; but she did know that the piano Josh talked of had drawn her to it ever since she'd arrived. Many a time, when polishing it, she'd lifted the lid and tinkled the keys, and inside her at such moments had been an excitement she couldn't have given a name to.

15

Frederick & Katrina

A Blight on the Start of Their Marriage

Today, her wedding day, had been lovely; even the weather had been kind, as the late June sunshine shone on her. At least, Katrina thought, she had that to hold onto, though she had to admit it hadn't been quite as wonderful as the day she'd been presented to the Queen. That had been an amazing experience. The first surprise she'd had was Queen Victoria's height. She hadn't known the monarch was so tiny – under five foot, she would guess, as she herself, at five feet four inches, was looking down at her. But the Queen's physical height hadn't taken away anything from the presence she had about her, almost as if she were not a being from this earth. You couldn't call her beautiful, but handsome maybe? Her dark hair was fashioned in a most becoming style, parted in the middle and falling into bunches of ringlets that covered her ears.

The second surprise was how easy it was to talk to her, and how the Queen didn't baulk at mentioning Katrina's father, even saying that she admired him. She also mentioned her mother, and said she was very pleased that she had managed to get her daughter back into the circles where she belonged. 'I think you will be an asset to the Earl of Harrogate, Miss Arkwright, and I hope you will both be very happy. My blessing is on your marriage, though I am afraid I cannot attend.' She did give them a present, though: a signed picture of herself, which Katrina treasured.

One thing had been accomplished that day, for the Parvoils and the Bellingers had been humbled. They were not invited to the introduction, although they could view it all. It gave Katrina a great deal of pleasure to know that they saw the Queen conversing with her for more than a few minutes, and then introducing her to all the elite in attendance upon her.

The Parvoils and the Bellingers were both in attendance today and had given Katrina her rightful place, and although they weren't friendly, they were at least respectful.

Daddy had done her proud by allowing her mother to have a free hand in preparing their home for the event. No expense had been spared, and all had been done to the very latest fashions that society demanded. And, to Daddy's delight, the cream of society had attended. Oh, and Daddy had tried so hard to speak with a 'posh' accent, as taught by her own and Marcia's old governess, brought out of retirement for that very purpose. Poor soul, what a job she'd had!

For the most part Daddy had managed very well, until Lord Bellinger had sought him out. Then he'd been unable to hide his anger and she'd heard him say, 'If I were you, lad, I'd watch me back, because I don't forget, and I've me own means of sorting the likes of you.' Frederick had intervened and had steered Bellinger away, but not before Daddy had said, 'And another thing: I'm after seeing me solicitor about having you, for slandering me daughter's name.'

This had sat like a dampener on proceedings for a while

– not that anyone other than herself and Frederick had heard, but Frederick had to spend some time with Bellinger to calm him down and smooth things over. It was then that something had happened that she hadn't expected. She'd looked over at them, wondering how things were going between them, when she'd caught Bellinger's eye. What she saw in his gaze had shaken her. He'd looked on her with longing and, to her shame, something had kindled inside her that triggered feelings Katrina could not comprehend. Even thinking of it now did the same. Her nerves jangled as Annie, her maid, fussed around her, giggling as she prepared Katrina for bed. It was the kind of giggling that told of Annie's knowledge of what was going to happen, as did the suggestive note in her voice and the knowing looks she gave as she tended to her. Katrina wished she was a party to that knowledge, too. *What is this mysterious thing that happens between a man and a woman?*

Annie had been with her since she'd turned thirteen, when Mother had decided that Katrina needed a maid of her own. She'd travelled with her to school, and to Belgium for finishing school, and – well, everywhere. They were friends, in the way it was possible to be friends with a maid. Annie was her confidante. They'd talked about everything, except . . . well, they'd never broached the subject of the man–woman relationship. Such things were just not spoken of, but Katrina had to find out from someone! Mother was hopeless, and though she suspected Marcia knew, as nothing passed her by, her sister had only teased her as to what she was in for, but wouldn't share the truth of it.

Marcia hadn't changed, although Katrina had missed her whilst she'd been away at finishing school, as her antics were usually a fun distraction from the everyday routines of life.

That is, except for her mischief-making! No, Katrina had been glad to have a rest from that for a while; and from the way that Marcia's jealousy of her manifested in wanting whatever Katrina had, and often going to great lengths to get it.

Marcia had this inbuilt principle that if someone crossed her in any way, they would pay; besides which – and Katrina wasn't sure if this trait was worse than the mischief-making or not – Marcia would do anything to get what she wanted. Today she'd shown signs of wanting Lord Bellinger! She'd planted herself wherever he was, had laughed a little too loudly at his jokes and had generally gushed over him at every opportunity. It was all very bad form, especially as he and Henrietta had now announced their engagement. Thinking of Henrietta, Katrina knew there was still a coolness between them that hurt. *Oh, but why am I thinking about Marcia and Henrietta, when the time for me and Frederick to come together is fast approaching? I must find out what will happen – I must!*

'Annie, leave my hair for a moment. I can brush it out. I want to talk to you.'

'Oh, Miss . . . Oh, I'm sorry, I mean Lady Katrina. I'm that excited! It's been a grand day and I've been the most important of all the maids; and, oh, you looked lovely, Miss!'

'Annie, please, this is important. We can talk about the day over and over another time, but there is something I have to know. I need to know what's in store for me.'

'Eeh, don't worry on that score, Lady Katrina.'

'What score? And what do you know about . . . well, about what will happen? I mean, what Lord Frederick will do to me?'

The brush halted in its progress through her long hair. In

179

the mirror in front of her Katrina saw Annie's face drop into an amazed expression, before colouring till it showed a tinge of scarlet on each cheek.

'I'm sorry, Annie. I shouldn't have asked. Look, just give me the brush. I will finish my hair. You've had a long day.'

'I'm all right, Ma'am, I – I were just shocked as you don't know. I thought your ma had told you. Mine did, as soon as my monthly show started. Gave me a right lecture, she did. But at the same time she made me think about the day I come to wed. It ain't owt to worry over, Miss – eeh, I'm sorry, I've been practising for a long time to call you Lady Katrina, but me tongue's not used to it.'

'Don't worry, it will come. I'm not used to it myself yet. Just try hard to remember if there is anyone present, otherwise they will think you rude. Now, tell me what your mother told you. I have to know.'

'It ain't easy to tell, but me ma said as it's sommat to look forward to – that is, if you get a good man as loves you, and I know as Lord Frederick will. How can he not love you? And he's a good man an' all. He'll treat you right, I'm sure of it.'

'Never mind all of that. Just tell me the facts of what happens. What can I expect? I am so afraid. I—'

'Don't be, Miss, it ain't nowt to be afraid of. Look, me ma said . . .'

What she heard over the next few seconds had Katrina reeling through so many different emotions. Fear turned to anticipation; ignorance turned to a realization of what the funny feeling was that she'd had at times, when she had caught a certain look from Lord Bellinger. But there was also disgust at herself for thinking that; and at him for doing such things with the whores she knew he visited. At the same time she wanted to experience these thrills Annie was telling her about, but then she became afraid again as to whether Frederick knew what to do and whether they would manage it.

And what of this pain Annie is now talking about? How bad is it, and will I be able to relax, as Annie says I should? And why haven't I felt the same desire when Frederick is near that, without doubt, I do feel when Lord Bellinger looks at me? Oh, it's all so confusing. Frederick is nice. He is handsome, and loving, but not in the way that suggests he wants to do this thing with me! Oh dear, does he even desire me? And what of Bellinger? Is what he shows me simply lust? It must be. Surely no one could do what he did to me, if he loved me?

'You're very quiet, Lady Katrina. I ain't upset you, have I? You did ask me.'

'No, no, really, Annie, I'm glad you told me. I can prepare myself for something I know is coming, instead of being terrified of the unknown. Leave me now. I – I want to be alone for a few minutes. D – don't tell Lord Frederick that I am ready just yet. Leave it another five to ten minutes.'

Annie did something she'd never done before. She put her hand out and touched Katrina's shoulder. It was a reassuring gesture, and she quickly pulled it away. The worried look on Annie's face told of her anxiety.

'Annie, please don't be afraid. I can handle anything, but only if I know what it is I am in for. Thank you for enlightening me. Everything will be fine, now that you have done so.'

But will it? In some ways I feel more afraid now than I have been of the unknown. Taking a deep breath, Katrina made her way to the closet behind the screen in the corner of the

181

room. An urgency had taken hold of her and she wanted not only to pee, but to touch herself there – to feel what she had between her legs, and to explore a little.

It came as a surprise to her that she had a bigger orifice than she had imagined, and that she could insert her finger without hurting herself, and even evoke a nice feeling as she touched a protrusion that lay just inside the front of the opening. The feeling spread through her body and filled her with anticipation.

Covering her pot, she glimpsed Frederick's bigger pot a few feet away. The sight confirmed to her that he would come to her bed. And something in her couldn't wait!

Hearing a noise outside her door, Katrina scampered across the room and dived into the bed. Its soft-feathered mattress allowed her to sink into its depths. This room was in the far west wing and was part of a suite of rooms that hadn't been used for years. Of late they had received a fresh coat of distemper to whiten the walls, and some very plush furnishings that her mother had found in a large store in London. They were French in design, which she had said Frederick would appreciate, as his mother, Lady Eleonore, had steeped him in her native traditions.

It was to France that they were sailing tomorrow on their honeymoon, staying with a cousin of Lady Eleonore's whose family still lived in Paris . . . *Paris! Oh, how I loved the place when I visited, and they say that spring in Paris is not to be missed; well, I'm sure it will still be just as delightful in midsummer.* These thoughts drifted away into the fast beating of her heart as the sound of someone in the adjoining bedroom – Frederick's apartments – reached her. *Oh God, he is getting ready. He will be coming in soon.* Anticipation and excitement scrunched her up into a ball, then a knock on the connecting door straightened her body. Her voice sounded husky in her own ears as she bade Frederick come in. Shock caused her to sit bolt upright as Lord Bellinger entered her room.

'Wh – what are you doing? Get out at once!'

'You don't mean that, my pretty one.'

'I do! Where is Frederick? Why are you here? Please go away. Please! Frederick will be here any moment. He'll think . . . Oh God, don't do this to me, please.' He was nearer her now. His face held a look that spoke of his intention. 'Stop it, stop now!' But even as she said this, she felt a strange fascination at his progress towards her. The bed sank under his weight as he sat down near her and reached his hand towards her. His fingers played with strands of her hair. Her throat tightened, as sensations rippled through her. How had she got so close to his face that she could feel his breath?

The tinge of brandy and cigar smoke didn't repulse her; instead it added to the anticipation she felt, making her want him to continue, to complete the move that would have his lips on hers. When he did, his touch tingled through her, and his weight bore her down, pressing her back into the pillows. His movements had him lying next to her, but something in her wouldn't let her protest or resist. When he lifted his head, her lips burned with a near-agony to have him kiss her again. His voice was different now, the tone thicker. 'Katrina, my Katrina.'

Her name held a promise she couldn't deny. Though she knew she was doing wrong, she melted into him and gave herself to the pleasure of his kisses, his caresses and the burning desire he'd awoken in her.

That burning turned to discomfort as he entered her, making her cry out. His apology held love; his holding back

183

helped. His lips snuggled into her neck, kissing and sucking. His hands kneaded her breast. Catching her nipple between his thumb and forefinger, he massaged it with a motion that had her writhing beneath him. She could take the pain. She needed to. She needed to have him sink deep into her. He responded with a thrust. The pain was momentary, the joy immense. Feelings she didn't know existed seized her whole being. She was shocked at this awakening – this exquisite joining of herself with the man she loved. Yes, she could admit it: Simon Bellinger was engraved onto every part of her, and would always be so. She opened every pocket of herself to him.

Then something strange and wonderful happened. His movements started a sensation creeping, slowly at first, but then gaining in strength, until she wanted all it had to offer. Drawing in her breath, she gasped his name and dug her nails into his flesh. He mustn't go from her; she had to have what her body promised. 'Yes. Yes . . . there, keep going. Please, my love.'

Her core burst in a cascade of wave after wave of the most exquisite feeling, which had her wailing with uncontrolled ecstasy and crying out her despair at its fading. But then it grew in strength again as Simon moved once more, thrusting himself against the delicate place that was the very heart of her, until she caught her breath, unable to bear any more, and stayed him by clamping him between her legs. Pulsating on him, she allowed her body to come down to a peaceful, spent state – a place that held her. The real her: the one that belonged in the arms of her man, this man . . . Simon Bellinger.

Without knowing why, sobs racked her body. Simon kissed away her tears and told her he was close to his end.

He asked her if he could stay with her when he came. Not knowing what he meant, but not wanting him to leave her, she whispered 'yes', then lay beneath him, unable to participate as he took his fill until he gave an animal-like cry of great joy and let his shuddering body lie fully on her.

Staying like this for a moment, with only the ticking of the clock and Simon's slowing gasps disturbing the silence, Katrina felt guilt creep over her. *What of Frederick? Where is he? Oh God, if he should come in!*

Simon rolled off her, as if sensing her distress and its cause, and then spoke in a more normal voice. 'Don't worry – Frederick is out for the count. I made sure of that. I gave him something with his drink, to knock him out. He's lying on his bed next door. When I get my breath back, I'll have him carried in here by my trusted men, who will first prepare him for his marital bed. When he wakes in the morning beside you, my darling, it will be an easy matter to dupe him into thinking it was he who deflowered you.'

Reality hit Katrina. All that had been now seeped into a dirty, disgusting place. 'No! Oh God, how could you?' Her body cringed away from him. Everything about him repulsed her now. *What have I done? Oh God, what have I done?*

'Don't. Please, my love, my darling, don't reject me now. You know we were meant for each other.'

'I don't deny that I am strongly attracted to you, but it is too late. I am married to Frederick. Oh, Simon, why – why did you do it? And if you love me, why didn't you offer for me?'

'My dear, I wanted to. But by the time I'd decided to, that bloody Bertram told me he had done so and had been accepted. I never dreamed that Frederick would act so swiftly, on Bertram's death. I know he is short of money, but

I didn't think he would stoop so low as to jump into his brother's shoes before he was even cold in his grave! Oh, darling, don't cry . . . don't.'

'I am ashamed of what I have done. I – I have behaved the way you expected, and I am not like that, I'm not!' Her tears were now ones of distress at the disgrace she had brought upon herself. *How did such a thing happen? How did I let it happen? And what of the future? Simon loves me, and I love him!*

Trying to come out of the sleep that held him felt, to Frederick, as though he had to fight through a forest of closely-knit bracken. His brain hurt; his body ached. Sweat ran from every pore, leaving his mouth dry and his throat sore. Turning his head only increased the pain. Opening his eyes threatened to bring to his mouth the vomit that was churning in his stomach, as the ceiling spun towards him. A strange ceiling – one he'd never looked up at before. *Where am I?*

Turning his head, Frederick let his eyes settle on a sleeping form next to him. Memory struck him, enlightening him with a rush of information that shocked him. *My God, I'm a married man! And I can't remember a thing about it. Well, not . . . oh, dear God, please let me have been gentle.*

'Katrina.' His voice held the fear that he felt. What if, in his drunkenness, he'd been rough and had done what Simon had kept urging him to do? 'Just get on with it, old boy, it'll be for the better in the end. Yes, she'll feel pain, but that will pass and then she'll be grateful every time you visit her bed-chamber. Pussy-foot around, and you'll be a slave to her every whim!'

He'd laughed and had joined in the guffawing, but hadn't

thought he would do as Simon had suggested. He'd rather be a slave to Katrina's every whim than hurt her more than was necessary. *How is it that I can remember that conversation, but nothing afterwards?*

'Katrina . . .'

Her stirring increased the dread in him, but when she opened her eyes, she smiled and rolled towards him. Moving his arm to enclose her brought Frederick's painful joints back to his attention, but her body felt soft and warm, snuggled into his. Still she didn't speak. He would wait.

He didn't have to wait long. A small sob escaped her. *Oh no, I hurt her!*

'I'm sorry, dear, really sorry. I didn't mean to hurt you. I don't know what happened, I—'

'No, don't be sorry. Please. I'm being silly. I – I'm so happy. But I need my maid to come to me now. Will you leave me?'

'Of course, but are you really all right? I mean—'

'Yes, I'm fine. I am just in a little bit of a mess. I need to get clean. I will come into your room when I am ready. That is, if you want me to?'

'I'd like that.' As he kissed the top of her head, Frederick's lips sank into her soft hair. Its touch reminded him of Ruth. Something stirred deep in his groin as his head cleared at last and, with the clarity of his every fibre, he wished it was Ruth in his arms at this moment. Shaking the thoughts from him, he pulled his arm from under Katrina and swung his legs out of bed and onto the soft rug beside it. Once more the queasiness hit him, and this time the vomit came into his mouth.

Staggering across the room, he made it to Katrina's dressing table. His stomach emptied into her washing bowl.

187

Humiliation withered him. Reaching for the pitcher next to the bowl, he poured the water from it over his head. Nothing helped. His legs gave way beneath him.

Somewhere a long way away he heard the tinkling of a bell. For a moment he thought he was dead, but the sound of Katrina calling out told him he wasn't, and he realized the bell was her summoning her maid.

'Frederick, oh, my dear. Forgive me. Oh God, I'm so sorry.' The scent of her told him she was near, but he had to keep his eyes closed, as the nausea would beat him if he didn't. *But why is she asking for forgiveness, when it is I who should be begging it of her?*

Another voice came to him, a rough-and-ready voice. 'Eeh, what's to do, Ma'am? What's happened? Eeh, look at you, you're in a reet mess – and look at me Lord Rollinson. What happened?'

'Annie, Lord Rollinson is suffering from the amount he had to drink. Can you do something for him, in a very discreet way?'

'Eeh, I can't understand it. He was fine when I told him as you were ready. I mean, he had the expected banter with his friends, and then that Lord Bellinger accompanied him to his room, saying he had his last duty as best man to carry out – helping to get the bridegroom ready for his bride and making sure he knew what to do. Everyone had a laugh. I even giggled meself. They must have carried on drinking. Anyroad, M'Lady, he looks fine. I'd be for just letting him lie there and sleep it off. That's the most discreet we can be. If I get a servant to help, it'll be all over the house what state he is in, and what was obviously a successful union between the two of you.'

'What do you mean?'

188

'Your nightdress, M'Lady . . .'

Frederick heard no more. His common sense agreed with Annie – he was best lying here until the sickness passed. With this, he closed his eyes.

Katrina's shame had her drooping her head, but when Annie asked, 'Are you all reet, M'Lady? Remember, I did tell you as this would happen, but are you hurt bad?' she knew she had to act differently, to minimize the gossip amongst the household staff.

'No, not at all, Annie. It was nothing. My husband is the gentlest of men. Now, you are to say nothing of this. You are my closest confidante and I want you to remain that way, but if anything gets out about what happened here, I will not take you with me as my maid when I move to Lord Rollinson's home. Now, see to my bath and I will dress. We will deal with my Lord Rollinson after that. He seems to be sleeping soundly again.'

Worry niggled inside her at Frederick's condition. His face had taken on a pallor that frightened her, and his sleep was more akin to a coma, as his whole face had slackened and his eyes and cheeks had sunk until he looked almost skeletal. She hoped with all her heart that he would rally in a while and the doctor wouldn't have to be called, as surely he would detect what had happened and then the whole sorry tale would come out. But then, was it a sorry tale? Part of her couldn't think that the coming together of herself and Simon was. A sensation zinged through her at the memory of it, and now sadness settled in her at the sure knowledge that she had married the wrong man.

16

Frederick

Finding Amy

'Well, lad, you've not made a good show of yourself, but I'm glad to see you're well now.'

'I can't apologize enough, Sir. I still have no recollection of events. The last thing I remember is going to my rooms with Bellinger and—'

'Well, I wouldn't tell Katrina that, Frederick. She won't be pleased, as by all accounts you managed to consummate the marriage, and it will be important to her that it meant something to you.'

It seemed that the world knew he had come together with his bride – even her father! He only wished he knew it himself, because whatever had happened on their wedding night hadn't been repeated. He'd just not been up to it, and hadn't visited his wife's bed since. His illness had meant they had missed their trip to France and had been stuck at his in-laws' house while he recovered. Never in his life had he felt as he had felt the last few days, though he hadn't taken up Arkwright's offer of having a doctor attend him. His father-in-law had done enough for him, as it was. No, the few days' rest had gradually cleared him of whatever had ailed him.

Katrina had visited him every day, and he'd learned more about her than he'd known before. She had a sweet, attentive nature, though he detected something amiss and felt sure he had been rough with her. Not wanting to embarrass her, he hadn't broached the subject.

Nothing about his body seemed different. Even now, when he felt well, he didn't detect anything in him that might suggest he'd taken on the mantle of 'being a man', in the sense of having experienced lying with a woman. It was disappointing in a way to feel like a virgin still, but he had no excuse to delay repeating the act, so tonight would be the night – why didn't that fill him with some sort of anticipation? Now, if it was Ruth . . . *Stop it! Stop being so damned silly. That can never happen! Ruth has gone; there is even a possibility that she could be dead.*

This thought brought a pain into the pit of his stomach that stabbed his heart. He couldn't bear the thought of that. He had to find out the truth about what had happened to Ruth. He'd start by getting a man to look further into that chap he'd met at the market in Pradley, and to look for Ruth's sister, too. He still felt guilty about her. Damn that bloody Bellinger! There was a lot he could lay at his door – his own state on the night of his wedding, for one!

'Maybe tomorrow you will feel able to come to the mill with me, eh? I can start to put you in the picture as to the workings of it, and give you a feel for it all.' This, from his father-in-law, drew Frederick from his musings. Agreeing with him and showing some interest – not that he felt any – appeased the man and suited his own purpose, as learning

191

the ropes would give him an excuse to stay around Blackburn a little longer, to put his plans into operation.

The door opened and his sister-in-law walked in. He didn't like Marcia or the way she carried on, often flirting with him in an open manner. The look on her face told him that something was brewing in her mind – he'd seen the same look many times over the last few days.

'What is it, Marcia? Can't we men have even a few minutes without one of you women folk disturbing us?'

'Sorry, Daddy. I was looking for Katrina and naturally, when I heard Lord Frederick's voice, I thought I might find her here. Though why I did so, I can't imagine. There has been no real young lovers' spark about the two of you.'

'Marcia, you should learn to hold your tongue, lass. I can't think why you have such bad manners. Your mother has spent many pounds of my money trying to make a lady of you!'

'Oh, Daddy, that is unfair. I speak my mind more than a lady should, maybe, but I *am* a lady and I am not bad-mannered. Oh, by the way, I bumped into Lord Bellinger whilst out for my ride this morning.'

The look, and the drawl she used to voice this, sent worry coursing through Frederick, but he couldn't have said why.

'I invited him to dinner.'

'You had no right, young lady. You should have consulted your mother. She is not best pleased with Bellinger; and neither, I imagine, are Lord Frederick and Katrina. He was the main instigator in making their wedding night a near-disaster.'

'Only near?'

Marcia's eyes flickered with a venom that chilled Frederick.

'Anyway, I rather fancy Lord Bellinger. Oh, I know he has spoken for someone, but Lady Henrietta Parvoil is no catch, not to speak of. Simon only wants her because of her social connections. Whereas I – well, I can bring him a lot more, as surely—'

'Marcia! Damnation, girl, does your tongue have naw bounds? I have told you there will be a handsome dowry for you, but all the holdings in the mill will pass to Katrina – to her husband, that is. It is done, and cannot be undone.'

'Daddy, there must be some part of it that you could pass on to me? What kind of a prospect am I? A dowry is nothing. The gentry are all suffering financially – well, most of them are. They all want a foot in the cotton-mill industry.'

'Well, they should have taken the opportunity when it arose, instead of trying to get in the back door by making marriages. They— Oh, I beg your pardon, Lord Frederick. Marcia, leave the room at once!'

Frederick had heard of Arkwright's temper, but hadn't thought to witness it, or to hear how he really felt about the marriage of his daughter. He was glad, though, that Arkwright had given him his title, in another person's presence. It boded well for his learning, and stood to remind Marcia of the respect she should show him.

'Please forgive my outburst. I . . . Look, I didn't mean that, lad. Me tongue wagged without me bidding it to. That daughter of mine – God alone knows where she pitched up from. Though likely she's taking after me: ruthless and stepping on all she needs to.'

'Don't concern yourself.'

'Naw, lad, it were unforgivable of me. It ain't even what I think, where you're concerned. You've given me daughter far more than we've given you. She now has the proper standing in life that she's entitled to. I stole that from me wife. But I have given her love. Her father sold her to me, if truth be known – another one desperate for me money. Eeh, here I go again. I'm like a mole digging a hole and piling the muck behind me, as I go.'

'It doesn't matter, really. You're an honest man. We both are. It's not easy, the way the world goes round in our circles. I hate most of it, but I love it at the same time. You won't lose out, or be sorry that I have taken Katrina. Neither will she. I will make her happy. I will give her and your family standing in society. As you say, it is deserved, through your wife's birth, and should be restored to her and given to your daughters. And I am not averse to you giving Marcia some share in the business, if it will make her happy and improve her prospects.'

'Well, I am. I love her very much, but I recognize the worst side of meself – and, yes, of her mama – in Marcia, and that will spell trouble if she has even a small hand in the business. I'll sort her out so that she'll be taken on by a good husband. Though this thing with Bellinger worries me. D'yer see owt coming of it? Marcia has a way of getting what she wants.'

'No, Bellinger wouldn't go against his word to Henrietta Parvoil. It would cause too much of a scandal and he'd be ostracized by society, something he couldn't face. Lord Parvoil is extremely influential in many fields of society and politics. He's even a favourite of the Queen, up to a point – and not as much as he'd like to be – but he could, and would, make Bellinger's life hell if he crossed his daughter. The most Bellinger could get away with is taking a mistress, as that is still the done thing and is acceptable, if conducted in a discreet manner.'

'Good God! I allus knew you toffs were a fickle lot. Well,

Bellinger hadn't better throw his cap in Marcia's direction with that in mind. I'd kill him. It may be accepted in your world, lad, but it ain't in mine. And while I'm on, don't you ever think of doing such a thing to my Katrina, or I'll take back everything you have coming to you. Aye, her an' all, if it comes to it. I'll not stand for it, thou knows.'

'You have nothing to worry about, Sir. I am an honourable man.' *Or am I? Why, if I am, do I even think of Ruth in that way?* With this thought came the memory of what he intended to do, for Ruth and Amy. 'On another subject, Sir, my wish to carry through obligations to others has put me in the position of needing your help. I want to engage an investigator.'

Without taking any heed of Arkwright's adverse reaction to this, Frederick went on to explain why, which further astonished the man. 'But that lot did for your brother, and caused harm and great stress and unhappiness to your mother. It beggars belief that you now want to help them!'

'I am not sure they did all they were accused of; and, if they did, they at least tried to help my mother. She would have died if they had taken the easy way out and run off. But they didn't. Besides, the lads have paid heavily; and don't forget they all lost their mother and little sister because of what happened. And that after losing their father and being evicted! So I do feel responsible for the girls' welfare. Setting them up with a position amongst my servants isn't much to me, but to them it could make the difference between dying and living.'

'Aye, well, lad – put like that. Here.' His father-in-law walked over to his desk and retrieved a calling card of the type businessmen generally used. 'This man tracks down folk as owe money, but his skills would be the same for this, so he could be what you're looking for. What does Katrina think of it all?'

'I haven't discussed it with her. It doesn't concern her.'

'Oh, but it does. That's the first rule you'll have to learn about being married – especially to someone as determined as Katrina can be. She won't be crossed, or left out of things such as this. I'd chat to her about it, if I were you, lad.'

This surprised Frederick and was alien to him. He had only ever known the man of the house to take decisions and do what he thought best. Women were capable of running the home, having children and taking part in the frivolous side of society without disgracing their husband, and of course servicing the husband's needs in the bedroom, but that was all. Well, it was for the women of his class, anyway. It seemed the Arkwrights hadn't completely prepared their girls for the world they wanted them to join! Oh, well, it would make no odds. Nothing would stop him from carrying out his intentions – and certainly not his wife's opinion to the contrary. He'd never be able to live with himself, and would be considered brow-beaten by a petticoat, if he allowed such a state of affairs.

A pain woke Amy. It stabbed her stomach and then settled to a dragging ache. The dampness between her legs that followed this told her she wasn't having a babby and brought on her tears – tears that had been frozen inside her. Oh yes, she'd shed some, but still there had been a lump of tears left that she'd been afraid to cry out of her, and it had taken good news to shift them; and, with their shifting, she lost all control.

'Shut your racket! Don't you think as we all wanna give

way to bawling our heads off? Some of us are trying to sleep here!'

Knowing she was disturbing the others in this cramped room, where row after row of beds accommodated the workhouse inmates, didn't help. She couldn't stop. The tears flooded from her eyes, but her whole body wept for everything she'd lost and all that had happened. Loneliness crowded in on her and fuelled her despair.

'For God's sake, put a sock in it, afore I put me fist in your gob. That'll stop you, alreet.'

'Leave her alone. Any of you touch me little Iva and you'll have me to contend with!'

Lil came over to her. She'd never call this woman loopy, as the rest of them did. It wasn't a problem to her that Lil still thought of her as her lost daughter. It made Lil happy, and that was all that mattered. Besides, it brought some comfort and love into Amy's own life, as did her friendship with Lettie. She was a good friend, was Lettie. She'd managed to get Amy a job working alongside her in the infirmary, and that had eased the load she'd to bear. She'd never have survived doing what most newcomers did: keeping the sewer free, emptying the slop buckets and rodding the cesspit. God, the fetid air when she got downwind of it made her feel sick, let alone swishing it about.

Snuggling into Lil's arms slowed Amy's sobs. 'Fetch Lettie for me, Lil. She'll be rising from her shift just now.'

'Naw, I can see to you meself. Tell me what's wrong, me little Iva. I'll sort it.'

'For fuck's sake, whoever sorts it, do it quietly, will you? I'm trying to get me last winks of sleep here. I'm warning the pair of you: shut up the racket, and shut it now!'

Lil leapt at the man who'd said this, her hands held cat-like in front of her. Spittle ran from her mouth; and her hair, grey and wiry, stood up as if she'd taken fright. But the man moved faster than she did. The full thrust of his fist cracked into Lil's jaw, sending her spinning backwards. The crashing of her head onto the iron bedstead behind her caused a sickening crunching sound, which resounded around the now-still and quiet room.

As if spilt from a bottle, blood seeped out from under Lil's head and snaked its way into a pool that settled near Amy's feet. Lil's eyes stared up at Amy. Her lips moved, but no sound came from them. Getting down beside her, Amy cradled Lil to her. Something inside her told her to call Lil 'Mam'. 'You're alreet, Mam, I promise. Me and Lettie will make you better.'

Lil's eyes held love and hope, but the rattle of her chest told Amy that all was lost, as did the trickle of blood running from the corner of her mouth.

'Mam, stay with me.'

'Naw, tell her to come to you,' a woman that she knew as Peggy whispered in her ear. 'That way she'll go happy, as there's no saving her, and in her heart she knows her Iva's gone.'

This seemed the right thing to do. 'Mam, come to me. I've waited so long. I'm in heaven waiting for you.'

'Eeh, lass, see that smile on her face. You did good. You made her passing from this world a happy one for her. I saw her eyes light up for just a second, when you said as you were in heaven waiting for her. She weren't a bad lass. Just demented, like. But she's gone to her rest now.'

'What d'you mean – gone?' The bully of a man whom Amy had often been afraid of, and who'd hit Lil, stood up, his stance aggressive. 'It were self-defence. She were coming at me, she—'

'You needn't have hit her like that. You could have held her at bay. She were a frail thing; it wouldn't have taken no doing.'

'You killed her alreet,' another voice chipped in, to the sounds of others agreeing and more accusations being levied, until the noise increased to a frightening anger of lynch-mob proportions. In one corner Amy saw the younger ones of her own age huddled together.

The man backed away, inching towards the door, all the time facing the crowd and telling them he'd take any of them on, if they liked. No one went so far as to tackle him, but when he reached the door he backed into Lettie. His arm lashed out, knocking her off-balance. Catching her, he held her to him, with his arm around her chest. For a moment all went quiet. her shocked and frightened expression urged on Amy's body and she lunged at the man, catching him off-guard. Stepping backwards, he stumbled with the weight of Lettie. Amy, on her knees now, sank her teeth into his leg. His scream was that of a babby, and he let go of Lettie.

Amy only had a second to be glad about this, before her head stung with pain as the man wrenched her off his leg by her hair. Before she could recover, the door shut with a bang. The man had gone.

No one moved for a moment. In the silence Amy was sure all could hear her teeth chattering and her bones shaking. Lettie spoke first. 'Amy, lass, are you all right? What's gone on here? Amy, you're covered in blood and . . . Oh, my God, Lil! Lil!'

*

All except the sewer workers were let off their duties and set to cleaning up the dormitory. Lettie helped Amy to sort herself, showing her where the rags, which were clean but still showed stains, were kept for the women on their monthly, and where to put the soiled ones. Hugging her, Lettie said she was pleased to see that Amy weren't 'caught for a babby'. 'Eeh, lass, giving birth is sommat bad to go through; but the taking of your child after – by, I've heard some wailing that'd cut your heart in two, and I wouldn't want that for you.'

Amy hadn't answered this. She couldn't think right now about what might have happened, but only of the task she and Lettie were carrying out. It wasn't a nice task, but they didn't mind and they would rather it was them than anyone else. As Lettie washed Lil's torso and Amy washed her arms, Lettie said, 'Eeh, she were a devil, but not in an evil way, God rest her. She'd like it that we're doing this for her.'

The still figure of Lil, once into everything that didn't concern her, lay peacefully now. Her waxen face, though sunken onto her cheekbones, bore the slight trace of a smile.

'I called her "Mam",' Amy muttered.

'Aye, someone said. Is that water still hot? We can get the worst off her back with it, afore we get some of it clean. Help me turn her. Have you put kettle on?'

'I have.' Crossing over to the stove to bring more hot water over, Amy had the sensation of the hair on her arms being brushed by a dozen fingers. 'Eeh, Lettie, I'm not liking this place. It gives me shudders. And the smell!'

'It's a morgue, that's why. There's still a couple of old bodies over there. Undertaker don't seem to bother to turn up when he should. I've had them rotting afore he's took them. It's on account of them being paupers. He don't get much for shifting them. They have no service, or owt like that, just being shoved in a rough grave.'

'Will Lil have a service?'

'I doubt it. She's no money as I know of. But we'll give her a send-off, eh? There's a few as liked Lil, so we'll get them all together and sing some hymns.'

'I don't know any. Does you know some, Lettie?'

'Aye, you've heard that "Amazing Grace", haven't you? I love that, and that clever bloke – him as is allus shuffling about and reading stuff; some call him "the professor" – he heard me humming it one day and were telling me as it was written by someone involved in the slave trade, and I reckon as that's what we are in, an' all. Only we're the slaves, we're not selling them, so I reckon that would be a fitting hymn. Besides, Lil would often hum it, so she must have liked it.'

Lettie began to hum it now and the sound made Amy feel better, as did their decision to have a service for Lil. She'd have liked that for Ma and Elsie, but she never knew what happened to them. Her da had a service. Sad it was, but nice. It was like a proper goodbye.

These thoughts had hardly settled when a lad put his head around the door. 'Warden said as Amy's to come at once to the office. There's a bloke asking after her.'

Lettie's face held a worried expression. 'A bloke? What kind of bloke? It ain't one of them police, is it?'

'Naw, he don't look like one.'

'Is – is he a toff?'

'Naw, he's young and kindly-looking. Phew, it stinks in here. How does you stand it?'

'Because we have to. How does you know he's kindly? You know a lot, for a messenger.'

'He ruffled me hair when I opened the door for him, and

201

said I was a good lad when I showed him to the warden. He talked to me like I were somebody.'

'Aye, well that's nice for you. Run along and tell warden we're nearly done here, and that Amy must change afore she comes up. Tell him what we're at, then he'll understand.'

As Amy prepared to go and see her visitor, she tried to imagine who the stranger was. She felt disappointed the caller wasn't likely to be the Earl. The lad would have known the Earl was a toff.

She'd never given up hope that he would come for her, but then she'd no way of knowing what that mean Lord Bellinger had told him about her. Who this could be, she couldn't imagine, but at the lad's description, she didn't feel afraid.

Wearing her clean apron – the one they were allowed to wear only once a week, on a Sunday when the vicar came to take a service – Amy stood in front of the stranger and waited.

'I'm Haydon Green. I find people, when others are looking for them. You're Amy Dovecote, I believe?'

'I am, Mister.'

'Well then, my mission is almost accomplished. I was commissioned by the Earl of Harrogate to find you and your sister. Have you any idea where your sister might be?'

The relief nearly brought Amy to tears. It was funny how good things had that effect on her, and yet she found it hard to cry at bad things. 'Me sister may have gone back to Pradley over Bowland Hills, or at least she'd have tried, I reckon. There was a bloke there as wanted her, and he had a lot of power, so he might have saved her. But I doubt she'd have made it.'

'Don't underestimate willpower, young lady. It can

surmount a lot of things, even a club foot, which I understand your sister is afflicted with. And I have it in good faith that there has not been a body found on the Bowland Hills, so there's a lot of hope. Especially as the police have given up the search for her.'

'What will happen to her, if you find her? Will you hand her over to the police, Mister? If you do, she could hang.'

'I don't think so. The Earl is considering her options and making deals. He is hoping that she will get no more than a short sentence and will then be released into his wardenship. He wants to find you both a job, and a home.'

'Humph! Seems a lot for an earl to do, for a couple of wenches who had a hand in the demise of his brother. What's his game?'

'That is not for you to know, Warden. The Earl's business is his own. He obviously feels responsible for these girls' welfare, and the whys and wherefores of that are for his own counsel.'

The warden reddened at this, but stood his ground. 'Well, that's as may be, but the welfare of this girl is my responsibility until she is released from these premises, under the conditions of the Poor Law that binds her here. So, my business or not, I must ask a lot of questions and satisfy those whose business it is.'

'The Earl's solicitor will see to all of that, man. You will receive a copy of his application for your files, but that is all the involvement you will have.'

'Have I to come now, Mister? Cos there's stuff I need to do. And I'd like to ask the Earl a question an' all,' Amy said.

It was the warden who answered. 'Well, you have a side to you. Naw, you can't leave here now – not until I have the proper paperwork from the court, which states that I can release you to this Earl. A funny business all round, if you ask me. I've never heard the like!'

The Earl's representative winked at her. 'Go along and get on with what you were doing. The warden is correct: you can't be released until all is in order, and I couldn't do anything about that until I found you. I have now, so it won't take long. Just be patient. Now, this question you have for the Earl, what is it? I'll pass it on to him.'

'It's about me friend, Lettie. She wants out of here. She's hard-working and she's only in here because the pox took all her family. It ain't what she's used to and—'

The warden snorted in disgust. 'Shut your mouth, girl. I'll not stand by while you make out there is sommat wrong with this place. It's better than the street, where the likes of you come from.'

'I – I didn't mean—'

'A civil tongue wouldn't go amiss, Sir! You may run a respectable place here and a much-needed place for the homeless, but that doesn't mean to say those shackled to it have to like it. Now, Amy, run along and leave things to me. I will of course mention your friend, but first I would like to meet her – *if* you have no objections, Sir?'

'Am I to bring her, Warden?'

The warden glowered. 'Very well. But any such meeting is to be conducted here in my presence, and I'm to be allowed to say my bit. Is that understood?'

The meeting had gone well. Lettie was shocked at Amy daring to ask for such a favour for her, but was thrilled, too. 'Eeh, Amy, lass, it's me dream to walk out of here. Fancy you knowing an earl and him looking for you! Put warden's nose out, that did.'

'Aye, I know.' Amy gave a giggle that came from the deepest part of her, which she never thought would laugh again. It set Lettie off, and soon they were doubled up and slapping each other playfully.

'Eeh, don't. Me sides hurt, but then who cares? We're getting out of here, lass. We're on the up and up.' With this, Lettie did a little dance along the corridor, and Amy copied her until they met in the middle and took each other's hands and did a jig together.

Then Lettie burst into the chorus of 'Amazing Grace', and Amy had never heard a sweeter voice, or a more beautiful and rousing song. 'Eeh, it beggars belief that a man as could sell slaves could write sommat like that.'

'Aye, well, he was converted to Christianity later and became very famous and was a good man, so he made up for it, or so the professor told me.'

This made Amy feel better and she joined in the singing, thinking the line 'That saved a wretch like me' was more than fitting for her and Lettie. She hoped it was for Lil, too, and that she had gone to heaven and was holding her Iva in her arms.

17

Marcia & Frederick

Marcia's Devious Plotting

Marcia looked peeved at the announcement that Bellinger had brought Henrietta with him to dinner. Now she would be the odd one at the table, with no one to sit opposite her. *How dare he, after flirting with me? I had every hope of using his attentions towards me to make Frederick at least aware of my presence and to see me as a woman – maybe even a desirable one!*

It seemed everyone except Marcia and Katrina knew that Henrietta was coming. One consolation was that Katrina's face was a picture, when she heard Henrietta being announced. It hadn't passed Marcia by that her sister had preened herself in an extra-special way before Bellinger's arrival.

It would serve Katrina right. That was a rotten trick she had played on Frederick. The poor soul still thought it was he who had deflowered his bride. Well, she knew differently. She had hovered around the west wing that night – she hadn't known why, and realized it was a strange thing to do – and, in doing so, had heard and seen what had gone on.

Stupid Katrina: naive to the point of being ridiculous. She had an air about her as if she were Bellinger's only conquest. Good Lord, the man's reputation was well known. Marcia herself could have him at the drop of a hat, but she didn't want him. No, Katrina had taken the man *she* wanted. How happy she'd been to hear that Katrina was betrothed to Lord Bertram Rollinson, for that news had opened up a dream inside her. It would have meant that his brother Frederick would be in close contact with the family, and she – Marcia – would have an opportunity to seduce him. But, with the twist of fate that prevailed, brought on by the handiwork of that bloody family who'd killed Bertram, all her own hopes had been dashed.

Her anger had shown this afternoon in her insulting the very man she loved – flaunting her flirtation with Bellinger in the hope of making Frederick jealous, and hinting to him the truth of his wedding night, in the further hope that he would seek her out, wanting answers. This would have given her the chance to expose his unfaithful wife and declare her own love for him. But he hadn't done that. Still . . . there was always tonight, and who knew what might happen?

The atmosphere rather pleased her, as it turned out. Henrietta and Katrina were still showing only a cold politeness towards each other, and Bellinger peeved Henrietta by being overly attentive to Katrina. That silly sister of hers couldn't handle such situations in the sophisticated way they warranted; spilling her drink and jumping whenever someone spoke to her made it obvious that she was distressed about something. Well, *she* knew what it was and would take every opportunity to hint that she did.

'Really, Katrina, what is the matter with you? You are as clumsy as a young girl in love in the presence of her beau, instead of acting like the married woman you are.'

Her mother's sharp rebuke of, 'Marcia, that wasn't called for, and was not a fitting comment to make in front of our guests' didn't embarrass her; she just giggled. And neither did it detract from the pleasure of seeing Katrina further confused, whilst trying to hide the deep blush the remark had caused.

Marcia hadn't missed the chance to hint to Katrina that she knew of her tryst with Lord Bellinger, so she knew her sister had taken the full impact of her remark to mean exactly what she intended. 'Sorry, Mummy, I was only playing. I thought to make a joke of Katrina's obvious discomfort, and help to put her at her ease.'

Frederick's bemused appearance at this further enhanced Marcia's enjoyment of the situation. She watched as he tried to catch Katrina's eye, his look quizzical.

Bellinger rose to the challenge, but then he would. 'My Lady Katrina – such an apt title for such a beautiful and deserving lady – please don't be uncomfortable in our presence.' He smiled at Henrietta, who graciously smiled back and nodded at Katrina.

Poor Henrietta. She has no idea . . . I could almost feel sorry for her, and now Katrina is blushing even more and stammering. It is all going better than I dared imagine!

'No, really, I – I'm not. I – it is all behind us now.'

Her father's scowl pleased Marcia even more. She was having a delicious evening; she had to keep it going. 'Surely, Lord Bellinger, it isn't for you to compliment a lady who is not your fiancée, and in front of her at that – and in the presence of her new husband, who hasn't done so?'

'Marcia!'

This from her father made her feel like a child. She wouldn't have been surprised to hear him tell her to leave

208

the table, but Mother stepped in. 'It was a nice compliment, Lord Bellinger. I am sure, though, that Marcia – like me, and surely Henrietta, too – is feeling left out of your flattery.'

'The opportunity hadn't presented itself, Madam. I am dazzled by the beauty and elegance around the table, particularly that of my fiancée, as I told her, the moment I picked her up tonight.'

His bow to Henrietta had her giving a pleased, good-little-girl-rewarded kind of smile. Marcia felt sick to her stomach at Lord Bellinger's ability to wriggle out of anything. And then, as if prompted, Frederick joined in. 'I have to agree. We are honoured to have the table graced by such beauty, and particularly Katrina's. My dear, you do look very beautiful tonight. I am so proud that you are my wife.'

Katrina's look of gratitude held what Frederick might mistake for something else, and his smile showed his fondness for his wife. If she didn't have the knowledge she had, Marcia would say they were a young couple in the throes of that first flush of consummated love – a picture that was the last thing she'd intended as the outcome of her mischief-making.

Though she had to admit that Katrina did look beautiful. Marcia was sure the extra effort her sister had put into her appearance was for Lord Bellinger's benefit. A natural beauty anyway, with her dark, sultry looks that emulated their mother's, Katrina wore a gown of peacock-blue tonight. The half-moon shape of the neckline showed off her pearl-like skin, from the nape of her neck to her bare shoulders. A single strand of black jade beads further enhanced her skin tone and provided just enough jewellery to complement her gown. The puffed-out short sleeves had a lace trimming to match that of the lines of lace on the bodice, which finished at the nipped-in waistline. The style showed Katrina's hourglass figure to perfection, as did the skirt, which, with its many petticoats and supported by a framed under-petticoat, had an exquisite bell-shape that finished in the perfect small bustle. Her hair, pinned on top of her head and falling in ringlets around her face, had been dressed impeccably, with pearl beads threaded through it.

Poor Henrietta; although she was a delicate lady with clear-cut features and a nice figure, her almost plain ruby-red dress buttoned up to her neckline made her appear slightly frumpy, and well and truly in Katrina's shadow. *As, I must admit, I am. And I made such an effort!*

The gown Marcia wore, and now hated, was of a beautiful pink satin in a style that gathered under her bust and flowed to the floor – no petticoats held it out, no bustle enhanced her shape. She'd chosen it thinking she would look vulnerable, and that it would attract the eyes of the soft-hearted Frederick. She had failed. His eyes and his attention were on his wife. *Katrina really doesn't deserve it! Besides, I am just as pretty as her, though I do have less delicate features, as my face is more clear-cut – something I like about myself. And everyone says that my dark eyes are beautiful and reflect my mood. Often that has been sensuous and drives men wild. Why isn't that so with Frederick!*

'Well, Sir, I must say, you put on an excellent table and we are honoured to be your guests.' This lie from the pompous Bellinger did have the effect of changing the subject.

'Thank you, Lord Bellinger, though it is my wife who sees to such things and is to be congratulated. Tell me, how are things in your corner of our industry?'

'My dear, if that is the turn of your conversation, I think we ladies will retire and leave you gentlemen to your port.

Come along, girls, I have some delicious sweet pastries laid out for us in the withdrawing room and a nice, delicate wine to wash them down with. We can talk about the fun we had on Katrina's wedding day, and hear your plans for your forthcoming one, Henrietta. I expect the arrangements are taking shape now?'

The men stood and bowed. Marcia saw a chance in the situation and hung back just long enough for the other ladies to get clear of the table. When she did follow, she intentionally brushed against Frederick and faked being unbalanced. A thrill went through her as he caught her. She held his eyes for a moment and then caught an amused look in Bellinger's as he stepped forward to catch hold of her, too. His wink held a promise of what he'd hinted at in this afternoon's encounter. She hid her contempt for him behind the smile that she gave him in return. 'Thank you, gentlemen. You saved me from a fall. I tripped on the leg of the chair. I hope I didn't hurt you, Frederick?' With this, she let her hand slide down his arm.

'No, Marcia, I am only glad you are not hurt.'

'And I'm glad to have helped, my—'

Bellinger was pulled up short by Henrietta calling his name and saying, 'My Lord Bellinger, please don't take chivalry too far. I am sure Marcia is perfectly all right.'

Mother came to the rescue again. 'Of course she is. Lord Bellinger, would you like to escort Lady Henrietta to the withdrawing room? And, Frederick, Lady Katrina is waiting for your attention.'

Both men jumped forward to attend to their respective ladies. As she watched them making obvious amends, Marcia's amusement reached its peak and a laugh escaped her.

'Are you drunk, Marcia?'

Mother's urgent whisper stopped her giggle. 'No, of course not, Mama. You know how these situations affect me. It's all a bloody farce!'

'What is? And please do not use such crude language.'

'All of it. Two lords and a "proper-born" lady dining at *our* table – besides other things, such as pretended love, which is tolerated out of respect! I hate the whole thing.'

'Oh, and will you hate it when you are betrothed to someone considered "a catch", then?'

'Mama, my catch has been caught. You and Daddy netted him for Katrina. You didn't even stop to consider me. You must have seen how I felt?' To her utter consternation, tears prickled Marcia's eyes.

'Oh, my dear, no. Oh, sweetheart, I am so sorry.'

The others had left the room, carrying on their charade, and Father was busy instructing their butler to bring the cigars, so for one moment she could be her mama's little girl and take comfort in the arm she put around her.

'It hurts, Mama, but don't worry, I will cope.'

'I know you will, dear, but please be careful how you do so. Being bitter and twisted, and throwing insults that make Katrina uncomfortable, will only make matters worse. Better that we find you someone of your own and that you have a big society wedding to someone of importance. Then you can throw your energy into the arrangements and get involved in all that your standing will bring you, and children and—'

'Mama! You're impossible.' But despite sounding exasperated, Marcia could see the funny side of her mother's reaction. Her tears dried and her sense of humour won the day as she laughed out loud.

'What are you two still doing here? And behaving as if you

have a conspiracy going.' Her father looked pleased as he said this.

'Oh, women's talk: I am just sharing a moment with my youngest. We are going now, and will send the boys back in.' With this from her mother, Marcia felt she could get through the rest of the evening, but as for the night-time? She didn't know. For surely tonight Frederick, now completely recovered, would visit his wife's bedroom? The very thought hurt her deeply.

Coming together with Katrina still held a little fear for Frederick and was tainted by his behaviour on their wedding day, and his lack of memory of their first time, but he knew he could not put off his duty to his wife any longer. Now he had to tell her that he had done something without consulting her – which, according to her father, she might not like.

He'd managed to put it all out of his mind, as he'd enjoyed the few hours he'd spent at the mill with his father-in-law today. He'd found the workings fascinating – the noise of the looms and the smell of the cloth – more so than he had the business side of things. His social conscience had been touched by the young ages of some of the workforce and the hours they had to labour: all in the name of saving money, which was abhorrent to him when the workhouses were full of able-bodied misfortunates who could be put to work for a decent wage and helped out of their plight. Yes, they would have to be paid more than the young ones, but the industry could stand the cost. It was just sheer bloody greed, as far as he could see. And although he hadn't won the argument, he had brought it up whilst they had their port and managed to voice his concerns.

All of this, though, didn't detract from the joy he'd felt

at Amy being found. Not least because it meant that Haydon Green had proved his worth *and* had found her so soon after being commissioned to do so. Admittedly, Amy wasn't difficult to track down and was where she would be expected to be, after he'd found out the truth from Bellinger. That man was a cad of the first order. Frederick no longer considered him his friend, but rather someone he had to watch out for, but couldn't avoid.

As it was, now that they had located Amy, and had Josh Bottomless's lead concerning Ruth's whereabouts, surely there was every hope that Haydon Green would find Ruth, too.

Frederick's plan for the sisters had changed, after hearing that Katrina might not be pleased to know that he was helping them. He'd decided to set them to work in the mill and find them lodgings, but this didn't sit easily with him. He wanted them in his household, especially Ruth. He'd convinced himself that just having her near would be enough. There would be plenty of jobs going: maids would be needed by the dozen, with his vision of running his life along the lines that it should be run. Beckstone Abbey would be fully opened up and decorated, the furnishings reupholstered and new carpets laid. Visitors would grace its corridors once more, and parties would be held. Shooting weekends would be arranged and, when the stables were up and running again, hunting weekends would be reinstated. He might even buy a racehorse and enjoy gambling in that field, as well as his poker games, which he would now host for the first time.

In due course children would run around the place and be schooled in the nursery – yes, a lot of staff would be required. Maybe Amy could be brought on as a governess; she'd showed herself to be a bright girl. And Ruth . . . *if only*

Ruth could be given the position I'd like to give her – oh dear, I'm off again; I must stop this ridiculous notion! Anyway, there would be a position for Ruth, something that didn't tax her too much; and for this other girl that Amy wanted to bring with her. And he'd have to content himself with having Ruth near him.

Katrina's maid opening the door to him, instead of his wife, disconcerted Frederick for a moment. Katrina had seemed in good spirits at dinner and had even flirted with him a little, once the embarrassment Marcia had caused had been handled. Though he had to admit he had no idea what lay at the bottom of all of that, and why Katrina had been so distressed by it.

Now that he was in her presence, all such thoughts vanished as his nerves had him begging: *Please don't let her cry off. And please don't let what I have done upset her.* His role of being married to her had to be sealed in his mind. He had to *feel* in every way that he was Katrina's husband. Maybe then he could cope.

At Katrina's direction, the maid scurried out after handing her the jar of perfume she'd had in her hand. While she waited for her maid to depart, Katrina kept her eyes focused on Frederick's, as she squeezed the soft bulb on the jar and released a spray of scent onto her neck.

His nervousness and sense of shame increased. 'Katrina, I am really—'

'Don't!'

Her finger felt soft on his lips – placed there to stop him making his umpteenth apology. She had almost run towards him, and her body was so near his. The crisp linen of her white nightdress had a fresh fragrance about it, vying with the delicate perfume she had just sprayed.

215

Reaching for her, he pulled her close to him, feeling her softness through his dressing gown – the only garment he wore. He drank in the scent of her and revelled in the sensation of having a woman snuggled up to him for the first time, though for a moment he was tinged with embarrassment, as he knew she must be able to feel the hardness of his response. Their lips meeting took away all such feelings of discomfort.

There wasn't anything he could compare to the sensation of their kiss. This was a measure of his naivety, but then no comparison was needed. The kiss had its own uniqueness. Caressing her came as a natural extension of the kiss. Katrina's willingness helped: she showed nothing but desire at his touch, and even led him to where she needed him to touch her, moaning her pleasure at his actions. His own pleasure and confidence grew, banishing the last traces of the anxiety that had plagued him, as a cascade of feelings like none he'd experienced before surged through him.

'May I join you in your bed, Katrina?'

Her giggle wasn't a mockery, but added to his anticipation.

'Of course, kind sir, but surely it is *our* bed?' Her voice held a note of seduction and the lids of her eyes lowered, giving her a look of the temptresses in paintings that he'd seen when they had visited a gallery together and she'd told him of her love of art. But what surprised him and affected him most was her removing her shift. She was beautiful. Her skin had a creamy texture, her breasts were soft mounds. Her stomach was gently rounded, and the curls of the soft down covering her vagina were dark and thick. Her thighs were slim and taut; everything – even her tiny, dainty feet

– had a loveliness about it. And it was all his, to enjoy whenever he wanted to.

For a fleeting moment, he wondered if Ruth would be
this beautiful. He knew she would, despite her foot, and he
wished . . . No, he couldn't insult Katrina like that. She was
his wife and he needed to give his whole self to her. She
deserved that of him.

The bed creaked as it took his weight. Katrina giggled
again. 'You look like a naughty boy who might get caught
out, but you don't have to worry. These quarters are far
from the rest of the house. Relax, Frederick. We'll fare well.
I – I mean, we did that first time.'

'Did we? I haven't been able to ask you, and I—'

'Don't. You have been clothed in shame ever since, and I
know it wasn't all your own fault.'

'You truly believe that?'

'Yes, I know it. Oh, Frederick, we must beware of those
who will harm us. We need to get to know one another and
look out for each other's back. And we have to grow to love
one another.'

'That won't be difficult, my dear. You are a very sweet and
beautiful person.' They were under the covers now, and he
had the superb sensation of her naked flesh touching his.
There was no need for further words – only the kind that
gave and accepted the pleasure of their union. Sinking himself into her, he felt that at this moment his world was
complete, and gave himself to loving her with everything
that was in him.

At first he thought he would burst into her before he had
satisfied her, but gaining control, he used skills that came
naturally to him. Holding back increased his pleasure as he
then allowed the urgency to build again, thrusting into her

slowly and deeply until she cried tears of joy, which he knew held relief, too. Instinctively he knew she was spent, and now he could abandon all thought of trying to please her and enjoy all she had to offer and the sheer joy of coupling with a woman. The pleasure of this abandonment had him calling out. No words – just hollow animal-like sounds, as he tried to cope with wave after wave of thrills that were almost too much to bear.

Katrina calling out his name – in a beautiful husky, but urgent voice – brought her back into his focus, and he realized he was pounding her unmercifully, but he couldn't stop. It was the exquisite, almost unbearable explosion of himself into her that finally brought his movements to a halt and left him drained and exhausted, with his legs trembling and his breath labouring, as he gasped for air and for some hold on what had happened.

Never, when relieving himself previously, had he known such intense pleasure at the moment of this release. How could he have forgotten experiencing it on his wedding night?

Rolling off her, he pulled her to him, hoping that holding her told her of his love, as he found himself unable to speak. The silence lasted only a moment; her sobs broke it. They took away the euphoria and filled him with concern. 'My dear, have I hurt you? Oh God, I am so sorry. I—'

'No, no, I – I am not crying because I am hurt. That was wonderful, the best. I mean . . . Oh, I don't know.'

Turning towards her, he cradled Katrina closer to him. 'Are you happy to be married to me? I know it was arranged and everything, and for reasons other than us falling in love, but I will be a good husband to you. We like each other; we are good with each other. Aren't we? You said—'

'We are. I'm sorry. I'll be fine. It's all new to me, that's all.'

'Me, too. But, for a couple of novices, I think we did all right. Come on, snuggle up, or am I supposed to leave you, now that I have had my conjugal rights?'

'No, don't leave. I feel safe with you here.'

'Safe?'

'I – I mean happy, relaxed. Oh, stop quizzing me. Talk of something else.'

'Well, I'm glad you said that, as I do have something I want to tell you. You remember the family . . .'

During his discussion her body stiffened, but nothing prepared him for Katrina's reaction when he told her he'd engaged a private investigator and that one of the sisters was found.

Pulling from his arms, she sat up and looked down on him. 'How dare you do such a thing? It is preposterous! They . . .'

Shocked, he listened to her raised voice telling of the distress it would bring her, for him to move his mistress into their home. Her tears were ones of pain now. Her words spat out, calling Amy and Ruth whores and telling him that she would not tolerate the situation.

Getting out of the bed and grabbing his robe, he could only wait for her to finish. When she did, she trembled with sobs once more, but although he felt pity for her, her outburst had angered him. 'Katrina, I do not have a mistress. What we just had together was my first experience – I mean, well, the first one I can remember. I am an honourable man, and it is not the place of my wife to tell me I can or cannot do something I wish to do. Your mother has let you down, in her upbringing of you. You should know that, yes, I will tell you of my plans, and yes, you can advise me, but the final decision in all matters is mine. And I will not be turned on this decision. I will bid you goodnight, and hope you have a restful one and that you will awaken in a better frame of mind!'

'Don't leave me. I – I'm sorry. I was told that you were in love with the one called Ruth.'

'Good God, you believed Bellinger? Damn that man!'

'Why should he say such a thing if—'

'Stop it, Katrina! You either believe me or you believe him. I would hope you believe me. You have been a victim of Bellinger yourself, so you know what he is like. For my part, I have had enough – I cannot endure his interference in my affairs any longer. Tomorrow I will talk to him. I have no idea why he is acting like this. He used to be my best friend, for goodness' sake! Now it is like he has some axe to grind and is using nasty tactics as his weapon with which to do so.'

'No! No, you mustn't . . . Please.'

This was all beyond him. Sinking back onto the bed, he took her hands in his. 'I understand why you are afraid of him, how he tried to ruin your reputation, but you have no need to be now. Neither of us has. Look, let's get you to my home. You will be away from Bellinger there. My mother will travel back with you, as I must spend some more time with your father at the mill. There is a lot for me to learn. You can spend your time familiarizing yourself with your new home and with the staff; and then, when I come to you, you can show me your visions of how you see each room. And we can make our plans from there. I will get Amy Dovecote and her friend over there, and you can ask our housekeeper to begin settling them in and teaching them the jobs she allocates to them, though it is my intention to have Amy schooled. She is very bright and, my dear, in the future we are going to need a governess for our children. I think she will be the perfect choice.'

'But—'

'Please, Katrina, make your mind up after you meet them. They are nice; they have good manners for their class, and I am certain they did not mean to bring harm to my brother. I feel responsible for them.'

Her nod didn't hold any hint of her not meaning it. The movement caused a stray tear to plop onto her cheek. She looked afraid, vulnerable and lost. He'd made a mistake in not talking to her first. Oh, he knew she would still have objected and would probably have had a tantrum similar to the one she'd had just now, but at least she would have felt respected. Pulling her close again, he admitted as much to her and promised he would not act in that way again. 'I'm a new husband, you know. I have some learning to do.'

'And I'm a new wife, Frederick. And I have a lot to learn, too. I will go to your home, but please don't be away long. And . . . will you stay with me tonight, please?'

'I will. Hotch up, but I warn you, I snore louder than Humbug's pigs, so on your head be it.'

This sent her into a fit of giggles. 'Humbug's pigs?'

He laughed with her as he told her the tale of one of his farmers who kept pigs and was called 'Humbug', as he always had one of those sweets in his mouth. 'It isn't just his pigs that snort, either; because of trying to speak while juggling the peppermint around his mouth, Humbug makes little pig noises the whole time he is talking to you!' Demonstrating this increased Katrina's laughter – a lovely, infectious sound that had him joining in. And in the way that folk do when they have come through a crisis, they giggled like children, and the silliness lightened the moment.

'I tell you what, I'll speak to your father and if he can delay my schooling in all matters pertaining to the mill a little while longer, I'll arrange for us to re-book our honeymoon to Paris. Yes, you and Mother get back to Northallerton together, so that you get a taste of life at Beckstone Abbey, and I'll do my best to arrange things.'

Her arms tightened around him and her head came onto his chest as she said, 'That would be lovely, Frederick.'

The seductive sound of his name sent a trickle of relit passion through his groin. She was right: they would get along all right. He would do his utmost to make it so, and for this he needed to rethink having Ruth in his life. *It won't work – it won't.*

As he found her lips, Frederick's desperation for this thought to leave him caused him to grind his lips into Katrina's. Her mouth opened and he was lost in her sweet sucking of his tongue into her mouth, and within moments he knew once more the ecstasy of those exquisite feelings to return, as he guided her on top of him – a position Bellinger had described to him.

Her cry of complete joy as she lowered herself onto him gave him the knowledge that she was a willing bride, and a passionate one, as she accepted Frederick into herself with a hunger that surprised him, but that boded well for their future. Just before he gave himself up to the joys of her, he told himself: *Everything will be all right . . . it has to be.*

18

Ruth

Witches' Fire: Pendle Hill's Curse

The sweet sound that came from the piano keys at her fingertips held Ruth in a place she never wanted to leave – *his* world, as she was sure this was the kind of music the Earl would listen to.

In the three months since she and Josh had made up their minds to be man and wife, it was as if music had been the thing her life had lacked and yet craved, without her knowing it. Josh had laughed at her enthusiasm, and sometimes baulked at teaching her the notes every night. 'Give over, lass,' he'd said one night. 'A man needs his rest.' Then he'd leaned forward and whispered, 'Especially as he now has a wife to keep happy, before he can go to sleep in his bed at night.'

With this, she'd learned that giving in to his needs could help her get what she wanted, and she had whispered back, 'Yes, but a man has to please his wife out of the bed an' all, to get what he wants in it.'

He'd looked surprised, but had grinned. 'Eeh, lass, I'd do owt so as not to have you stop our coming together at night. So you're now saying as I must earn it? Well, hotch up on that stool and let me get beside you. I think you're ready to learn a piece of music that is beautiful but simple to master, though it took me three years to get to the bottom of it.'

Listening to him tell how his grandmother taught him the notes and how he played by ear at that time, and then taught himself the meaning of the chords as they were written, had enthralled her. For him to do all of this on his own, and just from books, was magical to her. Once he had mastered them, he'd taught himself to play 'Für Elise' by a man called Beethoven, as he'd read that it was one of the easiest piano pieces to play.

When Josh had played it to her, it had touched her soul, and she had made it her mission to learn to play it herself. But her constant practising of the keys and learning of this piece, whenever she could, had got on Nora's nerves. 'Give over, lass,' she'd said. 'I can't hear me own thoughts.'

Ruth's look of utter disappointment had Josh saying, 'I'll put piano on that pull-all on wheels as I made, and take it out back to me shed. It's dry in there and, with the high roof, it will have good acoustics for you.' She'd had to ask what acoustics were and he'd told her, 'Them's like vibrations – sound. Oh, I don't know how to explain, but without them your music is flat and held back some.'

Feeling in awe of his self-taught knowledge had made her practise even harder. But still Ruth had a longing to read the squiggles that represented the notes, so that she could play anything she wanted to.

The door of the shed creaking open didn't stop her. Josh came up to her and sat on the bale of straw next to her. Glancing at him, she saw his look of wonderment, and this encouraged her and brought her back from dreaming of the

Earl. As she came to the last of the notes she'd mastered, she gave him a smile that held achievement.

'You were lost in that piece, and your face were a picture. I'd like to be where that took you, lass.'

She turned her blush at this into a laugh. 'Eeh, Josh Bottomless, you're a one. A farmer through and through, with a side to you that the world will never see – an artistic and very clever side. Seeing stuff in me face, ha!'

'By, that's daft. I'm not artistic. I never paint or owt. But you are. What you've picked up in a few weeks took me years. That piece has a structure, which in music books is described as . . . A–B–A–C–A. They say it ain't difficult, but I bet there ain't many as have never touched a piano afore that can play it within a month of doing so! So, lass, now you have got the hang of the piano-pedalling bit, I reckon we could go on to the next part of it. Shift off the stool and I'll play it for you.'

Watching his fingers in wonder, and listening to the intricate notes of the last half of the piece, Ruth thought she'd maybe take the three years Josh had taken, before she could play it. For now, she let the rapidly rising music seep into her. As she did so, it surprised her to know that this wasn't how it should sound. She knew instinctively that it could be better. *Oh, I must learn to read the notes somehow. As Josh said, he could teach me which key to strike and when, but he don't know where to start with the teaching of reading music. He's hardly got it all himself. And with me not reading and writing.*

Though Josh was starting to teach her this last. That is, when he could prise her away from the piano, which wasn't often, as that's all she wanted to do in her free time.

As the music came to an end and she stood to take the

seat again, Josh stayed her. 'I have a worry on me, lass, and I need to talk to you.'

Why fear jabbed at her stomach she didn't know, but something told Ruth that what he had to say held terror for her. Her legs shook as she lowered herself back down. Coming round to the other side of her and sharing the same straw bale, he took her hands in his. Calluses roughened his skin and told a different story from his music and the learned side of him. But though there was no clue to that part of him in his touch, his caring side was etched into it.

'Young Fin hasn't showed up in a while, and I found out today that he's took with the sweating-sickness and croup – the same as that lad had, who you cursed when he attacked you.'

The blood in her veins chilled, shivering her body. 'But they can't think as I had owt to do with it. I haven't seen Fin.'

'Naw, but he looked on you. He told his ma, before he got too ill to talk, that he were curious as to why he weren't allowed up here and he crept up one afternoon. He said as you were feeding chickens, but you stopped and stared at him.'

'I didn't, Josh, I didn't. I remember hearing a noise and looking to see what it was, but I didn't clap me eyes on owt. And I haven't got them powers they say as I have. Neither did I curse that McNaught lad. I only shouted at him in self-defence!'

'I know that, but the town is whipped up about it. I had them jeering at me and saying as I were harbouring a witch, and no good would come of it for me. I had to pack me stall up and come home early.'

'I hadn't noticed that you were early. I got what I had to

do done as quick as I could and came in here, and then lost track of time. Eeh, Josh, what're we going to do? They'll come for me, I can feel it.'

'Aye, some of the talk were of that.'

'What were they saying? Oh God, Josh, they burn witches.' All the breath went from her at the horror of this. Her throat burned as if the flames were already licking at it. Her 'Help me!' was a rasping cry.

'I'll think of sommat, lass. And I have me gun. I'll shoot the bastards if they show their faces near enough to me house.'

'Naw – I must go, Josh. I must. I'll make me way to Northallerton to find that earl. You have his card. We could contact him. He told you as he'd only meant well by me and that I should have trusted him. Well, now . . .'

'I can't bear it, Ruth. I can't lose you, I—'

'But, losing me is what will happen if I stay. I know them Pradley lot, and aye, you and Nora won't be safe either, not if they come baying for me and you try to stop them, you won't.'

His arms enclosed her, his tears dripped onto her hair. Hers wet her face, as a hollow despair locked her in its grip.

The first sound of a disturbance caused Ruth's unsleeping body to jolt to full alertness. Sitting bolt upright, she listened. Within seconds Josh had rolled off the bed and stood upright, causing the springs to groan and block out any further outside noise. Every part of Ruth became aware, as if honed ready for action, but inside she was stiff with fear.

'What is it, Josh? Can you see anything?'

Light flashed over his face before dancing on the walls of their bedroom in ever-expanding flickers, accompanied by a chant. A low, hum-hum chant. The barrel of Josh's gun glinted in what, she now realized, was light from torches carried by a walking throng of folk. Torches of fire!

A crack that resounded around the room blocked her ears and filled the air with gunshot fumes. Silence engulfed her, but as her hearing came back she heard Josh shout, 'Come any closer and I'll take you one by one – man, boy or woman. None of you are entering me home.'

A stone crashed through the window, just missing Josh. There was no time to react as a ball of fire followed it, landing on the bed next to Ruth. Her body cringed away from the searing heat as flames spiralled up towards the ceiling.

Sweat ran from Ruth. It snaked its way in trickles that wet her through, but still she hadn't moved off the bed as the roaring inferno held her mesmerized, unable to take a breath or find her voice to scream out. Someone else's scream filled the space around her. Looking in its direction, she saw Nora, her hair bound in a thousand knots of cotton, nightdress buttoned to her chin, eyes staring and mouth agape.

With her heart pounding and her body seemingly turned to stone, Ruth could do nothing, but a yank on her arm propelled her to action. 'Get hold of Ma and take her out back. Hurry, Ruth!'

Another crack spun her into a panic, but she held herself together. She must save Nora. Taking her ice-cold hand, Ruth tugged. 'Nora, come on. We'll get into the pigsty out back. Come on, we can hide there . . . Hurry, Nora, hurry!'

A wall of faces met them at the back door, blackened with coal dust – ugly, snarling faces with eyes red-raw and lips shining in the light of the flaming torches they held. 'You're coming with us, witch!' This said in a voice she recognized, but couldn't name, as her mind became strangled with terror. It was taken up by the group, as if they'd lost their freedom of thought and were now a hungry pack of wolves.

Hands grabbed her, tore at her, gouged her flesh and pulled her hair. Her body was propelled forward. Her foot dragged behind her, then her other one gave way and the hard ground scraped her skin, tearing her as if to shreds. Her wails of pain and fear went unheard. Dust and pebbles filled her mouth. Spitting them out gave her the taste of blood, mixed with her tears and snot. Every limb burned and her arms stretched, as if leaving their sockets. Her hair, pulled out at the roots, made her scalp sear with pain.

'Lift her. We don't want her dead yet. If we don't hear her scream the evil spirit out of her, at the agony of the flames, she'll not die – not ever. Instead her spirit will roam our streets and our houses and, unseen, she'll strike us down one by one.'

This cry she knew to be from McNaught, who still bore traces of his Scottish accent. Looking up at him and calling him by name, and begging mercy of him, did no good and was lost in another crack of Josh's gun. The sound hadn't died down before McNaught hit the ground with a thud that only a dead weight can make.

'She's killed him! Christ, she's killed him!'

With this cry a chant started up, 'Witch, burn the witch!' And another voice, a scream: 'Do it – do it now!'

Ruth's teeth clamped down on her tongue, and her eyes stung with the fear that seared her as they travelled from one hate-filled face to another. Everyone she looked on shrank from her. A woman fainted, causing a hush to descend. Into this a voice trembling with horror shouted, 'Get a sack to cover her face, so that she can't look on us. She's the devil incarnate!'

Horror seeped from all her pores, giving Ruth the feeling that her blood was draining from her. 'Josh – Josh, help me. Save me!'

'He can't help you, witch. He and his ma are dead.'

The words, spoken in a matter-of-fact tone, had hardly died on the lips of the speaker when a shaft of flame billowed into the air. All fight left her as she saw the house – the home Josh and Nora loved – enveloped in flames. 'Oh, Josh, Josh . . .' Along with this utter despair came the knowledge that truly she was a witch. She'd caused so much trouble and had brought pain to those she loved. Everyone she encountered either died or was killed, or something dreadful happened to them. Her cry for mercy now turned into a prayer: 'God, help me. God, help me . . .'

'He'll not help the likes of you.'

'Throw her into the fire!'

'Naw, we're taking her to Pendle Hill, like we said. It has to be done there.'

'But it's miles away. And don't forget, there's that valley to cross an' all.'

'Stop moaning and get the carthorse and hitch it up to that dray, then get her onto it. Tie her, so as she can't move; and, aye, cover her face.'

These were the voices of townsfolk she'd known all her life. Some had given her a wide berth, others had chased kids off when they tormented her, and still others had been good friends to her ma and da. And now they were intent on killing her. As the sack came over her face, two women stood in front of her. 'Hold it a mo. We have sommat we have to do.' Their spit hit her and mingled with her sweat and tears, as it traced a slow path down her cheeks. She looked from

Mrs McNaught to Mrs Finwil. Both had distraught expressions, holding more hate than she'd ever imagined existed.

Through the sack she saw the light of their torches, the house fire and the dark shadows of her persecutors as if cut into a hundred little squares. Her breathing became harder and had her sucking the hessian in and out of her mouth. The rough cloth took what spittle she had and tasted of dry, dirty wool. Her throat stretched, her stomach wrenched, but she pushed the cloth out of her mouth with her tongue and swallowed hard. If she was sick she would choke.

The wheels squealed their protest at having to force their way over the rough terrain – a sound she'd heard many a time as Josh had left for market. *Oh, Josh; poor, poor Josh. And Nora. Oh God!* Prayers seemed useless now, mocking even, as though God himself laughed in her face. Yes, he'd allowed her snatches of happiness, but was that only so that she'd feel the painful parts even more? At this moment she cursed him. And that left her even more destitute.

19

Ruth

A Horrific Event

The cart jolted and swayed, bruising Ruth's thin body and scraping the skin and flesh from her bones. Tears seeped into her ears and down her neck. Some left their salty taste on her dried tongue. Her mind screamed against the thought of what it would be like when flames licked her feet and then her legs. A cry of agony escaped her.

'Shuddup! No hollering's going to save you, witch.'

The voice sounded afraid more than aggressive, but still it held hate, leaving Ruth no hope of finding mercy. Heat built in her head – a red, searing heat that got her clenching her teeth until she could feel the blood pounding against her temples. With this came a sense of light-headedness. Her thoughts began to swim away from her. She couldn't hold onto anything tangible. She was sinking . . . sinking into a blessed oblivion.

Cold water brought her round. It splashed her face and neck and shuddered life back into her, bringing the realization that they had arrived at the place of her execution. *Oh God, no . . .* 'No!'

'Sit her up and take that sack off her. I want her to see

that her death-fire is all ready for her. I want her to know the curses she has put on us and our kin will soon just be ashes, as they will burn with her.'

The full moon sent an eerie, ever-changing light over everything as clouds passed over it, obscuring it slightly, then allowing it to shine fully. There, just a few yards from her, a huge black heap was silhouetted against the midnight-blue sky.

Madness entered Ruth at the sight. Snarls came from her, her wide-open eyes stung and spittle ran like froth from her mouth. 'You will all die and know the burning I have to suffer, but yours will be for eternity. I curse you. I curse every man and woman of you. And know this: this is my death-curse, not one that will die with me. The pox will take you all, you'll writhe and call out for help, but none will come. Your agony will be prolonged and unbearable and there will be no mercy.'

The gravel of her own voice hurt her throat. The words, alien to her, hadn't come from a conscious thought. A demon had possessed her. She had power; she could yet win! When she pulled her arms, the ties came away as if they had been loosened. The crowd shrank back at the sight of her flailing her arms around. One shouted, 'She's free. How . . . ?'

A scream of 'It's there – the fire of hell is coming for us!' silenced the crowd once more, and all eyes stared in the direction that a woman had pointed. A spluttering line of sparks made its way across the grass towards the heap that was to be Ruth's death-fire. When it reached it, an explosion of flames soared into the air. Her own hollow scream drowned the collective gasp of fear around her. The sound of rapid gunfire splitting the air stopped her screams, and for one moment the noise of the crowd died.

Panic set in. Folk ran in all directions, dropping their lighted torches, revealing a scene of fire all around Ruth, and filling her with the terrifying thought that the end of the world had come. But although she was filled with horror and fear, she remained in the same rigid position, sitting upright and staring at the fire.

Now, outlined against it, she could see the silhouette of a man: tall, slim and looking towards her. Her heart thudded, as her mind made her think this was the devil incarnate come to get her. Her body slumped. No inner demon helped her now. Everybody and everything had left her. She was nothing.

'Ruth. Ruth, it's all right, you're safe. They've gone. I won't hurt you. Don't be afraid. Let me untie you.'

She wanted to ask who he was, but she had no voice. In the light of the fire she could see a man whom she judged to be in his late twenties. His face held kindness. But who was he, and how had he come to be here? Confusion vied with the drained feeling and extreme tiredness that had overcome her. Something in her registered that she had been saved, but nothing would show her the sense of it.

Lifting her as if she weighed no more than a bag of chicken-feed, the man took her towards the fire. Cringing away from the horror it held for her, she clung to him. 'Don't be afraid. I'm only taking you nearer to give you some warmth. You've had a massive shock and have been through unimaginable terror.'

That terror cracked a little as the full horror of how it had begun hit her. 'But Josh and Nora – me husband and his ma . . . Look, over there on the other hill: that fire. They're caught up in it. They may be hurt or—'

'Your husband? You married?'

'No. Well, yes; we married ourselves, for fear of me whereabouts being known. I – I'm wanted for sommat as happened a while back, sommat as I couldn't help. And then there were them from Pradley, them as would burn me as a witch. But I ain't a witch. Things as happened were a co-incidence. I—'

'I know. I know what happened here, and in your past. I have been looking for you.'

'Oh? Are you some kind of policeman?' Even as she thought he was, no fear of him being so reached her. If Josh was gone, then her world as she knew it was gone, and with that her spirit would die. For at this moment she was so low that she didn't care about the prospect of facing the gallows. It would be a better death than the one she'd faced a few minutes ago.

'No, I'm not police. I'm an investigator. I find people for those who want them found. Mostly folk who owe someone money, but in your case, why an earl should want to find you was a mystery. But then I looked up all that had happened and realized he just wants to put things right. He is a rare being: a toff with a social conscience. A good man. And I never thought I would say that of any of the aristocracy.'

'The Earl! But I thought he would hate me?' Her heart pounded with an emotion other than terror, and for a fleeting moment she felt joy nudge away all the fear that was in her.

'I know, it would be natural to think his motives were other than good. I did myself, but I know now: he only wants to make amends, for you and your sister.'

'Amy! Have you found Amy?' All of it seemed incredible. This man had plucked her from death in a way that had seemed like black magic, and now he was saying he knew all about her past and was making her feel everything would be all right. But then how could it be, if Josh . . . ? 'Look, Mister, I'll be fine, I promise. Only thing as will help me is to get me back to Josh and his ma. We must try to save them. We must!' Pointing to where the sky was still lit by huge flames, she begged him, 'Ride over there. Leave me – just go. I can drive the cart back. I have driven it before. Please go and help Josh, please.'

'I am not leaving you, now that I have found you. Over this rough terrain it will take as long with a horse as it would with a horse and cart, especially as I don't know the way. We'll ride over there together.'

He had no urgency about him, which frustrated her, but she sensed she would not be able to change his mind. 'I know there is a road that winds around the bottom of here and passes the bottom of the track we have to ascend to Josh's farm, but that takes an age. The way the mob brought me is new to me, and I was bound and blindfolded. Oh, it is useless! Josh, my Josh.'

'Don't let go again, Ruth. You're doing well and I need you, if we are going to help them. I watched them bring you here, and they came that way.' He nodded towards the valley, before saying, 'Besides, we have the fire to guide us. We'll ride together on my horse, but our progress will be slow. I'm sorry.'

She had no other choice but to agree to this. During the journey he talked. Part of her wanted to scream at him to shut up, but she listened as she clung to him, and they made their way much more slowly than she wished.

She learned that his name was Haydon, and that the Earl had told him to begin his search at Pradley. When he'd arrived there at a late hour the evening before, he'd picked up on an atmosphere that didn't seem right. Huddled groups whispered to each other, but stopped doing so when he approached. Folk he asked questions of scurried away, shaking their heads. And then, whilst he enjoyed a jug of beer in the bar of the hostelry he'd booked into, a man came in and asked him what he wanted with Josh Bottomless. Disinclined to share his business, Haydon said he needed supplies on a regular basis and had been recommended to try Bottomless; and, having been told that he lived near Pradley, he'd thought it a good place to start. At this, the man had said, 'Aye, well, he lives a good ride from here, but on the morning he'll be down for the market.' The man who told him this had been McNaught.

The very name struck horror into Ruth, as she remembered McNaught's death. *Oh God, how will this all end?*

'Are you all right, Ruth? I can tell you another time.'

'Naw, tell me now. I have so much confusion in me.' She couldn't tell him that Josh had killed McNaught, and that the mob had thought she had done it. She couldn't dwell on that, or what they would find when they arrived at the farm.

'McNaught didn't hang around, but bade me farewell without making any other conversation, leaving me certain that something was afoot. Why should the folk of Pradley need a spokesman? Why hadn't one of the dozen or so others I'd asked given me this information? My investigative instincts took over, and I decided to make it look as though I was content to wait till market day.'

Listening to him, Ruth learned that with the skill he'd nurtured to glean information without seeming to want it, Haydon had found out where Josh lived from the barman. Armed with the knowledge the Earl had given him, regarding some folk thinking of Ruth as having powers that she used to hurt folk with, he'd begun talking to the man about the most famous event of recent history: the Industrial Revolution. It was a subject far from the one he'd wanted to talk of – Pendle Hill. Eventually the barman had come round to talking of it and had said there were still witches in the area, to his reckoning.

'What marks out a witch?' Haydon had asked, and had been horrified to hear that the locals still thought that the crippled or afflicted had been given extra powers, and that most used them for evil. A few jugs more had loosened the fellow's tongue further.

Haydon told her the words spoken by the barman: 'We had one living here, but we thought we had rid ourselves of her when her da passed on, as the family had to move. But she's back in the area and has caused a lad to take sick, and no one knows if he'll survive, and that after him just having got a job to support his family.'

Ruth felt a sick feeling churn her stomach. It deepened as Haydon told her that the barman had spat his tobacco into the brown-stained fireplace and had said something that, on hearing it, made the horror inside her settle into a pit of despair: 'A curse on Ruth Dovecote, curse on her. May she burn in hell.' How could folk think such things about her? And to the point they were prepared to – to burn her!

More ale, and the man had revealed that the community planned to rid themselves of her soon. 'I asked him: Where does this witch live then? And I told him I'd never seen one and would like to take a look at her.

'And then I had it! Confirmation that you lived with Josh Bottomless and his mother.'

'Confirmation?'

'Yes. The Earl had suspected that Josh was harbouring you.'

After hearing how the Earl had spoken to Josh, Ruth couldn't think why he hadn't told her. *Was it because he feared for me, or because he feared the Earl wanted to take me from him?*

Haydon continued, 'Once I knew where you were, it was a simple matter of a few more jugs of ale and a handsome tip, to get directions to Josh's farm.'

Walking out of the bar a while later, he'd come across some children playing. Their game entailed one of them being the witch and the others hounding her down. A farthing each had furnished him with all he needed to know.

Sitting up in his room, he'd waited. The main street of the town was visible to him, but nothing happened at the allotted time. Three chimes of the village clock told him that, if the children were right, somebody should make a move soon, but nothing happened. Then he saw it: a snake of flickering lights in the distance . . .

'They must have gathered somewhere at the back of the town. This filled me with fear, as I needed to get to the farm before they did, but how? Once on my horse, which I had left saddled and loaded ready with what I needed, I realized that my task was hopeless, so I changed tactics and headed for Pendle Hill instead.'

The very name of the place had Ruth holding him tighter.

Huddled against the cold, Haydon waited. All was ready. A chill had seized him when he'd arrived, as the full moon had lit up the shape of the huge bonfire and, on his approach to it, he'd found that one side was open, leaving a pathway to the centre. Here he saw a deep hole, with a huge stake protruding from it. The thought of the planning that had gone into Ruth's burning made his stomach retch and added urgency to his intentions to make sure he had everything in place. Then he'd waited and watched as the ever-swirling stream of lights had made its way up the hill opposite him, the cold steel barrel of his gun giving him reassurance.

'When the night was suddenly lit by a massive glow, I thought I'd done the wrong thing, as I'd felt certain the light meant the farm had been set alight – and maybe you with it. For a moment I thought I should have tried to catch up with them and stop them. But once I saw the lights head this way, I knew I had made the right decision; they were bringing you to the bonfire they had built, and I stood a chance of saving you.'

Then Haydon told her of his plan. He'd thought his only chance against such a crowd was to use an element of surprise and scare the life out of them. To this end, he'd used a technique he'd learned from a Chinese man, who made firecrackers on his children's birthdays. The noise from them was like gunfire. Learning how to make them had been a skill he thought he'd use only at friends' parties, as a novelty factor. He laid the crackers in the ready-built fire. This meant that if the crowd didn't disperse, he would have destroyed the fire they intended to use. 'Though I must say, your flailing about and cursing helped.' He chuckled at this, but Ruth couldn't join in. That moment was seared into her as a time when something had entered her and taken her over. It held extreme dread of what she was capable of. Did she have the powers they thought she had? She didn't allow herself to dwell on the question, but instead listened to Haydon's description of how the bangs that had saved her life had been made from gunpowder extracted from cartridges, and how he'd kept some of the powder and had laid a trail of it from the bonfire to the place where he waited.

'Ha, I can only imagine what went through the heads of that mob! No doubt most of them will have been sent mad, having seen what they thought was you bringing the wrath of hell down on them.'

Ruth didn't laugh. Her eyes stung as the smoke from the farm swirled around them. It clogged her throat. 'Ride faster. I will hold on. Please, we have to hurry.'

But still Haydon only walked the horse at a very slow pace, though she had to admit even that must have been a trial for the poor animal, as it wove its way over the rough terrain.

As they neared the farm the horse snorted in fear, lifting and shaking its head and stepping backwards. 'It's no good. We'll have to go the rest of the way on foot. Don't worry, I will carry you on my back. The horse is terrified and exhausted.'

The heat engulfed them at that moment. Sparks settled around them and threatened to set their clothes alight, but at least the wind had changed and now blew the flames and smoke away from them. In the light of the fire she could see the still figure of Josh lying on the ground. Scattered around him, some distance from him, lay three bodies. All, she knew, had been shot by Josh in his attempt to save her. One of them would be McNaught's.

Her mouth filled with spittle as they came up to McNaught's body. She gathered the spittle and spat it onto him with a hatred that contained venom for all of his family.

'Don't! If you fill your heart with bitterness, there will be no room for any happiness to enter you.'

'Happiness? I'll never feel that again.'

'You will. Your heart—'

241

Her gasp of pain stopped Haydon saying whatever he'd started to, as they reached Josh and she felt all hope of him being alive leave her. The handle of a butcher's cleaver stood out from his skull. The blade was embedded so deep it had almost sliced Josh's head in two. She realized that she hadn't seen Whalley Bradstone, but to her, this was evidence enough that it was Whalley who had killed her lovely Josh. One day – she didn't know when – she would get even with him, with all of them, for she doubted any of them would face charges for what they had done here tonight. The police hadn't done anything to stop it happening and they must have known. Nothing passed them by.

'Haydon, I need to sit with my Josh.'

'Right, but Ruth—'

'He needs me. Go and see if you can find his ma. Please God, she is alive. No, leave me. Find Nora. I'll be reet.'

She meant this, as she had a feeling that nothing could touch her any more, after all she'd been through. But when she sat beside her beloved Josh, all that bravado dissolved and sobs racked her body, as the realization came to her that she couldn't even see his face, and never would again. As her tears washed over him, she held his stiff, cold hand and told him of her love for him. Because, despite her feelings about the Earl being topsy-turvy, she had loved Josh, and with the kind of love that would have lasted them a lifetime.

'Ruth! Ruth, she's here. I have her. I'll come and get you.'

Nora lay not far from Josh, unconscious but alive. Her face, blackened by smoke, showed a deep cut running from her forehead to her nose. Whalley must have lashed out at her, too, but hadn't been able to finish his work.

As Ruth stroked her cheek, Nora let out a moan.

'Oh, Nora – Nora love, I'm here. I'll take care of you. Just get better, love. Everything'll turn out. It will . . .' *But will it? What does the future hold for me? Why has the Earl gone to so much trouble to find me?*

And what about the law? Would she be dragged up before the Assizes? But then what did it matter? She had Amy and Nora; and most of all, she had the Earl. For hadn't Haydon said the Earl's intentions had been to help her? Would he do that out of conscience alone, or had she been right when she read something in him as to his feelings? Were they like her own? But then if they were, what would he want from her? One thing she knew: he wouldn't take her as his wife. That would be unheard of.

Oh, why am I thinking of such things at a time like this? Maybe I am possessed – possessed by my love for the Earl. It must be that, because what will happen in the future shouldn't matter at such a moment! Telling herself this didn't help, however, because even though she was surrounded by death and destruction and held a broken heart inside her, it *did* matter to her.

20

Katrina & Marcia

A Seed of Doubt is Sown

'It's preposterous, Katrina, you cannot allow it. Frederick cannot do this to you. That woman is a murderer! It is enough that he had her sentence commuted to six months' hard labour, when she stood to face the gallows, but to bring her here to your home! She is his lover, for God's sake! How you even allowed Frederick to bring her sister here and have her educated, I just don't know.'

'Marcia, Ruth Dovecote is not Frederick's lover.'

'Yet! Katrina, are you mad? You know he is in love with the girl.'

'I do not. Frederick has told me that he isn't, and it was just part of the spite that Lord Bellinger meted out when—'

'Rot! Look at the evidence. Oh, I suppose he has given you reasons for his actions where that slut is concerned, has he? Explained why he paid someone to look for her, then engaged the best lawyer there is going and—'

'How do you know all this? In fact how do you know any of it, Marcia? All you are talking about is what Lord Bellinger contrived. I didn't tell you any of it, and I know Frederick wouldn't have . . . You've been seeing him, haven't you? You and Bellinger have . . .' The thought hurt so much that Katrina found herself backing towards a chair. Her legs shook and almost let her down. God, she couldn't bear it: Marcia and Bellinger. Her own sister!

The pain of this, she knew, was embedded in her own love for Simon Bellinger – a love she hated feeling, and would cut out of her if she could. He'd used her; used her and then moved on to her sister.

Marcia's face held a mocking smile. 'Did you think you were the only one for Simon? Silly Katrina.'

'What do you mean? I am not *for* him at all. I—'

'Oh, don't come the innocent with me. Your wedding night, dear sister . . . remember? It wasn't your husband who deflowered you, was it?'

'He told you!'

'No, he doesn't know that I know. I was hanging around your quarters, hoping to see Frederick. You know how I feel about him – you knew before you married him – but you still went ahead. Well, now I know things. And one of them is what happened on your wedding night. If you are with child, Katrina, it could well be Bellinger's, not Frederick's. And I know – and let me tell you, this hurts me more than it does you – that Frederick is in love with that whore who is now in prison, and wants to bring her here on her release.'

'No! No, Marcia, you don't know all of that. You have surmised it. You are more jealous of what Frederick does than I am. I pity you.' Katrina's thoughts were not those of pity for Marcia, but of fear of what she had said. *God, I hadn't thought of being with child! Please don't let me be. What did Annie say? That's it, I need to miss my monthly and then I will begin to feel sickly in the mornings. Well, my monthly didn't come – I'm weeks late!*

'Don't feel pity for *me*, thank you. Pity yourself, because when I tell Frederick the truth, he will drop you as soon as look at you. Oh, he'll keep up the charade, but he'll feel that he can openly take lovers and flaunt them in your face; and if I have anything to do with it, I will be one of them!'

This had Katrina defeated. Her head pounded. What had gone wrong? She'd tried to fight Frederick over having the sisters here. She hadn't minded Amy so much. She was a pleasant girl and, by all accounts, was learning fast and would be ready to be a nanny and then later a governess, when they had children. And Amy's friend was proving to be an excellent cook, which was invaluable, as the one who worked for Frederick had long passed retirement age and had been glad just to stay a while to teach the girl. But this other one, the cripple, was it true? Could Frederick be in love with her? No! Frederick was just being kind. But then why did he need her here? There was very little she could do around the house. Her affliction would prevent her from coping with the heavy chores. Even getting around this huge place would be a problem to her.

Frederick had asked, on his last visit, that she give some thought to a position for the girl, but as yet she'd only come up with setting her to helping the laundry maids – mending and ironing. But if . . . No, Frederick wouldn't do that. He wouldn't insult her in that way!

She and he were happy. Even falling in love with each other a little. Their lives were harmonious, and their love-making had blossomed as they'd become more experienced and was now at an exquisite level. All in all, they had been very happy, if not fully in love. They liked each other.

Frederick's visits home had been more frequent than he'd planned during this last month. He'd said he couldn't stay away, that he needed to be with her. And Katrina knew that she needed him – needed what they did together. They lusted after each other, and she'd thought that was enough. It had compensated her for being with the wrong man. God, why did she have these feelings for Bellinger? And he for her? Because he did, she knew that. He expressed them every time they came into contact. And now her heart felt torn to shreds on discovering that he was lying with her sister. Perhaps she should be more understanding of the possibility of Frederick being in love with this crippled girl. He wouldn't have asked to fall for her, any more than she herself had asked to love Simon Bellinger. Frederick probably hated himself for it just as vehemently as she hated herself – maybe he imagined the girl when they came together, in the same way she did Simon. God, what a mess!

'Are you all right, Katrina? You've gone very pale.'

'I – I'm fine. Please leave me a moment, Marcia. I've had all I can take of your spite for one day.'

'I'm sorry. I love you really – you know I do. It's just that, well, it isn't easy being the youngest. Father has not helped my prospects at all. You have everything, as well as the man I love. It just isn't fair!'

'Stop it, Marcia! Just leave me alone for a while. What with you and the noise of the men working on the decorating of this place, I am at my wits' end. I wish Mother had never suggested that you came with me. Why she did, I cannot imagine. Thank goodness Frederick will be home later this week, and that he and I are off to France next week. We will be free of the lot of you!'

Afraid that she'd gone too far, Marcia did as she was bid and left the room. As she rang the bell cord just outside the door, she felt a moment of remorse. She shouldn't take it out on Katrina; it was childish and unfair. None of it was her sister's fault – well, sleeping with Simon Bellinger was. Why she had, Marcia couldn't imagine, unless . . . No, Katrina couldn't be in love with Bellinger? But then Katrina's reaction to thinking Marcia was having an affair with him did seem to indicate that. *Good God! Well, all of this might just turn in my favour* . . . All she had to do was take Simon Bellinger up on his constant attempts to get her into his bed, then flaunt it in front of Katrina to the point where she sought out Bellinger – or, wait a moment . . . Wouldn't it be better to help Katrina get into Bellinger's bed and have them caught? Yes, that was it! Surely then it would be an easy matter for herself to become Frederick's mistress?

'You rang, Miss Marcia?'

'Yes, Annie. Lady Katrina is very upset. We had a silly sisterly falling-out, but I am worried about her. Will you please attend to her, as she is in the throes of one of her headaches? It's my fault. Oh, and can you ask someone to come to my room in about half an hour, as I have a telegram I want to send. Thank you.'

'Marcia, what is going on? I was just coming to join you and Katrina when I heard your raised voices. Is there something concerning my son that I should be worried about?'

'Oh, Lady Eleonore, you made me jump. I – I . . .'

'I heard some of what was said. I did not mean to eavesdrop, but what I did hear was very unpleasant. Be so kind as to come to my sitting room and explain.'

The uncomfortable feeling that now prickled Marcia crawled over her entire body. This was something she hadn't expected. She'd enquired of Lady Eleonore before she'd gone in to tackle Katrina, and had been told that she was taking her afternoon nap. The last thing she wanted was for others to know her true feelings towards her sister – or anything that Katrina or she had done.

'Please sit down. Would you like tea? Or maybe a glass of lemonade?'

'No, thank you, My Lady. I have a telegram I want to send to Mother and Father.' God, she hoped that lie was believed, but if not, it might trigger Lady Eleonore to reveal all she had heard.

'Very well. Please explain what you meant by telling my son the truth, and him not wanting to be with Katrina, but possibly making a mistress of you.'

The hot, prickly feeling rushed to Marcia's face. *Oh no! Oh God, how do I get out of this? Maybe the truth will help?* 'I am mortified, Lady Eleonore, that you heard that. I do apologize. I – it was a reference to my love for Frederick. I have been in love with him for a long time, and hoped against hope that when poor Lord Bertram married Lady Katrina, Frederick would come into my company more and . . . Well, it has hurt me badly that my sister married Frederick for the reasons she did, knowing the truth about my feelings. I am truly sorry. What I said, I said in temper. My sister has never had much thought for me or for my feelings. I – I childishly wanted to hurt her.'

'I see. So is that why your mother sent you here? Was she making sure you had no chance to be with Frederick, as he is staying with them?'

'I think so. I am sorry, I—'

'Please don't be. I understand. I am very sorry for you, my dear. But to be fair, there was no other solution than them marrying. Not for us there wasn't and . . .'

'But Katrina—' Biting her lip till it hurt stopped the

249

stupid outburst that Marcia was about to make, concerning her sister's misdemeanour.

'Yes? Katrina what? Is she in love with another? Has she had an affair? Or committed some other deed likely to harm the marriage?'

'No, Lady Eleonore.'

'Good. Whatever the truth, that is the correct answer. Now, put all of this behind you. And learn a lesson from it. Women of our class rarely marry the one we love. We have to make the best of things as they are. Look to finding a good young man for yourself – a titled one, to please your mother; and, if possible, one who will provide for you. But with your father's wealth, that isn't a major need. In fact I will put out a few feelers. You are a very pretty girl, and an educated one, too. Add that to your prospects as a provider of financial help, and you should have the pick of the crop. Oh, I know you think yourself in love, but . . . well, un-think it and concentrate on nurturing love with whomever you marry.'

'I will. Thank you, Lady Eleonore.'

'Very well, you may leave me and go and send your telegram, if you must, but please don't do so if your intention was to involve your parents in all of this, as that would be very upsetting to them.'

'I won't send it now. I am glad I have had this chat. I feel much better. I will see you at dinner, Lady Eleonore.'

'You will, my dear.'

Feeling very pleased with herself at having not only pulled off a deceit, but having gained some sympathy and possibly even an ally in Katrina's mother-in-law, while perhaps having sown a tiny seed of doubt in her mind as to Katrina's character,

Marcia smiled to herself as she wrote the telegram she'd intended to all along: to Lord Bellinger.

PLEASE VISIT BEFORE F ARRIVES HOME IN THREE DAYS'
TIME – STOP – NEED YOU – STOP – WANT TO SURPRISE
F – STOP. K.

She hoped Lord Bellinger would know that the last bit was a subterfuge, so as not to alert the servants or anyone else who had sight of the telegram. It would also provide him with a reason for accepting the invitation without having to mention it to Lord Frederick.

A clever plan, Marcia thought, though she had to admit to a little nervousness as to whether Lord Bellinger would see what she actually intended behind the message; and, if she was guessing right, that once he was here, Katrina wouldn't be able to resist him.

Now, if the first of these went well, she'd only have to put the second part into action: take Lady Eleonore out on a shopping trip or some such on the day, so that Lord Bellinger had a clear field with Katrina – and then plead a headache and return earlier than expected. Perfect!

21

Frederick

Increasing Ruth's Vulnerability

As he rode past the timber buildings on his left, Frederick
felt his stomach muscles knot in anticipation. 'Go past them
timbers down yonder and make a right,' the man he'd asked
directions of had said. 'The area past that will open out and
you'll see a field on your left. Opposite is Wakefield Correc-
tion House in Back Lane. Can't mistake it. It has scaffolding
around most of it, as they're extending it – making it a
proper jail, for all sorts to be housed in. Not welcome round
here, but nowt we can do.'

And there it was: a building in progress, with the west wing
housing some two hundred female prisoners. She was in there
– Ruth. Dear God, how he hated that thought, but there was
nothing he could do. Sentenced to hard labour, she'd be
breaking stones, no doubt. He didn't like to think of it, but
knew it was something that she'd cope with, as her upper
body had been strengthened by its need to support her when
walking. He could only thank God that the planned tread-
wheel – a wide, hollow cylinder composed of wooden steps
built around an iron frame, which would be powered by as
many as forty convicts – wasn't yet completed. The concept

of it was to punish in a productive way, getting the prisoners to grind corn or pump water wherever it was needed. Once the wheel was into motion, the prisoners would have no choice other than to continually step up onto the next plank as it came round. And they would be forced to do this for up to twelve hours a day.

If only he could get Ruth out before that contraption was built. She wouldn't stand a chance working on it.

The thought ripped at his heart. His only consolation was that at least he could give her the few things he'd brought for her comfort. And above that, he would see her. Be with her. That had to be enough.

'State your business, Sir . . .'

'Lord Frederick Rollinson, Earl of Harrogate. I have come to check on the welfare of my soon-to-be charge, Ruth Dovecote.'

'Of course, M'Lord, you are expected.'

The iron gate groaned on its hinges as it swung open. The sound filled him with dread. A putrid smell of rotting vegetables hit him, causing him to retrieve his handkerchief and hold it over his nose.

'That'll be the kitchen waste. The farmers from the local area are supposed to collect it on a regular basis. They use it for pigswill or manure, but they've not been nigh in over two weeks. Might get the governor to order the prisoners to shift it.'

'That's not women's work, man.' But no sooner had he said the words than he realized it would probably be a darn sight easier than what he was now witnessing: women in a long line, bent double over rocks, hitting them with all their might and making very little headway. 'Good God! What goes on here, Sir?'

'Them's hard-labour prisoners. Men prisoners break the stones to that small size, and these have to crack them to pebbles. Serves them right, by my reckoning. Load of murderers, thieves and whores. Happen as they got off light by missing the gallows, though some are losing their appeals. We hang five t'night.'

Shuddering as much from fear at the fate of these five women as from pity, Frederick asked, 'But what of Elizabeth Fry's reforms? This is horrendous!'

'I spit on the reforms. Them's hardened women who'd rob you and kill you. They're not fit for this earth.'

'They are human beings and deserve your compassion. Often it is circumstances that force them into crime. It is these circumstances that need sorting. Tackle the cause, and find the cure. Is Ruth Dovecote amongst them? How does she fare, with her club foot?'

'Aye, she's there. Yonder, near the wall. She has a hook to hold onto with her right hand – a concession, some say – then she strikes the rock with her left. Does a good job, she does.'

Frederick's eyes followed in the direction the man had pointed. Ruth was so close to him, and yet he hadn't spotted her. His heart somersaulted. She looked up. Her face held lines of pain, her hair hung in thick, greasy strands, her dust-crusted eyes stared, then blinked as the sweat-beads from her forehead trickled into them. They remained closed for a second, as if she was thinking that when she opened them he'd be gone, but when she did so, they filled with tears; and as Ruth nodded to him, those tears trickled down her cheeks, leaving streaks in the dirt clinging to them.

A woman's coarse voice broke the moment. 'Who's this then, Groydon? A stinking toff in 'ere, never been 'eard of!'

'Shurrup, Ginger, and get on with your work. Dovecote! Get yourself in and wash, then get ter visitors' cell.'

Something told Frederick not to interfere or to object. His instincts warned him that if he did, he would only cause Ruth trouble – if not with this warden, then definitely with the other inmates. Looking around at them, he felt pity etched into his heart.

The inside of the building had its own stench: that of body odour, bodily waste and stale air. Waiting in the small cage-like room, Frederick retched, but managed to swallow the bile back down. His throat stung and his breath felt tainted with the smell. Taking a humbug from his pocket, he sucked on it. The fresh taste had the desired effect.

A woman opened the door. Behind her, Ruth dragged her body. He had no other way to describe her slow gait. Her every movement was far worse than he remembered, making her appear almost hideous. Not that she could ever be that to him.

'Ruth?'

'M'Lord.' Her voice held oceans of tears, and some spilled over onto her cheeks.

'Don't – it will soon be over. Stay strong, my . . . I – I mean, well, you can do this. You have been through so much. You can get through this.'

'H – how's Amy and Nora?'

'Nora is pining to go back to the farm. Her physical health has improved, though she has aged. Her grief weighs her down. I went to the cottage hospital yesterday. She was pleased to see me and sends her love to you. She says she misses you. She realizes she cannot go back and is talking of selling. And I have plans I need to discuss with my wife.' Ruth's stare became more intense at the mention of Katrina.

If only she knew how she is never far from my thoughts when . . .
But then, he mustn't think of that. His disloyalty to Katrina
shamed him. 'I want to buy the farm, so that Nora benefits
from the money sooner rather than later. She says she wants
to buy a cottage where you and she can live in peace, as she
knows you will care for her in her dotage.'

'I – I'd like that. Yes, that is what I want to do.'

'But . . .'

'It's not an option for me to be in your house. I've
thought on it and know it is good of you, but—'

'I thought it was what you wanted.'

'Naw. I'll not be put under that strain. Nowt about working in service appeals to me. Working at mill is more likely
to suit me.'

This shocked Frederick, as did Ruth's question after he'd
told her how well Amy was doing, in an attempt to change
her mind. Pleased and relieved for Amy, she asked, 'Would
you think on educating me an' all, M'Lord? Cos I need to
learn music.'

'Music?' If she'd asked if he would put her in a convent to
become a nun, he wouldn't have been as surprised as he was
at this. He couldn't imagine where she'd got this notion, but
as he listened to her, he remembered Haydon Green had told
him that a shed of tools had survived, and in it was a piano.

'Maybe I can lift some of your sadness, Ruth. That piano
in the shed survived.'

'Oh, thank God! Josh . . . Josh would be pleased.'

'I will have it brought down for you and will have it
tuned. But I am amazed and don't know what to say. You,
playing the piano!'

Her head drooped. He followed her gaze: gnarled fingers
fidgeted in her lap.

'They can heal. Try to soak them every evening. When they let you wash, spend more time on your hands. Massage them.'

A small smile twisted her lips. It was a cross between amusement and a sob. Frederick's love for her tore at his heart.

'Ruth, I will help you. I will get you an education, and even a music teacher. I am sorry – desperately sorry – that everything you have been through was caused by your encounter with my family. I am grateful to you for saving my mother. If it had only been that, I wouldn't have had any problem in securing your freedom, but the jailer you attacked – he wanted you in prison.'

'I knaw. I'll be reet. Especially now as I knaw I can have me piano and learn some notes. Thinking of that will get me through. Will you do as you say, and get me and Nora a cottage?'

'I will.'

Her eyes lifted. Nothing had diminished the beauty of the blue depths of them, and in them he read a return of his feelings. 'Ruth, I—'

'Naw, you can't say it. You can't. I knaw it and so do you, but it cannot be. Take me love back to Amy and Nora. Tell Amy I can't wait to hug her. I wish . . .' A sob overcame her.

'Don't wish for what you can't possibly have. Remember what it was like when you did have the things you so want, and take comfort from that.'

'Aye, it's the only way. I knaws that. Help me up, I've to go. You've given me sommat to hang on to. And that'll keep me going.'

Touching her enflamed every part of Frederick, increasing the beating of his own heart and tingling sensations through him that he could hardly cope with. But these turned to horror as he steadied her and saw what he hadn't noticed at first: bruises purpling areas of her arms, gashes – some old and others still bleeding – and then, as he helped her to rise, he caught sight of her feet. Her club foot swelled over the huge boot she had on it. Blisters full of pus stood out on her ankles; some looked at bursting point, and the red-raw weals that traced a path along the sole of her foot looked infected. The agony of seeing her like this cut him in two and caused an anger to rise in him that he couldn't deny. 'Warden!'

The woman who had brought Ruth to him jumped back into his view. 'M'Lord?'

Ruth's whispered 'Naw!' seared through him, but did not stop him. Nothing could. 'I want Miss Dovecote to be taken to the infirmary at once.'

'Naw. I'll be reet. I will.'

'At once, I said. And if any of you try to punish her for this, you will be sorry. Just look at the state of her leg. She is verging on blood poisoning. If she dies, you will all pay: you will go to the gallows for murder. This is sheer neglect, and goes against the Prison Act. Arrange it – and arrange it now!'

'M'Lord, naw – you don't knaw . . . Don't.'

'I do. Well, I can guess. Don't worry, I will protect you.'

The noise the warden made told him she didn't think so, and for the first time Frederick regretted his outburst. But not for long. He had influence that he could bring to bear. He had already made his maiden speech in the House of Lords, indicating that he intended to be a reformer of the conditions the poor had to endure. He would go up to the House and speak on what he had seen going on here. Some-

258

thing must be done! In the meantime, if he could make enough fuss, the newspapers would carry the story.

'Madam, I warn you. You, as well as the conditions here and the way you treat the prisoners, will be in all the newspapers by the morrow! So tread carefully, or you may find you are on the receiving end of a heartless person like yourself!'

With this the woman huffed, but her manner changed. 'We are not heartless, M'Lord. We work with what we have and try to maintain order. It is easy to swan in here and make judgements. Dovecote's leg will be seen to, I can assure you, though also be assured that all the inmates see a doctor once a month and, as his visit is in ten days, the condition would have been picked up then.'

'Ten days! She would have been dead by then. See to it, and make sure a bath chair is sent to transport Miss Dovecote to the infirmary ward. I will personally supervise the move, so don't try and do anything different. I can assure you, Madam, this will be spoken of in the House of Lords this very week.'

There was no retort to this. The woman retreated in haste, and only Ruth's wretched sobs broke the uncanny silence. Frederick hadn't previously thought silence could ever prevail here, as there had been a constant background noise of prisoners calling out and crying in pain and despair, and of wardens shouting orders, not to mention the banging and clanging of the gated doors.

'Ruth, my love.' Oh God, he hadn't meant to say those words. She lifted her head. Hope shone through her tears.

'M'Lord?'

'You know how I feel about you. You do. I cannot help it, but I had no right to express it. I'm sorry. Oh, it's

259

hopeless. Look, Ruth, I have this love for you that is eating at me, and yet I can offer you nothing more than my help.'

'It's enough to know how you feel. I've allus known it. And it's like you say: it can't be helped. We didn't invite it. I loved Josh, thou knows. It were different, but I loved him and I was his wife in all but the marriage service, but—'

His gasp stopped her. He couldn't do anything other than show his shock, as the pain of her words was excruciating to him and caught him off-guard. 'You, and Josh?' *God, why didn't Haydon Green tell me this?*

'I'm not ashamed of what I did, and I would have stayed loyal to Josh. We had no other way. We wanted to be wed, but . . . Anyroad, Josh was a good man and loved me very much.'

'No, you have nothing to be ashamed of. I understand. I . . .' He wanted to say it hurt like hell, but he couldn't. He just had to find a way of accepting that she had been taken – no, had willingly gone to another. But accepting it and living with the knowledge were two different things. And something in him roused a thought. Maybe? 'Ruth, I – I could make you happy in the same way. I mean, we couldn't be married either, but—'

'Naw! I wasn't Josh's mistress. I will be naw mistress! He was me husband, and I his wife. It was done the only way we could do it, by taking our vows to each other, though none of it mattered in the end. They found me, despite us taking every precaution.'

'I didn't mean to insult you, Ruth, or your union with Josh. I just . . . well, I need you. I need you so badly.'

Her crying increased, and now he knew it to hold desolation. It told him that she felt the same way about him, but that she was a better person than him. When she could,

Ruth held on to her principles. Her life with Josh must have seemed as though it was always going to be that way, and this had driven her to accept a compromise. His shame at offering what he had crippled Frederick. Sitting down, he took her hand. 'Forgive me, Ruth. I will never mention it again, I promise. But know that I will always love you and be here for you.'

Her head nodded; her eyes held his. In them he read all he needed to know, even though she did not utter another word.

22

Katrina & Marcia

Treachery Rewarded

'My Lord Bellinger – what are you doing here?' The skipping of every other beat of Katrina's heart didn't help her confusion, as the butler announced Simon's arrival.

Lord Bellinger's head bobbed from her to her mother-in-law and then to Marcia. Marcia looked as surprised as Katrina felt, at this unexpected visit. After a moment's hesitation and, to Katrina's embarrassment, a quizzical look in Lady Eleonore's direction, Marcia stepped forward. 'My Lord Bellinger, how nice to see you again.' As Simon kissed her hand, she said, 'Though I must confess the moment you have chosen to visit is inopportune, as the dowager and I are just about to depart for Ripon. We have several appointments, all of which entail me spending money on myself. I'm in need of a new wardrobe to take me to all the engagements that my sister's elevated position in life has opened up for me.'

'Oh? Oh, well, I am sorry. I thought I was—'

'Of course you are welcome. You are always welcome, Lord Bellinger.'

Katrina could only watch as Simon took the hand proffered

by her mother-in-law, the dowager. His bending over and touching his lips to it was accompanied by a sly glance towards herself. His look held puzzlement.

'Have you planned for Lord Bellinger to stay for dinner and be an overnight guest, Katrina?'

Feeling like a cornered animal, with propriety forbidding her from saying that she hadn't invited him, when it seemed obvious that he considered himself invited, Katrina nodded. 'Of course.'

'And is this a social visit, Lord Bellinger, or are you on business?' the dowager asked, before answering herself, 'But of course you cannot be here on business, as Lord Frederick isn't here.'

'It is business, Lady Eleonore, but I understand of a secret nature that concerns a surprise for Lord Frederick, which it seems neither of you two ladies are party to, either. So you will have to wait and see. Maybe Lady Katrina will reveal all at dinner – I presume you will both be in attendance then?'

'Of course. How exciting, Lady Katrina, and fancy you not sharing any of this with me! I am your sister, after all, though I think you forget that sometimes.'

The ringing of a bell startled Katrina, and Marcia, it seemed, as she swung round and instantly received a look from the dowager that Katrina couldn't interpret. If she didn't think it preposterous and very unlikely, she'd have said the two were in cahoots! But that was impossible. *Oh, what is going on? How do I react?*

The butler attending, and her mother-in-law ordering that the carriage be made ready at once, took away the immediate need to do anything, but that changed as the dowager also ordered the butler to assign a man to Lord

Bellinger, to take him to his quarters and attend to his needs.

'No, I don't want you to see to that last instruction, Crowther.' There was a moment's awkwardness as the butler looked from Katrina to her mother-in-law. The moment had come for the dowager to relinquish the reins of running Beckstone Abbey in favour of Katrina.

'I – I beg your pardon, Lady Katrina, you must forgive me. Habit of almost a lifetime. My order for the carriage still stands, Crowther. Please see to it at once.'

There was another strained moment as the butler left. Everyone looked at Katrina, waiting for the next episode in this drama that she had no idea how to handle, but meant to try. 'Lady Eleonore, will you accompany me to my office?'

The dowager looked shocked. 'Really, Lady Katrina, we cannot both leave our guest.'

'Marcia, please see to getting a drink for Lord Bellinger and amuse him for a moment. I am sure you can do that for me.' Keeping her back straight, Katrina walked towards the door.

As soon as she had arrived at Beckstone Abbey, Katrina had taken a small room just off the hallway that had always been Lady Eleonore's office and had designated it as her own. It was only just big enough to house a desk and some shelving, although she intended to have the wall between it and another small room removed, so that she could have a comfortable chair installed. The other room had a large window that would provide light and a view of the garden – another project she intended to get to work on, but not until after returning from France. There were so many rooms in this house that it had been an easy matter to allow her mother-in-law to choose one, and to have it done up as her own private sitting room in any way she chose. It had been a relief to her when the dowager had chosen some of the pieces of furniture that Katrina herself hadn't liked.

Throughout these changes she and Lady Eleonore had remained on the good terms they had enjoyed during her growing up, but of late there had been a change of attitude. It was almost as if Lady Eleonore was on her guard.

On entering the office, the dowager expressed her concern. 'What is going on, Katrina? You cannot invite someone of Lord Bellinger's standing and then not offer him our hospitality. If he is offended, it could go very badly for you. He has already tried to smear your character once. Please don't give him the opportunity to do so again.'

'I didn't invite him – he is lying. I know nothing of a surprise for Frederick. I am afraid of him, Lady Eleonore, and I don't want to be left alone with him.'

'Oh dear. Why has he come? I don't like him, or that Parvoil. They do things to further their own cause. The thing is: what *is* his cause today? I will cancel my trip . . . Oh, but that won't do. He will suspect something, and that could be even worse. Look, my dear, I am not used to the goings-on that have occurred since you and your sister arrived here. I had to talk to Marcia after I heard you both arguing, and she intimated that you had things to hide.'

Katrina's throat dried. It was as if there was a conspiracy against her. Guilt reddened her cheeks. Her world – the one her mother and father had created for her and for themselves – looked as though it was about to crash. The shame would be immense. No, it could not happen.

'I have nothing to hide, Lady Eleonore. My sister is being silly. She is jealous of me and it seems she set out to discredit

265

me, as indeed Lord Bellinger has tried to do. I don't know how I will fare against them. I know Marcia's motives, but not Lord—'

'I think you do, Katrina. Is he in love with you?'

There was nothing for it. 'Yes, I believe so, but I haven't given him any encouragement. I—'

'Never mind that now. Love is an emotion that none of us can deny. We have to find a way of living with it, if it is thwarted. That is your task, Katrina. You have to somehow manage this latest trick of your thwarted love. We all have to save face. I suggest that you arrange some activity for Lord Bellinger this afternoon that doesn't involve yourself. Then we will be with you at dinner. Once that is done, I will stay with you until such an hour as we can all retire. How we handle this with Frederick, I do not know, but something will occur to us before he is home. Maybe we can arrange a surprise that would have needed Lord Bellinger's help, as that is the reason he seems to have conjured up for being here? I will give it some thought. I am used to men like him. You must school yourself in their ways, and learn to deal with them in any way that does not cause scandal. You have done well so far, my dear. Now you must cover up our disappearance, and taking me to task on his arrival, and we must do so in a very clever way.'

Life as a dowager wasn't easy. Lady Eleonore still felt responsible for her family – what little there was left of it, that was. She swallowed hard. *No time to think sad thoughts. Life goes on.* But what life? It felt as if she'd been put out to grass: not allowed to take any decisions, only give advice.

Feeling the sigh that she released coming from deep within her, she reflected on how difficult it was proving to settle into her new role. She had thought she knew these Arkwright girls, having seen them grow up – having helped, even, in the direction they should be schooled and made ready for what had always been Veronica's ambition: getting them their rightful place in society. Poor Veronica – a lifetime of being shunned because her father couldn't keep hold of the family money. Disgraceful!

Now it seemed that breeding had more to do with the way people handled themselves and the situations they found themselves in, as the girls were proving troublesome and Eleonore lived in fear, after just a short time of coping with them, that they would bring her family into disrepute. Oh, for the days of simplicity when a commoner here, and in her beloved France, was kept firmly in his place. A marriage such as Veronica was forced to make, and now her own son had taken on, was unheard of before the revolutions. No good would come of it.

At least Katrina had spirit, and by the looks of things, she would need it. If only she was more like Marcia – a sweet child. A little minx, but harmless. Katrina was getting in too deep. It wouldn't surprise Eleonore to find out that she *had* invited Lord Bellinger today, but that he'd arrived earlier than she planned. She would need watching. Whether to warn Frederick? That was the question. Maybe not. Better that she worked on Katrina and brought her into line.

On entering the withdrawing room, she had to admire Katrina and wondered for a moment if she was wrong, as Marcia was looking as if she'd won a victory of some sort and was enjoying her sister's plight. It was good to see Katrina handle it so well.

'My Lord Bellinger, forgive our leaving you just as you arrived. I had important matters to discuss with Lady

Eleonore before she left for the town. It was all to do with the surprise I am planning for Lord Frederick. You coming earlier than I had planned did not leave me time enough. Well, now that the person who should have known the details first – Lady Eleonore – is informed, I can reveal everything and then perhaps you can start to help me make it a reality?'

'Of course, Lady Katrina. I do beg your pardon. I should have let you know my travel arrangements in advance, but I had little time after receiving your telegram. What can I do for you?'

This shocked Eleonore and she saw, from Katrina's expression, that it had taken the wind out of her sails, too. *What is going on? Telegram? Did Marcia say?* Katrina interrupted her thoughts, but not before Eleonore had caught Marcia looking very sheepish. Surely not. Had she got everything wrong? There was no time to ponder this, for Katrina rose in her estimation as she regained control in an instant.

'I want to buy Frederick a wedding gift – a racehorse – and have no idea how to go about it. I heard there was a horse fair locally tomorrow, and I need help with what I should do and what kind of horse is best, and even how to bid! I believe prospective buyers are going this afternoon. I know that you own racehorses, very successful ones. And Lord Frederick has a groom who could take you to the event. It would be such a wonderful present for Lord Frederick. Please say you will do it!'

Well! Fait accompli, *as they say in my country. Well done, Katrina!*

'How wonderful. What a splendid idea, Katrina, and one well worth keeping a secret, my dear. My son will be delighted. Thank you so much, Lord Bellinger.'

Lord Bellinger bowed slightly in acknowledgement to her. Katrina might have managed the situation very well, but a feeling niggled inside Eleonore that there was more to come in the Katrina–Bellinger story, and this worried her. But for the time being she needed to support Katrina.

'Well, come along, Marcia. Let us take our carriage quickly. We will send the groom straight back. It only takes twenty minutes into town. Then, if you can make sure you are back from the horse fair by four o'clock, Lord Bellinger, the groom can come and collect us. Goodbye, and happy horse-buying! Goodbye, Lady Katrina.'

As soon as they had gone out of the door, Katrina rang the bell.

'No, not yet, Katrina, we need to talk.'

'I have nothing to say. How dare you come here on the pretence of receiving a telegram, and put me in such a compromising position!'

'But I did receive . . . Here, look, I have it with me.'

'But this is impossible! I didn't . . . Oh God, Marcia must have—'

'You rang, M'Lady?'

'Oh, Crowther, yes, I did. Please see to Lord Bellinger's comfort. We have bedrooms ready in the south wing, I believe? You must excuse us, Lord Bellinger. We are in the middle of a refurbishment, but I have tried to plan so that we always have some comfortable rooms available for unexpected guests. And, of course, Crowther will put a man at your disposal.'

'There is no need. I brought my man with me, and he has no doubt prepared for me already.'

'Of course. Is that so, Crowther?'

'Yes, M'Lady. I beg your pardon, but Lord Bellinger's man was very insistent, so I took the liberty of showing him to the south-wing suite.'

'That's fine, thank you, Crowther. Please inform Lord Bellinger's man that his master is ready to be taken to his rooms and—'

'But he is not. Thank you, Crowther. If you will be so good as to leave us for a moment, her ladyship will issue further instructions after I have had a few moments with her. I beg that of you, Lady Katrina?'

Furious that for the second time her orders to her own butler had been countermanded, Katrina could only give a polite nod. Crowther scrambled for the door. Poor man. She almost giggled. He had suffered the same fate as her. Well, maybe she could turn that into making him an ally for the future. She could do with someone on her side in this household.

'Katrina, what is all this about? I thought you wanted me here. Darling, I—'

'No, Simon, don't. Please. I had nothing to do with getting you here, so please don't play into the hands of whoever did – though I believe it must have been Marcia, although I don't have proof. But she knows.'

'Good God – knows about us? How? And what is she playing at? What is it to her? Oh Lord, what if she says anything to Henrietta?'

'We have to stop Marcia. She cannot be allowed to ruin all of our lives just because she wants Frederick. It is ridiculous. He doesn't want her. We—'

'Huh! Good Lord, no. He only wants his little trollop. You know he has visited her in prison, don't you?'

'No! He wouldn't, not without telling me. I – I mean . . .

look, Frederick's dealings with that girl are done purely out of kindness. If he decided he needed to visit her, then that is his business.'

'It becomes yours when there is talk, my dear, and that is what is beginning to happen.'

'Talk? Simon, you cad! How could you start a rumour of that nature, because if there is talk, you *must* have started it!'

'A word may have slipped out. You know how it is. Well, he deserves it. Anyway, it is expected, with an arranged marriage, that he will take a mistress, but he has chosen badly. This will be a scandal if he doesn't stop.'

'No, only you can make it a scandal, not Frederick. He is open with me about his dealings with the girl.'

'Oh? So you knew about the visit to the prison?'

'No, but . . . well—'

'Katrina, there is only one way you can stop me from discrediting that husband of yours, and that is by agreeing to be my mistress.' This shocking statement came as Simon stepped nearer her. When he was close to her, his voice lowered. The tone of his words shivered down her spine. 'You know we are meant to be together, Katrina. You know my love for you is strong enough to protect you from gossip. I have to have you.'

How she got into his arms, she did not know. All she knew was that it felt right. It was the place she was meant to be. And she couldn't resist the force that held her there, even though common sense told her she should.

When his lips met hers, all concerns left her. Her senses yielded to his. Her heart drowned in the sensations that washed over her. He was the other half of her. She could not deny him.

The door opening, and a gasp of shock and horror, broke

the spell that had captivated Katrina. Coming out of Simon's arms, she looked into the aghast face of Lady Eleonore. Next to her stood Marcia, her face a picture of satisfaction.

'Sorry, both of you. I – I left my purse, so sorry.'

The door banged shut.

Oh God! What now? What have I done?

23

Amy & Lettie

A New Life

The chatter around the kitchen table went from this to that, before the upstairs maid chirped in with, 'Eeh, there's fun and games with them lot upstairs! I were doing me banisters, when the dowager and that Miss Marcia returned not ten minutes after leaving. They went straight to the withdrawing room, as the new mistress has had done up, and opened the door. Well, you'll never guess in a month of Sundays what I saw!'

'Whatever it was, keep it to yourself or you might find you haven't a job. We don't have gossips here.' This from the new housekeeper as she left the room, carrying the thick notebook she took everywhere with her, stopped all conversation for a moment, and Amy was glad of it. She had a test to face this afternoon on her arithmetic, and she wanted to practise a few additions in her mind while she ate.

Counting the number of cups hanging on the rack that contained the upstairs crockery, and adding that to the number of plates on the lower shelf, occupied her for the next few minutes, until Mildred started again, only this time in a lower voice. 'I'm telling you, it was scandalous. The new mistress in the arms of that bloke what's visiting.'

'No!'

This, from the old cook, had the effect of running a thread of worry through Amy. *Are things going to change?* She couldn't bear it if they did. Her life had taken a turn for the better, to the point where some happiness now nudged the sad, heavy part of her and, with her future looking good, she didn't want anything to spoil it. The only change she wanted was for their Ruth to get to the end of her sentence and to come here, to be with her. Her world would be complete then.

'Eeh, lass, are you sure?' Cook had closed her mouth into a clamp and had her eyes fixed on Mildred as Lettie asked this, then went on to say, 'The poor Earl – and them not wed more than a couple of months. What happened? Were there a to-do?'

'Naw, the young miss just closed the door with a bang and said something like, "Oh dear, I didn't expect that." Then the dowager said, "What? We didn't see anything, did we?" And I never heard owt else from them; they just left again.'

'But what of the new mistress? Did owt happen? Did she come out of the room? Did he?'

'Aye, Lady Katrina came running out. She were crying, and she pushed past me and ran to her room. I reckon as she's still there, as I never saw her again.'

'Well, it ain't reet as you told what you saw, anyroad,' Cook said. 'First lesson in service is to be invisible, and to keep all you see to yourself. You'd do well to learn that one, Mildred. Now, tea break over – get yourselves back to work. We have a dinner guest and he's a lord, so everything must be reet. Have you all the silver in the dining room cleaned, young Tommy?'

'Aye, Crowther checked and said I'd done a good job. I've to help him set it up, as he wants me to learn the footman's job for the future, as he reckons he'll need a team of them, once all decorating is done and the family starts to entertain on a grand scale.'

'Well, that's good. Run along to Crowther and see if he has any other duties for you. And, Florrie, you see as all the fires are stoked. I'll get young Arthur to fill the coal buckets. Now, the rest of you, get out of me kitchen and back to your duties. Me and Lettie here have a good bit to be getting on with. Are them pigeons all plucked, Arthur?'

With the bustle of bodies scurrying away to their posts and Cook directing all and sundry, Amy had a moment to talk to Lettie. 'What d'you think, Lettie? I don't like the sound of it. Will the Earl leave her? And what of our jobs?'

'Naw, lass. Me ma used to be in service when she were a lass, and she used to tell me a tale or two about the goings-on. She reckoned as the gentry jumped in and out of each other's beds like rabbits going from one buck to another. Allus at it, she said. It ain't as if they marry for love. Don't worry; it'll be handled discreetly. That's if it happened how Mildred said it did. She strikes me as a bit of a gossip, that one. And one as would add on a bit here and a bit there to make her tale more interesting.'

Lettie patted Amy's shoulder and gave her one of her lovely smiles. Her teeth, even and white, always had a clean fresh look, which was surprising, as some folk only had one or two in their head by the time they were her age. Nineteen, Lettie was, and she had what you'd call a motherly face: rounded, well scrubbed and shining. It had a niceness rather than a beauty, and her cheeks dimpled when she smiled. Her eyes were kind – a soft grey colour, they twinkled with each different expression. Even if she was cross, which wasn't often, her eyes had a glint; only then they showed her temper. At other times they showed her amusement, but mostly her kindness. She was not very tall, and her figure tended to the roundness that spoke of her fondness for that extra bun, if she could get it, or finishing up what others didn't want.

Amy had asked her how she kept her teeth like she did, and Lettie said her ma had told her to eat an apple a day, if she could get hold of one, and to clean her mouth with salt water every night and every morning. The first time Amy had tried this she'd been sick, but she'd got used to it now. Getting hold of the apple was another matter, though, and this she'd only managed a couple of times a week.

'Come on, lass, get back to whatever you're meant to be doing. It's going to get hectic in here. I'll see you at dinnertime. Eeh, you're the lucky one, set to do your learning. I wish I could read.'

'I'll teach you if you like, Lettie? It ain't difficult.'

'Not for you, no doubt, but I reckon as I'll try your patience some.'

Walking along the back drive that led to the village, some five minutes later, Amy again began to count and add up – this time the number of birds she saw, added to the times she had to jump over a puddle. Though the August sun was hot, the air was fresh after a recent downpour. The child in her wanted to jump into the puddles, but she couldn't think of muddying her new boots. They were just one symbol of this new life she'd fallen into and, though it was a good life, she still couldn't accept it and often felt as if she was somewhere she shouldn't be. 'That'll pass,' Lettie had said. 'You'll settle, lass. Life's been a bit up and down for you. It's to be expected. You're bound to feel displaced.'

This went some way to helping Amy understand, but it was as if she hadn't found her place in life. She was happy enough, and loved learning all the skills she'd need for the job she was being prepared for, especially what Mr Rudderford, the village schoolteacher and her tutor, called 'her academic skills'. She sometimes felt like a sponge soaking up all the knowledge he gave her, and he was always full of praise for her efforts.

Her other lessons with Mrs Larkins, learning the skills she would need as a nanny, were all right, if a bit mundane. Mrs Larkins had a host of young 'uns from six months to ten years old, and a wealth of knowledge about their upbringing and how to deal with their ailments, besides what to feed them at different stages of their lives, what to dress them in, what amount of fresh air they needed and all manner of things – even how to monitor if their bowels were working properly! It seemed that she used to be nanny to the Earl and his late brother, and after each reached the age of ten and went off to boarding school, she married Larkins, the groom, and they were given a cottage on the estate. It seemed to Amy that Mrs Larkins had been engaged in building her own child-nursery ever since!

One of the big changes for Amy was that she never saw poverty any more. Not real poverty. There were the haves and have-nots, but the latter were well shod and had someone in their household working. They had all this fresh air to breathe, though the aroma that tingled her nostrils now – the farmer's manure pile – didn't add anything to that!

Food wasn't a problem. It grew all around them, and village life was like a community of support, from what she'd seen of it so far. Much like back at Pradley. Folk were poor, but happy.

None of this erased from her memory what she'd left behind, though. The plight of those in the workhouse, and of the homeless on the streets, still worried her to the point where she had thoughts of a plan to help.

Once she was a paid member of staff – and that depended on when the Earl's wife became pregnant – from that day on, she would have a role. She'd be preparing the nursery, ordering what she'd need from the housekeeper, and generally looking after Lady Katrina's needs where her health was concerned. But she would also have leave-days, and it was on these that she would buy some food and give it out to those on the street, or just buy some hot tatties from the man with the brazier and give them to the hungry. Perhaps Lettie and Ruth would help her, chip in a bit of their pay even, as they'd both known what it was like to be hungry. Poor Ruth still knew.

Eeh, it'd be a good day when Ruth came here. But would it all start again – would there always be trouble in her sister's path? Somehow Amy knew there would be, and the thought weighed heavily inside her. And with this thought a little fear entered her. Fear for her lovely, misunderstood sister, a fear that everything that went wrong would be laid at Ruth's door and would cause everything in their lives to spiral downwards again.

Kneading away at the dough, with Cook chuntering away in her ear, Lettie could have screamed. She hated the work in the kitchen – the smell, the heat and Cook's constant nagging. It had never been her ambition to do such work; she had just landed in it! Aye, her life was better than in the workhouse, but somehow she'd been happier there, nursing the poor, than she was now feeding the rich, even if it meant she was well fed and housed.

One good thing: she was free now. She could just leave. *Oh, Lettie, lass, stop thinking like this. Think yourself lucky. Them as are back there in the workhouse would love to change places. Sing, that's the thing:*

> 'Tell me the tales
> That to me were so dear,
> Long, long ago,
> Long, long ago;
> Sing me the songs
> I delighted to hear,
> Long, long ago,
> Long ago . . .'

'Eeh, lass, that's grand. You has a lovely voice, I could listen—'

The housekeeper cut off Cook by shouting, 'What's the noise? Who is it singing? I am trying to do my ordering, and I can't concentrate.'

'Sorry, Mrs Grimes. I was just passing the time.'

'Aye, and she sings like an angel. Don't be such a sour-puss. You carry on, lass. I was enjoying it.'

Not sure what to do, Lettie looked from one to the other. The housekeeper gave in first. 'Aye, right you are. It was pleasant-sounding, and I've nearly finished. Not used to hearing any such around here, that's all.'

'You should sing at the "Free 'n' Easy" down at the

tavern. Me and Crowther go sometimes and have a jar of ale and watch the show. Anyone can join in, and them as have a nice voice often get taken on by one of them touring companies. Go all over the world, some of them do.'

The thought of this sent a thrill through Lettie. Not just 'going around the world', but singing to others to give them pleasure – that settled in her as the place she was meant to be.

'When will you be going there again, Cook? I'd like to come if I can and, aye, I'd get up and sing an' all.'

'Well, if you do, you'll be lost to us and that's for sure. Anyroad, start up with your singing again, lass. I've never heard the like and it does me heart good. And, aye, we'll take you with us to the Cock's Crow, and be glad to.'

Though this pleased Lettie, she had her doubts about Cook's motives. *Happen as she'll be glad to get rid of me, as more than once she's given me the feeling as I'm treading on her toes . . . Eeh, why am I thinking like this? What's got into me the day? I'll be turning into a sourpuss like the housekeeper.*

24

Ruth

A Fight to Survive

Stomach pains gnawed at Ruth. The emptiness in her made her muscles clench and unclench as they begged her for food.

She'd been put on water only, and just the odd drip of that, and this was the fifth day of the order given by the governor. The bed she lay in held the dampness of her own urine. The stench of her sheets and the putrid smell of the other occupants of this ward – all lying on filthy beds, all starving, with their bony bodies near to death – had assaulted her nostrils in the first two days of being here, but now she was used to it.

And yet the pristine clean walls, painted white, looked saintly and belied the way they enclosed such human misery. For the people in here were considered the dregs of the prison population. This was the madhouse.

The governor stood over Ruth's bed, looking down at her. 'And what frame of mind are we in today then? Have we concluded that we're nowt special? Because having an earl for a friend does nowt to make you above any of the rest of them, Black Witch.'

'I – I knaws that, Governor, and I'm ready to go back to work.'

'That's good. Right, Matron, one more day of starvation should do it. She's cracking. She's not given any curses for two days now. I have a catalogue of her misdemeanours whilst in this hospital. Let's see: throwing the piss-pot at you, screaming a curse at Jackson, spitting in Jackson's eye, clawing Jackson, throwing the water you offered her over you. The list goes on. Any more trouble and I'll present it to the magistrate. That should put at least another year on her sentence, and well deserved.'

As he walked away, Ruth's mind screamed after him, *I never did all of them things, I didn't!* But she dared not say it out loud. That's what they were taunting her to do. Aye, she'd gone a bit mad, but the pain of the salt being rubbed into her wounds with a rough piece of hessian had sent her that way. As had Jackson's ways. She'd had to defend herself. And, yes, she'd clawed at him, but not without reason.

'Ha!'

Jackson's sarcastic laugh cut into her thoughts. Her body cringed away from him as he bent over her, his voice thick, his stinking breath wafting onto her face. 'So you've to do as you're told, eh? Well, you can start by opening them legs for me. Because if you don't, I'll add something else to the governor's list.'

This had been his mission from day one of her coming onto this ward. Looking up at him, Ruth could see the shape of his hardness jutting from his trousers. Should she just give in? What would it matter? But then she thought of Josh and the purity of her union with him, and she couldn't. Opening her mouth wide cracked her lips and her scream rasped her dry throat, but somehow she shouted, 'Governor!'

Jumping back from her, Jackson, a security guard for the hospital wing, went to turn away as the governor came back to Ruth. 'Have you sommat to say, Black Witch? You do know that wasting my time is another offence?'

'He . . . Jackson, he wants to rape—'

'So? What's that, to a whore who lived in sin? Jackson has every decent piece of woman that comes in here, and you look like you'd be good to have, despite your gammy leg. I may take me own turn after Jackson. I've never done it with a cripple, let alone a witch! Pity they weren't successful at burning you at the stake. If I'd have been there, the job would have been done, and no sorcery from you would have stopped me. You don't scare me.'

'So I have your blessing, Boss?'

'You do, Jackson. Then if nowt happens to you, I'll take me turn. Go ahead. And you let him, Witch, or I'll not only add to me list sommat like stealing from inmates, but I'll present it to the magistrate on the morrow!'

Despair crept through Ruth, leaving her knowing that she was nothing. At this moment she hated the Earl. Why? Why had he insisted she be brought into the hospital, and why had he made such a fuss about her treatment, then not come back to make sure she was all right? Yes, he'd left her in a clean, bright ward, with only a few well-cared-for inmates and a doctor in attendance, as well as crisply dressed nurses, but hadn't he known this would change? Why hadn't he listened to her when she'd told him her fears?

For a moment she had a feeling that she would curse him to hell and damnation, but stopped herself, as fear of her own powers showed her a vision of the Earl being hurt at her request – though power, if she possessed such a thing, wasn't helping her now as she cursed Jackson. 'Damn you, may you rot in hell!' And yet still he stood there, the grin on his face showing his blackened teeth, and his hands busy undoing his belt.

A moan from the bed next to her got her looking in that direction. An old woman lay with her face turned towards them, her distressed expression stretching her paper-thin skin over her protruding bones. Finding a smile from some-where, Ruth tried to ease the old woman's fear and mouthed to her that it would be all right.

Giving in was her only option. Fighting had no merit now, as she had no strength and no one was going to come and help her. The female warden had disappeared the moment the governor had given the nod to Jackson.

The bed creaked under Jackson's weight. Now that he was this near, she could taste his sour breath. Cringing away from the touch of him on her skin, her body stiffened so that he had to prise open her legs. Her resistance caused her pain. Desolation filled Ruth as he crushed her body with his. Within minutes he entered her, and his thrusting scrunched her inside with the agony and the filth of it. Looking towards the old woman, she tried to focus on her, through tears that blurred her vision as the violation went on and on.

Pale eyes looked back at Ruth. Eyes that had seemed unseeing, when the old woman's distress had shown, now looked alert and willed her to bear it, sending her an unspoken message that she wasn't alone.

At last it ended. Drops of Jackson's sweat dripped onto her trembling body as he rolled off her and stood up. A hate she'd only ever felt once before entered her and filled her soul. It seared her eye sockets and burned her eyes, as she directed it at Jackson. He shrank back from her, his satisfied smirk turning ugly as his features twisted in pain. Gasping for air made his eyes bulge and swelled his face. Clutching at his chest, he collapsed onto the floor.

A wail that started as a whimper came from deep within her. Footsteps, plodding and hurried, came towards her. She knew that tread.

'What the—? Oh, my God, she's killed him!' Horror slackened the female warden's facial muscles and a strangled cry of fear erupted from her as she looked at Ruth. 'You're a demon. The devil incarnate – a witch!' Turning from her, the warden ran towards the door. Her petrified and piercing screams of 'Help me . . . help me' drained all thought from Ruth, filling her mind and then her heart with fear.

That fear had her teeth chattering, as her whole body shook with the force of it. Vomit – consisting of what, she did not know – came from her mouth. She could not take her eyes off the prostrate figure of Jackson. He lay still; not one part of him moved, not even his chest. A blue tinge circled his open mouth, and his eyes stared back at her.

The governor's heavy footsteps resounded in the silence, coming nearer and nearer, his step hesitating once he could see Jackson's body. His face was a mask of horror, and his voice held incredulity as he asked, 'What the—? How did you kill him?'

'She didn't. The dirty bugger had his way on her, then keeled over. I saw it all.'

As he swivelled round to look at the old woman, the governor's mouth dropped open.

The old woman's voice grew in strength. 'He went down after he'd done her. I've seen it afore. It were too much for his heart. She didn't even struggle.'

'Shut up, Alice. You've not opened your mouth in four years, playing the deaf-mute, and now you've a lot to say.

She must've killed him. He stood large as life afore me, not ten minutes since. She's a black witch. They should burn her.'

'Naw . . . naw I didn't. It was as Alice said.'

'Don't open your mouth, either.' Turning, he shouted, 'Pauline, clean her up, and do a proper job. Don't leave a trace. Take Alice into solitary. I'll get the police. We'll let them deal with this.'

A hubbub of noise built to a crescendo of screaming – 'She didn't kill him!', 'She didn't!' – as all the weary occupants of the room tried to shout in Ruth's defence.

'Shut up, the lot of you. She's a witch! She doesn't have to do owt – just curse him. If you want bread and water for a week, carry on how you are, you mad idiots. Clamp them all to their beds, Pauline, and the black witch can go to solitary an' all.'

With this, hopelessness overcame Ruth. Nothing could save her from the gallows now. Nothing.

Washing her in cold water didn't cleanse her – not inside, it didn't, though the way the female warden dealt with her between her legs, you would think she was trying to. She doused Ruth time after time, and then shoved a rolled-up piece of hessian into her and twisted it. The soreness this caused got Ruth crying out, but it wasn't a cry of protest. She allowed everything that the woman wanted to do. She could almost taste the woman's fear as she worked, for her glances told of her terror. Ruth knew that with just a look she could stop her, but no. She wasn't a witch, she wasn't!

They had to carry Ruth into the Assizes. Looking around, she wondered if this was where the lads had learned their fate. But she dared not think of that time. All of her, even her soul, felt ready to give way, but she mustn't. She had no one to defend her. She needed to be able to ask questions. At the sound of someone knocking on a door, the male warden lifted her onto her feet. Her legs gave way. Catching her, he supported her with stiff arms that spoke of his revulsion.

'Stand for Judge Christian,' the voice of the clerk commanded.

Her hope was that his name stood for a Christian man, a fair man who would see through all the charges that were levelled at her.

'I can't stand without me crutch, Sir.'

Showing a small amount of compassion, the warden offered his arm.

As the proceedings began and they were all told to sit, Ruth willed herself to sit upright. The judge had been told of her affliction, and he allowed her to take a seat. Her heart raced as a list of her supposed crimes was read out. Murder had been added to the list of offences. Despair threatened to undo her, at the sound of the word.

Yes, she had killed – but not Jackson. The death she'd been responsible for had been the young Earl's, but it had been done in defence of her family. Oh God, would she feel the tightening of the rope on her neck tonight? A tremble of horror and fear left no part of her body untouched and set her head pounding.

'How do you plead, Miss Dovecote?'

Looking at the judge, she opened her mouth. Her throat dried, releasing what sounded like a croak, but it was snatched back in a gasp as a man's voice shouted, 'She cannot plead. She has not spoken to me; I have not advised her. I am her defence counsel, Your Honour!'

The warden's stiffened body next to her relaxed as his breath left him in a sigh. His growly whisper of 'You'll be all right, now, love' shocked Ruth as much as the man's interruption had. As she started to look at him, the warden said in a sharp whisper, 'Don't. Act as though I am telling you off.'

Cringing from him, Ruth hoped she gave the right impression. She could feel his concern. *What is going on?* A scene outside the court, when they had arrived from the prison earlier, came to her: the warden calling a lad over, looking all around and passing a note and a coin to the lad, then saying, 'If you get him here in time, there'll be more for you.' *The warden must have arranged this, but why?*

The words from the judge held her joy in check. 'Mr Cotram, I have seen nothing that you have filed as the defence in this case. Besides, it is cut-and-dried, from what I have read. There is no defence. It is a simple matter of murder.'

'I beg Your Honour's pardon, but there is nothing simple about an accusation of witchcraft!'

As he said this, Mr Cotram – a tall, thin man with a thick-lipped mouth and a huge nose that told of his drinking habit – looked around the court. His nod was directed towards a man scribbling away in the corner.

The judge brought his attention back. 'What witchcraft? Don't be so ridiculous. Are you playing to the journalists? There is nothing about such an accusation and, if there was, I doubt it would be lawful. Witchcraft has long been considered something of the past. Does your so-called client conjure up spirits?'

'No, she does not. It is said that she curses and bad things happen . . . Yes, I know, Your Honour, you may well smile.

I did myself, when I heard. Stuff of the last century and all conjecture, based on whipping up the fear of the crowd. I ask for an adjournment to give me time to talk to my client.'

In a voice that spoke of his disbelief, the judge asked, 'Does she even know she is your client? I doubt it, by the look on her face.' His drawl turned to a stern, 'Well, whether she does or not, I hope you can come up with a defence, and that this is not all a waste of my time. I will want witnesses and concrete evidence even to order a new trial.'

'Yes, Your Honour, but I understood this to be a hearing?'

'It is. But it is one, from what I have been told about the case, that could have ended in a judgement being passed, as there was no evidence to contradict her guilt. Now, I am not bandying points of law with you. You should have filed as the defence before now. I will adjourn for two weeks. At such time, if you do not present a case, we will go ahead without one.'

When the judge stood, the warden helped Ruth to. She could see from the judge's face how angry he was. But then her body crumpled, as the warden let her go with a rough gesture. 'Don't tell anyone I was involved or I'll never be able to help others. Good luck.'

Never had she been told good things in such a rough way, but she understood and, though she wanted to thank him, she didn't dare.

'Hold yourself together, Miss Dovecote. Everything will be all right. I will visit you tomorrow.'

Ruth looked up into the face of the lawyer who had come to her rescue. 'But I – I can't pay you.'

'You don't have to. There's a charity set up by those of us who care about the poor and getting them justice. The hardest thing is finding out when they are up on charges, as they won't let us hang around the court to pick up cases as they come in. Gardener, your warden, is one of our contacts. He gets information to us, when he can. He's a good man. He must believe in you, as he won't give us anything on anyone he doesn't think innocent. But he won't give evidence for you. He'd lose his job, and then we'd be back to not finding those in the prison who need our help . You have to start thinking of your own defence. Think of the names of anyone who witnessed anything. All I know about you is that you are up for murder, and they say you are a witch.'

'I'm not. I – I didn't mean owt bad to happen, not ever. It just does.'

'Don't talk like that. It doesn't. No more to you than to anyone else.' He'd come closer and she could smell drink on him. Some of Ruth's hope died as his nose proved that he was a man who liked his liquor, and she knew those who couldn't leave it alone couldn't always keep their promises, either. 'And don't look so distrustful. No one may ever have helped you before, but you have me on your side now.'

'I beg your pardon, Sir, but if that man you directed your comment at, about me being done for witchcraft, was a newspaperman, he might make things bad for me. My Josh said as those as can read newspapers are influenced by them. What if he makes folk hate me?'

'He won't. He is a friend. He will make it sound ridiculous. And who is Josh? Can he be of help?'

She didn't want to tell him everything, but knew he didn't believe her when she said that Josh had just been a friend.

'Rule number one: honesty with me at all times. My learned friend the prosecutor, William Thirsk, is very astute.

Now that he thinks he has a fight on his hands, he will get his men to dig up all there is to know about you. So I need to know everything. The good *and* the bad.'

At this, Ruth thought, *Most of it will be bad*. The picture her story would paint would put off even the kindest man – and that was how she'd come to think of Mr Cotram. Well, he must be kind, to do what he did for no pay. But was kindness enough? Did he have the skill to save her? And what of his obvious love of drink? Would that stop him doing as he promised? Ruth didn't know, but she had to have faith in somebody. And she knew she should have, as there were still good people left in the world. The warden who had brought Cotram to her had shown her that.

25

Frederick

Love is Blind

With his horse saddled and ready, Frederick looked forward to the ride home. It would take him all of seven hours, but for most of the way the scenery was spectacular. He would change his horse once he'd skirted around the Pennines and reached Threshfield, where he'd taken to leaving a mount at the inn and spending a night to break his journey. Not that he would have that much respite this time. He'd been away for weeks, and was missing Katrina and all she had to offer. That wasn't a gentlemanly thought, he knew, but he couldn't argue with it and so he intended to complete the journey in one go.

It had been two weeks since he'd visited Ruth, but he had received regular reports that she was doing well. The latest said that she wanted to go back to work. That boded well, and he felt satisfied that she was now being taken care of. Surely they wouldn't dare do otherwise, knowing that he was involved in her case?

His heart had yearned to visit, but he dared not show more than a passing interest in Ruth's welfare. Someone in his set would note it if he did, and would see that either

Lord Bellinger or Katrina – or, indeed, both – knew. Either would be a disaster, as Katrina must still have her suspicions about his feelings for Ruth, and Simon Bellinger would make mischief with the information.

The course he'd taken was the right one, but putting it into practice had proved – and was still proving – a little more difficult. *Bloody difficult, in fact!* because every part of him wanted to be with her. *Oh, Ruth . . . Ruth.*

The journey wasn't without heartache, as he had so much time to think. And most of his thoughts were occupied with what he'd learned about Ruth. His soul ached at the thought of what she had been through, but mostly he couldn't get her common-law husband, Josh Bottomless, out of his mind. Thinking of Josh, and how he had taken Ruth in a way he himself wanted to, compounded Frederick's hurt and somehow tainted Ruth. But he pulled himself up and refused to let the thought take hold. Ruth had seen her life panning out as she and Josh being together forever. The man had offered her everything she needed, and she would have made their union legal, if she could. She'd had no choice in the matter. He had to accept that.

At least his mind was at rest concerning Ruth's future. He'd checked with Josh Bottomless's solicitor and had found him to be a good, solid man, who had looked after Josh's family's legal requirements for many years and was capable of sorting out what Nora wanted to happen. The man had seen immediately to the transportation of the livestock to the farmers' market and made sure he got a good price for them. He'd engaged an agent to see to the tidying-up of what was left of Josh's property, and to prepare the tools and equipment for sale. They would go to auction. And he'd had the piano put into storage.

Ruth being musical was something Frederick still couldn't take in. Who would have thought it?

Although he was more than willing to pay for her education, as she'd requested, he'd found that Josh had recently altered his will to include Ruth. All in all, there was very little for Frederick to worry about, concerning her finances; she would be well able to educate herself, and she and Nora could buy that cottage Nora wanted and could live comfortably. This had put his mind to rest, but not his inner feelings. They would remain in turmoil, and he couldn't foresee a time when they would ever be at peace. But he had Katrina – an easy-natured woman and a passionate one – and he needed to settle down and be a good husband to her, and a father to their children, if that occasion arose. He knew he must also make his mind up that, once Ruth was settled, he would never seek to see her again.

With these thoughts to keep him company, as well as much concerning the cotton industry, which he had begun to find fascinating, Frederick made good time and reached the inn by two in the afternoon, with a good three hours of riding behind him. A jug of ale and a slice off a side of beef, with some onions and a chunk of the innkeeper's wife's home-made bread, beckoned him. He hadn't meant to stop to eat, but now he was here, he couldn't resist.

'Nice t'see you, M'Lord. Your fresh mount will be got ready for you. He's been sensing you were near and started to kick his stable door, so we had to let him out. He's a sight for sore eyes, galloping and whinnying whilst tossing his mane. I'd say you're in for a spirited ride on that one. So, whilst the groom sees to that, you will partake of some good food, won't you? It is all ready for you.'

Hearing about the high spirit of his horse gave Frederick

a tinge of excitement and an eagerness to get going. His next love, after gambling, was horseriding; and Dandy Lad was his favourite of all the horses he'd ever owned. Gallient, which had seen him safely thus far, was a steady ride, taking care and not wanting to test the waters and stride out. He could set a fair pace, but nothing like Dandy Lad, which was a thrill to ride. Dangerous and carefree. He took some handling and always left Frederick feeling exhilarated.

'Your ale is a fine brew, Innkeeper. It has slaked my thirst without making me want to snooze. I will be on my way, once I have finished this cheese – a nice finishing dish to the beef. Have my bill ready . . . Good God! What is that on the news-sheet you have there?'

'Just the racing results, M'Lord. I'm a keen follower, as you know.'

'No, on the page at the back of what you're reading. It can't be!'

'Oh, that witch's tale, aye. That's a funny one. Thought they'd all died off. Haven't heard tell of any, and those I have were probably just fantasy.'

'Hand it to me, man! Oh, I beg your pardon, I didn't mean to be rude, but I think the story concerns someone I know.'

The headlines flashed before him:

MURDER TRIAL OF A WITCH
Has witchcraft reared its ugly head again?

Instinctively Frederick knew it concerned Ruth. Frantically reading the story, he found that indeed it did: 'A girl being held in Wakefield Prison, Ruth Dovecote, is being accused of the murder of a security . . .'

God, Ruth, what have you done? Oh, my darling.

What was he thinking? If Ruth did this killing, and it seemed very unlikely, she must have been provoked beyond endurance or trying to defend herself. What did it say? 'The unexplained death . . .'

Did they really think Ruth used witchcraft? For goodness' sake, it wasn't possible. But even as he thought the words, he had to admit that strange things did happen around Ruth. *Stop this. It's ridiculous – they are all coincidences.*

Reading further, he found that the case had been adjourned. And he was heartened to note that there was a group of lawyers who were of a like mind to himself and believed that the poor should be helped. *Thank God!* This Cotram fellow had things in hand, by the sound of it. The trial was set for two weeks after the hearing, which had been held two days ago.

Frederick made up his mind to contact Cotram and tell him of his interest in Ruth, then he'd have the man checked out and get a better defence counsel on the case, if need be. In the meantime he needed to get home – to be with Katrina and try to put some normality into their lives. There was his honeymoon in France to finalize. The year would be out before they could go, at this rate, and that wasn't fair to Katrina.

Frederick could sense the atmosphere when he arrived home. Even though the house was empty of his family, the staff seemed on edge somehow. Sighing, he told himself it was to be expected, with three women left to their own devices. Mother would be trying to hang onto her role, Katrina would be fighting to take the reins, and Marcia . . . well, that little minx could have caused all kinds of mayhem, and no doubt the staff had been caught up in the middle of it all.

The first thing that met him on his desk were two piles of invitations. Glancing at them, he could see that the smallest pile consisted of invitations awaiting his answer, but the other invitations sat on top of a list of names – some with ticks next to them, others left blank – no doubt needing his approval. *Oh Lord, they have been planning a party!* A quick look at the date told him it was set to take place in two weeks. Damn and blast it – that clashed with the trial. He had to be there for Ruth, he had to be!

Striding into the hall, he found Crowther hovering. 'Where is everybody, Crowther? A man comes home after being away for weeks, and no one is here to greet him. It's bad form.'

'Yes, M'Lord. I believe the ladies are delayed in town. A messenger came to tell us to hold dinner for a while.'

'Bloody hell. Well, see that my bath is run. I will take it now. And have a stiff brandy brought to me. And make sure there is plenty of hot water, so that my bath can be topped up. I need to soak a while and ease my saddle-sores. Dandy Lad played havoc with me.'

Scurrying away in the only way butlers can, with an air of both dignity and finesse, Crowther left him. At that moment Frederick could have kicked something, as frustration vied with misery in him. Instead he returned to his office.

What should he do? Could he refuse to give his permission for the bloody ball that Katrina had arranged, just so that he could be with Ruth? No, he couldn't see a way that could happen. The invitations told him that a lot of planning had gone into the event – Katrina's first ball – and he couldn't thwart her. Picking up the top invitation, he read:

The Earl of Harrogate, Lord Rollinson, and Lady Rollinson extend an invite to Lord Bellinger and Lady Henrietta to their Late-Summer Ball.

As he read on, it became clear that this wasn't just a ball, but a whole weekend, as there was also a poker game in the afternoon of the day of the ball, for the gentlemen, and a croquet game for the ladies. The following day a shooting party was planned with, if the weather permitted, a picnic by the lake afterwards, when the bagged game would be spit-roasted for lunch! *My God, Katrina, why the hell didn't you contact me about this?*

But then he would have consented, and he must allow her to be mistress of his house and to have a free hand in that domain. *If only it didn't clash with a time when Ruth will need me!* And to see bloody Bellinger at the top of the list of invitees . . . That swine! *Oh, for goodness' sake, I must snap out of this. At this rate I'll be having my first argument with my new wife, and she least deserves the backlash of all that is going on in my life.* Calming himself, Frederick could see that the list was in alphabetical order, and that was the reason for Bellinger heading it. With a wry smile at his own little-boy tantrum, he made his way to his bedroom.

It was a familiar route, but one that had seen immense changes. How they had been accomplished in just a few short weeks, he couldn't imagine. Katrina had done well. He liked her choice of soft green on the walls of the hall, with the cornice and gargoyles in a stark white creating a pleasant contrast. The whole effect was complemented by the newly stained solid-oak doors and skirting, and created an excellent background to the French furniture and family portraits that lined the walls as he ascended the stairs – all of which looked freshly cleaned.

Admitting to a sense of relief at Katrina's taste, he found himself curious as to what she'd done with the rest of the house and couldn't resist turning round and going back to check out his favourite room.

Amazement seized him as he opened the door. Mother must have told Katrina how much he loved this drawing room, and she had kept it almost the same. The golds and silvers were richer, as the upholstery had been renewed. The carpet, the same wine colour as before, was new, though he had liked the old one, which was shabby and threadbare in places. But then he knew it would have looked awful against the freshness of everything else. His favourite pieces of furniture – his father's chair, the deep couch and all the occasional furniture – looked grand and very inviting, though he noticed that his mother's writing desk was missing; in its place stood a new one in the bay window. It was one in much the same style, with elegant bowed legs, an inlaid pattern of a lighter colour than the rest of the deep mahogany, and new desk accessories: a silver ink-blotter and inkwell and a cut-glass paperweight.

The only other real change was that where his mother's portrait had hung over the fireplace, there was now one of Katrina, looking very beautiful. He had a moment of feeling sorry for his mother, but she had prepared herself for this happening. At least she was still resident in the house and hadn't had to move to the dower-house, and he was sure Katrina would have given her a choice of sitting rooms for herself and would have allowed her to furnish it with what-ever she chose. That's probably where the desk and portrait had gone. 'Yes, Katrina, you have done well. This house is taking on the persona of being our home. Quite a clever achievement in such a short time.'

This he had said out loud to her picture, which he gazed at for a long moment, allowing his imagination free rein. His thoughts turned to the passionate first week of their union, and a longing for her set up a reaction in his groin that was more than pleasant, giving him an urge to lie with his wife as soon as he could, but at the same time leaving him asking questions of himself. *How can I feel like this about Katrina, when it is Ruth I love?* Having Ruth back in his thoughts, his desire increased, but soon turned sour. *What kind of a man am I? I have a basic sexual need for what Katrina gives me, but a longing to give that same experience to Ruth.* As he closed the door and headed back upstairs, he knew it was more than a longing to satisfy himself with Ruth; it was a need to make her part of himself, to give his soul to her, to protect her and enclose her in the greatest love he was capable of giving.

Relaxing back in the hot water a few minutes later, with the fire crackling to one side of him, his brandy glistening in the crystal glass, and his staff told to leave him until he rang for them, he felt his heart begin to bleed tears of anguish for his love. Without warning, these tears spilled from his eyes. *Why? Why has Ruth to suffer so much?* He had to bring an end to it – he had to. *But how?*

Katrina paced her room. She hadn't yet greeted her husband. He was in the adjoining room, she knew that, but she couldn't hear him moving around and didn't like to disturb him. The last couple of weeks of his absence had been uncomfortable, though made less so by Lady Eleonore's handling of the situation.

At first Lady Eleonore hadn't mentioned it, and the couple of days that Simon Bellinger had been here had passed relatively smoothly on the surface, except for Marcia's constant innuendoes. Simon had met Katrina in the garden the next day and had told her he'd tried to visit her, but had seen the dowager walking up and down the landing and so he had gone back to his own room. This had partly pleased Katrina, but alarmed her at the same time, as it showed he wasn't giving up, no matter what. How was she to cope with it?

Lady Eleonore had taken her to one side once Lord Bellinger had left and had said, 'My dear Katrina, I must mention an unfortunate incident. I know how it looked, but I also know you would not do such a thing. The Bellingers of this world are difficult to handle and can have any woman they want fall in love with them. Once it happens, they take what they want and then move on to the next conquest. You do know that Bellinger was making overtures towards Marcia that very evening? That is typical behaviour of his kind. Now, I don't want you to even think of telling Frederick. It would be disastrous. He already has issues with the man, and we don't want them escalating. Throw yourself into another project, dear, as your plans for refurbishing the house are all finished or well under way. A party – that would be the thing. And when Frederick is home, concentrate on all that is good about him, and you may find that you fall in love with him in a much more solid and sustaining way than your fancy for Bellinger.'

Katrina had tried to make an immediate protest. 'But, Lady Eleonore, I do not—' It had been cut off before she'd finished.

'Accept that you love, or think yourself in love with, Lord

Bellinger, Katrina, then you will be able to deal with the situation as it stands. Denial is a barrier to that. Oh, you won't be the first. It happens to most of us who have our marriages arranged, and I am sure it is happening to Frederick, too. It is a natural reaction to the feeling of being trapped with someone you didn't choose. It will pass, if you tackle it and do not give into it. I know Frederick won't; he will do his utmost to make you happy, and you must do the same for him. I will speak to the right people to stop Lord Bellinger's advances to you. Don't worry, it won't happen again.'

This had settled all discomfort between them, but had compounded Katrina's own guilt. If she could wipe away the events of her wedding night, she would. Just as she would work at not loving Simon, if she could, although she knew she couldn't. Maybe she should talk to Frederick. She felt sure he would understand. After all, he was in the same predicament, wasn't he?

A tap on her door made her jump. She wasn't properly dressed. Annie had helped her to bathe and then, donning her silk robe, Katrina had asked Annie to leave her for a while. Annoyingly, the silly girl had taken to giggling in such situations, and Katrina found it embarrassing. It was as if the girl thought she wanted to jump into bed with Frederick or something – not that she didn't, but the things on her mind were marring the joy that the thought of such an occurrence should be giving her.

The door opened slightly. 'Katrina, may I come in?'

'Of course. Oh, Frederick, it is nice to see you.' And, to her relief, it was. He stood there in the doorway, his own robe wrapped around him, looking sheepish, but with an anticipation about him that lit a similar spark within her.

302

They were in each other's arms within seconds, and it felt as though the world had been put to rights. Yes, she could love this dear, kind man, she knew that, and at that moment she wanted to show him how much, and be rid of the conflict inside her.

Words were not necessary between them. Their kisses spoke all that needed to be said, as he guided Katrina towards her bed. Having him on top of her, and entering her, was a natural progression, and one that her whole body welcomed and accepted, as the thrill of his thrusting deep into her drew a moan of abandonment, and endearments she never thought to utter to him. 'Oh, Frederick, my love, my husband. Oh God, I have missed you!' The words strangled in her throat as it tightened in response to the clenching of her muscles, while a sensation built in her that she wanted so much, and cried out for. 'More, please . . . more.'

His reaction of thrusting ever deeper and harder brought the feeling to a climax that she could hardly bear. Forced to push down, Katrina knew that her face had contorted. Sweat ran from her, and gasps that she didn't consciously compose came tumbling from her. 'Stay there, yes; yes, oh God, I love you.'

Exquisite pleasure washed over her, consuming her very being as it ascended to a delicate height she knew she couldn't hold on to. When her body released all she had to give, she fragmented into a thousand pieces, as the shattering experience exploded and left her spent.

Frederick had burst into her at that same moment, and his pulsating had pleasured her in a different way, as she'd still clenched him. But the vocal expression of his pleasure had shocked her further, as it held words of love – just as hers had done. Now he lay panting, not yet removed from her, but with his weight to the side of her. He was, she knew, just as fragmented and stunned into a sense of confusion as she herself was, by where their union had taken them.

How could that happen, when they weren't in love? Though she knew she did experience a love in her for Frederick. No one could give what they had just given of themselves to someone they didn't love. Yes, she understood that it might be possible to enjoy the act with anyone who had the skill, but that hadn't been skill; it had had a life of its own. What had given it that life? Not experience – neither of them had that. Instinct then? Animal instinct? No. She rejected that. Feeling? Yes. It had to be. Oh God, was she in love with Simon or Frederick? For the first time, Katrina felt doubt about her feelings for Simon and questioned how she felt about Frederick.

His movement had her tensing. As he withdrew from her and rolled over to the other side of the bed, she sensed there were things he needed to say, but she was frightened to hear them.

'Katrina! Oh God, Katrina. Are you feeling like me? Are you afraid of what we have unleashed?'

That was it; he had pinpointed it. Yes. They had unleashed something neither of them knew how to handle. Her 'yes' came out in a soft voice. She couldn't manage anything more.

'I – I have a confession.'

Turning towards him, she put her finger on his lips. 'No. Whatever it is, let us put all things behind us. We have a chance now. We have tapped into something wonderful. We both felt it, and know it was special. We both expressed our love. Let us build on that, from this point forward. We can, I know we can. If there is anything in either of us that we

304

shouldn't have done, or have felt for another, it is time to let it go. I can do that. You must, too.'

She saw Frederick's hesitation. It rekindled the fear in her, as she thought he might not listen to her.

'I know you are a man with a conscience and a strong sense of honour. I know you feel you must be truthful, but that can only harm the fragile link we have. Nothing is worth that. We have a lifetime together. It can be a happy one, if we go forward now. We shouldn't taint that prospect with confessions – neither yours nor mine . . .'

'You have some, too?'

She didn't get to answer that, as the sound of a door clicking shut, coming from Frederick's room, got them both sitting up.

'What the bloody hell? I'm sorry, I didn't mean to swear, but did you hear that?'

'I did.' Anxiety trickled through Katrina. *Marcia? Has Marcia been listening in again, as she did on my wedding night? Only this time has she dared go into Frederick's room? Oh God, no. Don't let that have happened. Don't let Marcia have heard all that has passed between me and Frederick, please.*

These thoughts trembled through Katrina as she knew what Marcia's jealous revenge might cause.

26

Frederick & Katrina

A Shattered Illusion

Before dinner, Frederick asked that Amy be sent to him. Waiting for her in an anteroom just off the housekeeper's office, where in the past his mother had instructed the staff and where he now assumed Katrina did so, he thought about the last two hours. He knew there was a passion between himself and Katrina that they could not understand, something that gripped them both and cemented their feelings for one another. He knew, too, that the feeling didn't come near what he felt for Ruth, but it would be enough. That's what Katrina had said. They should go forward from it, and he intended to. Somewhere inside him he did hold a love for Katrina, as she was proving to be a superb wife and was running his house to perfection – even managing his mother, who, to his shock and surprise, had stepped aside in the most gracious manner. How Katrina had managed that, he'd never know.

The sound of someone leaving his room had been a strange twist to the amazing encounter he'd shared with Katrina. Had one of the servants taken to listening in on them? For what reason? Was one of them a pervert? One thing he knew: none of them would have gone in there on legitimate business, when he had left strict instructions not to disturb him. Pondering the mystery made it become even stranger, as he discounted this and that as the possible reason. There just didn't seem to be any answers.

Amy's arrival with the housekeeper, and her bobbing a curtsy to him, brought him out of his reverie. 'You may leave us together.' He nodded his head towards the housekeeper, as he couldn't for the life of him remember her name. Her 'Humph!' at this request angered his already-fragile temper. Fuelled by the sneak in the bedroom and by his extreme tiredness, he acted out of character and did what on other occasions he would have avoided, and bawled her out in front of Amy, a lower-standing member of staff. 'Madam, do not show disdain at any order I give you. Never. You will carry out my orders to the letter, no matter what you think of them!'

'I beg your pardon, M'Lord. I'm sorry, I didn't mean to offend you.'

'Very well, but please do not act in such a way again.'

As she went to reply, he raised his hand. 'That will be all.' He didn't have the time or the inclination to banter with her. At last the housekeeper left, and he could turn his attention to Amy. 'Well now, Amy, how are you faring?'

'I'm doing reet well, M'Lord. I passed me test a few days back and I'm in for another one next week, Me test were on adding and subtraction, and this one is on fractions. I find meself dividing everything into portions – fifths and sixths – then taking pieces of them and adding them to other pieces. I think I have it mastered now.'

'Good, good. Yes, there was an excellent report on your progress in that field. But are you happy?'

'To speak honestly, M'Lord, part of me ain't. At least one-third of me.' Though this concerned him, he couldn't help but smile. Amy seemed to be applying fractions to everything, and this became more apparent as she continued, 'And whilst half of the other two-thirds is muddling along, the other half is still deep in the doldrums over everything that has happened.'

'That is understandable – the last half, that is: feeling in the doldrums.' He was doing it himself now! 'But why is it that the other two parts, the half of the two-thirds and the third, are unhappy and just muddling along?' *Good Lord, I'm confused now!*

'Well, M'Lord, I don't like the work in service, and I don't get no pay, though they put a good deal on me. I don't think they like me, as I am different to them in how you're educating me. That's the third. And the half of the third, one-sixth, is because I don't feel I am following what I am meant to do.'

'Oh? That is disappointing, as I had you down as an excellent nanny in the future, when I hope our need for one becomes a reality. And I have had good reports on your progress in that field, too. What do you feel you should be doing?'

Listening to her tale brought to mind Ruth and her extraordinary quest to learn music. Now, it appeared, Amy had plans that he would not have expected, either. Something or someone – maybe their mother? – had instilled in these girls the idea that they could achieve whatever they wanted to, though it seemed that Amy's desire to help others, and her plan to start to give to the homeless, once she was earning, had been influenced by the vision she'd had whilst in a coma brought on by illness. 'So, this little lady who spoke to you, you think she was the Mother of God? Well, now, she may well get her wish to have you better others' lives and make a difference. I have much the same desire. And just maybe, if you continue to improve in your education, you might be the person to help me with it. But to do so, you will need the skills my ex-nanny can teach you about the health of children, and you will need the level of intelligence of a tutor, which is what your schooling is aimed at . . .'

Frederick went on to tell her of his plans, and Amy seemed captivated – excited even – and showed great eagerness to be involved in his scheme to help the homeless. 'But as I said, that is for the future. I have too much on at the moment to do anything other than donate to those who are already trying to help. And, I am sorry to say, this is not what I have called you in for, Amy. I have some bad news for you.'

Her face turned ashen, and for a moment she looked as though she might sink to the floor.

'Sit down, Amy. There, that's right. Don't worry, it's perfectly all right to do so, as I have suggested it to you.'

'What – what is it, M'Lord? Has sommat happened to Ruth? I thought as she were safe in the cell? Or is it the lads? I don't know as I can take—'

'Look, it isn't the boys. It is Ruth, but I promise everything will be all right.'

Tears were tumbling down Amy's cheeks by the time he'd finished telling her what he knew.

'It will be fine. I will see to it. There is no burning of witches, or even hanging them now. At most, she will get a longer term in prison.' His heart split with pain as he said this. He couldn't bear it, he couldn't. He had to prove her innocence. *She must be innocent.* 'Amy, dry your eyes. I will have a man go and find out if these lawyers are any good. My man will come up with something; and if the lawyers are not right for the job, we will hire better ones. Do you understand?'

'Aye, I does.'

The weak nodding of Amy's head told him that she didn't altogether, but for now he could do nothing about that. He himself only had a few newsletter lines to go on. 'Now, about the boys. They will still be travelling to Australia. They only set off a week ago and it will take them eight to ten weeks to get there – probably more. I had news from the Governor on the Isle of Wight to say they had behaved themselves and caused no problems, so that bodes well for them. Once they land, I will contact the Governor of Australia and ask him to send me regular reports. I know him; we went to school together. A good chap who won't let us down.'

'Thank you, M'Lord.'

'Before you go, Amy, if I can arrange it, would you be willing to go to the trial and report back to me what happens? If Ruth comes out of this unblemished, she could be out of there in three months.'

'Aye, I would. I'd be scared, but I'd like our Ruth to see someone there for her who loves her. But if . . . *when* she gets out, where will she go then, M'Lord?'

At his telling of Ruth's plans, Amy showed no surprise. 'She's allus loved music. Not that we heard much, unless the fair came to our town, and then Ruth would be so happy. She'd stand for hours listening, and nothing bothered her. Not the pain in her back, nor her not being able to walk proper – nothing. Ma used to have to send me to fetch her home for her tea.'

This little snippet of information had Frederick longing to right all the wrongs in Ruth's life, and in Amy's – not just now, but in the past. And it made him more determined than ever to try to do something for others in the same plight.

'You may go now, Amy. I will let you know anything I find out. I am sorry dinner is to be served late, as that will mean you will all be working late, and you must be tired.'

'Ta, and aye, there's a few as are disgruntled, as they were planning on going to the "Free 'n' Easy" tonight. Me friend Lettie has a beautiful voice and they were to show her off. It seems as she can get took on with one of them travelling shows, but I don't want her to go.'

Not wanting to continue this conversation, but amused that Amy had relaxed so much she felt entitled to chat to him as if he were one of her own, Frederick just nodded and indicated the door. As she curtsied and left, it occurred to him that although he would never have thought it, the lower classes did possess talent, just as those of his own standing did. And, like Amy, they could be taught and educated, and surely that would be the direction in which things should go, as education would show them how they could better their own prospects. *What am I thinking? Radical thoughts like that will be frowned upon in most sections of the society I move in. Though I do know some who are of a like mind. Maybe I, with them, can make the difference that Amy's 'little lady' was talking about?*

As he escorted Katrina into the dining room, Frederick felt a moment of pride in her, and a tingle of anticipation as he thought of their time together and the promise of more to come, which he read in her smile. She really was the most beautiful creature and, from his experience so far, a really lovely one, too. He was a very lucky man.

After grace, Katrina looked towards him. Her eyes held a sparkle of mischief and he detected an air of excitement about her. 'What is it, my dear?'

'Oh, I can't tell you, not yet. You have to wait until after dinner, then you will see for yourself!'

Marcia sighed and shifted in her seat. 'Oh, for heaven's sake, just tell him, or I will!'

'Tell me what?'

'Marcia, I don't think it is your place to tell anyone *anything*!' No one could mistake the warning in his mother's voice as she said this. Alarm bells started up inside Frederick.

'If there is something I should know, Ladies, then please be kind enough to tell me.'

'It's a surprise, my dear Frederick, a surprise – but a nice one, I promise. But if you cannot wait . . . ?' Again, that sense of mischief, this time lighting up Katrina's nervous smile.

'Yes, I can wait, but I hope you haven't done anything too elaborate. I haven't brought anything back for you. I – I, well, there has been so much going on.'

'As there has been here. You don't know the half, dear brother-in-law.'

'Marcia, please!'

'I am sorry, Lady Eleonore, but this is all a farce – all of it. And you and Katrina know it!'

'Marcia, no. No, don't!'

At this, from a now very distressed Katrina, Frederick turned to his butler. 'Crowther, please leave the room and clear it of your staff. We will ring when we are ready to begin dinner.'

Once the room emptied, he looked towards his wife. 'Katrina, would you like to talk to me in private?'

'It is not a private matter. She is in love with Lord Bellinger.'

'Stop this at once, Marcia!'

His mother's voice would have halted him, but not so Marcia. 'I won't. Frederick should know. Your so-called wife slept with—'

'Marcia. Please stop. Please.' Katrina's plea should have made him halt this at once, but he couldn't. He had to hear it all.

'I won't stop. You don't deserve Frederick, and you should never have married him. I LOVE HIM. I WANTED HIM, AND YOU STOLE HIM!'

'Marcia! Oh, Frederick, bring this to an end, please!'

'Of course, Mother. I am sorry. Katrina, kindly accompany me to my study.' Rising, he shut his ears to Marcia's sobbing and marched out of the room. Humiliation stung him. Something told him this was all true, and with that realization came a shattering of his illusions. He'd been hoodwinked. *Katrina and Bellinger – my God!* It made him sick to think of it.

'Well?'

Why did this hurt her so much? The betrayal of this good man – why did she care? There was nothing Frederick could do to her, was there? But as she glared back at him and held his violet eyes, Katrina knew why. She loved him. How that had happened, she did not know, but it had. Lord Bellinger was just a memory – nothing to her. Nothing but a filthy encounter she wished she could tear from her. As this revelation hit her, it felt as if she'd been struck hard in the stomach. Her insides folded; her head swam. Hitting the floor was the last thing she remembered.

Frederick's voice, tender and caring, filtered through to her. 'Drink this, Katrina. Take a sip. It will all be all right. I'm here for you.'

Opening her eyes, she looked up into his. The hostility had gone. Back with her was the Frederick she knew, and knew she loved. 'Oh, Frederick. Can you forgive me?'

'Are you saying it is true?'

His hostility was back.

'I thought you had fainted because you were shocked at me challenging you. God, Katrina, how could you? When?'

Nausea washed over her. Sweat stood out on her face and seeped from her every pore. 'Frederick, I'm going to be sick!'

'I'll fetch Mother. God, this is a mess. I can't believe it. Bellinger – Christ!' The door slammed, only to be opened a few minutes later by Lady Eleonore.

'My poor dear, that dreadful sister of yours deserves a good slap. How dare she bring you into disrepute? I've talked and talked to her. Your mother has committed many serious errors in your upbringing, but in not schooling you in discretion, she has left you both vulnerable. It is a paramount requirement of our class. Yes, we have affairs, but no one speaks of them. Marcia is a damned idiot! She could have played it so differently and got what she desires at a later date.'

This shocked Katrina more than anything Lady Eleonore had said before, but there was something she needed to talk to someone about – something that had worried her since her wedding day: she hadn't seen her monthly bleeding at all. 'Lady Eleonore, I think I am pregnant. And, I – I don't know whose it is. I – I want it to be Frederick's. I love him. I love him more than life itself. I just took too long to realize it. Oh God, what have I done?'

Rising slowly, Lady Eleonore, for the first time since recovering from the accident, looked the epitome of a dowager. In one split second she had lost the regal stance of her youthful appearance and had taken on the look of her true age. Her shoulders slumped; her eyes glazed in a confused expression and her lips quivered. 'You mean, you had this affair *after* you married my son? Not at that cad Bellinger's ball, when he tried to discredit you?'

Scrunching up into the corner of the sofa in Lady Eleonore's sitting room, where Frederick must have carried her, Katrina felt like a cornered animal. Fear dropped like a lead weight into her stomach, and this time she did vomit. Undignified though it was, she could not stop the vile-tasting liquid spouting from her mouth.

'My God, I don't know what to say.' This Lady Eleonore uttered in a whisper as she pulled the bell cord twice.

Nothing could be resolved then. Everything was taken up with the cleaning, of both Katrina and the room. By a servant she knew as Mildred and the other one, whom she knew was part of *that* family. They helped her to her room.

Annie fussed over her, preparing her a bath, washing her tenderly and swathing her in a warmed, fresh nightgown. She even put a hot jar into her bed. And all without speaking.

'Thank you, Annie. Do – do you know?'

'Aye, I does, Lady Katrina. That wicked sister of yours

315

stood in the hall and screamed it out, after we brought you up here. But I told everyone – including the dowager – that it was a lie. That I had seen you to bed that night, and I seen Lord Frederick in your bed.'

'But you didn't. He was on the floor.'

'I told them he was in your bed afore he got up and fainted. No one knows any different, nor will they.'

'Thank you, Annie. I've made a dreadful mistake. I love Lord Frederick. I love him with everything that is in me. I found out too late.'

'I know, M'Lady, I know. And I reckon as he loves you, and don't know it yet! He was like a raging bull when you weren't here earlier, after he came home. And then . . . well, he were with you a long time, once you came home.'

'He was, and it was the best thing that has happened in my life. Surely my child will be his? It has to be. It was only the once with Lord Bellinger.'

'Aye, well, me ma says it can only take the once.'

'Oh, Annie, what am I going to do? I feel so miserable and I have brought it all down upon myself, and upon Lord Frederick and Lady Eleonore. Oh God!'

'I reckon as the least said and done is best. Lady Eleonore gave me this potion for you. She said it would help you to sleep. I'll fetch you a cup of hot milk and then you can take it. Things'll look better in the light of day.'

But nothing looked better when Katrina woke. The heavy, drugged feeling held her low. The news that Frederick had left for Blackburn, without saying when he would be back, punished her more than anyone could imagine. And despite her stubborn nature, which never allowed her to give in, she crumpled into a ball on her bed and wept.

Hours passed, before a knock at her door announced her mother-in-law. Lady Eleonore had regained her composure and looked younger than her years once more. 'Katrina, dear, this won't help matters. This is a dreadful situation, but it can – and has to – be handled. I have sent a telegram to your mother and received one back. She is on her way.'

'Oh no.'

'Yes. It is essential that we come together and contain this. The servants have all been briefed to the effect that your sister – that stupid girl – is ill. I have had Marcia removed to a friend of mine, until your mother can take her home, but in the meantime the staff believe she has gone to a sanatorium. Annie is a great help. She insists that she knows without doubt that you and Frederick slept together that night. I hope and pray that, with these measures in place, the staff are convinced, and this will not travel from servant to servant in house after house, as these things are inclined to. The staff believe that you are distraught about your sister's illness and that Frederick has gone to fetch your mother. Now I need you to play your part. You are to wash, dress and come down, with your head held high and with as much dignity as you can muster. I want you to attend me in my sitting room, where we will talk and you will tell me how all this came to happen. If I die trying, I am going to disgrace that – that . . . Ooh, I don't have words to describe him. But he will pay. Oh yes, Lord Bellinger will pay dearly for this.'

27

Ruth

The Trial

Ruth couldn't have said what hurt her most. Agony encased her whole body. Lying on the hard bench in this solitary-confinement cell had caused the pain in her back to flare up, and it radiated through her. But at least things had improved a little since the first hearing.

Initially the blanket darkness had enveloped her, making her feel as though she was in a coffin. Panic had quickened her breathing until she thought she would suffocate, but she had got used to it and had kept her eyes closed most of the time.

The worst was not knowing whether it was day or night. She'd tried to keep the hours in her head. She'd worked on the assumption that the night was when the rats' scurrying feet made a noise that was almost as loud as the clogs of the cotton-mill workers going to and coming back from their shift. Her screams, when the rats first appeared, had worn her out and made her feel as though she was going mad. Now, when they came, she scrunched herself up in the corner and waited, knocking the rats away from her if she felt their bodies touch her.

Dirt had matted her most of the time in those early days, and her slop bucket had overflowed or been knocked over by the rats, before anyone came to change it. The first time someone came she'd begged them to help her. Her sobs had hurt her chest with the vicious way they had flowed from her, but the man had kicked her away, knocking Ruth unconscious. His action held fear of her rather than malice. After that, she'd remained quiet and as far away as she could from whoever came to her cell.

Every few days or so – she had no way of marking the time – her door would open and buckets of soapy water gushed in, thrown with force by a person unseen. Sometimes it drenched her. And then for a little while afterwards the putrid air would lighten and she would feel a bit better. Her only food had been shoved inside her cell through the door: a basin of water and some bread. As soon as the door had closed, she'd made her way to her meagre meal, holding onto the wall and counting the bricks, moving slowly so as not to knock it over, and then lifting it and taking it to the bench. She eked out this ration, not knowing if she would get another. But it had come each day.

Tiredness had become her friend, and still was, as the more she slept, the less she needed to endure it all. After the first hearing at the court, things had improved. Now she had a bowl of water and a towel every day, and a candle and matches, which she made last by blowing the candle out every so often. Her slop bucket was emptied two or three times a day. This, she knew, was because she had a lawyer.

Through all of this she worried about Alice: how could an old lady like Alice stand this? But she had been afraid to ask. It had been the first thing she'd told Mr Cotram, but not even he had been able to gain access to her, even though

Alice was a key witness. When he'd said he would get an order, or some such, to force them to let him talk to her, they told him that Alice was too ill and was back in the hospital. He'd visited and had told Ruth that Alice wasn't conscious and was close to death. Hope had died at that moment, leaving Ruth sure of her own death; and yet her despair had vied with a wish that Alice, for her own sake, would die and know some peace.

After this Ruth had been convinced that she would hang – so much so that she tried to strangle herself, to see what it felt like. It hurt, and she hadn't even been able to cut off her breath. The rope would do that. The pressure would be so strong, the loop so tight . . . And then her neck would break, when the rope fell as far as it could go. Would she feel the pain of that?

Nothing had given her hope until Haydon Green had come. She'd held onto that hope as soon as she received the message Mr Cotram had given her from the Earl, saying that he had put Haydon onto trying to gather what information he could to help her. This went some way towards Ruth almost forgiving the Earl for not coming to see her. Though it was strange that he hadn't said why he hadn't been. Mr Cotram had no idea, and had been shocked that Ruth had such a friend and yet had suffered so much.

She wondered if it was because the Earl didn't want to be seen to be giving her too much attention. But she discarded this, as a man such as the Earl could do as he pleased, and no one would dare to stop him.

The key turning in her cell door, and hearing Mr Cotram's cough – the one he gave every time as he was about to enter – stopped her heart. Today must be the day. He'd said the next time he'd come would be the day of the trial.

Shifting her bottom and twisting herself till her one good leg hung over the side of the bench, Ruth tried to rise. Holding onto the wall and dragging her gammy leg, which was already hurting as much as she could endure, she groaned. It throbbed with even more pain as she lowered it over the side, too. It hurt both on the inside and the outside, as the sores, which were still not healed, ate into her flesh, exposing her bones in places; and they hung in pus-filled sacs of skin in others. Her despair deepened as she reached the door and the stench of ale-soaked breath hit her. Mr Cotram was drunk. His greeting confirmed this.

'Ulshers. That's what they are on your legs, girl. Ulshers, and they should be sheen to. You could get gangrene, then you'll be in a proper mesh, girl. I know ulshers when I see them. I've had enough, on account of my blood doeshn't go round fast enough, or so the quack shays.'

Anger at him, and at the plight he might put her in, saw Ruth talking to him in a sharp tone. 'Well, ta very much for caring about me, but I reckon as you'll more than likely not have to worry later, when they put the noose round me neck. No ulcers will matter then.'

'That won't happen. I have a defensh.'

If she'd been able to, she would have clawed at him, but not even her despair and anger could move her body. 'The judge will laugh in your face, the state you're in. I thought as you had more respect for the likes of me, but if you did, you would have made sure you were sober, so as you could give me every chance. I stand none now.'

All hope leaked from her as she looked at the lawyer, who'd given her the very hope she was now losing. His body wobbled on unsteady legs. Some pity came into Ruth for him, as his expression showed his remorse. His jowls hung, his eyes did not look at her, and his lips worked as if he was chewing something, but she knew this was his effort to control them, as they seemed to want to hang slack.

As she'd got to know Mr Cotram over the last weeks, she'd found him to be a kind man, a learned one, and one with his heart in the right place, with a desire to make the lot of those such as herself a little better. It was a shame the drink had taken him. It was this affliction, Haydon Green had told her, that had gradually lost him clients and put him almost on the breadline. Feeling the pinch, he'd begun to think what it was like for those who never even reached the breadline, and wondered how they got justice. He'd talked to other lawyers. And so the Union of Solicitors and Lawyers against Injustice for the Poor was formed. But it appeared that most of its members were too busy to participate actively, so they just put money into a monthly fund and left Mr Cotram to take up the cases he felt were most deserving. This made her wonder if the lawyers really cared, as they must know that, at worst, he'd not turn up at court when he should, and at best he wasn't really capable, as he couldn't leave the drink be.

'Look, I'm sorry as I snapped. It's cos I'm scared. From what happened last time, the judge ain't for me and would sooner see me hanged than look at me. And you coming today must mean that I have to go to court?'

'It doesh. But nothing will happen, I promish. I can shober up. The trial is the last of the day – two o'clock – and it is only twelve now. I just wanted to shee as you were all right and to get you these clothes.' The candle flickered from the draught he caused as he threw a parcel onto her bench. 'You're not to worry. Haydon has given me plenty of stuff and I have a good case. I'll go now and shleep this off, as I've all my papers in order for M'Lord judge.' With this, he swayed towards the door, where he turned, saying, 'I'll tell the warden as shomeone should dress your wounds.'

'Naw, don't do that. The more fuss is made of me, the worse they treat me. Does you know if the Earl is coming today?'

'He is. And he told me to tell you he has arranged for your shister—'

'Our Amy! Naw. What if I get to hang? He shouldn't have done that. It'll be too much for us both. She—'

'I can't stop it. The Earl is a law unto himshelf.'

There was nothing more she could say. It was all out of her hands. Just before he left, Ruth asked him to set the bowl of water and towel on the bottom of her bed. She'd have to make some effort to look better than she knew she must appear, if only for Amy's sake.

The door of her cell closed, enclosing her once more in darkness. She lay back down, careful to avoid the water. She'd become adept at moving around in the dark and sensing where things were.

The tear that seeped out of the corner of her eye trickled into her ear, as the folk she'd loved and lost came to mind. *And to think, Ma, that I'm to see our Amy today. But, eeh, I didn't want to see her while I'm like this. Help me, Ma, help me.*

Wiping the tear away did no good, as another followed. Inside she felt a hollow pit of despair. If this were her last day on earth, she would face it with courage, like her ma said: 'Build up your self-worth, me precious lass, as despite your gammy leg, you are worthy of folk's respect, but you'll only get it if you respect yourself.'

With this thought, she pulled herself through the pain to

sit up and set about washing and dressing herself. If for no one else, she had to look right for Amy.

It lifted Ruth some to have the same warden come for her. Though he showed no sign of knowing her, she knew this was to keep the help that he gave secret, and she respected that. Coming out into the light hurt her eyes, making it impossible to open them until they arrived at the court. It was the shock that overcame her, as the warden clamped heavy irons on her wrists and feet, that got her opening her eyes and looking at him. His look told of his pity, but his words were harsh. 'All prisoners facing the death-penalty have to have irons on, as the likes of such go mad sometimes, when the sentence is passed. This makes it easy to drag them to the gallows and get it done.'

'It – it would be that quick?'

'Aye, afore midnight usually. Now, shut your mouth. I ain't for talking to no prisoners.'

Again she knew this was a cover, but still it hurt. 'I've to say ta for everything.'

'I said you're to shut up!'

His hands grabbed her. Ignoring her cry of agony, he lifted Ruth and carried her into the courtroom. The sound of her name, on a gasp of pain, got her looking upwards. Amy was looking down at her. The sight of her beloved sister had Ruth's heart taking on the weight of a bucket overflowing with water. Tears threatened, but she swallowed them down and smiled. Trying to raise her arm to wave proved impossible, as the irons were too heavy for her, but at least she knew she looked the best she could in the grey frock, with a white bib insert. And somehow she'd managed to tug the comb that Mr Cotram had left for her through

324

her tangled, greasy hair. While doing so, she lamented the loss of her beloved ribbon.

Just along from Amy another dear face appeared. Lines of anguish creased it. The Earl! Ruth gave him a weak smile. Did she see him wipe away a tear? A loud sob cut through the silence, bringing her attention back to Amy. 'Don't cry, our lass. Be strong for me. Everything'll be all right,' Ruth muttered.

'Shut up. You're not allowed to speak. You can be done for Contempt, or trying to influence the jury. Just keep quiet.' This the warden said in a kinder voice.

They had reached the dock and he sat her down. The iron on her gammy leg chafed at her sores. Now she could see the front of the court. The bench on the left looked busy: two men shuffled papers. The one on the right stood empty. *He hasn't come. Oh God!*

A familiar voice brought some hope back into her. 'May I approach the prisoner, Sir?'

Haydon! *Oh, thank God.*

At the warden's nod, he leaned forward. 'Hello, my dear, don't be afraid. Everything will be all right. There's some good testimonies. Have you seen Cotram?'

'Oh, Haydon, he were drunk.'

On her telling of Mr Cotram's visit, Haydon's shocked 'Good God – damn the man!' ground Ruth's fear even deeper. 'Look, I'll sort something. I'll talk to the Earl. And, Ruth, you look nice. Nothing like a witch. Keep calm, and keep your head down. Don't look at anyone. Rumour has put fear into folk. The jury are all God-fearing people, so they won't be looking to believe in witchcraft, but we don't want them thinking you try to use your powers, as it is said that just the fear of this can induce death. That's the angle the prosecution is taking. Don't give anyone reason to believe it.'

With this, she knew her own doom. How could she convince folk that she didn't try to use her powers? If the prosecutors knew about the lads back in Pradley and . . . Oh God, she mustn't think about the deaths on that terrible night of the fire. *Josh . . . my Josh.* At this, she couldn't stop the tears. They flowed without her bidding. *Perhaps I should give in. Tell them I done the murders – all of them – because there is one that is laid at me door. Going to the gallows will atone for that, and aye, it will take me out of me misery and back to Josh and Ma, Da and little Elsie. Aye, that's what I'll do. I'm sorry, our Amy. Sorry to the heart of me. But you'll come to know it's for the best. Folk'll never let me live in peace.*

With this, a serenity of the kind she'd not known for a long, long time settled in her and she knew she'd made the right decision. Even the thought of the rope tightening, and the snapping of her neck, didn't change her mind. It would all be over in a second, but her release would be eternal. She was tired and in unendurable pain. This world wasn't for her. Lifting her head, she shouted, 'God have mercy on my soul!'

Silence clawed at her, then a hubbub started up all around. Above it all she heard Amy screaming, and the Earl calling out her name: 'Ruth, no. Ruth, don't give up. Don't. RUTH!'

This last followed her into the pit of blackness into which she descended.

Cold water brought her round. It hadn't been splashed onto her, but trickled gently over her. Opening her eyes, she looked into those of her beloved Earl. 'Ruth, come on. I will speak for you. I don't care what the world thinks. Come on, my love.'

'Aye, and I will an' all,' said the warden. 'I knows what went on, M'Lord. I don't care about me job, except as being in there, I can help them, in me own way.'

'I know your way, Warden, and it is a good one. But, you know, sometimes speaking up can help even more. As you know at first hand what goes on in that terrible place, and you will be listened to. Thank you – your courage will be rewarded. Ruth, there are people here from Pradley. They seek to discredit you, but don't react to them. They don't know it, but Haydon Green has been working through all the evidence, and he was witness to some of it. He has material that will send most of those who survived to jail – and some, like Whalley Bradstone, to the gallows. Life will change for you; it will.' His head drooped. 'I did wrong by you, Ruth, my love. I should not have arranged for you to go to jail. I should have taken you right away from it all. Hidden you somewhere you wouldn't have been found. Looked after you. I – I'm sorry. Oh, Ruth, I'm sorry.'

She couldn't even smile at him. Her heart had turned to a solid mass of impenetrable coldness. And her decision had been locked inside it. Nothing could change that.

'I – I killed your brother.'

'What? My God, Ruth, you're delirious. Don't say such a thing. You didn't, it was an accident. An accident.'

In this last there was a seed of doubt. It was up to her to make the Earl believe her, so that he could let her go. 'I killed him. I hit him with the butt of his gun and he died.'

This time the Earl remained silent, staring at her, but still a little doubt showed in his eyes. And, she knew, that was the way of it. If she told the truth, she wasn't believed; and yet they could lay vile things at her door and they would all be believed.

'It – it isn't possible. Ruth, he died from injuries he sustained: a bang on the—'

'Aye, done by me. Then we put him back in the carriage and pushed it over and set about saving your ma.'

Rising from his haunches, he looked up at Amy. Ruth looked up, too. Poor Amy, her anguish wasn't deserved. *I've brought it down on her. The moment I smashed that young earl to death, I brought everything down on them all . . . Elsie's death, and the lads being sent away, never to return, and Amy shoved in that cesspit of a workhouse. I deserve to die, and I know now that is what I want.*

In a few strides the Earl was climbing the stairs to the public gallery. 'Amy – Amy, I must speak with you. Go down those steps on the other side and through the door on the left. It is the lawyer's chamber. I will meet you there.'

Once in the chamber, he asked in a voice that didn't hold aggression, as he had no intention of frightening her, 'Now, Amy, tell me – and I want the truth of it – everything that happened. Tell me: did Ruth kill my brother?'

As he listened, he knew it was a true account. It hurt his heart that his loving brother should have come to such an end, and at the hands of the woman he himself loved.

'She had to, M'Lord. She had to, as he was going to send us all to the gallows. And we hadn't done wrong. We were only there because our Ruth could never have made it over the tops. He threatened to shoot us an' all. Ruth only did it to save us, and she didn't mean for him to die. She wanted to knock him out, then we could get away. Ruth said if we had got away, we would have sent help up to them. She'd have left a note at the police station. It hurt her. It hurt her bad that he died.'

'It was self-defence! Thank God. I know Bertram. He had a hatred in him for the poor. He couldn't bear them within miles of him, and threatened to shoot them if they were. Even as a lad, he would take me to the field next to the one where the peasants worked and we'd hide in a tree with our game-guns. He would frighten me as he aimed at the heads of those bending over the crops and pretended to pull the trigger. He would have done what you said.' *Oh, Bertram. Bertram, in the end you met your own death at the hand of one of them. And well deserved. You must have terrified them. They'd just lost their mother and only had Ruth, a poor cripple, to protect them. She did what she had to do. She took your life to save those of her siblings and her own. For me, that is reason enough.*

The door opened and, bleary-eyed, Cotram walked in. The Earl had to use all his effort not to bawl him out. 'Sir, you are late. There have been some disastrous developments. Amy, go to your sister. No one will stop you. I need to talk to Mr Cotram. He is Ruth's lawyer. Tell Ruth all is well. Tell her I know, and I believe, she had to kill in self-defence. Go on, tell her. Cotram, are you ready?'

'Yes, I have checked in, so there isn't much time. I have been told the judge is angry at the delay already. I'm sorry, M'Lord.'

'Never mind that. Listen . . .'

The proceedings went on around Ruth without touching her. She had been stopped from pleading guilty, as she had intended, at the desperate request of Amy, but she had no intention of defending herself and hoped everything would go against her. She just wanted to die. It would be good to do so knowing that the Earl realized the truth of all that had happened, and that he didn't hold her to blame.

'Call Mrs McNaught of Pradley.'

It went on and on. Call this one, call that one. Each telling one lie after another, damning her. If only they knew they were helping her. Even Ruth's pain eased as her body took on a numbness that shrouded her from all that could harm her. There was to be no further harm. She was leaving this world, one way or another. *There is nothing surer than that.*

28

Katrina

Making a Stand

'Mama, I have to go to Frederick's side. This cannot go on. Lord Frederick is doing the only thing he can. He is being true to himself. I must do that, too. I must release him from the marriage, if that is what he wishes, and settle on him an amount that he can go forward with. And I need to help him in his quest to save this girl that he loves. I betrayed him with a man I thought I loved. Now I can show loyalty to him, as the man I truly love.'

'Katrina, it isn't the done thing. If this woman is his mistress, then you should be discreet about it.'

'It is a bit late to teach discretion, Veronica,' said Lady Eleonore. 'I am still very cross with you for not dealing with this vital aspect of a woman's role as a wife in our society, when schooling your daughters. If you had, none of this would be happening – except my son's efforts to help this girl, of course, whom I *know* is *not* his mistress . . . Oh, I know, Katrina, it suits you to think she is, and to be forgiving of him. It appeases your own conscience, but that is all the merit there is in the accusation. Frederick is an honourable man and, even if he did love the girl, he wouldn't do anything other than he is: helping her to get through this and seeing that she has a good future.'

'I know, Lady Eleonore, and it isn't what I think. I just want to help him, that's all. Well, and to get his forgiveness. And surely my being with him will stop any gossip. There are those who are beginning to believe Lord Bellinger, and some of the snippets in the news-sheet are outraged at it all and could make life very difficult for him. The Queen even—'

'Queen Victoria should know the truth by now. I have friends at court whom I have told everything to. Yes, everything. They are very discreet, but they will gossip about it with the Queen, which is exactly what I wanted. I doubt Lord Bellinger will ever have an audience with her, or be anywhere near anything that she attends. I am sure the Queen is watching this case very closely, and I think you are right, Katrina: you should go to him. It will look good that you are standing by him. In his last message Frederick said the trial had run for two days and would be in session again tomorrow. I believe there is only the girl's testimony to come, as she wasn't well enough to give it.'

'Is it a good thing it's lasted so long?'

'It is, Mama. It means that a lot of evidence has been heard.'

'Yes, you're right. This is a proper trial, not like some when, if the defendant is poor, they don't even have a say,' Lady Eleonore said. 'This girl has a lawyer, and Frederick hired a man to dig into everything. There are others being arrested for what happened to her previously. Frederick thinks it looks good for her, but he is worried sick about tomorrow. He says the girl has resigned herself to her own death, that she sees it as a way out. She believes she will never have any peace from the torment that got her where she is. I feel so responsible, as does Frederick. Those children should never have been arrested. They helped all they could, when we had the accident. The new police force is over-zealous, not to mention too costly.'

'If that is the case, I will go immediately to Frederick,' Katrina responded. 'Mama, can you stay here a little longer? I don't want Marcia to be at your home whilst I stay there. It will take me a long time to forgive her for what she has done.'

'Do you think you should travel? I mean, what if you *are* pregnant?'

'Is there any doubt? Can there be, Mama? I thought that—'

'Yes, yes, dear. Oh, I do wish you girls wouldn't talk so openly about things of that nature. It is embarrassing.'

'Oh, Mama! How am I supposed to know anything if I am not told? How did you know? Did you just guess it all?'

'No, I – I, well, your father knew everything. He told me, his class . . . I mean . . . Anyway, I also had Eleonore as a friend.'

'Yes, and I am French, and we French are not so stuffy about it all. I had a lot to unlearn, to fit into the English society, but I did so. I can never understand you English being so prudish about such a natural thing. Of course it is possible you are not pregnant, Katrina. You could have missed your monthly for several reasons, but it is not probable. I would say, from the way you have taken to that side of human nature, that you must be very careful or you will have babies by the dozen, and by as many fathers.'

'Eleonore!'

'Well, it is true. And good luck to the girl. I was the same

– couldn't get enough – but I had my tricks. I will tell you about them, Katrina. In fact I have a duty to do so, otherwise our family will be constantly embroiled in scandal.'

Katrina wanted to laugh at this. Lady Eleonore was a madam sometimes, but so down-to-earth and understanding. She could never think that Eleonore was, or might be still, a woman who would lie back and think of England – or, in her case, France. No, she was a woman of the same ilk as herself: passionate and capable of reaching great heights, when she was with a man she wanted to be with. Now her mother, she wasn't so sure about. Maybe she and Daddy had got along in their own way, but . . . *Oh, I must stop thinking about such things.* The very thought of her mother and father doing it was embarrassing; and besides, thinking about anything of that nature wasn't good for her, as she missed Frederick so. They had only been together in that way so few times, but when they had— Oh God, it was all a mess. She had messed up something that was the most beautiful thing in her life.

'Katrina, why have you come?' The coldness of Frederick's remark sliced her heart.

'I have told you.'

'I know, but it is all too much for me to deal with at the moment. The last day of the trial begins in half an hour. I have to go, but I cannot think of not being there.'

'I will come with you.'

'No! Good God, what on earth are you thinking of? It is no place for a lady!'

'Well, I don't believe I am a lady, Frederick. I am a woman, that is all. And my husband is the subject of gossip-mongers when he least deserves to be. I want to show I am solidly with you on this, that I know all about it. Besides, I too want to help Ruth Dovecote. This is a ridiculous charge, and we women should stand shoulder-to-shoulder.'

'I should applaud you. That was a good speech. As for the rest of what you have told me, though it sickens me, you are my wife and will remain so. We will think of the child you are carrying as *our* child. I am its father. As for the way we conduct our lives in the future, I do not know as yet how we will do that. It may suit us both to have affairs. We will work it out between us. But this is not the time, and I wish you hadn't come.'

The words sounded cruel, but to Katrina they were a joy to hear. *So he does intend to carry on being my husband?* Well, that would make things easier. The affair thing – no. She would fight that every way she could. At least he would never have *her* consent to do so, and she didn't think he would enjoy doing it in a clandestine way. It just wasn't him. 'I am happy you intend to stay with me, Frederick. Thank you. As you say, the terms we will have to settle. For now, Ruth Dovecote is more important, and I am coming. Whether you give me a lift or I come in my own carriage, you will not stop me.'

'Good Lord! Oh, very well. You can come with me. But I want no reaction to anything I might do.'

What he might do, she couldn't imagine. But a small part of the hurt inside her melted. *I think I won a small victory there. But, girl,* she told herself, *don't for one minute think the battle is won. There is a long way to go.* The main thing was that she was ready for the fight. She'd fight until the end of the world for Frederick. Her love for him was that strong.

The courthouse held no shocks for Katrina. She had imagined it being worse than it was. The cold of the place struck her most. Pulling her shawl around her neck, she looked up at the high ceiling. A streak of autumn sunlight came through the skylight, but it held no warmth and did little to lighten the dingy mustard-coloured room. The smell of paraffin lamps and of the sweaty bodies in the public gallery tinged her nostrils, but didn't overly bother her. The atmosphere held tension and filled her with a strange anticipation, to the point where she felt akin to the knitting ladies who attended the beheadings in France, during the Revolution.

France. Would they ever get to visit there? Or would Frederick go on his own to complete an ambition he had had for so long, to visit all the places his mother's family once owned? Still, this wasn't the right time to think of lost honeymoons. The clanging of gates below and the sound of the rattling of chains told her they were bringing the girl up.

It was shocking that they should put Ruth in irons. As she understood it, there was no possibility of her escaping. The girl could hardly walk, or so she had been told. When Ruth appeared, being carried by a warden, this was confirmed. When the warden turned at the top of the stairs, Ruth looked straight up towards Frederick. Her expression registered shock as her eyes moved on from Frederick.

She is looking directly at me. Now what do I do? I don't want my appearance here to upset her, not least because that will confirm Frederick as being correct when he said I should not attend!

The moment held awkwardness, but the thought occurred to her that maybe a smile of encouragement might ease the situation for the girl, and let her know she was there to support her, not condemn her. The girl didn't smile back, but some of the stiffness went out of Frederick and he gave

Katrina a grateful glance. *Small titbit, but I feel better for Frederick's reaction.*

As the warden sat the girl down on the bench in the dock, Katrina was able to get a better look at her. Painfully thin and with dark, sunken skin under her eyes, she looked desperately ill and a pitiful sight, but one that held a waif-like beauty. Something in Katrina wanted to go down and take the girl in her arms and give her comfort. A big part of her prayed the girl would not send herself to the gallows. A lot depended on her testimony. Frederick had said on the way here that Ruth still held a death-wish and wanted her life over. He had a plan, though – something he'd arranged that he hoped and prayed would change Ruth's mind.

His 'something' now appeared, in the shape of an old lady. The distinct squeak of bathchair wheels announced her arrival. Frederick sat up and looked over the balcony, his countenance one of hope. Ruth gasped. Frederick turned and whispered, 'Mrs Nora Bottomless.' The lady was someone very important to Ruth, he'd explained, but although he had told Katrina about her, he'd declined to explain the connection. He'd seemed almost gruff about it, for some reason.

Katrina watched, fascinated, as the old woman and Ruth stared at each other, then a powerful voice, as if from a much stronger woman, came from Mrs Bottomless. 'Ruth, lass: live for me and for Josh. I need you, and Josh needs you to take care of me.'

The warden spoke to Ruth, obviously warning her about talking, so she didn't answer, but a young girl's voice came from behind Katrina. 'And live for me, Ruth. I need you.' Turning, she saw it was Amy. Katrina didn't know her well, of course, but she had interviewed her as a prospective nanny and had found her pleasing, though her accent and command of the English language left a lot to be desired and needed correcting.

Whilst she tried to catch Amy's eye to offer a smile of comfort, another voice had her turning round. The chap on the other side of Frederick, whom she understood to be Haydon Green, Frederick's investigator, had spoken. 'And I do, Ruth. I need you.' At this, Frederick turned sharply towards Haydon, but didn't say anything.

For a moment the tension in the room rose, especially in herself as she willed Frederick not to say anything. The girl was now staring at him, and he had turned back towards her and held her gaze.

Katrina could feel her cheeks warming. *Please don't let him speak. I don't think I can stand the indignity.* A head appearing at the top of the stairs caught their attention. Lord Bellinger! *Oh God, no. No . . .*

'Excuse me.' This Bellinger said to the man who had spoken to Ruth. The man got up and gave his seat to Bellinger. 'Freddie, my boy, and Katrina. Well, this is pleasant. I heard you were here and that you, Frederick, have been attending the trial every day? I thought I would join you. Been quite a high-profile event. Reported in the news, and your comings and goings noted by all. What's it all about then?'

'What this is about is justice for an innocent girl. It is not a side-show, Lord Bellinger.'

'Uh-oh, you're cross with me over something. Sorry, old friend. Whatever it is, I'll make amends.'

'Not this time, you won't. I want nothing more to do with you.'

'All stand.' This, from a self-important man who had

come through a side-door on what Katrina was now thinking of as 'the stage', stopped the appalling conversation.

The judge entered, his wig immaculate, his cloak of the finest satin and his medals of office gleaming as they caught in the flicker of the lamps. Katrina held her breath. How would this day end? Please, God, not with her and Frederick further estranged; and not with the outcome that Ruth desired.

After a brief summary, Ruth heard her name. She was the one being called now. The warden lifted her and carried her forward. On giving her name, a hissing started up above her. The judge called, 'Order' and the silence was immediate.

'Ruth Dovecote, do you believe you have special powers?'

'No, Sir.'

The prosecutor who'd asked this had a pompous attitude that she'd only seen him use with those who spoke for her: a man from the prison hospital, the warden who had helped her, the Earl and Haydon Green. None of them had been intimidated by the prosecutor and all had stood firm.

'How, then, do you account for two boys suffering grave illness after you cursed them, and one man dying?'

'I can't, Sir.'

'So you are not denying that you cursed them then?'

'Not cursed, but I hated them for what they did to me.'

'I say that is a curse, and a curse can give such fear of the likes of you that it can cause death!'

'M'Lord, may I say that my learned friend is suggesting that hating someone who does wrong by you is tantamount to a curse; and, further, he is suggesting that a curse can maim or kill. I say that is poppycock. How can a curse cause the pox such as the boys in question fell victim to? I have cursed you, M'Lord – yes, I confess I have, on many occasions when you have ruled against me, but you are still in good health, are you not?'

'I accept the objection of the defence. Furthermore I, for one, have heard enough. I see no evidence of this girl using any powers, or even thinking she has powers. I believe, as Lord Rollinson, the Earl of Harrogate, said yesterday, that it is just a myth whipped up by ignorant folk who would have us believe that someone with an affliction can hold powers that could be used to harm. I see this girl as having been harmed, rather than harming others. I am dismissing the case and ordering that Ruth Dovecote be released from prison to the wardenship of the Earl of Harrogate – immediately.'

Shock held Ruth rigid. Shouts of 'The witch has got away with it!' and 'The wrong ones have been arrested – she cursed them, so they would be so!', and more along those lines, had her looking up at the gallery. Aye, she could see people who cared about her, but mostly what greeted her was a sea of hate. She could take no more. 'No . . . no! I want to go to the gallows. I want to die. Please, I want to die.' Her screams silenced everyone else's, leaving her voice echoing back to her, thick and slurred and spraying the spittle that had foamed in her mouth. 'I *am* a demon. I bring sorrow wherever I go. Please, let me die. Please.'

The hammering of a gavel quietened her. 'I will not have this uproar in my court. And I forbid that the defendant's last words be included in the records. Ruth Dovecote, you are a very sick girl. You are not evil. I may have come across as thinking that, before I heard all the evidence, but now I know you are sinned against, not a sinner. And take note, all of you in the gallery who would lynch this girl: not one of you will be spared a jail sentence if you even try to harm her. This case has set a precedent and has shown that the poor should have a fair trial. You should be grateful to Miss Dovecote for that. And to Mr Cotram and his fellow lawyers, who have believed so for a long time. I, for one, hope they have more successes in the future. This case is dismissed and closed.'

'All rise.'

This, Ruth thought, was a phrase she would never forget hearing. Every day it had meant the end of her ordeal for a little while, but today it meant it was over. Letting go of the little strength that had sustained her, she slumped against the warden.

Frederick sat staring down at Ruth. At the judge's words, his world brightened, but with Ruth collapsing it crashed again. He couldn't go to her. It wouldn't be right. He had to deny that longing, for the sake of Katrina. Whether she deserved it or not, as his wife she commanded respect from him in public.

'Well, well, winners all round, eh? Nice for you, Frederick; now you can do as you please with her.'

'Don't even attempt to mark me as being like you, Bellinger. My little finger has more honour in it than you have in your whole body. You have gone too far this time. You are a first-rate cad! And as I was saying before, neither I, nor any of my family, wish to have anything further to do with you.'

'I think, Lord Frederick, your wife should be left to speak for herself on that subject.'

'My husband speaks for me, Lord Bellinger. If I never see you again I would be all the happier. There are stronger words than "cad" that suit you; we are just too polite to use them.'

'Maybe, Frederick, you will use them if you know that your wife loves me and has slept with me, and only recently invited me to her home on a pretext.'

'You are not worth it. Damn you, Bellinger!' Frederick erupted.

'And I am not in love with you,' Katrina went on. 'You duped me. I am in love with my husband, and always will be. Even if your plotting makes it so that we are not able to stay together, I will still love him – and I will never, ever think of you other than as a vile creature. Don't come near me ever again!'

This shocked Frederick. Katrina had said she loved him as if she meant it. And her daring to speak whilst he was engaged in an argument . . . This wife of his was proving to be a handful that he wasn't sure he needed or could deal with.

At her words, Lord Bellinger had risen and left. His small laugh as he did so caused Frederick to worry. Concern crept over him and got the hairs on his arms standing up. Bellinger could cause trouble, and would enjoy doing so. No doubt he would let others know that he'd had an affair with Katrina – not so that Henrietta heard, but their peers would enjoy a snigger at Frederick's expense. And what of Katrina? Her reputation would be in ruins. Every time they attended a function there would be whispers and innuendoes. He didn't want that for her. He'd have to stand by her, even though it was painful to do so.

Below, the witness box was now empty. Ruth had been carried back downstairs. Looking to his left, he saw Amy, her head in her hands; and, glancing down again, Mrs Bottomless

– or Nora, as she'd asked him to call her – was taking a similar stance. So much despair around him but, with Katrina by his side, he didn't feel he could help any of them. Her words changed that.

'Frederick, you must go to Ruth. I will look after Amy and Mrs Bottomless. Instruct your man to give me a hand. Is that him over there?'

'It is. Katrina, I'm sorry I couldn't protect you.'

'I don't deserve you to. We will talk it all through, but it isn't our lives, my love, that are the important ones at the moment. I suggest you get Ruth to Dr Parker, who has been our family doctor for a long time. He has a small cottage hospital. Here, I'll write his address down. He'll take care of Ruth – tell him to charge it to Daddy's account. I'll forewarn Daddy.'

'Thank you. I – I wish—'

'Later. Just do what you have to do, and do it with my backing and love.'

Frederick couldn't find a way of answering this, but her words and Katrina's concern for Ruth's welfare chipped a little off the hard crust that had formed around the place where his feelings for her lay. *Maybe we could sort something out? I hope so, as what I really wish for can never happen. Maybe it will, for Haydon Green. Funny how he said what he did – and with such emotion. Oh God, life is complicated.*

29

Frederick

Facing a Devastating Settling of Scores

Life should be good, Frederick thought, as he sat in the office above the factory floor and watched the looms churning out rolls and rolls of linen. The conditions for the workers had improved, although urging his father-in-law to take on workers from the workhouse had backfired. It did seem, on the face of it, that they just didn't want to work, but he had a feeling that wasn't the real truth. Some, he knew, feared being released from the institutional life they had become used to, while others had an apathy they couldn't surmount. There should be something in between for them, a sort of rehabilitation programme. *Oh, I don't know – there's so much needs doing! Well, maybe now I will have more time to do it, but first I have to tackle the Katrina problem. I must sort that out tonight, I must!*

Feeling tired, and wanting to bathe and go to bed rather than talk, he was rather sorry Katrina had stayed on at her parents' home with him. But as he couldn't take leave from the office for a few days and he'd had so much time away already, Katrina had said that putting miles between them

344

now would be disastrous. He agreed, but although it had been two days since the end of the trial, they had done nothing other than be polite towards each other. For himself, he hadn't even been able to think things through. Her unfaithfulness – *and on their wedding night* – had devastated him. Why did Katrina affect him so much? Just knowing she was in the next room gave him feelings he didn't understand and confused him, and he couldn't square those emotions with how he felt for Ruth.

Knocking on Katrina's door, he felt as if he was back at school and had been summoned to the headmaster. His legs wobbled and the nerves in his stomach jangled. It beggared belief that she could make him feel like this. She was his wife in an arranged marriage, and there was no love involved – at least, not on his side, not now. Strange that she had declared her love for him.

When she opened the door, Katrina was alone. He'd rather hoped her maid would be with her, as she had brought Annie along on this trip. Annie would have caused some distraction or other to get over the first few minutes. 'Katrina, I think—'

'That it is time? Yes, but what took you so long? I have been waiting for you.'

'I know, I am sorry. I had feelings to sort out. I am still confused. Why did you do it?'

'Frederick, I could try to justify myself, but would it do any good? You must justify it, if such a thing is possible. You must look inside yourself and, with the feelings you have, ask if you would not have done the same, in the same circumstances? The difference is that the one you might have done it with would never put you in that position, while the one I mistakenly believed I loved would, and did. He plotted and

345

schemed, he drugged you and came to me when I was waiting for you. I was already expectant of what would happen and longing for it to happen.'

'So you are saying it could have been anyone?'

'No! No, that is not what I am saying. I thought myself in love with Bellinger. Ugh, the very idea repulses me now. I shudder to think of it. How could I have fallen for his words of love, for Bellinger saying that he had wanted to offer for me?'

This pulled Frederick up. That bastard! Bellinger had had no such intention of offering for Katrina, and had laughed at Frederick for having to offer for her, for the sake of saving his family name. That man was capable of anything. Christ, it hurt, though, that Bellinger had taken his wife, spoilt their first union. *Christ!* His body folded; his legs wouldn't hold him. Sinking onto the end of her bed, he could only stare at her. Tears streamed down his face, and he could do nothing to stop them.

'Frederick, darling, don't. I'm so sorry. I love you, my darling, and I'll never hurt you again, never. Please believe me.'

Her endearments and pleas for forgiveness increased his crying. He had so much to cry about. So much.

Being in her arms helped. He found comfort in Katrina's loving of him. His thoughts went to Ruth. She was being cared for at last, and all at his bidding; and, yes, he had to admit, if such a thing had happened to him, he would have taken Ruth, even though he'd just wed another. Understanding entered him at this, but still the rawness persisted.

'Darling, as this is hurting you so much, is there a chance you do love me? Would it matter so much if I was what I was meant to be – a wife of convenience?'

The time had come for Frederick to be as truthful as Katrina was being. 'Is it possible to love two women?' Her silence frightened him. 'I'm confused, Katrina, very confused. I love Ruth, you know that. She is not my mistress – I was truthful about that – nor will she ever be, but I love her. She has a special place in me. But well, yes, I am in love with you, too . . . It's madness! Madness!'

Still she remained quiet. She hadn't moved away. Her arms encircled him just as lovingly, as he continued, 'I know it is terrible for you to come to terms with. I am having that difficulty with what you did, but the question is: can we do it? Can you live knowing I have this love for another? Can I live, knowing you once felt a love for another that went to its limits? I don't know.'

'I am willing to try. Are you, Frederick? Yes, I knew you loved Ruth. And, yes, I believed you when you said you weren't taking her as your mistress, but hearing you in such despair over it all hurts me. Knowing you love me helps. It is a sandy foundation we have, one that's soft and likely to slip. We will have to keep shoring it up, but I am willing to build on that, if you will help me.'

'Oh, Katrina, I just don't know. You are a good person. You don't deserve me. Let's leave it a while. Let's carry on as we are, showing a united front, being polite, but that's all. I am not ready for anything else.'

Coming out of her arms, Frederick stood. He had to get away from the close proximity of her. If he took Katrina now, it would be a vile act, feeling as he did. It would be a long, long time before he coupled with her again, if ever. Why did that decision hurt so much? He didn't know. He just knew it had to be so.

*

347

The door closing behind Frederick put a final stamp on all Katrina's hopes. Her determination hadn't been enough. *But no, I won't give in – I won't.* Annie knocking at her door stopped the tears that threatened. 'What is it, Annie? I am ready for dinner. I just need a few moments and I will be down.'

'Your ma is home, and she wants you to attend her in her sitting room. She has Miss Marcia with her, M'Lady. She said there's nowt to worry over, and that she has delayed dinner and has asked for another place to be set.'

'What?' Katrina's astonishment stopped the smile she usually gave when Annie related anything her mother had said, because trying to imagine her mother saying anything in the accent Annie had was very amusing. But this news didn't allow any room for humour. 'No! I didn't want this. Oh, never mind. Thank you, Annie. Go off and have a break. I won't be needing you until I am ready to retire.'

'Ta, M'Lady.'

The other source of amusement about Annie happened then as she attempted to curtsy, which was a funny action with crossed feet and a wobble that made her look as though she would topple over. Whether she would ever perfect the curtsy, Katrina didn't know, nor could she give her attention to it at this moment in time. *What was Mother thinking of, bringing Marcia here! She has caused enough trouble and is likely to cause even more, if she is given the chance.*

'Mama! What are you doing home?'

'I'm here too, Katrina.'

'Yes, I know. But why, I can't imagine. It is good to see you, Mama, but you, Marcia, I had hoped not to see for a very long time.'

'Katrina, don't. Marcia wants to say she is sorry.'

'It is not enough. The damage you have done, Marcia, cannot be undone by a word. You—'

'I know what I did and I am very sorry. I was eaten up by jealousy. I won't cause any more harm, because I am over Frederick now. You can have him. I have realized who my true love is – *and* he doesn't need to buy me. He loves me, too. He has all the wealth he needs, and he has given up his intended for me.'

'Not . . . Good God, please don't say—'

'Lord Bellinger? Why not? What he had with you is nothing to him. It was merely a victory over Frederick, whom he despises and always has. He has accomplished that now, and has no need to do anything else.'

'Mama?'

'Marcia has made me see that you were very much at fault. I cannot think as Eleonore does about these matters. Marriage is sacrosanct. You could have screamed until someone came, instead of giving in to Lord Bellinger. You made his quest easy for him. I am not happy with him, not at all. He has caused a great deal of unhappiness, but I believe he is genuine in his love for Marcia. Why else would he risk a scandal by giving up Henrietta?'

'Oh no, you are wrong, so wrong. Poor Henrietta, poor you, Marcia – you stupid girl. What is it with you? You don't love him, you don't; it is impossible! How . . . ?'

'Huh, so all that is good is for you alone? Well, it isn't. Lord Bellinger sought me out. He said he was sick of your games and the way you try to discredit him at every turn. Yes, he did that on your wedding night, but it wasn't because he felt any attraction towards you. And it was as Mama says: you could have stopped it. Come off your pedestal, Katrina.

349

You have built it too high, and that is why you are tumbling. It is nothing to do with me.'

'Nothing? Good God, you listen at my bedroom door, and you plot and scheme against me. Why, why? I can't help being the eldest. I too think it unfair that Daddy plans to divide everything, but I have no say in it. And it is all done now. You cannot change it . . . My God – that's it! You think that by partnering Bellinger, together you can break us, and together you can get Daddy's empire. You do, I know you do. You know about the clause that says that if my marriage breaks down, then all Frederick is entitled to as my husband reverts to the estate. But how do you plan on getting rid of me? Because whatever you do, I am still the eldest.'

'Katrina, stop this. You talk as if Marcia is the devil. You should be pleased for her, not ranting on about the greatest poppycock I have ever heard in my life! Marcia has a handsome settlement, and Daddy reallocated some of the shares in the business to her. In any case, Lord Bellinger has more than enough money for them and huge business interests, so why should they want what you have? You are being ridiculous. Yes, Marcia did wrong, but she is sorry. She has a love of her own, and her infatuation for your husband has gone. Try to accept that, and for goodness' sake try and behave in the manner in which you were brought up. You are a disgrace.'

'Mama, I – I— Oh, Mama.'

'Oh dear, here come the tears. Leave her, Mama. Katrina can see that all of her spoilt-brat tactics have failed and she is going to be left with nothing. Because surely Lord Frederick will not want her now.'

'I do, actually.'

The door between this room and the adjoining withdrawing

room burst open and Frederick came through it. Katrina stood still, as if turned into a statue. He must have heard everything. She hadn't known he was downstairs. She held her breath.

'I love Katrina, and I am remaining her husband. I know she loves me, too, and that we have some things to work through, but we will surmount them.'

'What? Even when Lord Bellinger claims his chi—' Marcia's blank look of horror at her own words spoke of her never having meant to utter them.

'What were you going to say, Marcia? Because if Bellinger has any plans to cause my wife harm, by spreading gossip about the paternity of our child or about his – his conquest, then he had better take care. He isn't the only one who holds a good hand. I have some trump cards up my sleeve, which I could pull out and ruin him with. However, I am appalled that we are even having this conversation and that you, Mother-in-law, could be party to it against one of your own daughters. Have you lost all the decorum and training of your youth? Because it seems to me that you have failed to pass any of it on to your youngest daughter. We will leave at once. Please have some food prepared for us to take with us.'

'Oh, naw, you won't. Nor will you speak to me wife in that tone.'

'I apologize, Father-in-law. I – and to you, Mother-in-law. I am very sorry. I should not have said what I did, or spoke disrespectfully to you. Marcia's behaviour triggered a response I never thought myself capable of. But I will leave, because being in her company any longer is abhorrent to me. From now on, when she is in residence my wife and I will not be guests in your home. We would very much like to visit you at any other time, and of course I will continue with my work at the office.'

'Naw, that is not going to happen. I will not stand by and see me family split. Marcia, if Lord Bellinger is planning what you have hinted at, then he will not become a member of this family.'

'He isn't, Daddy. They had me all wound up, between them. Katrina's behaviour has caused all of this. Lord Bellinger loves me, and I love him. We just want to marry and live in peace. We don't want all of this. Mama will tell you: it was Katrina's nastiness that started all of this, not to mention her sleeping—'

'That's enough. My wife did not start all of this. I heard everything from the beginning.'

'*I* will say when owt is enough or not, young man. Now, this is getting us nowhere. Feelings are running too high. Apologize to each other, Katrina and Marcia, and do it at once. Your poor mother is distraught.' When none of them moved, he shouted, 'Now!'

'I apologize, Marcia. I shouldn't have reacted to your engagement in the way I did. Please forgive me.'

It was a long moment before Marcia gave in. 'I'm sorry for what I said, too, but you should not have reacted as you did. You made me say things I hadn't intended to say.'

'I accept your apology, and I am sorry if I have caused you hurt, Mama. I would wear sackcloth all my life if I thought it would undo everything I have done to you all.'

'You have no need to wear it for me, Katrina. I understand and forgive.' This, from Frederick, lifted her spirits. She could cope with anything if he forgave her.

'Nor for me, my darling daughter. I overreacted to your response to your sister's good news. Let us all forget it and begin again. Darling husband, would you see to it that drinks are served and that dinner is ready in fifteen minutes? Thank you, my love.' Katrina watched her mother rise as she said this. She came over to her. Snuggling into her arms took away some of Katrina's hurt.

The next few moments of polite conversation over drinks had a calm surface, but underneath a strong current raged inside Katrina. *How will all of this end? What game is Bellinger playing? How could he drop Henrietta?* But then she knew Bellinger would only do so if he thought there was a bigger fish for him to net. That bigger fish wasn't in marrying a second child who wasn't an heir, so he must have a wider scheme. What was it? Unless . . . Unless he thought to bide his time and eventually take everything from Frederick. *No, now I'm being silly. How could he possibly do that?*

The more Katrina thought of the possibilities, the more afraid she became. Summing it all up to herself didn't help. *Yes, I have Frederick's love; and yes, I am willing to fight for our future, but how will Bellinger settle the scores that he feels are owed by us? This is all a devastating twist that I don't know if I can cope with . . . I feel sick.*

30

Katrina & Frederick

Something Settled, but Not Concluded

'May I come in, Katrina?' Frederick was wearing his dressing gown and looked vulnerable somehow. Fresh and innocent. He smelled of soap and the oils that he added to his bath. He'd told her once they were from India.

'Yes. I – I . . . Oh, Frederick, that was awful – I'm so sorry I had to leave you. It seems babies in the womb can react to all sorts of things. I couldn't stop being sick when I came to my room.'

'I know, dear, your mother told me. I hope you don't mind me visiting you, when you have taken to your bed?'

'Of course not, and I haven't "taken to my bed". It was just more comfortable and stopped my queasiness when I lay down.'

'I would have come earlier, as I didn't feel like eating, but out of politeness . . . Anyway it was best that I stayed, as it turned out, because after a couple of glasses of wine everyone relaxed and something like a normal atmosphere prevailed.'

'I'm glad. Marcia came up after dinner for a few minutes. I'm worried, Frederick. I think Bellinger means to hurt you, and I don't think he will be a good husband to Marcia.'

'Marcia knows what she is doing. Whatever they are planning, she is fully aware of it. She's not in love with Bellinger. We will just have to take care and watch them closely.'

'Oh, I've brought so much down upon you, and you least deserve it.'

'You haven't. It isn't all your fault. I was up for having drinks with my friends on our wedding night, I was that bloody nervous. I shouldn't have done that. I should have spent the evening by your side, then no harm could have come to you.'

There seemed nothing more to say. What had happened would always mar their relationship – that, and Frederick's love for Ruth. Katrina knew she had no weapons with which to fight the pain this caused her, or to stop his love for the girl. What could she do? If it was another woman in their own circle, she would have an even chance, but with Ruth – a beauty, yes, but crippled, poor, uneducated and still loved by Frederick – there was nothing she could do. And it hurt. It hurt so much. All she could hope for was that one day he would wake up and realize, as she did with the hateful Bellinger, that he wasn't *in love*, it was merely a fascination. *Please God, it doesn't get as far as I allowed my relationship to go!*

'Well, dear, I'll leave you to sleep. You've had a lot to cope with tonight. You did very well. The situation was appalling, but you remained the lady you are.'

'Thank you. Will you stay awhile until I am asleep?'

'Very well. Move over. I'll lie on top of the bed.'

Acutely aware of him, Katrina lay stiff and unable to relax. But making an approach would be unfair. Lying on her side facing him, she saw that he was staring up at the ceiling. Watching him, she thought how dear he was, how kind and caring, and she wished she could cut out of her the ugliness of her unfaithfulness with Bellinger.

Unwanted thoughts visited Frederick as he lay beside Katrina. Thoughts of what they had enjoyed together. Thoughts of how that would be with Ruth, and of how he would fight Bellinger, if it was his intention to take everything away from him.

They would have to go home soon to Northallerton, maybe tomorrow. His work at the mill was at a stage where he could leave for a few days. In a week's time he would meet their chief buyers; he would go back for that. And afterwards, when he had the experience of selling and haggling over prices that he intended to gain from the meetings, he would introduce some customers of his own. He had a lot of contacts abroad, and he thought export would be the next big step for Arkwright's.

Feeling his eyes begin to close, Frederick glanced at Katrina, but instead of being asleep, she was looking at him, her dark eyes misted over, her look full of love for him. Against all he wished to do or to happen, as he held her gaze, familiar and not-to-be denied feelings crept into his groin. She was so beautiful, and passionate. She held in her a yearning for satisfaction. He wanted to give and take it, but could he? Was her look one of trust or *I am available to you*? Pulling himself together, he went to rise.

'No. I mean, I – I . . .'

Looking down at her, there wasn't a conscious moment when he intended to kiss her. It just happened. Katrina's response drank him in, sucking all resistance from him. He needed her. She was like the completion of him. How that was, he didn't know, but his whole being wanted to take all that Katrina had and drown in the ecstasy of her.

Their kisses deepened, his hands exploring her softness. Kneading her breasts, he played with her nipples. Katrina responded and her soft moans encouraged him. Caressing her, Frederick let his hand find the heart of her sexuality, played with her, brought her to orgasm, then knew an urgency he couldn't deny.

He needed to enter her. He had to strengthen their future together as man and wife, from this day forward. Climbing onto her and plunging himself into her, he didn't just take from her, but gave to her all that he was.

Lying with her in his arms, his whole self drained, Frederick knew this union with Katrina would be enough. It had to be. Soon he would go and see Ruth and say his goodbyes.

Into the silence Katrina's soft, pretty voice came to him. 'We will be all right, Frederick. The foundations are getting stronger.'

'They are, my dear. I know that.'

'Will it be enough?'

'What we just did isn't all that we have together. It is simply the cementing of the love we have for one another. I do love you, Katrina. And I like you. That's important, too. Do you like me?'

'I like and love you.'

'Well then, it is enough. And, yes, it is a strong enough love for us to build on. We'll go forward, and any man who tries to put us asunder had better watch out. Even Bellinger!'

'Don't mention him tonight, or at any moments we share in the future. We will only talk of the good things at these

357

times. We can discuss him and what he is up to, and that horrid sister of mine, at other times.'

'I agree. Now I must leave you and get some rest. Good-night, darling.'

Her little giggle told him this endearment pleased her. Now he must think of Katrina and of her alone, and he must not leave her, only to go to his bed and think of Ruth . . .

31

Ruth

A Shock Arrival

'Nora, does you like this cottage? Are you happy?'

'Aye, but it's nowt like home, lass. I'd give what I have left of me front teeth to be back there.'

'I would an' all, and I don't see why we can't. It can be rebuilt. We'll have the money between us, won't we?'

'Aye.'

'Well, then? We could keep enough livestock and chickens for our own needs and rent off the bottom fields. And we could rent this cottage for an extra income.'

'It sounds a good plan. But would you be safe, lass?'

'I think I would. That judge said that anyone trying to harm me again will pay for it. And that lot at Pradley are scared. They still think I caused the devil to come to me that night when . . . Anyroad, I reckon as none of them will dare to come near.'

'There's one thing you're forgetting, lass: your piano-playing. You'll not get educated up there, as no one can get there.'

'But I could come down. Twice a week, like Josh did.'

'Naw, lass, I've other ideas. You've a long life ahead of

you and I have been looking at ways of securing it. Making sure you're safe. We've had a good offer for the farm and the market business. I want to put that money into the factories.'

'What?'

'Aye, I know it sounds mad, but them factories are growing in strength. Josh often read out bits about it to me. And he said as he was considering investing. Well, you know an owner, in that Earl bloke. We should ask him about it.'

Ruth listened in awe as Nora outlined what Josh had planned. He'd intended to put money into one of the smaller factories. Help it to become bigger and learn the trade. 'He didn't want to stay up there,' Nora continued. 'He always dreamed of a time when he could fetch me down here, and of him being a proper businessman. I think, if you get an education, you could do that for him. Make a better life for yourself, lass. Don't go backwards. Leave behind you all that hiding from folk. You're worth more than that. When you are somebody, nobody will dare harm you.'

'But Josh allus said—'

'What he said to you was done to protect you. While he had you, and you were in danger, he was allus going to stay up there, and he wanted you to think he wouldn't have it any other way.'

The idea settled in her. Oh aye, she'd have a lot to learn. But she could. There was nothing that could stop her from learning. She'd start by getting a job in the mill. The Earl would see to it for her. It'd need to be in the mill that she and Nora invested in. She'd have to learn all of it, from the spinning to the weaving and where it was sold, and where the cotton came from to spin the yarn – everything. And at the same time she would get her education. She could do that at night.

'Eeh, Nora, I feel that excited. It's like a new life could open for me.'

'Well, don't tire yourself with it all. You're still not well. Lie back and rest, while I get you some milk. And I've to dress that leg for you. It's coming on nicely now. You're on the mend, lass, you're on the mend.'

Aye, and I have me plans to think about an' all. Exciting plans – plans as will take all the space in me head, so as I can't think on other things. And Amy's visit to look forward to some-time soon. Eeh, life is good.

'Eeh, our Amy, lass, it's good to see you.' The feel of Amy's arms around her almost undid Ruth, but she pulled herself together to greet the girl who'd come with Amy. 'And you'll be Lettie? You're welcome, Lettie. How long can you stay, our Amy?'

'We've three days altogether, but one and a half of them are taken up with travelling. We've had to walk most of the way, then we picked up the mail carriage for the last leg. He told us he leaves tomorrow afternoon at two, so if we're down bottom of the hill, he'll pick us up there and take us as far as Threshfield, then we should be able to cadge a lift from there. We'll make it. We're not to be on duty till the next day.'

'Well, Nora'll be in soon. She's made a lot of progress and can get down to the shop using her sticks. She's taken great care of me. She does me dressings, washes me and does all the chores. I can't wait to be well, so as I can help her. She'll make you a brew when she's back.'

'We can do that, lass. And we can give Nora a break and do your leg an' all. We were nurses back at that workhouse.'

'Ta, Lettie. It'd be good to give Nora a rest. Eeh, our Amy, come here and give me another hug. I've so much to

361

hear from you. By, love, we've been through the mill, and now we have to carry on without so many as we love . . .' Her voice broke on a sob.

'Naw, don't go down that road, our Ruth.'

They clung together. Holding her sister once more brought everything they'd been through back into Ruth's mind, and with the memory came the tears. Amy's joined hers and together they sobbed.

'Come on, me lasses. You're through it all now. And you both have a good future ahead of you. Never look back. Look to the road ahead, eh?'

It took a few minutes for them to calm down, but when they did, they agreed with Lettie; and as Ruth told them how her future looked, they cheered up.

'If you want to come here, our Amy, lass, you can. Are you happy where you are?'

'I'm not altogether happy, our Ruth. I'm not for all the chores I have to do, but I'm looking forward to being in charge of babby when it arrives.'

'Lady Katrina is having a babby!' This news sent a pain through Ruth's heart, but she suppressed it and made herself feel glad. She couldn't have picked anyone nicer for her earl than Lady Katrina.

'Aye, she's only a few weeks off having it now. She's been staying with her ma, here in Blackburn, but is coming home today. I've been trained . . .' Amy told Ruth about the preparations she'd been through to become a nanny. 'Lord Frederick's old nanny trained me. Eeh, she's a tartar! I won't be doing half what she's telling me to do. She used to swaddle the babbies up that tight, it's a wonder they could breathe, poor mites. Anyroad, what I really want to do with me life is help them as are like us.'

As she listened to Amy's plans to feed the poor and home-less with her wages, Ruth wasn't surprised. Amy had always been a caring lass, and neither did it surprise her when Lettie chipped in that she wanted to help. Lettie was nice. She'd taken to the lass as soon as she'd smiled, and was halfway to liking her even before she met Lettie, on account of know-ing that she was looking out for Amy.

It was a good thing Amy did, to get the lass out of that workhouse; and it was a good thing they were planning to do together. 'I'll help you with that, our lass, as I'd like to help them who are suffering as we once did. As I've told you, I've money coming to me, and I've prospects.'

'That'd be grand, Ruth. Eeh, you in business! I hadn't taken that part in proper. By, I'd love to join you. It sounds a lot better than being a nanny and a governess.'

'Aye, and I would like to join you an' all, Ruth. I'm not for cooking and doing. I enjoyed me work in the workhouse more than what I do now. I loved looking after the old and the sick.'

'Well, let's bide our time, eh? We've all got settled for now. Let's keep it that way and work towards what we really want to do. Maybe, Lettie, if the Earl does start sommat up, as Amy said his intention is, you could do your nursing of the sick then?'

'That'd be grand, and in the meantime I'll start with put-ting kettle on and making us all a brew.'

When Lettie left them, Amy said, 'That's not what she'd really like to do. She has a massive musical talent.'

'Eeh, our Amy, that's funny you should say that. I'm for having a talent along the lines as you'll never guess of: I can play piano.'

'I know – I heard it from the Earl, but it didn't sound real until you just said it. The piano! You can play piano? Well, our Ruth, you'd not have surprised me more if you'd have told me you'd grown another leg.' They both laughed at how ironic this was. 'Anyroad, Lettie's talent is her voice. You should hear it. It makes your hair stand up.'

'Lettie, sing? Ha, we'll make a good pair, then. I could play sommat, if you and Lettie could help me to the piano; and if Lettie knows owt as I play, she could sing. Me piano's in the parlour.'

Ruth hadn't played for more than a few minutes when Lettie began to sing. It was a popular tune that Ruth had learned from Josh. The words Lettie put to it, and the sound of her beautiful voice, tightened Ruth's throat. 'Amazing Grace, how sweet the sound . . .'

None of them had heard the parlour door opening, but they all heard the deep groan that came from just inside the door.

'Eeh, Nora – Nora, don't take on. I'm sorry, I shouldn't have played. I should've known it would hurt you.'

'Naw, lass, it were beautiful. It just made me think of our Josh. He loved that piano and he loved teaching you how to play it. He said as you could play in them concerts, if you could learn the music. It was going to be his next job, to teach you to read and write.'

There were more tears. Nora came over to Ruth and bent over, taking her in her arms. Ruth felt a breaking of her heart at this – at the loss of Josh, and the guilt she felt at bringing all she had down on him and his ma.

The two girls allowed them their grief, comforting them as best they could. It was Ruth's cry of pain that stopped it all. The holler came from her without her bidding it, as the pain shot across her back, then clenched her stomach as if a vice had clamped on her.

'Ruth – eeh, our Ruth, what is it?'

'I don't know, Amy, but . . . Oh, dear God. Oh, help me!' Sweat stood out on Ruth's face as the pain washed over her again. Holding her stomach, she doubled over.

Lettie took charge. 'Let's get her back to bed.'

As they tried to support her, another pain built inside her to unbearable proportions. This time she uttered a scream that echoed back at her, as Amy cried out in anguish, 'Ruth, Ruth.'

'Amy, stop that! Come on now, lass. Help me get Ruth back to her bed. Pull yourself together, we have to help her.'

The shout from Lettie did the trick. Amy calmed down and helped Lettie get her sister to her bed. As they did so, another pain seized Ruth and with it came an urge to draw up her knees and push.

'My God, it looks like lass is having a babby! Ruth, are you pregnant?'

'Naw, naw, I – I . . . Oh God, help meeeee!'

'She is, she's having a babby. Waters have broke. Get kettle on, Nora. Eeh, sorry, Missus, I'm Lettie – I'm a friend of Amy here, as I think you've met afore. I'm a nurse of sorts. Don't worry: me and Amy'll sort this. You get some clean towels and sommat to wash babby with, when it comes out.'

'Aye, I gathered who you were. But a babby! Ruth?'

'It's not unheard of. By the sounds of things, your Josh was a man to be proud of. Well, it seems he's left his mark on the world. Hurry, now.'

'Oooh, oh God!' The pain rose again. That was the only

way Ruth could think of it: as rising. Starting badly, but rising to a peak she could hardly bear. Screams and curses came from her, and spittle ran down her chin.

But through it all, she felt a joy, because what Lettie had said could be the truth. It was nine months since she'd first lain with Josh. She'd not seen her bleeding since, but she had put it down to all that had happened to her. And she'd noticed that her belly had rounded, but again it could do that with the way they had starved her. At this, another horrific thought came to her: what if her babby were harmed . . . maimed, like her? It was more than a possibility, as no care had been given to it. 'No. No. Please God, noooo!'

'There's worse things than having a babby, lass. Now, stop worrying and get on with bringing your child into the world.'

This, from Lettie, made her angry. 'I'm not praying not to . . . Aghh!' With the scream that came from Ruth at the next pain, her whole being bore down.

'It's coming, it's coming. Eeh, our Ruth, I can see its head. It's . . . Oh, Ruth, it's here!'

There was a moment of relief, a moment of silence, then another scream shattered the air – a babby-scream, the like of which Ruth had heard many a time back home with her ma.

'By, he's a good pair of lungs on him, I'll say that.'

A boy – oh, my Josh, we have a son. 'Is he . . . is he all reet, Lettie?'

'He's a smasher. A bit small, but little ones have a habit of growing into giants. And he has a todger on him that'll keep many a lass happy.'

'Lettie! Ha-ha. Eeh, Lettie, you're a one.'

This, from Amy, and her infectious laughter took the edge

366

off the shock Ruth had felt at Lettie's remark and she joined in the laughter. She had a boy . . . a son. She and Josh had a son.

'Lass, lass, I don't knaw what to say.'

'I know, Nora. I'm in shock meself, but it's a nice shock, eh? And, if it's alreet with you, we'll call him Josh, shall we?'

'Aye, me Josh would have been so proud of him, and you. By, lass, we have our Josh back. Well, at least a big part of him, we do.'

As Lettie passed Ruth her son, all wrapped up in a huge towel, the tears flowed, but this time as she looked down at the little red and swollen face of her child, they were tears of joy. Nothing could have healed her like the love that now gushed from her. She'd go through it all again – the threat of burning, the starvation, the . . . Well, she'd not think on the rape, but the trial. Everything. Aye, she'd go through it all for this moment, which was making all of it pale in comparison. For little Josh had made her a whole person again, just as his dad had.

'Reet, lass, hand him to his grandmother. We've still work to do. I've to help get afterbirth away, as it don't seem to be coming on its own. You know about that, don't you? It's what's been feeding babby, but you have no use of it now.'

'Aye, I know. I helped at all me ma's births from when I were nine years old.' This brought Ruth tears of real sadness – cloying sadness that she couldn't control.

'Cry it out, lass. Every new mother does, whether they've sommat to cry about or not. It's just a reaction. Now, let's see how we're doing.'

32

Ruth & Frederick

Time to Say Goodbye

They were on their third cup of tea and little Josh had already suckled at Ruth's breast when a knock at the door stopped them all in their tracks. Ruth instinctively knew who it was and embarrassed herself by asking, 'Do I look alreet? Is me hair tidy? Is—'

'Well, I don't know who you're expecting, but aye, you look a picture. Glowing, you are, and Amy's done a reet good job with that tangled mess you call hair!'

This had her laughing again. *Eeh, that Lettie! I don't know about being a singer, but she could be a comedienne for sure.*

Hearing Amy exclaim, 'M'Lord, is owt wrong?' got Ruth's heart thumping. If she had colour in her cheeks from the effort of bringing her son into the world, she felt it deepen to a crimson, knowing for sure it was him. *What will he think of it all?*

'Oh, Amy, hello! I'm just as surprised to see you here. I called to see how Ruth was doing, and if she and Nora were settled in now.'

'I'm on me days off, M'Lord. I just got here this morning and I go back tomorrow. Lettie's here an' all.'

'Ah, I see. Well, how you made it here I don't know, but if you must be back tomorrow, I can help with that. Lady Katrina and I are travelling home in the morning. You can travel with Annie, as she is following us in the luggage carriage. There's plenty of room.'

'Oh, that'd be grand, M'Lord. Ta.'

'Well now, can I come in?'

Ruth held her breath at this. The hope that had flipped her heart had already died when she heard him saying he was going back to Northallerton tomorrow.

'Well, there's sommat as you have to know, afore you go in to Ruth.' Amy's next words lifted Ruth again, as the way she put it, it all sounded natural and a good thing that had happened. 'Our Ruth's just given birth to hers and Josh's son. So it's a happy day we're having, and you'll find our Ruth full of joy. A good day to visit, I would say. Though she's a mite tired. Come on through, M'Lord.'

The expression on the Earl's face told Ruth of his feelings. Astonishment vied with pain, but he didn't put any of this into his voice. 'Ruth, it is so nice to see you sitting up. And this is your son? I didn't know. I – I had no idea. How . . . ? I mean, why didn't you tell me?'

'I didn't know, M'Lord. Little Josh here arrived not an hour since, and hadn't announced his coming at all. How he's survived, I don't know, but he has. His coming were a shock – so much so that poor Nora has had to go and lie down. I can call her if—'

'No, it is all right. Well, well! I haven't heard of that happening before. Maybe it is for the best in this case, because knowing would have made everything much harder for you, if that was possible. And look at him. Even though no one

369

has worried about him, he looks very well. What about you: are you all right?'

'Eeh, I'm feeling grand, M'Lord. Them at the cottage hospital looked after me a treat. Thank you – and thank your wife for me, for looking after Amy and seeing she was reet. She's a grand lady. You're lucky to have her.'

Frederick's eyes always searched for hers, but she didn't like looking at him. She couldn't. Things that could never happen visited her when she did, so a swift glance was all she managed every now and again.

'Yes, I am lucky to have her, thank you.'

This reply held more politeness than conviction. It fuelled Ruth's hopes, but she doused it with her own common sense. Never in a month of Sundays could owt come of the love they felt for one another. Because she was sure he still loved her, even though he'd never spoken of it since that time in prison. The thought of that place made her shudder.

'Are you all right? You haven't got a chill?'

Everything and anything, other than what we want to say. Well, this had to be the way of it, she knew that, so she sought to change the subject. 'Have you news on me affairs? Josh's will and everything, M'Lord?'

'I have, and on other matters concerning Josh, too. The court has ruled that he was murdered, but it is proving difficult to pin it on Whalley Bradstone, the main suspect. Yes, it was his cleaver that was used to kill poor Josh, but Whalley denies doing the deed. He is saying someone must have picked it up, when the crowd called at his house to get him to join them. He swears he didn't take it with him, or hit Josh with it. He'll do time in prison, as will all who were involved, which is good, but it isn't the justice you wanted Josh to have. I'm sorry.'

'It can't be helped. I didn't see what happened, and if anyone did, they won't say. Nothing can bring Josh back – well, not proper; but little Josh here is bringing him back. Carrying on for him, so to speak.'

'Yes, the child is Josh's legacy and a good one. Nothing he could have left you could be better than his own son. You will be fine now, I'm sure.'

'Oh, aye, I will. I intend going into business. Nora and me, we have plans.' The Earl didn't interrupt while she told him what they had been discussing. 'So, soon as I'm well enough, I'm going to be seeking a job that will help me to know the ins and outs of how the mills work. And I will study at night to get me reading and writing skills.'

'Good Lord, you *have* thought this through! I wish you all the luck in the world with it.'

But he hadn't said he would help her. 'M'Lord, Nora and me, we were hoping you would help us. Tell us which small factory to invest in, and help me to get a job.'

Looking away from Ruth, the Earl asked Amy and Lettie to leave them for a moment. After they had gone, he brought a chair up to her bed and sat down. 'Ruth, I cannot. I – I . . . We have to go forward. We cannot carry on being in each other's company or having any contact.'

'But I need your help with this. I don't know where to start, and I can't . . . I – I mean, please, M'Lord, just this one last thing?'

'I'm sorry, it isn't possible. Besides, I know so little myself and am still learning. Send a message to your solicitor. Tell him to come and see you, and discuss everything with him. He is a good man. He admired Josh very much, and has a good deal of respect for Nora, as I am sure he will have for you, when he meets you. I have already instructed him to deal direct with you from now on. I am sorry.'

Her throat tightened. He'd looked hurt, when her only reaction to him saying they should have no further contact was to beg him for a little more help. It hadn't been how she'd felt, but she had seen the Earl helping her as a way of keeping him near her.

'Ruth, my . . . Ruth, it has to be. Your solicitor will give you good advice. And as for learning the trade, you should educate yourself first, then study books on the subject of cotton mills and their workings. There are a number around – I have been learning from them myself; but it is out of the question that you go to work in a mill. You would never last in that environment. They would crush you. Anyway, you have your son, so you will need to be at home for a few years. Nora couldn't cope with him.'

'What about Amy, she—'

'Amy will come and stay with you on her leave-days. I will see that she can get here. She wants to live with you, I am sure, but I think she should continue her education. She is doing so well – and, well, my wife is also expecting a baby.'

The gasp that escaped from Ruth on hearing this held her pain. Even though Amy had told her, hearing it from the Earl had far more impact on her. It was the confirmation of the Earl and Lady Katrina making love that hurt. But then, what was the matter with her? Of course they would. But she couldn't think about it, and to her horror a tear trickled down her face.

'What we want cannot be, my love.'

The endearment cut through her rather than comforted her. 'I – I knaw.'

'Amy is training to be the baby's nanny.'

'Aye, but it ain't . . . I mean—'

'It's not what she wants to do? Yes, she has told me. Her heart lies in helping others. I am thinking up ways of doing the same, and of having Amy help me with the work. She knows that. But just in case she changes her mind, it is good for her to be trained in a vocation. She will soon be attending elocution lessons – learning how to speak properly, as it is necessary that she does so, for our child's sake. And that, too, will help her in the future. It won't change who she is, but the way she is perceived and received.'

Ruth couldn't argue with him. It was what her ma had wanted for Amy – for her to get an education. Ma had known that Amy was the bright one.

'Things have changed so much for you, Ruth. You are part-owner of a cottage, which will become yours eventually. You can afford to educate yourself and study the music you so desire to learn. You're protected by the law, as ordered by the judge. And now you are looking to the future and have good prospects, not to mention having become a mother. Let change happen for Amy, too. Encourage her to follow the plan I have for her. She has a lot to forget and put behind her, and she is doing that. Don't change the course of her life so that she is in your shadow, working for you and—'

'She would never be that! I wanted her to be in partnership with me. She's more brains in her little toe than I have in me whole head. We could go places together, me and Amy. I could learn the practical things and she could be the business mind.'

'I see. Yes, well, put like that. But she needs life experience first. Leave her where she is for a while. Let her gain her education, begin work, and then maybe I could take her into the office in the Arkwright mill. She could learn the business there. But remember, this is Amy's life we are talking about, and she has the last say.'

Ruth thought about what he said and could see the sense of it. In his office Amy could learn so much they would need to know. Anyroad, however she looked at it, it would be a couple of years before she could be released from full-time care of Josh, so she'd have to shelve everything for a while.

'You're very quiet, Ruth?'

'Aye, I was thinking. And you're reet: I'll not put pressure on Amy to come and be with me, but will you promise to get her into your office as soon as you can?'

'I will. I will speak to Lady Katrina and her father about it. It won't be until our baby is walking, as Lady Katrina will need to place a helper with Amy, who could take over once our child has learned his or her early skills. But in any case, it will take you a few years to get to the stage when you are needing Amy with you. Hopefully by then your other prospects will have risen. In the meantime, have you anyone who could come in and help you? Josh will take a lot of care, and you're far from well.'

'I have Nora.'

'Nora's quite frail herself. She won't be able to help you much. And I know that she was hoping you would care for her, once you were up and about. I worry about you both. You have strong minds, but neither of you is in good health.'

It occurred to her then to ask if Lettie could stay with her, but she didn't. Though it was a good idea, it was something to discuss with the girls first. Amy depended on Lettie a lot, and it might not be right to take that prop from her. 'I'll sort sommat.'

There was silence again. The Earl was the one to break it

374

once more, and what he said cheered Ruth so much that she almost forgot her problems. 'Changing the subject, I've other news for you. The boys, your brothers – they both arrived safely in Australia.'

'Oh, thank God! Will they be alreet?'

'They will. They've to work hard and will be apprentices, then employees, to an engineering firm. They won't have it easy, but from what I saw they're strong lads, so I'm sure they will fare well. I'll send news of them from time to time, and will work on them being allowed to send a letter to you and Amy, once they can read and write.'

This gladdened her, and yet in his telling she sensed something wasn't quite right. It was as if he was trying to make the lads' prospects sound good, just to cheer her. And then there was foreboding in her that the Earl was tying up all the loose ends, and this was his goodbye. That knowledge left her heart feeling heavy. Oh, she'd always get news of him from Amy, but it wouldn't be the same. Still, she had to help him go. They both knew it had to happen.

'So, that's it then? I've to thank you for so much. I don't know how to do that. There's nowt would come near to thanking you enough.'

'You have no need to thank me. I have gained so much by knowing you, Ruth. I will get news of you, through Amy, and will send news about the boys when I hear anything. And if you are to thank me, the best you can give me is to get well, follow your dreams and learn music, as is your heart's desire. And, above all, be happy.'

Allowing herself to look at him, Ruth's gaze held Frederick's eyes. His showed his anguish; hers, she hoped, told of her love for him. And in that moment of looking at him she tried to savour all of him. Imprint him on her memory, so that forever and a day all she had to do was think of him and he would be in front of her, looking as he did now, with his heart hurting at leaving her.

How could she ever live without him? A whimper roused her from this thought. She could; she could do it for little Josh. She'd concentrate on building a future for him – a happy future, aye, and a prosperous one. He'd never know the hunger or pain she'd known. Not if she could help it, he wouldn't.

As the door clicked behind her earl, her instincts got her scrunching up her body, but she straightened and put her mind to all the other things she would do. She'd get their Amy out of service, and get the lads back from that place. And there was sommat else to add to her list. She'd see to it as that Lettie had a chance an' all. She could be one of them opera singers, she could.

A giggle escaped her. *Eeh, Ruth, lass, you've a mountain to climb with that lot, but better that than have time on your hands to think. Better that.*

Brave as this thought was, she couldn't help the longing in her heart; or the tear that plopped onto the bedcovers as she leaned forward and saw the Earl glance back as he reached the gate, then turned and climbed into his carriage. He'd hesitated. He'd seen her looking. He'd wanted to come back, she knew that. And knowing it was going to have to be enough. But would it be?

PART TWO

The Passing of Time
Unsettles and Yet Heals

1861

33

Ruth

A Letter of Sadness

Ruth hobbled along the path, leaning heavily on her crutch. The letter in her hand crackled as the wind caught it and flapped it back and forth. She needed a quiet place to sit and read it.

When she reached the bench at the end of her long, land-scaped garden, Ruth looked back at her house. Perched on the top of a high brow on the outskirts of Blackburn, its many windows reflected the golden hue in which the autumn world was clothed. It was a beautiful house, which stood for all that she and Amy had become in the ten years since she'd said goodbye to her earl. But at what cost? And would they lose it all?

As she lowered herself to sit down, she tossed the plait that she'd fashioned her hair into over her shoulder and gazed out at the rugged hills of Bowland.

Standing majestic in the distance, they looked beautiful with their snow-capped peaks glistening in the light of the sun. Gold and red heather wove wonderful patterns along their craggy slopes. Scant, dancing clouds played with the light, giving an ever-changing kaleidoscope of colour as their shadows splashed here and there. It was a view Ruth never tired of, and yet those hills still evoked memories she'd rather forget.

Turning her attention to the letter, Ruth retrieved it and held it in front of her. Its crinkled appearance reflected the long journey it had taken from the distant land of Australia, as evidenced by the stamp on the envelope. But how she even came to be holding it was a miracle, as it had been sent to the post office in Pradley, some thirty miles away. Someone must have posted it on.

Eeh, Seth and George. Me lovely brothers. You'll be grown men now. I can't believe you've got in touch at last!

It had been a while since she and Amy had heard anything about how the lads were. Haydon, who had remained her friend over the years, had passed on a message from the Earl telling them they'd been released from the colony, and that he no longer had any contact with them. He'd said they'd both done well and had secured jobs. She and Amy had made themselves content with that, but had prayed that one day they would hear from their much-loved brothers themselves.

With the Earl of Harrogate coming to mind, Ruth felt something clutch at her heart, akin to an ache and ever-present. She lived with it, but it came to the fore at times such as this. She had never stopped loving him.

And now she was his equal. Well, in wealth, that was. Not in class; she'd never equal him in that. She'd done as the Earl had suggested the last time she'd seen him, just after her son had been born, and had taken up her learning. The basics at first, and then, finding she had a good brain, going on to experience a love of knowledge.

With the money that Josh had willed her, and what was

added to it when the lovely Nora passed on, some two years after Josh, she and Amy had bought a rundown mill from a man who had been suffering ill-health for a long time. Together, they had worked hard building up the business. Now that mill was one of the finest in Lancashire. But would they survive the current crises?

The civil war raging in America meant that raw cotton wasn't being harvested there. There had been no shipments into Liverpool for weeks now, and their stocks were running low. There was, of course, finer cotton from India, but it was far more expensive and had a limited market. Already they'd had to lay off a dozen or so spinners, and it wouldn't be long before they would have to cut the numbers of weavers and dyers.

But although it pained Ruth to think of the hardships this was causing her workers and their families, and she feared for her own and Amy's future, she agreed with the principles of the war. Slavery needed to be abolished, and she hoped with all her heart that the Yankees would win and set free the black people, who it was said led terrible lives, suffering regular beatings and unbearable hardship.

With a sigh that held all the frustration of her conflicting emotions over the situation, Ruth turned her attention to the letter and dispelled her worries for a moment, as she looked at the thin paper covered in a spidery child-like scrawl. A picture came to her mind of the two young boys her brothers had been before they'd been sent to the penal colony in Sydney, New South Wales.

Seth would be twenty-four now. A grown man. Ruth tried to picture him and knew he would be handsome, maybe tanned from all that sun, and perhaps even married with babbies? And George would be just as good-looking. Eeh,

381

he'd be a strapping young man of twenty-three. Did he have a wife and maybe a family, too? *Oh, me lads, me and Amy have never forgotten you both.*

Steeling herself and swallowing hard, Ruth opened the letter:

> *Dear Ruth, Amy and Elsie,*
> *I'm doing all right. I hope that you get this letter.*

Shock held Ruth still for a moment, and she closed her eyes. *Oh God, the lads don't know about Elsie's passing!* Though her mind screamed against the lie the Earl had told her about keeping the lads informed, she forced herself to read on:

> *I've learnt me letters in a school set up in the colony, and the bloke teaching me has promised to post this for me. As I don't know where you are, he said to send it to the last place the family were known.*

Fear trickled through Ruth. Somehow she knew in her heart there was a deeper pain to face. Why was Seth saying 'I', and not 'we'? And how come the Earl had told her they had left the colony?

Forcing herself to read on, Ruth tried to ignore the voice screaming in her head that she had been deceived – and by the man she loved most in all the world. *Why, why?* But her pain at the Earl's deceit was nothing compared to the agony that seared her at Seth's next words:

> *I expect you know most of what has happened to me, as after I arrived here, the Governor of the colony told me*

that the Earl had requested updates on our progress, so I
trust he intended to keep you all informed about us. But,
you know, though it were kind of him and seemed like a
lifeline to me, the Earl's intentions didn't do me any
favours. It marked me as someone who would have to be
kept in his place and had to learn that I weren't above the
rest of the prisoners. I've suffered more than me share,
because of it.

Sometimes it seemed worth it, as it gave me hope
thinking that if the Earl knew of me plight, he might one
day help me, but that help never came. And this set me
wondering: has he told you the truth, or does he even know
how it really is in here for me?

I trust, though, that he told you about George's passing,
though I doubt he told you the truth of how he died.

My grief is still raw all these years on, as I know yours
will be, and I've thought on as to whether I should tell you,
but then decided it was reet that you should know that our
George didn't have a peaceful passing, and the memory of
how he died visits me in me dreams. The poor lad were
flogged.

'Naw . . . naw!' This protest strangled Ruth's throat. Her
body shook with her sobs. *George. Oh, George!* Memories of
his stubbornness came to her. *Eeh, me lad, what did you do?*
What did you do?

Reading more of the letter told her how her brothers had
been locked in the hold in the bowels of the ship, with hun-
dreds of other convicts. How the sanitation was appalling
and how the older, hardier prisoners stole food from the
girls, women and young boys. George wouldn't put up with
this, and a fight broke out as he tried to stand up for himself

and rallied others to join him. When the master took them all to task, the blame was laid on George's shoulders.

He took twenty lashes. They did it up on deck and made us watch. It were meant to be an example to us all. George never murmured, though his back was torn to shreds. He were a brave lad.

When a woman screamed and another fainted, a big man stepped forward who'd been kind to us both. He told the captain that George were only thirteen. The captain was shocked and, due to the size of George, hadn't questioned his age when passing sentence. He apologized, which calmed the crowd, and then said that George was to receive the finest medical attention they could offer. But it were too late. George never recovered. They let me go to him in his last hour. He fought hard to stay with us. But death took him, as he flailed against it.

A wail came from Ruth. Her agonized cry sent birds soaring into the sky, squawking in protest at having been disturbed. Tears rained down her cheeks. Putting the letter between her knees, she clawed at her shawl, as if releasing herself from its encumbrance would release her from all her pain.

But it was as she read on that the last shreds of emotion were torn in two, as realization dawned that if she'd have known of his plight, she could have helped Seth.

Being on me own's been the worst thing. I could have coped better with our George by me side and knowing we had to look out for each other, but the stigma stuck with me that I had someone in high power taking an interest, and I suspect that only good reports were being given about me welfare. But I've lived a hell on earth.

When me five years were up I had nowhere to go, so I'm stuck here, but I'm not unhappy. I'm a free man, and that has made a big difference. I still work with the gangs, but have become a ganger in charge. I'm allowed to come and go, and I met me wife, Christie, when I went out one day. She were fetching supplies. Her family live in a remote place. They farm acres and acres of land. But they don't approve of me, even though Christie has told them I'd be willing to work for them; so Christie has no more to do with them, and lives with me and our family on the edge of the colony. It's not much of a place, more like a shack really. Me and Christie had a son. He's six months old. I want better for him, but it's not easy to get on when you have the stigma of having been a criminal.

Me lad's named George, and he's reet bonny.

I long to hear how you all are. I feel helpless as to how to make things better for you, and I've feared for you all for a long time, especially for you, Ruth, but I had to keep faith that the Earl helped you, as he seemed a decent bloke back then. I only hope that you're all together and have found some happiness, and all that went on is behind you.

I will try to write when I can. Please try to send a letter back to me. I've included the post-station address. I'll look in our mailbox every time I go to town and hope every day that there's a letter from you.

I want to say soppy things, but that will make me blub, and I'm a man now. So, I'll just say: I miss you and think of you all every day. Seth x

Ruth stared through her tears at the Bowland Hills. Now they seemed to close in on her, as if the treachery that had started on their slopes, the day she and her ma and the young 'uns were walking along that highway, was happening before her eyes.

Brushing the thought away allowed bitterness to creep into her. The Earl had promised to see to it that the lads fared well. He'd even promised that they would serve an apprenticeship and would prosper. If only she'd known. *Why? Why didn't the Earl tell me, as I had money and could do sommat to put things reet?*

Doubts began to gnaw at her as to whether the letters she and Amy had written, and entrusted to the Earl to send, had ever reached Seth, as he didn't acknowledge that *their* lives had changed.

Though weary from the shock and deep sadness that had settled in her, Ruth shoved the letter into the pocket of her frock, took hold of her crutch and raised herself to a standing position. She had to keep strong. Today was the anniversary of Nora's passing and she had to keep to her plans to go to the cemetery, for she'd feel as if she'd let Nora and Josh down if she didn't.

'Ruth?' Haydon's voice came to her as if he was a long distance away, but in truth he was just along the garden path. Ruth looked up to see him striding towards her. 'You'll catch your death out here, lass. That wind's keen enough to slice you in two.'

'Ha, I'm hardier than that, Haydon. Now don't start fussing. I've a lot on me mind.' She told him about the letter, and asked if he knew of a way to get money to Seth.

'Oh dear, that's sad news. I'm sorry, Ruth. And it's so unfair. Why you are sent so much to bear is beyond comprehension, but don't worry: there is a way. I'll look into it for you. Now sit back down for a moment, you look all in.'

'Naw, I'm reet. I need to cut some flowers.'

'I'll do that, as I know I'll not be able to dissuade you from going to the cemetery.' He took hold of her arm. 'Now, no more protests. Sit down, young lady!'

As she sank back down on the bench, Ruth thanked God, as she had done many times, for the loyal and loving friendship that Haydon and his wife, Lilly, showed to her and Amy.

Haydon had come to pick up little Josh, as she always referred to her son. Although he'd had his tenth birthday in January, she still didn't like to subject him to the sadness the cemetery held. Instead she kept his dad's memory alive in a happy way, telling him of the life they'd led in the hills and about the farm, and of his dad's way of making her laugh. Looking after Josh for her, whenever Ruth needed them to, helped Lilly, too, because although she longed for a child of her own, it hadn't happened.

As he cut the winter chrysanthemums, Haydon said, 'Lilly and I are feeling more and more concerned for your welfare, Ruth. You need to get someone to help Amy run the factory – it's too much for you, going in every day.'

'Naw, I'm reet. Amy does most things. Besides, finding the reet person would be difficult. They'd need to know so much about the running of a mill.'

Haydon was quiet for a moment. When he sat on his haunches to look at her, she could see that he had something else on his mind. 'Ruth, I've some news for you, lass, and it's not going to cheer you.'

Ruth held her breath.

'The Earl of Harrogate lost his wife.' Her gasp got

Haydon standing and coming to sit beside her. 'I'm sorry. I know how you feel.'

Ruth swallowed hard. 'Naw, I – I'm alreet. The news shocked me, that's all. I liked Lady Katrina, she was a lovely lady. What happened?'

'Childbirth. Four days ago – she was buried yesterday.'

'Eeh, that's sad. How come I never heard of it? Why didn't you tell me? Did Amy know?'

'She may have heard, as she still has contact with some of the staff over there, but she too has seen how worn out you are, and thought you'd take it better coming from me.'

Amy was right in her thinking. Had she told Ruth, her emotions would have spilled over. But with Haydon, she could keep herself together. 'Did the child live?'

'Aye, another daughter. Though he told me she's not likely to survive. Born too early, by all accounts.'

Ruth wanted to scream against the injustice of this, but kept calm. They'd reached the house before she felt able to ask, 'How is he?' A simple question, which hid the strong urge that filled every part of her: to run to her earl and hold him and shield him from hurt.

All at once she understood that that was what the Earl had been doing, by holding back the truth about her brothers – shielding her from hurt. It hadn't been his best judgement, as she and Amy had a right to know the truth, and she could have at least helped Seth if she'd known his plight. But didn't his action show that he still felt something for her?

With this thought, Ruth's heart, though heavy with sadness, lifted a little at the hope that entered her.

'He's taken it badly. They were a happy couple, and he fears for his new baby.'

Ruth hung her head in shame. Yes, she'd known the Earl had found happiness with Lady Katrina, and though it had hurt to know this, she'd been glad for him. Now she realized he must be a broken man. *How could I have let me feelings give me such powerful hope, when I should have been thinking only of his pain?*

34

Ruth & Frederick

Loss, and a Love Rekindled

As Ruth dropped onto Nora's grave the flowers that Haydon had tied in a bundle for her, the sadness in her deepened. 'Eeh, Nora, I miss you. What I wouldn't give to be cuddled in your lovely soft arms at this moment. And Josh, me poor Josh.' As she said this, she bent over as best she could and gently stroked Josh's name, which was engraved above Nora's. The sight of it brought him back to her.

Glancing around and checking that no one could hear her, Ruth did as she always did on her visits to the graves of her loved ones, and told them about little Josh's antics and his progress in his lessons. 'He's getting on fine – he has your brain, Josh, and he is so funny. A proper comedian.' As she moved on to tell them her worries, tears flowed as she related the news Seth's letter had given her. Always at these times she felt comfort from sharing, and a feeling that Nora and Josh were listening and would find a solution, but this time her desolation didn't lift. Drying her eyes, she turned away. She mustn't despair. Haydon would sort out sommat for her.

A sound stopped her. Her name, softly spoken, in a voice

that was so very dear to her. For a moment she thought she was hearing things, but then it came again: 'Ruth. Ruth, over here.'

Peering towards a clump of trees, Ruth could just make out a shadow. Her heart jolted joy right through her. Lifting her skirt with one hand and leaning heavily on her crutch, she hurried towards the figure. But then stopped within feet of the Earl, as embarrassment and shyness overcame her.

'Ruth, how are you?'

'I – I, I'm fine, thank you, M'Lord.'

'Just fine?'

Looking up into his face, Ruth saw a shadow of the man she'd known. She wanted to say she was sorry for his loss, but the words wouldn't come. She wanted to berate him for not being truthful with her, but she felt suspended, unable to control her emotions.

As if not noticing his effect on her, the Earl carried on making light conversation. 'I'd hoped you were really well. I'd heard such good things about your progress. The mill you bought is doing as well as those of the best of us. Funny that we're now rivals in business.'

She didn't want to talk about mundane things. She wanted to dispel the pain that she could see etched on his face, and could hear in his voice.

'I'm sorry. I'm intruding. I know the sadness you are experiencing. I – I'm here to visit Lady Katrina's grave; she – she lies in the crypt over there, with her late mother and her ancestors. You do know that I lost her?'

'Yes, M'Lord. I just found out today. I'm reet sorry. She were a lovely lady. Is your babby doing alreet?'

'Not really. Her breathing is weak. They say she – she—'

'Oh, M'Lord, don't. I – I knaw what you're going through, but . . .'

His sobs undid her, and his bent body called to her. Getting to him as best she could, she touched his arm and held onto it, never wanting to let go.

Slowly he raised his head. 'Oh, Ruth. Ruth, I've needed you so much.'

'Don't. Don't, M'Lord. It ain't reet.' Her hand dropped to her side. 'I've to go. I feel for you, and wish I could do sommat to help, but I can't.'

'Ruth, don't go.' She stood still. Then watched as he brought out a huge handkerchief and blew his nose loudly. 'I'm sorry. My behaviour was appalling. It was just seeing you, when I'm so vulnerable. Forgive me.'

'There's nowt to forgive.'

'You're right. Does one need forgiveness for loving another, beyond anything you think yourself capable of? Because that's how I love you, Ruth.' His hand came out to her.

Compelled by a force she couldn't fight, Ruth didn't try to move when he stepped forward. Her body swayed towards his. His arms encircled her. This was where she was born to be.

'Ruth. Oh, Ruth.' His tears dampened her hair.

Neither of them saw the woman slip from the shadow of the Arkwright crypt. Her cough startled them. Ruth almost lost her balance, as the Earl let her go and swivelled round. 'Marcia, what . . . ? How—?'

'My Lord Rollinson, I came to visit my family's grave, to be with my loved ones in a moment of peace. It is shocking in the extreme to find you, the so-called loving husband of

392

my darling late sister, in the arms of a – a slut, when Katrina's body is hardly cold! You disgust me.'

'Ruth is not a slut, Madam; she is a friend who was offering me comfort. Something you haven't even tried to do. Nor would I want you to.'

'Ha! A friend, eh? You call that – that thing – a friend? She murdered your brother, and umpteen others, remember? The witch of Pradley! She's your mistress. Go on: admit it. Well, we shall see how this will sit with my father. He can change his will yet, you know. I can still gain what is rightfully mine. Remember the clause that if you brought his beloved Katrina into disrepute, you would lose all? My husband will see to it that you do. Good day, My Lord.'

Fear held Ruth still. Was it all starting again? Would her presence always bring down wrath and bad fortune on others?

'Ruth, I'm sorry. Ruth . . . ?'

Somehow she managed to move away from him. As she did so, she looked up at him and felt the pull of his dark eyes appealing to her, but she had to get away. She had to get to Amy and then home, before Haydon brought Josh back to her. She didn't belong in the Earl's world. She knew that. She only wished her soul knew it, too.

The Earl didn't try to stop her. When she got to the horse and trap that had brought her here, she didn't speak to Denzal, the lad who did odd jobs for her and acted as her driver. He knew where she needed to go next, and he was used to her being distressed when she came back from visiting the graves.

The jolting of the trap usually soothed her, as did going through the busy streets of Blackburn, but today nothing could settle her. *Did that really happen? Did the Earl really tell me he loved me?* She knew she should be feeling happiness coursing through her, but instead she felt afraid and despairing.

Lady Marcia and her husband had a reputation. The two of them were ruthless. They were driven by greed, and took what they wanted by any means they could. Lord Bellinger had owned three mills, and now he owned five. The two he'd acquired had been taken by treachery. One, as she understood it, had been by means of blackmail. Haydon had told her the story. A fellow investigator, whom he knew well, was engaged by Bellinger to find everything he could about the owner of the mill, a John Brazin. The man had a large family and adored his wife, but Lord Bellinger had enticed him to one of the brothels and had then proceeded to extort money from him, on the threat of Lady Marcia telling Mrs Brazin. The poor man committed suicide, leaving debts that his wife couldn't cope with. Lord Bellinger stepped in and bought the business, before anyone even knew it would be for sale.

The other mill he'd snapped up after a mysterious fire had destroyed the looms and the owner couldn't afford to replace them. Haydon was convinced the fire was started deliberately. He'd made it his mission to keep an eye on Lord and Lady Bellinger, as he feared they might do harm to Ruth one day. *Oh, dear God, have I just given them their chance? Naw, don't let it all begin again.* Terror streaked through her as Lady Marcia's words resounded in her ears: *The witch of Pradley.*

Naw . . .

Frederick paced the bedroom in the west wing of his father-in-law's house. His pain for Ruth filled him with guilt. How could he even have considered doing what he'd done? Because he had to admit he'd deliberately stepped out of sight when he'd seen Ruth arrive, and had then crept over to the trees to watch her. And now his actions had put Ruth in danger. Oh, he knew that he, too, stood to lose a lot. Marcia would have a field day, but that didn't worry him as much as he feared for Ruth.

Marcia had never released him from the jealous spite she'd shown at Katrina winning his hand, when she herself had held such hopes of becoming his wife. *Good God, the very thought of such a match fills me with horror, and yet I might well have fallen into it, if Bertram had lived.*

Now he'd given Marcia what she'd been waiting for – a stick to beat him with. His heart felt heavy at the thought that her beating might be aimed at Ruth, as Marcia knew that's where she could hurt him most. Influencing her father to change his will would be a blow to him, but hurting Ruth in any way would be unbearable. *Why? Why does this feeling for Ruth still consume me? I loved Katrina – I did!*

Seeing the bed that had been at the heart of all their love and passion, Frederick crumbled. The soft feather mattress received him as if it was Katrina holding him. Sobs racked his body. His heart was broken, and yet it held hope. It was a contradiction that was tearing him apart.

A sharp, angry-sounding knock on the bedroom door woke Frederick from the exhausted sleep he'd succumbed to. As he lifted his heavy, pounding head, it pained him to call out and ask who it was, as he already knew who it would be.

The door opened. 'What the bloody hell have you been up to? Is it reet what Marcia says: that you're having an affair with that woman who murdered your brother? Good God, man, I've allus had you down as a decent bloke!'

Frederick dropped his head in his hands.

'I take that as an admission then? And I thought you were different from the rest of your lot.'

This was said in a voice that conveyed deep regret. When Frederick lifted his head, it was to see Arkwright slumped in the high-backed chair that stood by the window and had been Katrina's favourite. She'd sat there for hours, watching nature play out in the huge garden. Or delighting in watching the now ten-year-old Rosina playing with her dolls, innocent of her true parentage, accepting him as her father, with a love that he returned as if she were indeed his daughter. The picture triggered Frederick's grief once more, and more tears fell from his gritty eyes. Rosina was the only child to survive from the four pregnancies that Katrina had had.

He stared at his father-in-law. Unable to speak, he shook his head.

'What, man? Are you saying it isn't true?'

Taking a deep breath, Frederick at last found that he could answer. 'It isn't true. I remained loyal to my dear Katrina, and I mourn her loss. My heart is breaking. You know that I was very fond of Ruth, and her sister, and I helped them all I could, after the dreadful things that happened to them as a result of the accident that took my brother. But that was all I have ever done. Today I came across Ruth when I was at a very low ebb. She comforted me. Nothing more. However, I can see how it looks, but I am trusting that what you know of me, and what you know of your youngest daughter, will show you the truth of the situation.'

'Are you daring to blight the only kin I have left in the world? How dare you? Aye, I know Marcia has her faults –

that's if you can call getting what she wants in life a fault – but she don't tell lies to her father. You, on the other hand, are like all toffs: so far up your own backside that you think you can ride roughshod over everyone you consider beneath you!'

This hurt Frederick. He knew this was the opinion Arkwright had held of him in the beginning, but he'd thought that over the years he'd gained his respect. Well, he would command some now.

'Marcia isn't your only kin. You have three grandchildren, Sir. Two of them sired by that scoundrel Bellinger. Granted, you never see one of them, as Marcia leaves her son with her in-laws' nanny, and my only child is fighting for her life, but they are your kin, coming from your daughters.'

'*Two* of them! Good God, what are you saying, man?'

'"My Lord", to you, Sir. And you know very well what I'm saying. Marcia was at pains to inform you, the day after my wedding. She knew what had really gone on. And it is obvious to all that Rosina was sired by Bellinger. She is the very image of him and his family.'

The moment the words were out, Frederick regretted them. Not only because they were a betrayal of Katrina and Rosina, whom he loved dearly and looked upon as his own child, but because Arkwright was struggling to breathe and his face had turned a horrible purplish-blue.

Rushing over to him, Frederick loosened Arkwright's collar. 'I'm sorry, Sir, that was unforgivable of me. Please forget I ever said it. No matter what happened, Katrina and I were very much in love and had forgiven – and from the very beginning had been understanding of – each other. There was nothing we didn't share.'

Arkwright calmed. Gradually his breathing became normal.

Frederick poured him a glass of water from the pitcher on the table next to the chair. 'Drink this, Sir. It will help.'

After a sip, Arkwright studied Frederick for what seemed like an age. Neither spoke. It was for Arkwright to decide how he would accept what he'd been told.

When he did speak, it was to say, 'That bastard!'

'Exactly. There isn't another word for him. You know how Bellinger operates.' Frederick wanted to say that Marcia was no better, but he'd learned his lesson. Where the Arkwrights of this world were concerned, blood really *was* thicker than water.

'It seems to me that you're all the same. Marcia says you were holding the – the . . . witch-woman as if you were lovers. What do you have to say about that then?'

Frederick hung his head. It was time for the truth, no matter what the consequences. At the end of his telling, relief flooded through him. He no longer had to deny Ruth.

'Good God! And Katrina knew?'

'She did. She understood, but she also trusted that I would do nothing about the way I felt. And she knew that I loved her deeply, and Rosina, whom I accepted as my own.'

'I've never known the like. Well, Rosina ain't yours; and if the poor mite in the nursery don't make it, then you're nowt to this family. I should start packing, if I were you. I'm not condoning your way of acting under my roof.'

'No . . . No, you can't. It's ridiculous. It's inhumane. Rosina is my daughter. I won't let you separate us.'

'Won't let me! By your own admission, the child isn't yours. But she *is* my grandchild, and I don't intend to let her anywhere near the likes of you ever again.'

Defeated, Frederick crossed the room and sank back

down on the bed. The reality – that this man had never liked or respected him – was etched into the words he spoke and in the look of hatred on his face. What this would mean for his own future, he couldn't comprehend. All he could see was the black hole his life would be, without his little Rosina.

Left in the room on his own, he tried to absorb the shock of what had happened, and its implications. He was still by no means a wealthy man. No property had been officially handed over to him, and wasn't due to be until after Arkwright's death. Yes, he was in a better position than he had been, when he first came into this family. Katrina had used her personal money to revive his estate, and had even bought back some of the land for him. But he still numbered only five tenants who were bringing in revenue and paying regular rent. It had been the generous allowance made to him by Arkwright that had kept them, and the estate, together. And the awful thing was that Arkwright no longer needed him. He had only needed Frederick in the first place because he'd wanted a lord in his family, to lift his status for his beloved late wife, Lady Veronica. But he now had a lord in Bellinger. And Bellinger had risen in standing over the years and was even accepted at court now. Something Mother was powerless to stop, though she had vowed she would. But how could she, given that Bellinger had married her best friend's daughter – the hateful, scheming Marcia. And now Bellinger was successful and thriving, whilst others waned. *Oh God!*

Wearily getting up and crossing over to Katrina's chair, he sat down in it, hoping to feel some comfort from it. Looking out of the window, he saw Simon Bellinger's carriage arriving. Marcia was already here. No doubt Marcia had sent a messenger to Simon to come as quickly as he could. She must have known how fragile the relationship was between himself and Arkwright. She had probably been working away at eroding it, without him realizing. And here he was, thinking he'd done a good job in the mill and had Arkwright's respect and liking. How wrong he was.

Across the lawn a squirrel scampered up a tree, no doubt after acorns to stock his winter bed with. *What of my winter bed? What of the rest of my life?*

Shaking himself out of his morose mood, Frederick decided to go and sit a while with his new baby girl. A little nameless child – his only child? No, he mustn't think like that. Arkwright was in a temper. He'd calm down and realize the cruelty of what he'd said.

As he went towards the nursery, he knew that he would name the child Katherine, the English version of Katrina. Some peace rested in him at this decision. His little daughter was no longer someone he hadn't connected with. She was his life. *God, let her live. Please let her live.*

35

Marcia

Jealous Revenge

Marcia stood in the shadows of the house that she looked upon as tacky. Ruth's house.

Along the road and round the corner, where it was unlikely to be spotted, her carriage awaited her. She'd come because Frederick had left the house before dinner and hadn't returned. She'd wanted to follow him, but that would have been too obvious. Even Bellinger, with his liberal ways, wouldn't stand for his wife openly pursuing another man. But she wasn't going to lose Frederick a second time.

She had to have him. That witch mustn't be allowed to get her claws into him!

Stamping her feet to dispel the cold she felt, Marcia began to wonder if she had misjudged the situation. She'd assumed Frederick would be making for here, but although he had left an hour or so ago, he hadn't yet appeared.

The icy wind bit through her cloak. She'd have to give up. Pulling her bonnet further forward to shield her face, Marcia bent against the wind and scurried in an unladylike way back to where her driver waited.

It was as her carriage pulled away and turned into the

street where Ruth's house stood that she saw Frederick's carriage approaching. *I knew I was right. That bitch – you won't get away with this, you sorcerer!* Brought on by her anger but fuelled by her frustration, her tears stung her cold cheeks as the house receded into the distance.

'Marcia, where have you been? Your father is going out of his mind. Do you know where Frederick is?'

'I will tell you later where I have been, Simon. And yes, as it happens, I do know where Frederick is. Why, what's wrong with Daddy?'

'The baby – it died.'

'Oh, is that all? We knew it wouldn't survive. You couldn't even call it human, really. Does Frederick know?'

'God, Marcia, you're callous at times. Yes, he knows. He returned here and was with the child. He hadn't left her side since he and your father had a row. The nursery nurse told us that he brought in a vicar and had the child christened: Katherine Ruth. He beggars belief sometimes. Apparently he left the house without a word to anyone, soon afterwards. Your father is still furious, and I think his wrath is also directed at me. God knows what that bloody Frederick told him.'

'He couldn't say anything that Daddy doesn't already know.'

'Well, Frederick's put himself out of favour, that's for sure. By all accounts, his bags are packed and already loaded in the carriage. His driver is just waiting to hear when and where he should take them.'

'Frederick's leaving? He can't. I—'

'What can't he do, my scheming little wife? What are you conjuring up? Don't think for a minute that I will stand by

402

and allow you to pursue an affair with Frederick. Anyone else, but not him. Understand?'

'Keep your voice down, Simon. No matter what Frederick has said, we have Daddy eating out of our hands, and you don't want to spoil that. With what I told him about Frederick and that witch of a woman, I think he's on the verge of changing his will. And if they rowed, that's all to the good, although I don't think Daddy has seen his solicitor yet. If he gets a whiff of our plotting, he'll leave the whole lot to some benefit society or hospital. We need this estate, you know that. The Arkwright mill and the bloody Dovecote one, owned by that scum and her sister, have the best of the market. And they may be the only ones that survive this present crisis. If we play this right and become the beneficiaries of Daddy's estate, we will gain credence with the bank – and, God knows, we need it. We are very near bankrupt.'

'Don't you dare insinuate that the state we are in is all my fault. I didn't start the bloody civil war.'

'No, but you gambled too heavily and played too recklessly. You should set your sights lower and go back to the whorehouses, as you can't afford to keep in tow the costly bloody mistresses that you have.'

'Marcia, show some decorum. It is not fitting for a wife to mention her husband's mistresses. I forbid you to speak to me in that manner!'

'Forbid? You dare to forbid me to pursue the man I love, and now you forbid me to speak my mind? Tread carefully, My Lord Bellinger. Tread very, very carefully.'

Livid, Marcia turned away from her husband and stormed out of the room. In the hall she met the nursery nurse carrying a bundle. 'What have you there, girl? Are you not meant to go down the back stairs to the kitchens? Don't you know that you should not be seen by the family?'

The girl bobbed her knee. 'It is the body of the baby, M'Lady. Mr Arkwright has asked for it to be brought to the front drawing room, until the hearse comes to take it away.'

'Really! What is my father thinking?' No sooner had she said this than it occurred to Marcia to make sure she cemented her position with her father and curried even more favour with him. Reaching for her handkerchief, she sniffed into it. 'Oh dear, I can't bear it. I can't. My poor sister, and now my dear little niece.'

'I'm sorry, M'Lady. Do you want me to ring the bell and have someone come to help you?'

'No. I'll just follow on behind you. I cannot think of my father receiving his dead grandchild without me present. I'm all right, I have composed myself now. Please walk very slowly, out of respect.'

'Yes, M'Lady.'

As they entered the drawing room, fear clutched at Marcia. Her father looked so old. And very, very grey. Remembering to sniffle, she walked over to him and put her arm around him. 'Lay the dear child on that chair next to Mr Arkwright, please, Nurse. And thank you for your care of her. You may leave us now.' Again she gave a slight sob. Taking her father's hand, Marcia knelt beside him and placed her head on his lap, as she used to when she was a child. 'Oh, Daddy, how are we to bear it?'

'Be strong, my dear daughter. You and the grandchildren are all I have now, and I need your strength.'

'I'm here for you, Daddy.'

Her father cleared his throat, and his hand stroked her hair. 'You have your mother's hair. Dear, dear Veronica, thank goodness she didn't live to suffer this pain. We should have listened to you, my dear. You tried to tell us what was going on. Well, I know now, and that scoundrel of a husband of yours has a lot to answer for.'

No, Daddy. Simon isn't the one to blame. Remember, I heard a lot of what happened on Katrina's wedding night. But now isn't the time to talk it over. Please don't blame him. He has the greatest respect for you, and is ashamed of what happened. He was very young and easily led.'

'You're right, we mustn't talk about it now. Where is that damned Frederick? Couldn't he at least have the decency to have stayed to see his child off to the chapel of rest – or to have gone with her?'

'I know where he is, Daddy. I made enquiries. He is with that witch.'

'Good God, curse the man! He will never set foot in this house again. I'll leave instructions that if he returns, he is to be turned away. I'll tell his man to have everything shifted to the local inn. I can't bear to look on his face.'

'But, Daddy, he is the beneficiary of your will. He'll take all this from us when—'

'That isn't going to happen! I will see my solicitor tomorrow. Now, let us remain quiet for a while and sit with Katherine. All of this makes me think the poor soul is better off not to be in this world, with a man like the Earl of Harrogate for a father.'

In the silence Marcia pondered on her father's hatred for Frederick. The intensity of it shocked her, for they had always seemed to get on – admired each other even. Was it due to his grief for Mama, and the more recent pain of losing Katrina and now her child? Would he heal and begin to see that he'd been mistaken and had directed his pain at someone who didn't deserve it? She knew he felt disgust at the way the aristocracy carried on. A hard-working, self-made man, he found it difficult to accept that the lords and ladies of this world swanned around, over-indulging, and then, when falling on hard times, poached the money of those who had made good by their own merit.

Is that what Frederick was doing? Knowing that he might fall from grace, perhaps he thought the witch might come good for him. After all, she had money. Married to her, he'd be secure. *No, I won't let that happen. I'll destroy the Pradley witch first!*

Getting ready for bed, later that night, Marcia pondered everything once more, though none of it had left her head all evening. She was determined to discuss it all with her husband.

'Simon?'

'Call me Lord Bellinger, my dear.'

Marcia sighed. This meant Simon wanted to make love to her, and she wasn't in the mood. He had this quirky thing that he wanted her to act subservient to him during their sexual encounters, and her earlier outburst would have fuelled his need for her to appear unworthy of him, while he took her. This was the reason he gained so much pleasure from going with whores, because he knew they weren't worthy of him and, if they thought they were, they paid for it by being beaten.

Simon often told her how he enjoyed beating lower-class women; and that they were nothing but scum and should bow to his wishes and respect him. She agreed, as it happened, and hated that her father was also from the same class as the women, though the fact that he was gave Simon great pleasure. He could truly lord it over her, whereas Marcia longed to have his respect.

Theirs was a passionate union, and very satisfying to her. Simon often indulged her own quirk – he knew that she enjoyed hearing about what he did with his whores and how he treated them, which was usually badly, especially if they were virgins. But she drew the line when it came to talking about his mistresses. She hated them. They had Simon's respect; he cared for them and spent a lot of money on them. Far more than he did on her.

Many things had come into her mind earlier, as she'd sat at her dressing table in her bedroom and waited for Simon to come and say goodnight to her, so that she could discuss with him the plans that were forming in her head. She needed his help to destroy the witch. To her, the Dovecote woman was the only obstacle to her achieving something that had never died in her – her need to be loved by Frederick. Now she wished she'd talked to Simon in the carriage on their way home, as there would be no opportunity to do so at the moment, with him in an amorous mood.

Simon stood behind her now, massaging her neck in a sensual way, which helped her to relax. His body was close to hers. Marcia could feel his need. A spark of response warmed her, then lit a flame of desire as his hands moved to her breasts. But the pressure he used began to hurt. 'My Lord, not so rough – this is your Marcia. Be gentle.'

'You've crossed me, Marcia, you need to learn respect.'

Her horror at his next action made her forget to address him by his title. 'Simon, no!' Her head stung as he pulled her by her hair towards the bed. 'Let go, you beast! How dare you?'

'How dare I? I dare because you are a whore. A lower-class

bitch, and I've put up with you for long enough. You humiliated me tonight, and you've to learn that you can never, ever do that.'

Pain seared through Marcia as her head and shoulders landed on the mattress, her back hitting the wooden bar of the bed frame. Her scream fuelled his desire, rather than deterring him. He ripped her nightdress from her neck down to her waist, exposing her bruised breasts.

'Stop now, Simon, or I will tell Daddy, and then you will lose everything. I'll divorce you and make public how you trea— Agh!' The slap stung her arm. 'Avoiding my face, eh? Think that will stop me? I'll show Daddy my naked body, if I have to.' Lifting her leg, Marcia kicked out at him, catching him in the chest. Simon's eyes glared down at her, and in their depths she saw a desire she'd never witnessed before: a raw, animal-like hunger. The same kind of desire lit up in her. *God, I want him, but I don't want to be hurt.*

Lifting her roughly by her arms, Simon placed her so that she was sitting on the bed, then positioned himself between her legs and pushed himself at her in a bruising way. Taking him gave her exquisite pleasure. His holler told Marcia this was also true for him. Now she could enjoy him, the battle won. But then Simon shocked her again. Pulling from her, he turned her over and, holding her arms behind her with one hand, began to slap her buttocks, rendering them hot and stingingly painful. Her breath caught in her lungs, her moans begged him to stop, but the more she did so, the more he beat her.

Her sobs weakened her, till hatred of him seeped into her and her temper rose. Wriggling with all the strength she could muster, Marcia loosened his grip on her. Escaping, she rolled over and kicked and kicked with all her might. Catching Simon off-guard, she managed to get off the bed and stand up. The thought in her mind was to kill him!

Where her strength came from she didn't know, but grabbing her heavy dressing-table stool, she lifted it by one leg and smashed the leather-bound top over Simon's head. He slumped to the floor. For a moment the silence held a deep fear for her. But gathering her wits, she bent and checked his breathing. Relieved that she hadn't killed him, she backed herself towards the easy chair that stood near the window and slumped down into it.

Sweat poured from her. Tears of temper and humiliation gushed from her eyes. Simon had taken what dignity she'd clung onto. Oh, she knew how she was viewed: the daughter of a self-made man, with one foot in the lower classes. But she'd commanded some respect through her mother's connections. Now the last shred of that tenuous cord had snapped. She was nothing. Her husband had dared to beat her in the manner he did his whores!

Well, he would pay. She would see to that. She would win Frederick's love, and flaunt their affair for everyone to see. Lord Bellinger's humiliation would be complete. Then she would divorce him. Leaving the room and passing through the door to the small sitting room-cum-dressing room that connected their bedrooms, she made her way to his drinks cabinet.

Her body was aflame with pain; she needed a drink, and then a bath – though this last she would have to forgo, and for days to come. She couldn't risk her maid seeing her bruises. She'd have to make some excuse for wanting to wash herself down, as gossip would be rife if any of the maids got a whiff of what had happened tonight.

She poured herself a whisky, a drink she knew she

shouldn't be partial to, but had been since the night Simon had brought a bottle to her room and got her drunk – another sexual game he liked to play. He said she was very pliable when she was drunk and he could do what he liked with her. What that was, she couldn't remember the next day, although she guessed, from the way her rear was sore for days. After the second time, she'd avoided letting him get her drunk.

As she sat down, a murmur from the bedroom got her standing and rushing to the door. Locking it, and then the one to Simon's bedroom, from which he could gain access from the landing, made her feel safe. With this done, exhaustion overcame her and it was all she could do to pick up her glass of whisky and make it to the sofa that stood against the far wall. She'd just have to sleep on it tonight. *Damn Bellinger – damn and blast him!*

Taking a sip of the golden liquid warmed her and helped to settle her trembling body. Relaxing back, Marcia let her mind explore the ways she would destroy the Dovecote woman. It had to be by fire. *Ha, that worked before and how very appropriate that we should destroy the Dovecote mill – and, hopefully, the witch that owns it – by fire . . .* Well, that's what witches deserved, wasn't it?

With Ruth out of the way, she could work on Frederick. Maybe she should start doing so now. Go to the boarding house where she knew he was staying. Confide in him how Bellinger had treated her. Show him her injuries to gain his sympathy. *Yes, it is all perfect.*

All feelings of being a weak victim left her. She'd show his Lord and Mightiness, Simon Bellinger!

Moving silently over to the bedroom door, Marcia listened. She couldn't hear a sound, but she needed to be sure. She turned the key. Fear zinged through her at the loud click the final turn made. Bellinger had got himself onto the bed. His snores told of his deep sleep.

Finding an outdoor outfit wasn't easy, as she'd never had to go into her wardrobes before; nor did she find it easy to dress herself, a task made more difficult because of her sore arms, chest and back.

Once downstairs, she summoned the butler using the bell cord near the fireplace. 'Get Armington up, and tell him to bring my carriage round to the front. Then bring my cloak. But do not disturb Lord Bellinger. I will be back before he rises.'

'Yes, M'Lady.'

The night wind was even more bitter than the late afternoon had been. But the journey didn't take long. There were still lights on in the boarding house, an imposing place used mainly by the rich who were visiting businesses in the area.

Conducting herself with as much dignity as she could muster, under the scrutiny of the manager, who must wonder why she was here to visit a gentleman guest at this hour, Marcia tried to calm her nerves. She didn't have to wait long, for soon the bellboy came back from his errand to enquire whether Frederick would see her, and asked Marcia to follow him.

Though Frederick's face held anger and dislike, he was polite until the bellboy left them, but then, his voice full of disdain, his words cut through Marcia. 'What do you want? I cannot take any more of your games! I have nothing but extreme dislike for you. Say what you have to say and leave.'

'Oh, Frederick, help me – please help me.' As much to her own surprise as to Frederick's, Marcia burst into tears.

It was very convenient and was not put on, for suddenly she felt the weight of everything: Katrina's death, the baby, the way Bellinger had treated her, the financial plight they were in, which no one knew of; and, most of all, her love for Frederick – and Frederick not even liking her.

'My dear, whatever is the matter? Marcia, don't. Come here.'

She was in his arms. She wanted to snuggle in and yield to him, and have him yield to her, but she had her plan to carry through. Wincing, she eased herself away from him. 'I need to sit down.'

He helped her gently to a chair and used his handkerchief to wipe her face. 'Tell me, Marcia. What is troubling you? You seem hurt.'

Telling Frederick made her realize the enormity of what Bellinger had done to her. Yes, she was strong and could get over it, if she wanted to, without anyone knowing; and she could use it to her advantage to keep Bellinger in tow. But now she realized that what he'd done to her was unforgivable.

'No! My God, that man is depraved!'

'It – it's worse than that. I – I can't tell you about it, but sometimes he gets me drunk and does unspeakable things to me.'

'Oh, my dear, I never dreamed.' He was kneeling in front of her. 'How can I help?'

'I want to leave him. Divorce him, but I have nowhere to go. If I stay at Daddy's, it will be too much for him to take, and Lord Bellinger will be hounding me. But I have to work everything out. If I can get free in a month's time, can I come to yours for a while?'

Frederick looked shocked.

412

'I know I have been a beast to you. I'm sorry. I'll make it up to you. I'll tell my father that I was mistaken about what I saw in the churchyard, and about seeing you go to that woman's place this after—'

'What! You told him that? But how did you know . . . I – I didn't visit her. I was going to, but . . . Anyway, none of this is your business. What are you *really* doing here, Marcia? Is this part of the game you play? Are you trying to trap me?'

Her tears came again. 'No. I'm not lying – look.' She lifted her blouse, making sure he had a peep of her ample breasts.

Frederick gasped at the sight of the bruising covering her upper body.

'And my back is bruised, as well as . . . Well, he – he spanked me, not in a playful, sensual way, but in a way that hurt me very much.'

'Oh, my dear, I don't know what to think. On the one hand, you present as a vulnerable woman; and on the other, as a conniving bitch. I'm sorry, but you do, Marcia. And you have done ever since Katrina and I got together. You're a mystery to me.'

'I was horrid at first, because I loved you. You know that. I was jealous, but then Bellinger has driven my actions since. He recognized my nature and he has forced me to try and make you look bad in my father's eyes. He wants all that Daddy has got. If I refused, he beat me. He – he has even made me follow you. He said he was certain that you were having an affair, and that we needed more proof. Oh, Frederick, I can't take any more.'

'You don't have to. Where is Bellinger now – how did you get away?'

Not telling Frederick the truth about how she'd knocked

413

Bellinger out, Marcia told him that she'd left when he fell asleep.

'Well, you can't go back there. I'll book you a room and—'

'No, I must go back. I have to plan. Running away now isn't the answer. Now that I know you will help me, I will put everything in place. Besides, I cannot let my father suffer any more shocks just yet.'

'But what if Bellinger hurts you again?'

'He won't, at least not for a while. He's always remorseful and attentive afterwards. I have to handle this in the right way. I'm scared of his reaction if I just leave. I need to put a lot of things in place, and then I need to be somewhere he won't think of looking. He'll never guess, in a hundred years, that I would go to you. Once I am safely in your home, I can see a lawyer.'

Back in her own home, Marcia was filled with glee as she climbed the stairs to her bedroom. Her body held the memory of Frederick holding her gently to him once more and apologizing for having misjudged her, and for not realizing what was going on. He'd told her that she must send a messenger if she needed him, as he was leaving for home the next day.

Perfect. Just perfect. I'm a clever girl – a very clever girl.

36

Amy & Ruth

A Surprise Visitor

'These are worrying times, Ruth. We need to invest more of your money to keep us going. That way, I think we could survive for a couple of years. The merchants are taking advantage of the supply situation. Raw cotton is twice the price it was. Exports are getting more difficult, as most bought from us because of our cheap prices and we haven't half the orders now that we had. Then there's the lowering of sales here at home. Wholesale prices are being cut to the bone. It's like we're working for nothing to keep the work-force in jobs.'

'I can't give me mind to it, Amy, love. Me heart's that heavy with me grief for George and thinking of our Seth's plight. I've to leave it to you to decide.'

'Eeh, Ruth, lass. You've to be strong. My heart's breaking an' all, but I keep going, and you must, too. We've got through a lot of bad times, and we know that sticking together and taking a day at a time helps.'

When she was upset, Amy often forgot to keep up her nice way of speaking that she'd learned from the elocution lessons she had attended in the Earl's employ, and lapsed into her natural northern accent. Ruth liked to hear it; it felt good. Like she had her old sister back. Not that having a posh voice had changed Amy. And neither had her responsibilities, which were a heavy burden for a young woman; though what she lacked in age, Amy made up for in intelligence, and she fared well. Ruth was proud of her.

Amy had grown into a bonny lass. Her hair, which had been the bane of her life, now hung in neat ringlets, held back by a mother-of-pearl clip, though achieving this meant that she looked a funny sight in the rags she wore her curls in at night.

Ruth and Amy were sitting in what they called their parlour, but the toffs would call a withdrawing room. They both loved this room and had chosen the furniture and colour scheme together. The rich-looking but cosy sofas in soft silver-greys, with cushions filled with feathers, were Amy's choice. The occasional furniture and a deep oak cabinet holding beautiful ornaments had been chosen by Ruth. They gave the room elegance. Amy had guided her, as she had seen such a room in the Arkwrights' house when she was nanny to Lady Katrina's child, and had wanted to make this one similar.

The walls they had covered in silver-grey silk, and the carpet set everything off, with its royal-blue colour with a pattern of sweeping grey pampas grass woven through it. Never had Ruth dreamed that she would sit in such a room, let alone own one. And yet it all seemed to fit her and Amy. They spent hours in here. Often with Ruth sitting at the grand piano in the corner, playing classical tunes, while Amy read a book or did some beautiful embroidery – one of the many skills that had been part of her tutoring to become a teacher. Ruth often wondered if Amy regretted not going on with that career. But then the schoolroom she'd set up for the workers' children was a joy to her, and she could often be found taking one of the lessons, if she had time on her hands.

There hadn't been much call for the charity work that the Earl had organized and that Amy loved to help with, though the need for it was increasing again, with the numbers now out of work. And it seemed likely that she and Amy would be putting more folk out on their backsides. *Eeh, what am I thinking, but what else can we do?*

'You're quiet, Ruth. Are you all right?'

'Aye, but I've a couple of things on me mind. Both are tugging at me heart.' She hadn't told Amy about her encounter with the Earl, afraid that voicing it would taint the episode, as it was difficult to describe how it happened without it sounding sordid – happening, as it did, so soon after Lady Katrina's passing. But now she felt the need to unburden herself. When she'd finished telling the story, Amy was aghast, but not for the reason Ruth thought she would be.

'You mean, he actually said he loved you? Eeh, our Ruth.'

'I knaw. I never expected it, but now I don't knaw what to make of it. It's unsettled me.'

'But you should be joyous.'

'I am, but I'm also afraid that's not the all of it.' She told Amy about Lady Bellinger and her threats. 'And then, a couple of days ago, the Earl delivered a note to me, telling me that he was going back to his home in Northallerton. He left an address and asked me to visit him now and again. He said he needed time, but hoped we could rekindle the feeling we both knew we had for one another.'

'But that's wonderful. Oh, Ruth, you should be happy. I

know it's sad that Lady Katrina and her babby died – I loved her very much. And I know she and the Earl were happy, so he must be grieving badly. But this shows that although he loved his wife and made her a good husband, he never forgot you.'

'That's just it. What kind of man is he? I mean, he could have done just as he liked, for his class get away with owt. But he chose to abandon me, and to marry another because she was rich.'

'Eeh, Ruth. The Earl was already betrothed to Lady Katrina when he met you. That isn't something he could have got out of. And I think he was just as torn, as he did love Katrina. And, you know, he had to take on a great deal. He had to leave you behind, and forgive Katrina and take her child as his own.'

'What are you on about, our Amy? Are you saying as Lady Katrina had an affair?'

'I am. And with the worst one she could have . . .' Ruth listened in amazement to what Amy told her. 'It was during a furious row, going on between Lady Katrina and her sister, that I heard it, Ruth.'

Ruth shuddered with fear as she listened to the cruel words spoken by Lady Bellinger to her own flesh and blood: 'Don't think for a moment that you and Frederick are ever going to get your hands on Daddy's money. Your child is my husband's bastard, and you know it. You only have to look at her and your wedding-night debauchery stares you in the face. Well, I'm going to make sure that Daddy knows. I'm just waiting for Frederick to fall out of favour. And he will. The tug of the heart is stronger than loyalty, and you know – and I know – where your husband's heart lies. Haven't you noticed how that witch is gaining in wealth?

You don't think for one minute that she's done that on her own, do you?'

'Oh, our Amy. I can't believe it. That woman frightens me.'

'She's a nasty piece.'

'Poor Lady Katrina. To have such a threat hanging over her.'

'Aye, and I reckon that's what made her miscarry her second babby. That night, she fainted and began to bleed. There wasn't a nicer person, Ruth. Lady Katrina were lovely. Talk amongst the staff had always been that it was Lord Bellinger who took her on her wedding night, and not the Earl. But I'd never listen to the tales, so I don't know why it was said. But I have to admit, the child does look like Lord Bellinger. And especially like his sister, who came to visit once. But, you know, the Earl loved that little girl and treated her as his own, so that says sommat about him, doesn't it?'

'Aye, it does. I were daft to doubt him. Oh, Amy, he's in a bad place.' Ruth told Amy more of what the Earl had said in his note about how he had been cut off by the Arkwrights.

'Eeh, Ruth, the way them lot go on. That Lord and Lady Bellinger are underhand, and are trying to grow their empire at everyone's expense. Though there are rumours that they're failing and, if they're true, that could make them even more dangerous.'

'I've been thinking the same. She could make trouble for us. We're to be on our guard, Amy.'

'We are, I agree. But how we will know what they intend – if anything – I do not know. Now, what was the other matter? You said you had a couple of things playing on your mind, Ruth.'

'Aye, I have, Amy love. What d'yer think of us closing the factory? Just until the troubles in America are over. And then me and you could go to Australia and bring our Seth and his family back and—'

Amy's look of complete shock stopped Ruth from continuing. A silence fell. Ruth waited, not wanting to push for an answer. She knew Amy needed time to absorb this. Amy never made snap decisions, unlike herself.

When Amy did speak, the guilt Ruth already felt about her proposal deepened. 'If we did that, Ruth, we'd put the rest of our loyal workforce out of work. Eeh, Ruth, it's been difficult as it is, making the cuts we've had to. The number of homeless folk is growing by the day. I've seen to it that the charity work started by the Earl has begun to thrive again, and that the hungry are fed, as much as we can. But to put more out. No, I can't do it. I suggest we carry on as we are. I can manage with . . . I – I mean. Oh, anyroad, the civil war can't go on forever.'

Martha Bardacre, a motherly figure who took care of the house and cared deeply for the sisters' welfare, came through the door at that moment. 'We've got a visitor!' Her tone held excitement. 'Eeh, me lasses, you'll never guess who it is.'

'Give us a clue at least.'

'She sings like a bird, Amy.'

Amy jumped up and hugged her. 'Eeh, Martha, you had me going there. Where is she? Is she all right?'

'I am, Amy. Hello, you two.' Lettie breezed through the door. 'I'm reet as rain, me lasses. Eeh, don't get up, Ruth. Come here, me Amy.'

As Ruth watched the joy of Amy and Lettie's reunion, her troubles seemed to halve. Just taking in the sight of Lettie, in her long purple frock with a red feathered boa around her neck and red boots, got her smiling and wondering if Lettie had become colour-blind or if this was the way they dressed in London. Because it wasn't just her clothes. Lettie's hair was piled high and clipped back into a bunch of ringlets, and her face was painted with rouge. Though she'd have said Lettie was a mite too thin.

When the pair finally parted, Lettie had left traces of her red lipstick all over Amy's face. Ruth laughed out loud, but then found herself spitting Lettie's feathers out of her mouth, as Lettie bent over her and enclosed her in her arms.

'It's wonderful to see thee, Lettie. More wonderful than you can imagine! Me and Amy have a lot to tell you. Sit down, and I'll get Martha to fetch us some tea and cakes.'

'Eeh, bugger the tea and cakes, haven't you any whisky? By, I could down a reet good swallow of that.'

This caused alarm in Ruth. It wasn't the whisky, but the way Lettie had said she needed one, as if her life depended on it. Something was amiss.

'Are you really all right, Lettie? Has something happened? Your last letter said that you were doing so well.'

Lettie sank down onto the sofa next to Ruth. Her eyes filled with tears and her head shook. 'It's all over, I – I have—' A spasm of coughing seized her. Her hand rummaged in her bag, and the handkerchief she pulled out and put to her mouth was blood-stained.

37

Marcia

Sowing the Seeds of Vengeance

There was so much to do, so much to accomplish, but, Marcia thought, no time in which to achieve it all.

Her urgency stemmed from the need to strike whilst she had the upper hand. Lord Bellinger was putty in her hands. His remorse seemed genuine, though she suspected his motive was fear of losing the prospect of taking over all that Marcia's father had; this was his only hope of surviving in business and keeping his position in society. He'd even given up his mistresses, paid them off and closed the houses he kept for them. A triumph, indeed, for Marcia. But there was another reason that she knew she must act – and act now.

Dropping onto her knees the embroidery she'd been pretending to be engaged in, she looked over at her husband. Already dressed to go out, Simon was sitting in his usual chair next to the fireside. He was about to pay a visit to their bank manager, and had been telling her how his worries weighed heavily on him. Not that she cared unduly. The only thing that mattered to her was to complete what she felt she had almost accomplished – getting deeper into Frederick's affections. For that, she needed that witch out of the way; and now was her opportunity to gain Simon's help.

'Simon, we need to move fast. Daddy is softening up. He spoke to me this afternoon about whether he'd been too harsh on Frederick. He said he had a conscience about the fellow. And that Katrina wouldn't have wanted him to act as he had done, as she herself had forgiven Frederick his feelings for that witch, and Frederick had forgiven Katrina for her indiscretion with you. Daddy actually asked me if I would write to Frederick asking him to come for a visit, to sort everything out. God, if that happens, Simon, we are lost.'

'And how do you propose to stop it happening? What wicked scheme are you conjuring up?'

'I have a letter from Frederick.' The letter was the last thing she wanted to share with Bellinger, and yet it was a gift.

Over the last two months she had been writing to Frederick, keeping alive the friendship that had stemmed from her visit to him on the night Bellinger attacked her.

Bellinger's look of surprise, and then anger, unnerved Marcia. 'A letter? Why should Frederick write to you. You were arch-enemies.'

'And still are, but I use everything to my advantage. Your despicable attack on me didn't break me, as it would have most women of my upbringing, but instead gave me a weapon to wheedle myself back into Frederick's affections.'

'What! How? My God, if you've told him, I'll—'

'What? Hit me again? Subject me to the vile humiliation you carried out that night? Just you try it. And this time I won't go to Frederick, but to Daddy. Now, stop being a fool and listen. My ploy worked. Frederick has opened up his heart to me – and in writing. He wants me to approve of him having that bloody Dovecote girl over for a visit to his house. It's valuable evidence that will cement Father's hatred of him, and give me the chance to get Daddy finally to do something about changing his will.'

'Uh, I have as much chance of marrying Queen Victoria as you have of accomplishing that! Your stupid father is holding guilt about breaking his promise to Katrina, and you bloody well put me right out of favour by telling him that I fathered Katrina's first child. What were you thinking of? I've done everything for you. Everything!'

Anger caused his voice to rise. Marcia knew she had to calm him. She needed her revenge on Simon just as much as she needed to rid herself of that blasted witch. Only then could she go to Frederick, with everyone who stood in her way dealt with, and with Daddy's money coming to them. Her plan was a good one, but she needed Bellinger's help to carry it all through.

'You're not out of favour. You need to stop this attitude you have towards Father. I have smoothed all of it over. I've convinced Daddy that you were two young people who thought themselves in love and used the forgiveness that Frederick showed Katrina, and the way he took your child as his own and loved her. Trouble is, I have done too good a job of getting you back into a good light. Daddy now thinks he was wrong about Frederick keeping up an affair with the witch during his marriage, as he thinks that if it were so, Frederick wouldn't have shut himself away, as he has done. I can change that opinion. I plan to go weeping to Daddy to tell him that I too have forgiven Frederick and have been trying to support him – when Frederick shatters all that by asking me to help him nurture his relationship with that vile woman!'

Bellinger's expression changed. 'Go on: so far you are making sense, but why do we have to destroy the witch? What will that accomplish? Surely, if we leave well alone, Frederick will blot his own copybook by taking up with her?'

Marcia knew this and had to think quickly. Nothing must stand in her way, and the witch did.

'Because I want to destroy Frederick. Don't you? He has lorded it over us for years. He's even taken actions in business that have been detrimental to us. He holds a grudge against you, for what you did to him on his wedding night. And he has made you suffer for that. Look at that deal we set up with the government to supply all the uniforms for the forces. Frederick took that from under our nose, using his friendship with the Queen.'

It hadn't happened quite like that, as Marcia knew. Frederick had already secured the order and, not knowing this, Marcia had persuaded Bellinger to butter up the influential Major Stanstal, thinking that he could swing the deal their way. After much money had been wasted and much time spent, they had learned that Frederick had won the order. Marcia immediately convinced Bellinger that he had done so in an underhand way. She had got away with it, and it was now useful fuel to stoke Bellinger's hatred and have him wanting to exact revenge on Frederick. Just in case, she added, 'And didn't he steal the love of your life? Look how he moved in that disgusting way, offering for Katrina's hand before the body of his brother was even cold! You had no chance to act. You'd seen that such a match between a lord and the daughter of a self-made man had been accepted in society, because of our mother's standing, and saw a chance when Katrina's betrothed was killed, but Frederick stole your thunder. No one expected that!'

Her ploy worked. Bellinger's protests turned into a passionate desire for revenge. 'You're right, the mighty Earl needs to be brought low. And by us. What is your plan, my clever wife?'

Marcia had an order for the events she planned, though none of it would benefit Bellinger, but he had the right contacts. And she needed him implicated. 'Another fire. We have to destroy all that the witch has – and her with it.'

'You mean: murder! God, Marcia, no. That's going too far. Destroying her factory will be enough.'

'It won't. She has money. She can rise up from the loss. Frederick will go to her aid. He will land on his feet again.'

'But then we will have your father's favour. I don't understand why anyone has to die. I will agree to the fire, but it must be done at night, when the building is empty. My man can make it look like an accident, as he did before. It was an easy job setting fire to some rubbish in the area we needed to destroy.'

This wasn't working out how Marcia had planned. Bellinger had logic on his side, whilst she was driven by intense desire. 'We want Frederick destroyed – not getting all he has ever wanted!'

'But in a way, he will be destroyed. He won't be accepted in society ever again, and that will hurt him.'

'It won't. Not any more. He has already decided none of that matters. If he can have that witch, whom he calls "his dear Ruth", he says his world will be complete.'

'I see. In that case, you're right. I don't like it, but then she is no more than a whore – and we will treat her as such.'

Marcia could see, by the glint in his eye, that Simon relished the prospect of being part of the witch's downfall. She knew what he meant by treating the witch like one of his whores, and the thought excited her. 'Do what you think fit, but make sure it works. I want her dead, and her business destroyed!'

The vehemence with which this came out shocked Marcia. *God, what have I become?* But then she knew that whatever she wanted in life was hers for the taking if, and only if, she plotted for it. And she wanted Frederick, and always had done.

38

Ruth & Frederick,
Simon & Marcia

The Consequences of Thwarted Love

Ruth stood holding onto the back of her sofa. Could she dare to hope?

Frederick smiled a small, encouraging smile. 'Please, Ruth?'

Her name sounded different on his lips. Musical. But what he was proposing wasn't clear.

'We could go away together. My mother understands. She has known for a long time about you, and has given me her blessing to spend the rest of my life in happiness. My dear Katrina knew, too. Not that I didn't love her – I did, very much – but she knew that my heart lay with you, and always has. She wasn't unhappy. We were very happy together, and I will grieve her loss forever. But I want to be with you. I need you, my darling Ruth.'

He stepped nearer to her, his expression one of a man in turmoil. It was only weeks since he'd buried the woman he said he loved very much, so could he really know that he wanted to be with her? Did he mean marriage? He hadn't mentioned the word. Maybe she wasn't worthy of that status.

'Say something, Ruth. I – I don't know what you are feeling. Have I overstepped the mark? Or mistaken how you feel? If you would have me, I would love your son as my own. And I would see that Amy has all the help she needs to carry on without you. I have a man who has worked with me for a long time and knows everything there is to know about running a mill. He is young, but he has been working in Arkwright's mill since he was a boy of thirteen. I took him under my wing, and he is loyal to me. I know he would be willing to step into your shoes.'

'You have everything sorted then? Me life is to be taken over, it seems.' It wasn't what Ruth wanted to say. She wanted to go into his arms and hold him close. She wanted to tell him: yes, she'd go to the end of the earth with him; but were these the terms she wanted? He wasn't offering her marriage, she knew that now. He wanted her to go away with him, as his mistress.

'No, I haven't everything sorted, Ruth. I'm sorry if I sounded that way. Oh God, I'm making a mess of this. Forgive me. I—' His body seemed to fold before her eyes. Without even knowing how she made it to him, she was by his side holding him, her heart aching with her love for him. He'd been through so much.

'Sit down, me love.' Her endearment undid him. Tears flowed from his eyes. 'Eeh, naw – naw, don't. I do love you, and always have. It's just the terms you seem to be putting to me. I'm not for being your mistress, Frederick.' It seemed strange, calling him that. 'I knaw that's how I lived with Josh, but we had no choice. I were hunted and couldn't bring attention to meself in the legal world. But now I'm free. And if I go to a man, it will be as his wife.'

There were a few moments when all that could be heard

were Frederick's sobs. Ruth held him close. It was all too soon. *Is he clutching at owt that might relieve his pain, by coming to me? Have I pushed him too far?*

As his sobs lessened, he took out his handkerchief and wiped his face. 'Forgive me, I . . .' He looked up at her, his beautiful dark eyes holding so much love. 'Will you marry me, Ruth?'

Happiness engulfed her. All her worries surrounding Seth and Lettie left her, as he pulled her down onto his knee. His kiss made her whole. Nothing could mar the complete and utter joy that she felt.

But her happiness was short-lived. The door opening and the sound of Lettie screaming wrenched her from her blissful state. Frederick's lips left hers and his arm lifted her to a sitting position as, joined in shock, they stared at Lettie.

'There's a fire!' Lettie bent over in a fit of coughing. 'A – a fire! The . . . the factory!'

'What? Naw. Our factory? Oh God, naw. Amy! Amy's still there!'

In one movement Frederick stood both himself and Ruth up, holding her shaking body to him. She stared at Lettie.

'There's smoke – and the sky is red above where your factory is. A lad knocked on the door and shouted that the factory is on fire, and that his dad's in there. Oh, Ruth . . . Ruth.'

Lettie's fit of coughing was pitiful to hear, but Ruth could devote no attention to her. 'Get me crutch, Frederick: we have to go. Amy's in the factory; she had four men working late to complete an order that was urgent. She – she said she'd stay till it was done. Oh God, not me Amy. Naw . . . naw!'

'Calm down, darling – we'll help nothing by panicking.

I'm sure Amy will be fine, she has . . . Look, my carriage is around the back of the house.' Turning to Lettie, he asked her to help Ruth with her coat and hat. 'I'll go and summon my man. We'll go to the factory, Ruth; just hold yourself together, darling. We'll get Amy, I know we will, she – she's not alone, so don't worry.'

Ruth stared at the closed door, wanting to believe him, but her heart pounded fear around her body and she couldn't think what he meant, by Amy not being alone.

Getting to the front door with Lettie's help, Ruth was surprised by the sharp rapping of the knocker. Lettie opened the door, only to be shoved aside by Lord Bellinger.

Shock seized Ruth, and she couldn't speak. Her mind wouldn't give her any reason for him being here. His expression held contempt, and his voice mocked, 'Huh, going somewhere, are we? Well, you're too late – your factory is razed to the ground. Ha! The witch is ruined by fire.' His laughter sounded hideous, but Ruth could only stare at him. 'Well, now, my little whore, you are brought low to the position you should be in, and I'm going to bring you lower.' The slap he gave her knocked Ruth back against the wall, and her crutch fell to the floor. Bellinger raised his fist, but before he could land the punch he aimed at her, Lettie bent down, grabbed her crutch and hit him a blow that caught his shoulder.

'You bitch!' Grabbing the crutch, Lord Bellinger shoved it hard into Lettie's chest. Her body staggered and her face turned deathly pale. Her body sank to the floor. 'Naw! Lettie – Lettie . . .'

Lord Bellinger's painful grip on her arm stopped Ruth from going to Lettie. 'Leave her – you're coming with me.'

Excruciating pain zinged through Ruth's head as he

431

grasped her hair and dragged her along the hall. Kicking the sitting-room door open, he shoved her inside. She landed on the floor and her breath left her body, leaving her unable to protest. Every bone of her trembled as she stared up into the evil face of Lord Bellinger. His movements showed her the horror of his intentions. He was unbuckling his belt. 'Naw . . . naw. Don't—'

The lash he meant to give her never landed. Frederick caught his arm and twisted it behind his back. 'What the blazes are you doing, Bellinger? You bastard!' Shoving Bellinger hard against the wall, Frederick brought up his knee and rammed it into Bellinger's groin. His wail told of his agony as he slid down to the floor. His face held shock as he looked up at Frederick's face. 'You . . . b – bastard. It – it's all true then? You are having an affair with that . . . that witch!'

Frederick grabbed Bellinger's collar. 'No, it isn't true – not that it is any of your business. Why are you here, Bellinger? What on earth possessed you to attack my future wife? God, you were going to whip her – why? What has she ever done to you?'

'She's scum, she's bewitched you. Marry her! God, Frederick, have you lost your mind?'

'No, but you seem to have lost yours. You'll go to prison for this.' Frederick went to grab Lord Bellinger by the collar, but, recovered now, Bellinger kicked out. Frederick lost his balance and fell backwards. Seizing the opportunity, Bellinger rose and ran from the room.

Ruth crawled over to Frederick. Reaching for her, he pulled her to him. 'I'm sorry, so sorry, I brought this down on you.'

'Naw, it weren't your doing. Oh, Frederick, what he said

about the fire made me think he had something to do with it. But why? Why would he want to hurt me?'

'I don't know, but I can guess who's really to blame. Are you all right?'

'It's not myself I'm worried about, it's Lettie and . . . Oh, Frederick, me Amy – me sister. What if . . . ?'

Raising himself and lifting Ruth up, he sat her on the sofa. 'I'll check on Lettie, wait here.'

When he returned with Lettie in his arms, Ruth's fear increased. Lettie's face had a blue tinge, and moans of agony came from her. Frederick laid her next to Ruth, putting her head in Ruth's lap. 'Lettie. Eeh, Lettie, me little lass, where does it hurt?'

Lettie moaned again.

Frederick spoke. 'She seems in a lot of pain. Is this normal for her condition?'

'Naw. Not like this, she's usually weak and short of breath, and her bones ache, but . . . Oh, Frederick, that Lord Bellinger shoved me crutch into her. Oh God!'

'I wouldn't put it past him. Have you anyone you can send for a doctor? Someone who can get there fast. Only I have to go to the fire – I must find Amy.'

'Martha's in the kitchen. She looks after us. She can go next door and ask them to fetch the doctor. They're lovely folk; a bit offhand with us when we first moved here, but when they got to knaw us, we gained their respect.'

Within seconds Frederick was back in the room, with a mortified Martha following him. 'Eeh, Ruth, lass, I'm sorry. When I left you with the Earl, I went into the kitchen and fell asleep, I didn't hear a thing . . . Eeh, me Ruth, what happened?'

'Never mind that now, Martha; go round next door as fast

as you can and ask them to fetch a doctor. Tell them it's urgent.'

As Martha left the room, Frederick bent and kissed Ruth's forehead. The touch of his lips trembled through her. On the one hand, she was experiencing extreme happiness, but on the other, her heart bled with anguish.

'I'll be back as soon as I can, darling. Everything will be all right, I promise.'

Ruth nodded, but as she looked down into Lettie's beloved face she knew, with a sinking heart, that she wasn't long for this world. She wanted to hold Lettie and tell her everything would be reet. 'Lettie, lass. Eeh, me Lettie, how has it come to this?'

Lettie stirred. Her eyes opened. 'He – he k – kicked me.'

Tears ran down Ruth's face. She didn't have to ask who. To the Bellingers of this world, folk like her and Lettie were scum. 'The doctor's coming, Lettie. He'll make you better. We'll get you booked into that sanatorium he spoke of last time he came. And then, if they can get you well enough, we'll see about the rest of his plan to take you to Switzerland. They say the air there works wonders for them with the TB in their lungs.'

Lettie's eyes stared back at Ruth. They held a glimmer of hope. A small smile played around her lips. 'If anyone can m – make it happen that I get bet – better, you can, Ruth. You c – can do owt you put your mind to.'

In the hope that Ruth knew she had given Lettie, she herself felt only despair, as saving Lettie was something Ruth knew she couldn't do.

The door bursting open, and Amy standing there, shocked these feelings from her and replaced them with joy. 'Amy, lass – Amy! Where did you come from?'

Amy's coal-black lips widened in a smile, then quivered. A tear traced a path through the black smut that caked her face, leaving one clean pink trail.

'Eeh, our Ruth, it's all gone. All of it . . .'

'Don't take on, me lass. It's alreet. You're here and that's all that matters. Eeh, me lass, I thought I'd lost you.'

Amy hurried over to Ruth and flung her arms around her neck. Putting an arm around Amy, Ruth could feel the trembling of her body and this set all her emotions in turmoil. Her beloved sister was safe, but what did they have to face where Lettie was concerned? As for the factory, at this moment it meant nothing to her. As long as . . . 'Amy, lass, did everyone get out?'

'Aye, they did. Eeh, Ruth, it were bad . . . bad.' Seeing Lettie at that moment, Amy lifted her head from Ruth's shoulder. 'Lettie! Eeh, Lettie, what's to do?' Amy looked from Lettie to Ruth, and her face now held fear of a different kind – fear for the friend she loved dearly.

'We've sent for the doctor. Don't worry. A lot has happened here. The Earl was here – he went to fetch you.'

'I knaw. We met him up the road. He turned back, so he should be here in a mo. Ruth, there's someone I want you to meet.' Going to the door, Amy called, 'Come on in, Larry, and meet me sister. This is Larry, our Ruth. He – he's me friend. I – I didn't tell you of him; he, well, the Earl introduced us a while back, before . . .'

Ruth couldn't take this in. Frederick had introduced them? When? Why? Her mind went back to what Frederick had said earlier: that he had someone who could help Amy. *My God, I didn't even knaw as Amy had seen the Earl lately.*

Frederick came in at that moment. 'This is the young man I mentioned. I – I took the liberty of asking Amy to let him work beside her, when you weren't around. I'm sorry, I didn't want you to find out like this. It had nothing to do with you and me, at the time. Katrina was still alive when I heard that you were struggling to cope. I spoke to Amy. It was my idea that she should train Larry, but should keep my plan to transfer him to your employment a secret for now. I thought you might thwart it, but once you saw how efficient Larry was, you might be more inclined to hand over some of your responsibilities to him.'

'I kept it secret from you, as I wanted to see if I got on with Larry. I – I, well, I agreed with the Earl that you were doing too much,' Amy confessed.

Ruth was astounded. She hadn't dreamed her sister would go behind her back like this.

'I'm sorry, Ruth. It all seemed a good idea. And, well, once it began, it was fun and . . . well, me and Larry, we—'

'We fell in love.'

This from the young man – and Larry taking Amy's hand while giving her an adoring look – more than confirmed his words. But the joy Ruth should have experienced at this was marred by the feeling of having been deceived. She looked over at Frederick and knew, by his expression of deep love for her, that although some of his actions were not what she wanted of him, everything he did stemmed from that love. All these years he must have been keeping a close eye on her. The thought warmed her, but the knowledge that his information probably came from Haydon further hurt her, as she had looked on Haydon as her friend while, unbeknown to her, he was just doing his job.

None of it sat well with her. She liked openness and honesty, and this way of going about things was dishonest and left her unsure of anything – not even of her beloved Earl, no matter what his motives.

'Ruth, don't look at me like that. I'm sorry. I couldn't help myself. My love for you drove me to try and protect you.'

Martha coming through the door, announcing that the doctor was here, gave Ruth no chance to answer.

Lord Bellinger rode across town, his horse picking its way through the cobbled streets of Blackburn. The air hung heavy with smoke, and a glow coming from the east of the town, where the witch's factory was, gave him the satisfied feeling that at least – though it was all over for him and his detested wife – it was over for the witch, too. Ha! And for the despicable Lord Rollinson . . . *Marry that scum! He'll be shunned by everyone. Christ, why didn't Marcia know Rollinson would be there – or maybe she did? Maybe she wanted me to turn up with rape in my heart, only to be confronted by Frederick.*

'Damn and blast!' His own voice came back at him. Tears of anger and fear stung his smarting eyes and, as the lowering smoke caught in his lungs, his voice rose. 'I'll kill you, Marcia, you slut – I'll bloody kill you!'

Reaching his home, he handed his horse to his man and took the steps two at a time. The door opened without him knocking on it. Shoving the butler out of the way, he demanded that a bottle of whisky be brought to his study. He needed to think.

Watching the golden liquid being poured, Bellinger sat in the high-backed winged chair near the blazing fire. 'Where is Lady Marcia?'

'She's in her sitting room, M'Lord.'

'Don't inform her that I am home. I want a few moments to myself.'

'Very well, Sir. Do you need me to stay in attendance?'

'No. Just leave the bottle there. I won't need anything further tonight.'

The whisky went down in one. Its warmth did nothing to soothe the anger that was boiling like a furnace inside him. Grabbing the bottle, he lifted it to his lips and drank more than half of its contents without taking a breath. Rage tore through him now. The drink churned and fuelled his irrational thoughts. His hands itched to be clasped around Marcia's neck: he'd squeeze the life out of her.

Marcia jumped as the door crashed open. Terror clutched at her. 'W – what happened?'

'You know what happened, you bitch! It was all a trap.'

Simon leapt across the room towards her, slamming the door with a force that seemed to rock the whole room. Putting her hands up to shield herself, Marcia screamed, 'Don't touch me, I – I warn—'

His hands grabbed her hair and she was forced to the floor. Simon was on top of her. Her scream was strangled in her throat as his hands grabbed her neck – she couldn't breathe!

'I'm going to kill you, my fair scheming lady. You're going to die! Do you hear me?'

Her eyes bulged and felt as if they would burst. She tried to move, but all her strength had gone. The last thing she saw, before going into the blackness that called her, was Bellinger spitting in her face. She never felt the glob of spittle land.

*

Sweat rolled off Bellinger. His heart pounded. Beneath him, Marcia's face looked ugly, contorted. She was still; very still. Her eyes stared, unseeing. He'd done it! *God! I didn't mean to. I – I didn't . . . I was just going to punish her.* The vomit projected from his mouth as he stood up. *What now? What now? Oh God!*

Only one solution presented itself to him.

He passed no one on his way to the stable. Entering, he turned to the left, to the place where his guns were stored.

The bang shook the stable building.

39

Frederick & Ruth

A Deep Loss, but a New Beginning

Ruth took Amy's hand. It had been two months since the fire. And now they stood in the churchyard, within sight of the grave that held those who had caused it all, but Ruth felt no pity for them.

A tear plopped onto Amy's cheek. Larry stepped forward and took her into his arms.

'Ashes to ashes . . .'

Is that what our Lettie is? Ashes and dust? Naw, she'd never be that. A sound filled Ruth's head: Lettie's beautiful voice singing 'Amazing Grace'. She smiled. That's what Lettie had shown – a beautiful grace that carried her through the last weeks of her life; and she felt proud that she and Amy had been able to help her.

Amy stepped forward and threw a handful of earth. The sound reverberated through Ruth. An arm came round her, and she looked up into Frederick's beautiful face. She'd forgiven him for trying to manage her life for her; and for his misguided protection of her, in not telling her the truth about the boys.

Her attention came back to the proceedings, as her turn

came to help Lettie on her way, by throwing earth onto her coffin. She left Frederick's side and walked with as much dignity as she could to the end of the grave, ignoring the pain the movement cost her and leaning heavily on her crutch. Frederick didn't try to help her, for he knew this was something she wanted to do on her own for Lettie.

With the thud of the dirt hitting the coffin, she imagined Lettie smiling – happy that both she and Amy were settled now.

Looking up, Ruth saw that Mr Arkwright was standing next to Frederick. She hadn't noticed him at the service. A young girl pulled her hand from his and moved closer to Frederick, who lifted her up into his arms. His face lit up with happiness.

There had been some forgiveness. It seemed that Lady Marcia had visited her father on the day she'd died, the day of the fire. She'd told him that all would soon be resolved. That she was leaving Lord Bellinger and was going to stay with Frederick. That she and Frederick were in love, and always had been. She'd told him it had been Bellinger's scheming – and the hold he had on her – that had caused her to tell lies about Frederick and Katrina. She told him that she feared what Bellinger was planning. That their factories were failing fast, and that Bellinger sought to gain all he could by discrediting Frederick.

Mr Arkwright now knew the truth, but the knowing had taken its toll, as had losing all of his family. Frederick had tried to step in and help him, but the most help had come from Lady Eleonore, whom Ruth now saw step forward and take Mr Arkwright's hand. He smiled down at her. They had long been friends, through Eleonore's connection to Arkwright's

441

wife, and Ruth hoped that their friendship would deepen now and they might become more than a prop for each other.

It hurt Ruth to think that Lady Marcia must have plotted for her to be attacked, and even killed, if what Frederick surmised was correct. However, taking care of Lettie had overridden that, and Frederick's love had helped her through it all.

As they left Lettie behind in the churchyard, Ruth's heart was heavy. The sound of Amy's sobs made her sorrow seem hard to bear. But then, when she looked back at her sister and saw her in Larry's arms, and remembered his devotion to Amy and how they planned to marry, some of Ruth's pain lifted.

Later that evening the fire cracked and spitted, its glow giving out a comforting warmth. They were alone: Ruth and her earl. Amy planned on spending the night at her Larry's house. 'His mam's away, so we'll have the place to ourselves. And I reckon as that's what you need an' all, our Ruth – a bit of time alone with Frederick. I've told Martha to go to bed and leave you to yourselves.' The little twinkle in her eye as she'd said this had amused Ruth.

Frederick sat next to her on the sofa, his arm pulling her towards him. She went willingly into the comfort he offered and raised her head to him. Their kiss held all the promise of their tomorrows. A quiet wedding was planned in a month's time, and then they were going to sail to Australia to see Seth and his family and set him up in a new life. Frederick had seen to it that money was sent to him, and they had heard he had plans to buy a farm.

The insurance payout on the factory had been settled,

and the building of a new one on the ruins of the old one was in progress. The ownership had passed to Amy and Larry.

All of these thoughts floated from Ruth, as she lost herself in the deepening kiss that lit her body with a passion she knew she'd only ever touched on in the past.

As they came out of the kiss, Frederick stood. She watched as he removed his shirt. His nod told her to undress, too. As she did so, his eyes never left her. They burned desire into her, which took away her shyness. To her, Frederick was magnificent. His beautiful body glowed, and his desire for her was there for her to see. Her love for him filled every part of her.

Once all her clothes had been removed, Frederick lifted her off the sofa and laid her down on the soft rug in front of the hearth. His hands stroked and kissed every part of her, lingering to caress her club foot as if it were a thing of grace and beauty, while his soft voice spoke of his love for her, and how lovely her body was.

Inside, she burned with her need of him. When at last he entered her, Ruth's world came together. All pain was forgotten. She had known love of all kinds – her ma's, her da's and that of her siblings. Dear Lettie's and Martha's love. The love of her beautiful Josh and his ma; and yes, Haydon's and Lilly's love. But nothing compared to this. Her body responded with all that she was.

She heard her own voice hollering the coming-together of her body and soul, as wave after wave of sensations overcame her, splitting her into a thousand fragments, then putting her together again, making her a complete and whole being. Now she was no longer 'the cripple' or 'the witch' – she was Ruth, the woman of love.

That's what her earl was giving her.

She took all he gave, as she cried out, 'My Earl. My love, my life . . .'

Author's Note

Researching this book was an enjoyable experience, as it took me on some of the most beautiful car journeys not far from where I live.

Ambling around the countryside, and over the stunning Bowland Hills, discovering tiny hamlets that time had forgotten, didn't feel like work. Neither did a visit to see a working mill in the Saddleworth Museum and Art Gallery in the beautiful town of Uppermill, Oldham, which was followed by a leisurely boat trip along the canal, and then lunch. The latter wasn't part of the research, but hey ho.

The reason for the trip across the Bowland Hills was to trace the journey that Ruth and her family would have taken and to find a spot where it was possible for the accident that changed her life to have happened. I eventually found a place, and was excited to do so – until I remembered what I was finding it for! Then I closed my eyes and brought the scene alive in my mind, and shed a tear for what Ruth and her siblings had to face.

A lot of imagination goes into a novel and, along with it, emotions are tapped into and released, as the characters that are created become real and their dilemmas affect me personally. But it is important to me that the story is based on solid research, as this keeps me realistic – everything I write, despite being fiction, has to be proven to me that it could happen. Then I can write with confidence, and allow the story to flow.

I hope that shows through in *The Street Orphans*, and that you have enjoyed the book. My very best wishes and love to you all.

Acknowledgements

My thanks, as always, to my darling husband, Roy. You are my rock and give me a love that I am privileged to have. And to our children, Christine, Julie, Rachel and James, their husbands and partners, our grandchildren, and our Olley and Wood families. You always encourage and support me in everything I do. Thank you. I love you all.

To the wonderful team at Pan Macmillan: my editor, Victoria Hughes-Williams, and her assistant, Jayne Osborne; Laura Carr, Editorial Manager, and her team, especially Mandy Greenfield. And Kate Green, Senior Publicity Manager. I am grateful to you all. Without your faith in me, the support you give me, and the expertise you bring to my novels, I would not succeed. I especially acknowledge how you bring a clarity to my work where I may have muddied the waters, and yet retain my voice, and the care that Kate gives me when I am on tour. You all possess a special skill, and are a special team.

To my agent, Judith Murdoch. Thank you. You always go the extra mile for me, Judith, and keep me enthused. Problems are halved once you begin to tackle them, and I feel in capable hands, as you have my best interests at heart. One in a million.

An extra special thank you to my daughter Christine Martin and my son James Wood – both read so many versions of this book when it was in progress. They advised me on what was working, and held me back when I ambled down the wrong path. Your patience and enjoyment of my work helps me to keep focused. Thank you.

An acknowledgement to those who helped to bring this book into being isn't complete without thanking those who helped me in the days when I self-published: Rebecca Keys, freelance editor; Julie Hitchin, proofreader; and Patrick Fox, author and cover designer. Your support and help is never forgotten. Thank you.

And lastly, but by no means least, a huge thank you to my readers. Especially to those who follow me on Facebook and those who have subscribed to my website. You bring me joy and encouragement every day with your comments and I love the happy community-feel that we have. I would like to give a special mention here to Katrina Stevenson, a reader and a friend. When we met, Katrina's name inspired me to create my character, Lady Katrina. Thank you. Much love to all. Together, you help me to climb my mountain.

If you enjoyed

The Street Orphans

then you'll love

Brighter Days Ahead

**War pulled them apart, but can
it bring them back together?**

Molly lives with her repugnant father, who has betrayed her many times. From a young age, living on the streets of London's East End, she has seen the harsh realities of life. When she's kidnapped by a gang and forced into their underworld, her future seems bleak.

Flo spent her early years in an orphanage and is about to turn her hand to teacher training. When a kindly teacher at her school approaches her about a job at Bletchley Park, it could turn out to be everything she never realized she wanted.

Will the girls' friendship be enough to weather the hard times ahead?

Available now

Tomorrow Brings Sorrow

by Mary Wood

You can't choose your family

Megan and her husband Jack have finally found stability in their lives. But the threat of Megan's troubled son Billy is never far from their minds. Billy's release from the local asylum is imminent and it should be a time for celebration. Sadly, Megan and Jack know all too well what Billy is capable of . . .

Can you choose who you love?

Sarah and Billy were inseparable as children, before Billy committed a devastating crime. While Billy has been shut away from the world, he has fixated on one thing: Sarah. Sarah knows there's only one way she can keep her family safe and it means forsaking true love.

Sometimes love is dangerous

Twins Theresa and Terrence Crompton are used to getting their own way. But with the threat of war looming, the tides of fortune are turning. Forces are at work to unearth a secret that will shake the very roots of the tight-knit community . . .

Available now

All I Have to Give

by Mary Wood

When all is lost, can she find the strength to start again?

It is 1916 and Edith Mellor is one of the few female surgeons in Britain. Compelled to use her skills for the war effort, she travels to the Somme, where she is confronted with the horrors at the Front. Yet amongst the bloodshed on the battlefield, there is a ray of light in the form of the working-class Albert, a corporal from the East End of London. Despite being worlds apart, Edith and Albert can't deny their attraction to each other. But as the brutality of war reveals itself to Albert, he makes a drastic decision that will change both Edith and Albert's lives forever.

In the north of England, strong-minded Ada is left heartbroken when her only remaining son Jimmy heads off to fight in the war. Desperate to rebuild her shattered life, Ada takes up a position in the munition factory. But life deals her a further blow when she discovers that her mentally unstable sister Beryl is pregnant with her husband Paddy's child. Soon, even the love of the gentle Joe, a supervisor at the factory, can't erase Ada's pain. An encounter with Edith's cousin, Lady Eloise, brings Edith into her life. Together, they realize, they may be able to turn their lives around . . .

Available now

Proud of You

by Mary Wood

A heartfelt historical saga with a compelling mystery at its heart.

Alice, an upper-class Londoner, is recruited into the Special Operations Executive and sent to Paris where she meets Gertrude, an ex-prostitute working for the Resistance Movement. Together they discover that they have a connection to the same man, Ralph D'Olivier, and vow to unravel the mystery of his death.

After narrowly escaping capture by the Germans, Alice is lifted out of France and taken to a hospital for wounded officers where she meets Lil, a working-class northern girl employed as a nurse. Though worlds apart, Alice and Lil form a friendship, and Alice discovers Lil is also linked to Ralph D'Olivier.

Soon, the war irrevocably changes each of these women and they are thrust into a world of heartache and strife beyond anything they have had to endure before. Can they clear Ralph's name and find lasting love and happiness for themselves?

Available now

The People's Friend

If you enjoy quality fiction, you'll love "The People's Friend" magazine. Every weekly issue contains seven original short stories and two exclusively written serial instalments.

On sale every Wednesday, the "Friend" also includes travel, puzzles, health advice, knitting and craft projects and recipes.

It's the magazine for women who love reading!

For great subscription offers, call 0800 318846.

twitter.com/@TheFriendMag
www.facebook.com/PeoplesFriendMagazine
www.thepeoplesfriend.co.uk